Unraveling Timelines

LISE BREAKEY

Candlemark & Gleam

First edition published 2017

For information, address
Athena Andreadis
Candlemark & Gleam LLC,
38 Rice Street #2, Cambridge, MA 02140
eloi@candlemarkandgleam.com

Library of Congress Cataloguing-in-Publication Data
In Progress

ISBN: 978-1-936460-75-5
eISBN: 978-1-936460-74-8

Cover design by Eleni Tsami

Book design and composition by Athena Andreadis
Typeface: Calisto MT

Editors: Athena Andreadis and Kate Sullivan

Proofreader: Kelly Jennings

www.candlemarkandgleam.com

For the beloved dead—
Dad, Gram, George, and Maryanna.

CHAPTER ONE

One Thursday in September, as if to make up for his entire life to date, Peter Chang experienced two extraordinary events in a single evening. At 8:42 pm, he fell in love with a girl who walked in through the wall in his boss's office. At 9:19, her brother shot him through the chest for no apparent reason. Later he was called upon to save her from the consequences of her father's sins—but at 6:07 pm, he was bending over the printer in his cubicle on the third floor of the Palazzo Building, entirely without a clue.

The printer clicked, hummed, and covered the sheet with—to Peter—barely comprehensible gibberish before putting the page into the tray. It refused to be rushed.

"Client's waiting," Elaine said over the cubicle wall.

"I'll be right there. It's just this last, uh, fifty pages," Peter said.

"Well, while you're waiting, here." She thrust the financial pages under his nose. The NASDAQ was up, the Dow was down, everything was as it should be as far as he could tell. "Pick a stock."

"Can't we give that a rest?" She was always asking. Co-workers egged her on. At first, it was as if she thought he must have some uncanny ability to pick stocks, having been hired at Varian Financial with no other apparent qualification. Then it had become a joke, and now it was probably so that everyone would know what not to invest in.

"Just one, Pete."

She wouldn't go away until he did. He let his forefinger stab something at random.

"TNR Design." She shifted the paper out from under his finger and pecked it with her own. "Never heard of it." She was sharp-nosed, bird-thin, and always dressed in magpie black and white. "Now, it'd be nice if you could get me the Andersen report before you leave tonight."

"Right, of course," Peter said as worms of panic wiggled through his insides. "I'll get right on it." He thumped the printer. "Let's go!"

The clicking and humming stopped. He had turned it off.

"Try not to screw this up." Her black-and-white nails dug lightly into the fabric of the wall. "Now that the old man's hanging around the office so much, you need to look sharp."

"I'll, um, I'll do my best." He turned the printer back on and respooled the document from the last page. "One for the team," he added. She flared the holes in her elegant beak and disappeared.

Peter Chang wore wire-rimmed glasses, through which he blinked owlishly, and a rumpled just-out-of-bed expression. His suits seemed slightly too big for him even though they weren't. Women thought him cute, but forgot about him the instant they looked in another direction. As a baby, he'd been abandoned (mysteriously, inside the orphanage rather than on its doorstep) and adopted by the Changs.

The Changs consisted of one fourth-generation Chinese American and one sixth-generation Scottish-Irish American. They were to parenthood what Michael Jordan was to baseball: that is, they assumed they'd be good at it based upon their achievements in every other arena of life. "Corey" Chang Kong-li was a Silicon Valley success story, a business-savvy computer engineer who somehow always managed to ride out the extreme up- and downturns the industry was prone to. He said "whatever" a lot, bought Peter computer games, and took him along on business trips to Europe, Hong Kong, and the Philippines, where Peter passed the time alone in hotel rooms playing with his latest game system or watching television in strange languages. Destiny Moonchild McGee-Chang was an acclaimed writer of children's books (the popular *Penguin and I* series). She told Peter his parents would always love him no matter what he did with his life.

Peter's report cards, filled with Bs and Cs, were hung on the refrigerator. His parents took him for ice cream after every soccer game, even the one where Peter scored the winning goal for the opposing team. He grew from a baffled, polite kid with few friends to a baffled, polite young man who lived at home all through college. Nothing extraordinary had ever happened to him before, except for getting hired at Varian Financial. Shortly after he got his B.A. (in photography) and just as he contemplated flipping burgers or asking Dad for some menial data processing job, a Mr. Theodore Slinky called him up. Mr. Slinky said his resume looked good, and would he come by the firm for an interview for a job as an investment broker.

Only he hadn't sent the firm a resume. He hadn't even posted it on the career placement department website yet. Further, nothing in his background said "broker." He'd taken no business classes and his last job, unpaid, had been on the university newspaper, taking pictures at football games.

Nonetheless, he brought his resume along and Mr. Slinky looked at it for a moment or two. He was the office manager: a short, round, impeccably dressed black guy, as impassive as a boulder. He gave Peter a psychological test consisting of questions like "If you knew that terrorists were going to hijack commercial jets and crash them into the World Trade Center but you had no proof, what would you do with the information?" Peter had no idea how to answer that—he'd been nine years old back then, for one thing. He came away with the impression that the interview had not gone well. But the next day, Mr. Slinky called again and gave him the job.

Peter moved out of his parents' basement and got his own apartment—in San Francisco, no less. He filled it with game systems and cameras, and even some furniture. He went to work every day on Market Street and did what he was told as best he could and wondered why he was being paid for it while hundreds of his peers with better grades and more ambition were hustling for internships. He didn't have any feel for the stock market. He had no gift for foresight generally. He was not reckless, but life continually blindsided him.

6:14 p.m. The printer spat out the last few pages of the report. Peter scooped it up, a package so heavy that the bottom third of it promptly escaped his grip and hit the floor. With a groan, he dropped to his knees, grabbing pages as fast as he could. The firm dealt with an old-school breed of client: wealthy people not comfortable with the increasingly abstract nature of wealth—thus everything was printed out on dead trees rather than displayed on a tablet. He didn't attempt to put the pages in order, but shoved them into his briefcase and ran for the elevator.

The old Palazzo Building suited the firm perfectly, and its elevator was a case in point—a gilded cage, circa 1900, standing exposed from the cracked marble walls of the building in its own fenced-in shaft that pierced the floor below and the ceiling above. *Rattle, creak, bing*, it arrived and Peter jumped in with a nod for Abe Slinky, the head of security and maintenance. Abe resembled the office manager (his son) but was tall and lean and elderly. When Peter had first started the job, Abe had made him uneasy by often seeming about to speak to him, then walking away. But he soon stopped doing that and became just part of the ambiance.

There was also a girl in the elevator, dark-haired and unsmiling, with figure-concealing clothing and a beret pulled over her eyes. Peter felt himself flush because he could still tell she had enough of everything in the right places, and because at that moment he noticed he had trapped the end of his tie inside his briefcase. No contortions of body or shifting of grip could conceal this fact. Fortunately, she barely glanced at him. *Creak-creak, bing, rattle*, the gilt wire gates parted on the mezzanine level.

Peter jumped out and was just about to dash for the conference room when Abe said, "Here you are, miss," and she answered, "Thanks, I know my way." He looked back to see him usher her through the tall old teak doors that separated the rest of the firm from the office suite of its owner, president, and CEO, Mr. Benedict Varian, who—despite hanging around the office more often these days—was not currently in.

Peter went around the corner, waited until he heard the elevator start up, then crept back. He leaned against one door and pushed it open a crack. The outer office was empty as he expected, having just seen Elaine on the third floor. But the shades were up and the inner office, he could see through the glass partition, was also unoccupied except for the girl.

She was inspecting the antique walnut paneling. A paint-smudged smock hung under her open coat. She had exuded a faint scent like varnish. Maybe she was an interior designer and Varian Financial was going to join the 21st century, decor-wise. That didn't explain why the head of security had escorted her up, operating a manual winch-and-cable elevator like a hundred years of progress in vertical transportation technology and civil rights had passed him by.

She ran her fingers over part of the wall, traced the edges of a panel. Then she pushed it on with both hands and it swung open, swinging out on hinges, revealing an opening just big enough for an adult to pass through sideways. Light glimmered as if from the far end of a tunnel. It looked like daylight. She slipped through, closed the panel flush behind her, and was gone.

Peter let the outer door close and leaned against it.

That panel was set into an interior wall. And he had simultaneously seen darkness and streetlight through the windows.

He remembered the times Mr. Varian had emerged from that office when Peter was certain the boss wasn't in the building. The way he would go in sometimes and neither Peter nor anyone he talked to ever saw him come out. That very morning, Peter had been in the outer office waiting to talk to the boss when a stranger emerged. A bald guy in an old brown suit, whose expression reminded Peter of Mr. Slinky—the same closed-off imperturbable look. He wouldn't have noticed except it was 9:00 am, Peter had seen Elaine unlock the office, and if the guy had been in there first, he must have waited overnight or come out of nowhere.

He screwed up his nerve and reached for the door again. But there was a creak as another door opened on the mezzanine and voices spilled out, making him jump and sneak away. Around the corner, Mr. Slinky waited outside the conference room as Peter hurried over.

"Glad you could make it, Pete."

"Sorry, the printer was giving me trouble and—"

"Never mind, you're here now. Go along and meet the client so I can get home. And Peter…"

"Yeah?"

"Better take your tie out of your briefcase."

The new client—Mr. Sanders—proved to be a bloodless-looking man with a tight, clammy handshake. In fact, he was reluctant to let go of Peter's hand once he fastened onto it, and seemed almost to be drawing him into a damp sort of full-body embrace. Peter had to suppress an impulse to beat the man off with his briefcase. But when the client released him from his leech-like grip, he relaxed and the meeting went smoothly.

At least, he thought that the meeting went smoothly. Mr. Sanders didn't mind Peter's tardiness, or the fact that he barely knew what he was talking about. He was an okay guy in spite of his overly smooth, shell-like face, dead-looking eyes, and bespoke tailoring the color of cold volcanic ash. He was a guy you could talk to. He was trustworthy, was the main thing. Peter remembered that distinctly.

The problem was, he remembered it in the elevator, taking Mr. Sanders down to the lobby. Everyone else had gone home and the evening security guard didn't feel that running the clunky old lift was in his job description, so Peter was operating it. That was what he remembered. But he felt as though he had just woken up with his hand on the brass lever. A cold sweat was trickling down under his shirt.

The client was speaking into a gold-cased smartphone. "No, it's early days for him. We can proceed as soon as there's an opportunity." He disconnected, slipped the phone into his breast pocket, saw Peter watching him, and showed his teeth—possibly a smile. "Putting your good advice to work, Mr. Chang."

Peter couldn't remember what his advice had been. Nor could he think of anything he might have said that Mr. Sanders could not have found out faster and more cheaply with an online search. "You must be technologically challenged or a complete moron," he said. The client smiled thinly and Peter felt heat rush to his face. He couldn't believe that had come out of his mouth. "Uh, I mean, um...God, I'm sorry, uh..."

"Are you all right, Mr. Chang?"

"To be perfectly honest—" Peter felt a strange compulsion to be perfectly honest—"I feel like I blanked out somehow. I...don't remember what we talked about." The lift arrived on the ground floor with a grinding and a jolt because he hadn't been paying attention to the controls.

Mr. Sanders gave him an appraising look. "You didn't have a lot
to drink recently, did you? You don't look like a man with substance
abuse problems. You're a bit young for dementia. I'm not familiar
with blackouts associated with coprolalia. Vitamin deficiency, maybe?
Brain chemistry is a funny thing. Too much of one enzyme, not
enough of a particular protein...if you don't get enough tocopherols,
that can cause memory problems."

"Are you a doctor?"

"I used to be. Let me recommend you drink a lot of water and
take some vitamin B12." Mr. Sanders patted his shoulder with a damp
hand. "Works wonders. Everything comes down to chemistry, in the
end. Even love. Infatuation is chemical. It wears off. Remember that."

Peter walked him through the vaulted foyer to the front door. They
shook hands—briskly and briefly this time—and the guard buzzed
them out. Peter held the door and watched the client descend the front
steps and cross the street. Strange how he was such a great guy, so
friendly and easy to talk to, but Peter didn't like him very much.

It was dark now, definitely quitting time. He went back upstairs to
get his coat. Mr. Slinky was long gone, but Elaine swooped down and
cornered him in his cubicle. "Hey, knucklehead. Steve could really use
that report before you go."

Peter looked at the clock. "It's seven-thirty. What would he do
with it if he got it?"

"Hey, you know how important that report is—"

"Yeah, I know how important the Jones report is."

"Jones report?" Elaine said. "You mean the Andersen report,
right? She laughed and cocked her head sideways. "I swear, if you've
been working on the wrong one..."

"All reports are the Jones report," Peter said. "Haven't you
noticed? They're all the same report. And they're all boring as hell."

There was a glint of amusement in her sharp dark eyes, but she looked at him as if he had sprouted donkey ears. "What's with you?"

"I don't know," Peter admitted. "I feel a little weird."

"Hey, if you're not happy working here, just say the word."

"I, uh, um..."

"Well, as soon as you can manage to say anything at all," she said, and flapped away.

He had been on the verge of saying that of course he wasn't happy, but managed to strangle it into a stammer.

He fired up the spreadsheet program on his computer. The report would never see the light of day by tomorrow, but working on it might restore some sense of normality. First he went to the water cooler and drank off three or four paper cups worth. He found a bottle of mixed vitamins in his briefcase, but it didn't include any B12s.

An hour went by as he checked row after row of figures and the few people still in the office closed up and went home. The open-plan floor, with an old vaulted marble ceiling over a space like a warehouse, became dark, quiet, and ominous with echoes, until the mere clatter of a dropped pen was enough to spook him. At last he closed the Jones report—or was it the Andersen report?—shut down his computer, grabbed his briefcase, and left the cubicle.

He was not anxious to go home, where nothing awaited him on a weeknight but beer, TV, and online gaming. Car chases and gunplay, or wandering an apocalyptic wasteland killing monsters. Or his mom would call and invite him to a late dinner, and he was no good at putting her off, especially with his foot going into his mouth with alarming frequency. It was like he'd shed all inhibitions against blurting out the truth and he wondered what kind of vitamin deficiency could cause that.

He stopped the lift on the mezzanine and stared at the boss's office suite door. The whole floor was dark and silent. He tried the outer door and it was still unlocked. So he went past Elaine's desk and tried the door of the inner sanctum. It also opened.

Humans remember their animal selves in the dark, and Peter was no exception. His senses sharpened and he fancied there was a trace of scent like varnish or oil paint in the air. He closed the door behind him and crossed to the windows to close the blinds. Mr. Varian's antique lamps and bookshelves loomed around him, expensive and fragile, threatening him with their vulnerability. Now that he was in here, he dreaded getting caught. He found his boss intimidating and, thanks to the mysterious door to nowhere, unpredictable.

With a sense of transgression that mere trespass had not evoked, he flipped on the light. Then he went behind the desk to check out the panel the girl had gone through. He was pretty sure which one to examine because it was worn and a little shiny at the natural level for a hand to push on it. He pushed, but nothing happened. He ran his hands over the smooth surface and all around it. No hidden catches or levers around the edges. He tried moving nearby objects—perhaps the door opened when you pulled out the right ledger or twisted a knob on a cabinet or something. But nothing continued to happen. He pushed it in several places, testing. It gave a little in the center, just like the others did, but that was it. He could feel resistance, like a masonry wall behind it.

There must, he thought, be something incredibly obvious that he was overlooking.

He pushed it again, and this time it popped open. He lost his balance, but recovered and found himself nose to nose with a girl.

The girl.

發

On the morning of the day her father was murdered—"day" in this context meaning a period of personal time during which she was awake—Nikkole Varian concluded that she was not capable of keeping a relationship going longer than three months. Three months was the record. She'd gotten that far with Lorenzo Bernini. But that was history—so to speak. That morning, after five weeks in *fin-de-siècle* Paris, she broke up with Edvard Munch.

He had spent the night in her studio. A new version of *Madonna*, destined to become his second-most recognizable composition, hung completed in his apartment on the Rue Lafayette. "I am trying to capture a powerful and sacred moment," he had explained during the weeks she modeled for his figure studies. "The woman when she gives herself to become the mother of new life. Her face contains all the earth's beauty. Her lips part as if in pain…a corpse's smile. The chain binding the thousand dead generations to the thousand generations to come is linked together." Well, he'd done it with his rendering of the passionate red-haloed nude, subtly different from the versions he had done with Dagny Juel as his model, but now he was in a slump and Nikki (as she preferred to be called) didn't know what to do with him.

She had a surreal painting of the cathedral to work on, but couldn't do it with him so ostentatiously sulking. Giving up after awhile, she cleaned her brushes and got a baguette, Roquefort cheese, sausage, and a bottle of red wine to assemble lunch from. But she couldn't stand the silence. Finally she made him put the newspaper down and tell her what was wrong.

Munch, who all these weeks had been paying for the cafés, cabarets, galleries, and theaters they attended and had even offered to pay her rent, now told her that he did not know when or if he would receive a scholarship from the Norwegian government that year. Stiffly, he explained he would have to cut his expenses, at least until he knew where his next income would be coming from…

Nikki made the mistake of offering to pay for everything for a while.

She hadn't realized she'd been loading straw on her lover's back all this time, until now, when there was an almost audible snap. Munch paced away, not far because the room was tiny and cluttered with easels, tools, and canvas. When he turned back, the shy, quiet man—"the monk," his friends called him—was gone.

"Who are you, really?" he demanded. "Where would you get the money?"

The reasonableness of this question was emphasized by the shabbiness of her studio—a garret barely furnished and unadorned except for theater posters nailed to the support beams. They slept on a mattress on the floor. A paint-flecked mansard roof window let in pale sunlight.

"I never said I was poor. I've got some money." She sat on the floor with a board across her lap and started cutting up bread and cheese and sausage.

"All this time," he said, "you have been letting me think I saved you from the gutter, and you have actually been well-off?"

"Is that what you thought?"

"You are forcing me to express myself in a way I despise."

"I never lied to you! You lied to yourself."

She had given him ammunition. "Perhaps you have not lied, but you have not told me anything of importance either. You represent yourself as a woman without a past. Do you expect me to believe it?"

"What you failed to believe was the truth when I told it to you!" This was a low blow. She had told him the truth expecting that he would not believe it.

"Nikki...how could I? How can I?"

This was where she could have offered to prove it. But she'd tried that before with unpleasant results, and she was stung by what he implied. "It's easier for you to assume I'm a prostitute!"

That knocked the wind out of him. "American women!" he said after a stunned pause.

"Victorian men!" she shot back. Then, remembering he didn't know the cultural baggage that would one day be associated with that epithet, she added, "Scandinavian provincials!"

He occupied his hands with rolling a cigarette. "It would not matter what you once were as long as you were honest about it." She went on slicing cheese, but everything blurred, the knife, the round of Roquefort, the cutting board. "Dear girl. Can't you see..."

"What? What can't I see? Weren't you the one who hated for 'a woman to cling to a man and drain his strength away?'"

"What are you talking about? I never said that to you!"

"You don't have to say it—"

"You read my journal!" he interrupted.

"Well, yes," she said, "but not until after it was published. So now you lose—" she was about to say *your cool*, but changed it to, "—your temper because I'm not dependent on you?"

She was on her feet now. He was pacing. "You are incomprehensible to me, I admit, but surely two who love each other can tell each other the truth!"

It was the first time he had said the word "love," and he didn't even realize how manipulative it was to use it now. "I did tell you the truth. You either accept it, or you don't."

"I cannot," he admitted. "I enjoyed your fantastical stories, but I want to move forward on a firmer foundation!"

This was the moment she could have proved the truth to him, but she felt it arrive with a sensation of fear, of her back up against the wall. To let him see everything about her—no, she couldn't, and brilliant men tended to get so angry when wrenched out of their comfortable junctures and world views. In a burst of panic, she pushed back hard. "Just tell me one thing. How can so much genius and so much self-pity exist in the same person? Or is it that people in this benighted decade mistake self-pity for genius?"

She regretted that the instant it came out of her mouth. His blue eyes widened and turned to ice and he was free to say everything he'd only been thinking up to then. "This has all been some sort of diversion for you, hasn't it? You always had some other life you intended to resume when I ceased to amuse you. Don't try to defend yourself!" he snapped as she opened her mouth. "Your eyes betray you. You always look elsewhere, never at what is right in front of you. Your work betrays you too!" He turned to the table where some of her canvases were stacked and swept them onto the floor.

"You jerk!"

"Doors and windows and bridges! Why didn't you seduce an architect?"

"'Seduce?'"

"If the hat fits, *M'mselle*!" (They were fighting in French, the only language they had in common).

Nikki threw the sausage at him, snatched her coat, and stormed out. He followed as far as the door, calling her name, but did not come after her. The door slammed. She ran, spinning down the narrow spiral. Halfway to the fifth floor, she had a flash of *l'esprit d'escalier*, and realized that throwing him out would've made more sense than leaving herself. But then again, she intended to walk out of the entire juncture, not just one room, so maybe he had more claim to occupy it than she did. Her paintings were still there but she could go back for them any time…

She clattered past her landlady's door and down another half-flight of stairs, then stopped. She put her hair up under her cap, went back, and knocked on the bright enamel paint. The landlady answered at once. "Just dropping off the rent—" and Nikki fumbled in her pockets, smiling through the effort of not crying.

The landlady blinked pouched and watery eyes. "No hurry, *chère*. It is not due for a week."

"Uh, yes, but, I'm going away for a bit."

"Ohhh. Oh, dear." Madame glanced upstairs. The floor between their apartments was thin and sound traveled well. "Not giving notice, I hope?"

"Oh, no," Nikki said truthfully. She was not giving notice, she just wasn't coming back. "Just…might miss the day, you know. In fact," she added, having a good view of the garret behind Madame's figure, more bare and cheerless even than her own, "I'd like to advance another three months' rent, please."

A certain tension went out of Madame's face. Nikki had preconceived ideas of a widowed Parisian landlady, but she had lived up to none of them: she was soft and plump, with hair like angora fleece, and constantly worried that Nikki wasn't eating properly or her coat wasn't warm enough. "Well…if you wish. If it isn't too much trouble." She lowered her voice. "But what of your friend?"

From that question, Nikki realized Madame had thought Munch was paying her expenses—which meant Nikki hadn't been fooling her at all; she knew she was renting to *une femme*. "…I don't think you'll see him again," she said.

"Ah," the landlady sighed. "These artistes. So temperamental. I hope it was not so serious as that."

Nikki remembered meeting Munch, in a Left Bank dive with red velvet wallpaper. The flare of a match lit up his face across the room and she recognized the image—*Self-Portrait with Burning Cigarette.* From the way he stared at her, she realized there was danger of starting a new timeline, so she'd fled. He'd followed, caught up halfway across the Pont de l'Archêveché, actually grabbed her arm.

"You are a woman," he'd said. He was a Victorian man; naturally he'd made this sound like an accusation.

"I'm afraid so," she told Madame.

Downstairs, outside, she found a cheerful day in early May on the streets of the Île St.-Louis. Pigeons flocking, urchins running, lovers walking, fishermen with lines off the limestone quay, cyclists and cab drivers swearing at each other, painters trying to catch the quality of light dancing off water, drunkards adding piss to the smell of the river...

To be fair to Munch, it was illegal for women to dress in men's clothes in La Belle Époque. He must have thought she was on the run from some bullying pimp or former lover. To believe otherwise would put a strain even on his free-love principles. She had known it would in advance; it wasn't her first time in this benighted century.

But now he was accusing her of slumming. She stalked across the bridge connecting the Ile St. Louis to the Ile de la Cité, silently ranting about bohemian anarchist painters who thought themselves so liberated and avant-garde, but who were so repressed you could blow them up like balloons. By the time she reached the other side she was fighting tears. She headed into the park in the vast shadow of Notre-Dame.

The chestnut trees, their masses of blossoms shifting in the wind, nearly hid the river and the limestone quay opposite. The old cathedral rose into a serene sky with a high, thin layer of cloud, broken by the wind so that spots of sunlight hit the old yellowed gray limestone, the voussoirs, buttress towers, and jutting gargoyle mouths. She sat on a bench near the Vigoureux Fountain and got herself past the crying jag.

"Trouble in paradise?"

She jumped, gasped, dragged her coat sleeve across her eyes. Erik lounged at the other end of the bench and she hadn't seen or heard him arrive. "How the hell did you get here?"

"You entered this timeline into the engine records," he reminded her.

"So? I didn't leave coordinates!"

"You gave the year and the city and your famous boyfriend's name," he said. "All I had to do was shadow him until you made contact."

Ice struck down her spine. "You've been following me? Spying on me? For over a month? Dressed like that?" There were few locals near enough to notice his black trench coat, motorcycle boots, mirrored shades on top of his head. He looked like he had once been the kid nobody expected to bring a thirty-aught-six to middle school.

"Couldn't contact you before you entered the record. Then you might not have done it."

"You're darn right I wouldn't have!"

"Sounds like you're afraid of seeing me. I wonder why."

"Erik. Number one, you're my brother."

"Half-brother."

"And number two, you're a sociopath."

He stood up slowly, as if to avoid sudden moves that would give her an excuse to run. "But I am also a Timewalker. So are you. You can't be happy with one of them."

"One of who?" she asked, deadpan.

"You know. Ephemerals. Stationaries. Figments. Whatever you like to call them."

"We're not a different species!"

"Of course we are." Drifting closer. "They're all ghosts. Fragments of probability. They don't even exist unless we find them."

"They're still real. They still bleed, and die, and—and leave relatives squabbling over their stuff…. How did you get access to my records anyway?"

"Dad sent me, actually. Some nauseating reconciliation scene."

She scowled. "We've got nothing to reconcile about. What do I care if he married again?"

Erik shrugged. "I just took advantage of the opportunity to find you." He took another step and she flinched back. There was an electric heat generated by his proximity that she had to ignore. He took a hand-rolled cigarette out of his pocket, dribbling a few bits of tobacco, and lit it with a flare from a death's-head Zippo. "Seriously, Nikki, I have missed you."

"Seriously, forget it. I'm saying goodbye now."

"I'm going with you. What entrance are you using?" She walked away across the grass. "You think you're untouchable?" he called. "No one is. Not even us."

"Goodbye now," she said.

She found her father in the vineyard. He must be taking a break between capitalist forays into other people's timelines. The sun was beating down, the earth on the southern slope of the hill was warm and dry and smelled like cinnamon, and he was working on the spring vines with billhook and grafting knife, looking like an illustrated parable or allegory of something in fustian smock and sandals. Benedict Varian had the robust build and features that only sculptors under patronage give to old men—big, gray-bearded, and stern, he could have been a model for Zeus or Jehovah. But he looked around and his expression softened so much that she felt it as a shock.

"Welcome back." He rested the billhook in the dirt.

They took care of *how are you* and *fine*, and he said nothing about what she was wearing or how she'd avoided him while creeping into the house every now and then to access the engine records. Despite that encouragement, her gut churned and she let him go first. "You wanted to see me?"

"Yes, Nicoletta." Against her mother's wishes, he used an Italianized version of Nikkole. "It's time for you to come home."

"You mean permanently?"

"It is not safe for you out there. And I miss you. It is time we mended our quarrel. I would forgive and accept you—the best I can—the way you are."

"You'd forgive me?"

"And I am prepared to listen to your complaints," with a sigh that seemed to add *however unreasonable they may be*, and the next thing he did was to turn back to the vines. "What, out of my catalogue of faults, would you like to discuss?"

This was too good an opportunity to miss. "Well, picking one at random, why did you let Erik see my engine records?"

He seemed surprised. "Why should I not have?"

"Thought I made it clear I didn't want anyone but you and Alex to be able to find me."

He rolled his head, popping his neck. "I feared you would not listen to me. He seemed certain he could persuade you to return. I have not always been pleased with him; he was an undisciplined, vicious boy—"

"Well, we agree there."

"—but I felt that time and adventure had matured him."

"I'm thinking not," Nikki said. "Did you know I first met him outside?"

"...And?"

"And he didn't mention we were related."

She meant to say it straight out, but couldn't grit her teeth enough. Still, her tone warned him and he raised the grafting knife as if to ward off ill fortune. "And?"

"And we had an affair." Her feet twitched; she wanted to take a step back. "Until I figured out he was a Timewalker too." She remembered the tang of second-hand smoke. 'Let me show you what I am,' she had said to him once. And how impressed he had pretended to be under a mask of insouciance that turned out to be his real face. A face that once too often had five o'clock shadow at noon or a slightly different haircut or a complete change of mood for no apparent reason.

Her father seemed too nonplussed to be outraged. He put a hand to his head as the storm began to gather around the edges of his face. "You are sure?"

"That I slept with him? Yeah, Dad, I'm pretty sure."

"And he knew who you were?"

"Definitely. It might have been better if you'd mentioned, you know, that I had a brother named Erik?"

"It would have been better by far if you had remained in Santuario!"

"Dad, you really can't blame this on me."

The storm arrived and broke in the same instant. His face went florid, frozen to boiling in three seconds flat. "That incestuous *figlio di puttana* made a *troia* out of you, a Varian? I should have strangled him in his cradle!" He swung the billhook at the base of a grapevine, cultivated for centuries, and chopped it half off its roots.

"And don't freak out and do that affronted patriarch thing!"

"And you? How could you?" He threw the tools down, almost snorting. "Even though you did not know he was your brother—" Nikki backed away, seeing him react exactly the way she expected him to—but then, "No—no, wait," he added in different tone. He wiped his brow and made a pacifying gesture. "I forget. This is not the way to raise one's daughters any longer. I—please, do not go." To her astonishment, he put one arm around her shoulders and drew her close. "Forgive me. I curse the discretion that brought this shame upon you. If I had foreseen…" Speechless, she almost relaxed against his powerful chest. He smelled of earth, wool, and sugar-cured tobacco. "Never mind now," he added, releasing her. "The question is what to do about this…outrage."

"What are you going to do?"

He picked up the tools, shoving the knife into a wide leather belt and shouldering the billhook. "Well, he is no Absalom to me, girl, I assure you. I will call on him to explain, to defend himself, if he can."

He was leaving the vineyard; she followed, trying to get her breath back. "And if he can't?"

"Exile."

"Why would he care?"

"No access to the engine records? No safety from the Hunters? No chance to inherit what I have built here?" He encompassed the whole estate in a gesture. "He will care." They reached a shed where he put the tools away on their hooks. "You will see." He gave her a smug smile. *Father knows best.* "You will see."

He closed up the shed and began climbing the hill, through the steeply terraced gardens and the labyrinthine jasmine hedges toward the villa and again she followed. "Dad...whatever happens, this isn't a birthday party, not something I'm looking forward too, woo-hoo, big surprise, okay?"

"I understand it is not anything pleasant for you. But you should witness it nonetheless."

"Oh, no. No. No way. All I want is for him to stay out of my records and away from me." *It wasn't rape*, she wanted to say, but the distinction would be lost on him. The issue to him, beyond the fact of incest, wasn't her consent, it was unauthorized spoilage. "The rest is between you and him. It's not my problem."

"Then you do not intend to stay?"

"No. But I'll say hello to Alex."

"You should greet your mother as well."

"Stepmother."

"Stepmother, yes. Whether you approve or not, I have married again." Full of his success, he went on: "She is from Milan, the same timeline as the servas, so she is used to them already. And you will have a new brother or sister soon."

"Oh...congratulations," Nikki said, and wondered if that event had anything to do with his softened attitude, although neither his previous marriage nor Alex's birth had worked any such change.

"Thank you." They went through an archway in a hedge wall and followed the path upward and widdershins, reaching the eastern slope where the air was cooler and dew sparkled on turf soft as jeweler's cotton, before he urged her again. "Stay. Erik may be lost to me. Alex is a good boy, but no Timewalker; he cares for nothing but engines. My other children are long grown and have never come back. And you are not settling down as you should."

"Not in the sense you'd like."

"Not in any sense," he said dryly. "I do not require you to marry. But your first duty is to your family. I insist. You are too young. This affair proves it. I should never have let you leave in the first place."

Now she could summon outrage to her defense. "How do you know how old I am? I've spent years in other timelines. I could be nineteen going on fifty!"

"Anyone who uses the phrase 'going on' is too young," he said, even more dryly.

From the eastern slope, there was a good view of the aqueduct, three stacks of arches high, spanning the valley from its far wall to the summit of the central hill, imported stone by stone from ancient Hispania. In a trick of temporal physics Dad had never explained, it brought fresh water from Santuario to Santuario—and sometimes she felt her life was a similar Möbius strip. "Dad...I can't live here, knowing how you built the place."

"Not this again."

"You were a colonialist, a robber baron, you looted history, you were involved in the slave trade—"

"That was a long time ago!"

"It's still tainted! You're still probably using—"

"The whole Earth has that taint!" he snapped. "What I do is for you, for my children, for your protection! You do not know what I faced, what I had to deal with!" He was quiet a moment, breathing fast and even, until the thunderous purple receded from his face. "The Hunters will discover you sooner or later."

"I've never even seen one." The Hunters were childhood bogeymen. "You said it's been a hundred years since they made any trouble for us."

"Do you confine yourself to the last hundred years?" He shook his head. "They were diminished, they are not gone. And there are other dangers. The Telepaths are too reclusive to worry about, but the Seers...it's nearly impossible to guard against one, should he become your enemy."

"I have no plans to become anybody's enemy," Nikki said.

"And there are hazards in timewalking itself. Some even I do not understand."

They began to climb Santuario's northern slope. Ancient olive trees loomed over the path, each thick and twisted old stump supporting long, thin black fingers of new growth. Their shade was dark and cold by contrast with the glare. Chilled, she picked up the pace. "Dad. I'm sorry. It's nice to see you. It was easier to talk to you this time. But kids leave, that's life, it's normal. What are you going to do, lock me up?"

There was a pause before he said, "No. Never."

"I'll pay respects to the latest—to Lady Varian. Then I'm gone."

發

Peter stared at the girl, the hair prickling on the back of his neck. "Oh!" she said, as startled as he was. "Sorry, were you going through?"

"I— no," he said, with more honesty than presence of mind, "because I didn't really think it would open."

"Then would you mind letting me out?"

"Of—of course," Peter said, and staggered back, pushing his glasses more firmly onto his nose.

"Thanks." She stepped out and closed the panel behind her with a firm click, but not before he caught a whiff of dank underground scent and glimpsed an absolutely real dark stone tunnel with bright daylight at the far end.

She had limbs and eyes and breasts and so on. Curly dark hair, a dusting of freckles. She wore jeans and a blouse, but the same coat— short for a coat but long for a jacket—and she looked overheated in it, a glow in her cheeks. "Where did you come from?" he blurted.

"My dad's place," she said tightly. "Don't go in. He's in a mood."

"Your—your dad?" He gave the panel another push when she wasn't looking but it didn't budge. He followed her into the outer office. "Your dad has what, an office in there?"

"Among other things." She glanced at him sharply. "You *do* know my father?"

There was something familiar in the turn of her head and the shape of her face. "Mr. Varian, you mean? My boss."

"…But you aren't supposed to be here, are you?"

"I work here," he protested. "And I saw you walk through the wall!"

"Oh, Christ." She stared at him and sighed. "Now this is the part where I either warn you away for your own good, or tell my father that you were poking around." Peter gulped as stark vistas of unemployment opened up before him. Then she added, "But you know what, I really don't give a goddamn. And I don't know what good it would do. It's like, hello, Dad, do you know anything about human nature?"

She stalked out into the hallway. Blinking, he went after her. "Excuse me. Why are you supposed to warn me away?"

"It's a secret door, right?" She pushed the call button for the elevator. "Maybe my father would like it to remain a secret?"

"Then I suppose it would be futile to ask you why he has a secret door?"

There was a minute tilt to the corners of her mouth. "Completely."

There was only one elevator, so he wasn't following her when he got on board. She sent them rattling and grinding downward and studied him with a little frown. She still had a trace of that scent. Turpentine maybe. He had to think of something else to say. It had to be amusing, distracting, and non-threatening.

"I'm Peter Chang." Well, one out of three....

She extended her hand and shook his firmly. "Nikkole Varian. Or just Nikki. Were you the guy with the tie?" The elevator binged at ground level and she added, "Nice meeting you," before heading through the foyer for the front door.

He had to go out the front door same as everybody else, so he still wasn't technically following her. She stopped on the front steps, looking around at Market Street, the river of traffic, buildings ghostly, streetlights burning through a light mist. Why did she hesitate—not knowing where to go, or was she waiting for someone? "Do—do you need a ride?"

"Not a ride, no, thank you," she said, and went down the steps. She had a direction now: away from him.

"Or anything else?"

A direct stare. "You're following me."

"Yes I am, now. Er." He winced. What was wrong with him that he kept blurting out the truth? "Look, I'm sorry I was prying just now. I've been trying to figure out if there's another way into that office for weeks. It's been driving me crazy because...well, there isn't any space that someone could just vanish into."

"How do you know?"

"I spent a couple of nights working late with a tape measure and a set of blueprints." He was going to have to do something drastic. He didn't know what. He opened his mouth to see what would come out. "Listen, there's a coffeehouse across the street. If you would like...I won't ask you any more about it. I would really like to just buy you a coffee and get to know you better."

She looked at him severely and he continued wondering what was wrong with him until he noticed that almost invisible curve to her mouth again. "Okay. Why not? I should keep an eye on you anyway."

Peter's heart went *thud thud churn churn*. They crossed Market Street—she had a long, loping stride like somebody used to covering distances—to Cosmos Coffeehouse. His favorite piece of graffiti was scrawled on its outer wall: QUESTION EVERYTHING, under which someone had scribbled in smaller letters: *Why?* A crazy homeless man in a gray coat crouched on the sidewalk nearby, muttering to himself in the manner of crazy homeless men. As they passed, a few words came clear. "Go away. Beat it, you moron."

Peter opened the door for her, making a cheerful bell jangle. The place smelled good and had purple walls. It featured local art, scrawled manifestos, recycled paper napkins, beautiful tattooed waitpersons, conversation, and coffee.

Nikki staked out a table near the front while he stood in line to get two cups of steaming dark liquid, cream, sugar, a raspberry scone, and his change. He managed to get these items, plus his briefcase, back to the table without spilling more than a little liquid from one cup.

"So," he said, mopping his sleeve with a napkin, hoping to kick the conversation off to an exciting start. He wondered what they could possibly talk about while she sawed the scone in half with a plastic knife. She wasn't, objectively speaking, extraordinary, but she was a girl, he had just pulled off a Hail Mary pass, and she was actually sitting there prepared to have a conversation with him. They could fall back on the usual subjects, he supposed. "So what do you do? Most of the time?"

"I do some painting," she said in an off-hand way that he recognized from his photography days as meaning she did not make a living at it. If she considered herself successful, she would say "I am a painter."

"What's your subject?"

She gave a little snort. "Architectural features, mostly. Archways, doors, windows, bridges, that sort of thing."

Her default expression was serious, but excessively serious, as if she were trying not to laugh. "Why is that funny?"

"Is it?" she asked, and it seemed to be a direct question: *Do you think it's funny?* "Here." She passed him his half of the scone.

"Thanks." He tried a bite. "Well...why? What's the attraction?"

"It suggests possibilities. Further horizons. New worlds." A pause and she added, "Moving on."

That sounded like she'd appreciate a change of topic. "So why haven't I seen you around before? Are you just visiting?"

"No, I live in San Francisco, but I travel a lot. I don't see Dad very often. So infrequently that I have no idea what he does here." She chewed her half slowly. "What's going on in the Palazzo Building these days?"

"It's, uh, it's a brokerage firm." And according to the company literature, it had been a brokerage firm for over a hundred years.

"So you're a broker." Again there was a faint upward tilt to the corners of her mouth, as if she found that idea intensely funny but was too polite to laugh at it.

"I'm not, really," he said. "I mean, I'm learning a bit, but...that's just my job title. It's like... kind of like trying to do advanced research in an area you have an honorary degree in."

"Oh." She put the scone down. "Did my dad give you the job?"

"...I guess he must have. Do you know why?"

She propped her forehead against her knuckles and sighed. "Patronage." As he probably looked bewildered, she went on. "He has old-fashioned ideas. Like...a man in his position is supposed to look out for the people under him, you know, people he's responsible for. Same way he's supposed to look after his family. Especially the girls."

"Is that so bad?"

"Not if you grew up in the seventeenth century."

"It couldn't be that in my case. Why me? I never met him before I started working here."

"You could ask him."

"At the same time I ask what's behind that door, maybe?"

She licked a bit of raspberry off her upper lip. "I love scones. They're sweet, but not too sweet, and they're tough, you know? I like food that requires an effort to eat. Like good, crusty bread, or brownies that have been in the pan too long."

Peter took a drink of coffee, which he needed after a long, weird day. During this pause in the conversation, she seemed to be really looking at him for the first time. Since he could get self-conscious in the same room with a potted lisianthus, he put the cup down before anything could happen to it. "What?"

"Okay. What do you want to ask?"

"Where did the extra space come from?"

For the first time, she smiled. "Do you really want to know? You could go on thinking of it as a mystery. The explanation might be very dull, you know. Disappointing."

"I doubt that. Secrets are usually kept for a reason."

"Or from force of habit," she said, and the smile blew out like a candle. "On the other hand, it might be very upsetting. It might disturb your idea of the universe so much that if you accept it—which you probably won't—it'll leave you wondering out in the cold and the dark whether your life matters even slightly."

"I don't think it could be that bad," he said. "I think you're stalling."

She started to answer, then looked through the window over his shoulder and froze like a rabbit. Her face went paler under the freckles, and her eyes, which at this precise moment Peter realized were grayish green, went dark with fear.

He twisted around and saw nothing to get spooked about. The street outside was dark and foggy and full of traffic and pedestrians. "What's wrong?"

"I have to go." She stood up. "Don't follow me."

"What?" he protested. "But—"

"Don't follow me!" The bell clattered as she went out.

Peter was not the sort of person who, when told not to follow someone, did the exact opposite. Assuming that a person's requests were within the bounds of reason, he was usually compliant. But this time, he jumped right up and went to the door. Nikki was cutting slantwise across Market Street, in terrible danger, he thought, of being hit by an oncoming bus on a night like this. "Hey!" He dashed after her, but was forced to stop when one such oncoming bus tore between them, and she didn't hear him. "Wait!" he called, and followed.

She went up to a man in a long black coat leaning on a streetlight. Peter slowed as he realized that she was talking to the guy, and his heart went *thud thud churn churn* again even though she didn't look pleased to see the man. *He* was now in terrible danger of being hit by an oncoming bus, but luck was with him and the next one did not go by until he set foot on the sidewalk.

"You must know he wants to see you so he can tell you off!" Nikki was saying.

"So you told him," the guy answered. "Good. He could use a shock to his complacent marital bliss." Peter got a better look at the man and instantly loathed him, from the mirrored shades resting on top of his spiky blond hair to the squared-off tips of his motorcycle boots.

Nikki was glowering. "Why would you want to listen to that, unless you're up to something?"

"Because I thought I might run into you."

"Well, you were wrong. I won't be there."

The man looked over her shoulder at Peter and examined him the way a hungry lynx sizes up a stray goat. "Is that your new ephemeral?"

"Peter, I told you—" Nikki broke off and glared at the man. "None of your business. And stop using that word!"

Peter broke in with, "Are you okay?"

"Fine," she said tightly. "Go away."

"Why shouldn't I call him that?" the man said. "Especially if you aren't going to introduce him."

"Erik Varian, this is Peter. Peter, my brother, Erik."

"Half-brother," said Erik.

Peter wasn't as relieved as he thought he ought to be to learn that the man was Nikki's brother. He started to tell Erik he was pleased to meet him, then remembered that he was having trouble lying and changed it to, "Hi."

"So, is he your new ephemeral or not?"

She stamped her foot at him. Peter had never seen anyone do that in real life before. "Dammit, Erik—"

"We jus—we just met," Peter interrupted, "if it's any business of yours. Nikki, take it easy. I don't know what he means, so I can't be insulted by it. I'm sorry if I intruded."

"He doesn't know what it means," Erik echoed, and very white teeth appeared in his repellently beautiful face.

"No, and I don't care," Peter said.

"It means," Nikki's brother said, "that if I killed you, she could step back a few minutes and find you again. You could replace him in ten seconds flat, Nikki, and there's plenty more where he came from."

"Excuse me?" said Peter.

"Should we show him? It'll save you some trouble and explanations later on, won't it?" Erik reached into his coat pocket, produced a semiautomatic pistol, and pulled the slide back.

"…Christ!"

"No!" Nikki lunged for her brother's arm.

Peter felt a hard blow to his chest and his eardrums imploded. He staggered back under the impact. He wasn't sure what had happened until he tried to take a breath and couldn't. It felt as though his whole ribcage had been crushed and there was no space into which he could draw air.

He knew he should not grab his chest and look down, because that was what people always did on television, and if he did, he would find a great deal of his own blood on his shirt, and then, like a cartoon coyote discovering that he had been standing on thin air for the last ten seconds, he would fall. But he was panicking from being unable to breathe, so he did it anyway. There was a lot of blood on his shirt and on his hand, and more pulsing out every second from a hole that had no business being there. He didn't yet feel as though he was going to collapse, but he thought he should sit down.

He looked up at Nikki's white face, her fingers digging into her brother's arm, and at her brother as he lowered the smoking gun. He said, "Hhughh," which meant, "I can't breathe, please help me."

"You shit!" Nikki said to Erik, and she blurred or perhaps everything blurred as she moved toward Peter—

He was lying on the grass under a blossoming camellia tree, kissing her passionately. Bright sunlight filtered through the petals, striking him blind in staccato bursts. A busker was playing "Stolen Moments" on alto saxophone on the sidewalk nearby. She had one arm wound tight around his neck and the music seemed to move her against him in lapping waves. He could smell pine scent in her hair. Something awful had just happened. He couldn't remember what it was. He closed his eyes, trying to think—

發

When he opened his eyes, he was standing on the foggy dark sidewalk on Market Street, looking at Nikki's brother over Nikki's head. Erik had both hands in the pockets of his long black coat. There was no sign of a gun. Nikki was not kissing Peter. She never had. She hugged him briefly and stepped back. "Thanks for the coffee, Pete," she said. "I've got to run now."

"What?"

"I've got to go now," she repeated.

Peter hadn't meant "What did you say," but rather, "What just happened?" He could breathe. His lungs weren't collapsing. He wasn't bleeding to death—there was no blood on his shirt, no pulsing hole in his chest at all.

"I've changed my mind," she said to Erik. "Let's go see Dad. You need to hear what an asshole you're being."

A single realization cut through the mass of conflicting data screaming for Peter's attention: Nikki was leaving. "Wait! How— how do I see you again?" he stammered. That was important. Seeing her again. Not more important than getting shot, certainly. But more important than thinking he had gotten shot, where that belief was flatly contradicted by the simplest observable facts.

"Don't worry. I'll see you around."

"Unless I see you first," her brother said.

They went up the front steps of the Palazzo Building. Erik opened the door, Nikki went in, he followed with a smirk back at Peter, it glided shut. He was left standing on the sidewalk among some dead leaves the wind thought appropriate to blow into his vicinity at that moment for reasons known only to itself.

All his life, Peter had felt that somebody was looking out for him—not because he deserved it, but because it was somebody's job.

Good things had come his way with no effort on his part, although it must be said he never got anything that he would have chosen for himself. But he never had to prove himself, and he lived in a state of perpetual anxiety because he had no idea how or when his entitlement would come to an end. Someday the ground would shift under his feet and he would not be ready to cope.

This, the day he'd finally seen something he wanted, appeared to be that day.

CHAPTER TWO

Peter got his Honda out from the Palazzo parking garage. He wanted to go to the police, but what on earth would he tell them?

He drove home in a series of short waves of traffic, piling up behind each stoplight. A small, closed-in gray universe traveled with him. The city had vanished in fog and cars honked warnings to each other in what seemed like meaningful patterns, as if in a code that everyone except Peter understood.

With a merciful minimum of circling he found a parking spot on Geary Street, realizing as he got out that he had left his briefcase behind at the coffeehouse. He stopped by the corner hole in the wall for Thai takeout. He climbed the two flights of stairs to his apartment and let himself in with the house keys he found, by some miracle, still in his pocket. He listened to his mom on his old landline answering machine telling him to come over for dinner ("Tortellini, your favorite."). He got a bottle of beer from the fridge, turned on a football game, muted it, sat down, and started shaking.

The shock seemed as bad as if he really had been shot. Adrenaline raced around his system like an ambulance with a green driver, trying to find the emergency, then hung around turning sour in his stomach. He could not begin to understand what had just happened. His life had been safe but dull, then, since he started working for the firm, a little odd, but still dull. Today, it had reached a crescendo of the surreal. He tried to reconstruct events in a way that made sense, but they kept crashing into each other and sinking out of the rational part of his mind.

So after a few minutes spent picking at his food and guzzling the beer, he went over to Jack's place.

Jack was the guy with whom Peter had hung and sometimes clung since they had both been picked dead last for dodgeball in middle school. In theory he was Peter's best friend, but Peter thought of him more as the ground state of his own being—the person that he would have become, had he not gone to college and gotten a job. Going to see him was like regressing to a safer, more explicable childhood world.

Jack lived in his parents' basement, four blocks away. When Peter walked in as he usually did, without knocking, it looked and smelled like a large animal had trampled everything except the TV down flat to make the place comfortable—fusty blankets, wadded towels, crumpled t-shirts, Y-front briefs, half-pairs of socks, used coffee mugs, dried-sticky plates, chip wrappers, energy drink cans. Somewhere under it all, like logs under rainforest growth, were a game system and a couch. With his mind resting on the former and his body on the latter, Jack, a recumbent young walrus in shape, posture, and facial hair, looked around at the change in light and air quality.

"'Sup, Nine to Five?"

Peter put a beer down next to him and picked up the other game controller. The thing about games was immersion, beyond anything except what a good book or a really good movie could provide. Outside thoughts did not crash the party. You couldn't play and think about something else. Self was lost in action, and that was exactly what Peter needed right now.

Better still, Jack did not expect conversation. Theirs was a friendship of extended silences. Most of seventh grade, for example, had been spent wordlessly trading comic books. They finished a major questline and emptied another bottle each, and their babes in body armor were being hailed as the scourge of New Angeles before Peter got around to saying anything.

"I met this girl today."

"You don't need that."

Which was what he would say. And though Peter wasn't convinced it was true, it was a relief to hear. If he didn't need her, he didn't have to put up with the complications: her brother, her way of coming and going, the hallucinations that occurred in her vicinity, or the fact that she might not like him.

They played for another hour before he begged off, and he was no longer sick or shaking by the time he got back to his apartment, just hungry and unsettled.

He'd left the TV on, the Raiders and the Packers rampaging soundlessly in replay. The rhythms of violent motion were so familiar as to seem peaceful. He did some gentle deep breathing, mixed with gentle silent football and punctuated with swallows of warm beer and cold pad Thai noodles. If he took the seemingly impossible occurrences in chronological order maybe they wouldn't crash into each other so much, and he might make some headway brainstorming their explanations.

Thanks to spotting Nikki (*crash!*) in Mr. Varian's office, he knew now that there really was a secret passage, even though there was no room for one. He had measured the floor carefully, and that panel ought to open on to the human resource director's office. So either he'd made a mistake in a late-night pursuit of an obsession or there was another dimension in there. Nikki knew how, why, and where to, and she might have told him if (*crash!*) they hadn't been interrupted by her brother. He could ask her, if he ever saw her again.

Then came the meeting with the new client. It had been weird, but the good thing about Mr. Sanders was that he didn't have any apparent connection to any other event. Peter could think about him with less crashing. The meeting had gone really well, only…

Only Peter could not remember what, exactly, had gone so well. He couldn't remember anything except the initial handshake and then being in the elevator. So he had suffered some kind of blackout right after meeting the man, and then he had been blurting out embarrassing truths ever since. He'd even dared to let a girl know that he liked her, sort of.

What did that suggest?

As much as anything, the loss of inhibition suggested he had been drugged. What was the last thing Mr. Sanders said to him in that burst of medical jargon? *Take some B12.* Peter had heard somewhere in his college days that B12 was a good thing to take to let you down easy after dropping acid, among other things. So had he hallucinated being shot and kissing (*CRASH!*) Nikki? He had never tried anything stronger than pot, but he had heard about the symptoms of hallucinogen use and was experiencing none of them. No dry mouth, no trance, no visual traces, flashes, or distortions.

Just in case, he went into the bathroom, took a couple of B-complex tablets, and washed them down with tap water. He cleaned his glasses, then looked at himself in the broad mirror. His pupils were normal-sized and his tongue was a healthy pink. If he had hallucinated being shot (*crash!*) by that obvious sociopath who was the brother of the girl he might be falling in love with (*CRASH!*), then he had better check himself in at Fremont, because the sensory quality of his hallucinations was just as good as the real thing.

Finally, after the meeting with Mr. Sanders came the girl. The girl who emerged from the impossible passage. The girl whom he might be falling in love with and might never see again.

CRASH!

Peter jumped. That one hadn't been in his head. It came from the living room. A crash, as of something heavy and breakable hitting the hardwood floor. It was followed by a thump, as of something heavy but not breakable hitting the rug.

Like many apartments in San Francisco, Peter's was one-sixth of an eighty-year-old faux-Victorian house with turrets. His bathroom was in one of the turrets, making it an awkward seven-sided shape. The lightbulb was set naked into the ceiling because he had broken the globular cover and never gotten around to replacing it. Between the shape and the lighting, the room was stark and weird; he didn't enjoy occupying it at night while unnerved. He edged toward the door while his imagination ran on about what the noise could've been—a minor earthquake, he hoped, or a very clumsy burglar. He grasped the handle and eased the door open with a long, confounded squeak, inch by inch. Then he turned the bathroom light off, thinking he should have done that before opening the door.

The hallway to the living room was floored with boards that creaked abominably when he stepped on them. He was walking with heavy deliberation, like the tick of a great, slow clock, and tried to make himself quit it. The chill in the air was only the furnace going out, he thought, until he remembered that it was September. He eased past a precarious stack of packaged game disks with words like *slaughter*, *bloodbath*, *massacre*, and *carnage* in their titles, reached the doorway to the living room, and hesitated. Surely anyone in there had heard him coming.

He was hesitating, he knew, because he was terrified of seeing Nikki's unspeakable brother again. The place in his chest where he remembered being shot was throbbing.

Finally, he peered through the doorway into the room, where his armchair and couch seemed to float in the dim light of a single lamp. His other lamp, the kitschy china penguin that his mother had given him for Christmas, was in pieces on the floor. The door to his darkroom was open. Someone was crumpled on the rug in the shadow of the couch.

Peter went in and turned the person over. It was Nikki. Her blouse was soaked with blood. Her eyelids fluttered. She gave him the faintest smile and went limp again.

"Oh, jeez!" He peeled off her coat to find out where she was hurt. "Oh, jeez! Nikki—"

"Mm." She looked pale beneath a smudge of dirt on her cheek, but she mumbled, "It's okay, it isn't—the blood isn't mine."

Peter got the coat off her and said "Oh, jeez," again. She had a dart stuck in her chest, through her blouse on the left side, just under the collarbone.

After looking close to be sure it really was a dart and not some kind of steampunk-inspired brooch, he pulled it out. It was an ornamental brass and glass thing with tail fins and a stinger-like needle. Held to the light, a trace of clear yellow liquid slipped around inside the ampoule. He dropped it as if it were a poisonous insect.

He turned toward the phone his mother insisted he have in case of a quake taking out all the cellphone towers and the internet. "I'll call 911. You'll be all right."

"No," she protested. "No hospital...."

"Why not?"

"'Malright, 'mnot hurt. Just sleep..."

Peter picked up the dart again and showed it to her. "Look at this. Somebody drugged you. I don't know what this is, it could be dangerous. You need a doctor."

"No doctor...please..."

"Well..." But she was out again.

He dithered for a minute between the phone and the girl. Then he checked her pulse. It was slow but strong. He put his arms under her and lifted her onto the couch. She seemed light and he felt strong and protective for a moment, in spite of a panicky voice in his head telling him not to be an idiot. He wondered if she had been hurt without knowing it. But the blood seemed to be drying, not freshening. He took a blanket from the bedroom floor where he had kicked his covers off that morning and covered her with it. He found the dustpan in the kitchen and swept up the fragments of his lamp.

The strange dart had landed on the coffee table. It had eyes—tiny knobs of gleaming brass above the needle—that increased its resemblance to some nasty little wasp or hornet.

Without realizing he was doing it, Peter changed his mind. He picked up the phone and dialed. He got through on the fourth try.

"Emergency 911."

"Yeah, uh, there's this girl in my apartment and I think she's been drugged. She's unconscious and I found a sort of dart…"

"Location, please."

"In her shoulder."

"Your location."

Peter gave his address. "Apartment six, the third floor."

"Someone will be there as soon as possible. What drugs did she take?"

"Uh…I don't know. I just found the…I didn't see anything else. I don't think she took it on purpose. Somebody drugged her."

"Is she breathing? Heart beating?"

"Yeah, she's just out cold."

"Somebody will be there as soon as possible."

The line went dead. From watching cop shows, Peter had gathered the impression that 911 operators were supposed to stay on the line until help arrived. Maybe that was only when somebody was dying. He checked Nikki again. She didn't seem to be dying. He watched her chest rise and fall. He wondered if he had done the right thing. He wondered how long it would take. He fretted. Finally, his eyelids got heavy and he let them close for a moment.

He jolted up as somebody knocked sharply at the front door. Somebody rang the buzzer as well. He shook his head to joggle the pieces of his brain back into place, ran to the door, and yanked it open.

They were not paramedics. They were a stooping, haggard man in a shabby gray coat and a golden-blonde woman in a brown flak jacket.

"Yeah?"

"Good evening," the man began, grinning in a manic, toothy way. He looked a bit familiar in the way any lunatic flasher might be, while the woman was, hands down, the most gorgeous Peter had ever seen—paramilitary clothes ripped and sort of tied around her, like the female lead in a post-apocalyptic roleplaying game. "Mr. Peter Chang?"

The guy clearly wanted to convey the impression of being harmless and annoying. But while Peter accepted annoying, he could not buy harmless. He seemed haggard to the point of derangement. "Uh, who wants to know?"

"You can call me Mr. X, and this is my associate, Ms. Y." Without giving Peter a chance to ask if they'd chosen their own names, the man added, "We're in the missing persons business."

"You're private investigators?"

"No, just missing persons," said Mr. X. "Right now we're trying to locate this person." He showed a photograph of Nikki with longer hair and a green sundress, standing on the front steps of the Palazzo Building. The photo had a ridged surface and acidic color, like a seventies-vintage Kodak. "Seen her?"

"No, I haven't." Peter didn't know what was going on, but somebody had attacked Nikki, drugs and blood were involved, and this disturbed-looking man and beautiful woman were not paramedics, police, or even Homeland Security.

The man's smile turned into a sneer. "Puppy love." He gave the woman a nod. She shoved past Peter into the apartment.

He didn't know how she did it. One second he was in her way, and the next he wasn't. "Hey!" he shouted, wheeling around. "You can't just barge in!" But Ms. Y went on down the hallway flinging doors open—bathroom, coat closet, kitchen, linen closet. Peter followed, feeling like a yappy little dog. "Hey! Get out of my apartment!"

"Shit," Mr. X said.

Ms. Y reached the living room with Peter on her heels. The room was empty. Nikki was gone. Even the coat and blanket were missing.

Ms. Y went to the doorway to Peter's darkroom. Trying to assert some control over the situation, he grabbed her arm. "Excuse me—" Then a burst of red and black light went off in his brain, his head snapped back, and his legs buckled and dropped him. She had hit him in the chin with the heel of her hand. At least, he thought she had. The only things he felt certain of were the pain in his head, the ringing in his ears, and the hardness of the floor.

"Bad puppy," came the voice of Mr. X as if from far away.

"Shoot him up," came the woman's voice.

"Forgettable won't do it." Mr. X, louder and closer. Ms. Y was moving around the apartment—he heard the squeak of his bedroom door and the clack of a light switch—but X's voice stopped traveling. "You've had too much impact on him. The brain doesn't easily forget the circumstances of trauma. They become hard-wired even though blotted from the conscious mind."

"She's not here."

"She was, then she wasn't, but she's coming back." There was a pause, then X raised his voice. "As for our friend here, the best we can do is extract the memory and leave him with a frighteningly indistinct impression of loss and pain. It's a lot of trouble, though...."

"If you're bothered about trouble," Y replied, "a broken neck is no trouble at all."

"Let's shoot him up first." X came toward Peter, whose vision had cleared.

He sat up and scrambled backward on his ass. "Now wait just a min—" The last syllable turned into a grunt as Y plunged the toe of her boot into his solar plexus. He gagged and the room spun. Something rattled and clinked, then X bent over with an odd-looking syringe in his hand. Peter tried to roll away, but Y braced her boot on the juncture of his neck and shoulder and put him down.

X held the syringe in front of his eyes. Peter wished he hadn't. The needle looked heavy enough to pierce bone. The shaft, plunger, and three-ring grip had a greeny-bronze patina of tarnish, like it pre-dated stainless steel. Peter scrabbled to get away, but Y increased the pressure. X grabbed his head and ran hard fingers through his hair, exploring the shape of his skull. "I'll tell you what, we could give him enough to make an amnesiac out of him, if you want to hurt him for an hour or two."

"Sounds good."

"Unless you'd care to put in an appearance, Miss Varian," X suggested.

Peter flailed. Mr. X's fingers pressed hard into his temple. "Told you to go away, moron," he said, and raised the needle...

...then lowered it again, looking around. "Shit!"

"What?"

There was a bang on the front door and someone shouted, "Emergency Services! Somebody call 911?"

"Somebody called 911?" X said. "Somebody thinks he's very clever. Somebody's going to find out what his own kidneys taste like!" He rose and kicked Peter hard in the ribs. Peter screamed.

The pounding got louder. "Hey, open up! We've called the cops!"

"Now what?" Y said.

"Ambulance jockeys want to play vigilante," X said. "They're going to break in. Deal with it. I'll watch things here." Y took her foot off Peter's neck and left the room as the pounding changed to heavy, rhythmic thuds. X kicked Peter again, aborting his attempt to yell for help. He rubbed his finger over his lips, gazing into space. "We didn't check the closet, did we?"

The thudding broke off. There was a smack, a yelp, and a crash, followed by another smack, a scraping noise, and silence. X got a weird relaxed smile on his face, like...Peter didn't know what it was like, but it made him want to crawl under something. X drew a baroque, gun-shaped gun out of his coat. "Don't go away," he said, and went through the bedroom door.

Peter sat up with a groan, rubbing his head, rubbing his ribs, and gritting his teeth as he crawled to the phone. His second attempt to reach it knocked it off the end table and he saw the cord had been cut. His smartphone was...in his missing briefcase. "Oh...jeez!"

"Shh!" A hand reached out and grabbed his arm—Nikki! She wiggled out from under the couch wearing one of Peter's t-shirts (Photographers Do It in a Flash). The blood and dirt had been washed off her face. "Come on! Get up!"

Mr. X reappeared in the doorway. "No you don't!" Pointing the strange gun, he pulled the trigger. There was a pop of compressed air, and a dart hit the back of the couch—another nasty little thing with eyes, Peter saw. "Y!" X shouted.

Nikki pulled and Peter jumped up in a rush of glorious adrenaline fueled by primitive protective instincts that nearly got him shot. X fired again, but the dart stuck in the wall a few inches from his head. Ms. Y appeared at the end of the hallway, another gun leaping into her hand. Then Nikki yanked him through the door to his darkroom.

And everything changed.

發

A cheerful bell jangled. There was light. Nothing ostentatious—just ordinary subdued lighting supplied by metal-shaded industrial pendant lamps—but there wasn't supposed to be any light in Peter's darkroom. Hence the name. Further, the room was too big and had too many tables and chairs and an insufficient number of chemical tubs and file cabinets. Plus he had never painted any wall that shade of purple in his life. It looked like Cosmos Coffeehouse. He looked back and there was Market Street, a foggy night and a few pedestrians—no one trying to kill them.

Peter let out a strangled yelp. None of the customers, late-night caffeine junkies hunched over tablets and laptops, even looked up, but the barista was staring. "Hey, where'd you come from?"

"Schenectady," Nikki said before Peter could open his mouth enough to scream. "Can I get a coffee for my friend here, and one of those chocolate-chip muffins? He needs to get his blood sugar back up."

"Um…I meant… sure." The barista's decision not to ask was writ large on her face; even Peter could see it. "Hypoglycemic? Is he okay? He looks like he was in a fight."

Nikki punted the question. "Are you okay?"

"Uhh," said Peter. He swayed.

"I think he'd better sit down."

"Go ahead, I'll bring it to you."

Nikki took Peter's shoulder and steered him to a table, one well away from the windows this time. He felt his knees threaten to give way and dropped into his chair like a spontaneously collapsing piece of lawn furniture. The barista, short and pretty with a bleached patch in her hair and "Lindsey" on her nametag, followed up with coffee, muffin, and ice wrapped in a towel.

"Okay." Nikki took the chair opposite and slumped over the table. "You take a few minutes and let me know when you feel better."

Peter vibrated. "D–does it have to be that soon?" he managed.

"Sure, why not? You're coherent again already."

"What the fuck just happened?"

"Calm down. Breathe." She sighed as if to illustrate. "My family can open doors to times past, or places that we've seen before. I did that just now to get us out of there."

"...Ah," said Peter, when it became clear he should say something to that.

"Yeah."

"And before that? Who were they?"

"I don't exactly know." She folded her arms around herself, looking pale and small.

"This is the part where I ask if I'm hallucinating." Peter touched his chin. It hurt and felt puffy. His ribs sang pain every time he shifted. "But I'm not, am I?"

"Drink your coffee. That should help. You're suffering a little displacement shock."

Peter tried it. Very strong and too hot. "Don't you want any?"

"No, thanks, I had a whole pot at your place," she said. "Raided your fridge too, though I don't think it's healthy to live on pickles, beer, and cold pizza."

"What?"

"This afternoon, while you were at work. I cleaned up and slept off whatever they shot me with before I came back for you." She ran fingers through her hair, combing out dust bunnies from under Peter's couch. "Sorry. I didn't want to go to my apartment in case they were there earlier."

"...Ah," said Peter again. He tried more coffee, held the towel-wrapped ice to his chin, and asked a question he hoped he would understand the answer to. "What did they want?"

"Well, I think they want to kill me."

"You need to be more specific than that."

She looked away and closed her eyes. Suddenly she seemed very shaken. "I think they mur—murdered my father," she blurted. "And my brother and maybe my stepmother, I don't know…."

"What?" Coming out of one shock and straight into another. "Those two—they killed your dad? My boss? And whatsisname, Erik?"

"No—well, maybe him too, but I meant Alex. He's—he's the decent one." She was gripping the table so hard it wobbled. "And I don't know if they did. It happened so fast. …I need to get back."

"Tell me," he urged.

She laughed in a way that sounded like a sob, then said, "Okay, so Dad had just called a family meeting to chew Erik out about…well, that's not important…."

They had been in her father's study, which was book-lined and austere and twice as long as it was wide, with the Book of Days chained to his massive desk next to the engine terminal. Nikki and Alex stood on one side of the desk, wanting to be somewhere else. Lady Varian, in a muslin gown embroidered with pomegranates, was doing her duty on the other side. Her father presided in his tall chair behind the desk. Erik sat propping his ass on one corner of it. Both of them were at their worst—most authoritarian and most rebellious, respectively—and shouting at each other. Erik had just called Lady Varian a brood cow and her father, looking like he might burst a vein, was in the middle of telling him to get out and never come back when the gray man and the golden woman walked in.

Nikki had barely noticed. They were in her field of vision but they were unimportant, as if they were supposed to be there, like the furniture or the servas. Which was impossible. She'd never seen them before and nobody but a family member could get into Santuario uninvited.

The argument had trailed off as the strangers stood there waiting to be noticed. When they finally registered, she was struck speechless. *Who are you?* Erik demanded, and Alex said *How did you get in here,* then her father stood up.

"Would you like to tell me who sent you here? And thereby save yourselves some excruciating pain?"

The gray man laughed. The golden woman said it would be unprofessional.

"Leave," Benedict had said to Lady Varian. "You too," he said to Nikki. Then he fugued across the room—

"Did what now?"

"We'd be here all night if I tried to explain fugue. Let's just say nobody could've reacted fast enough to beat him. But they did."

For a few seconds Benedict existed in two places. One version stood behind the desk holding the eyes of the gray man and golden woman. The other appeared twenty-five feet away, right behind them, turning around to whip a long, thin blade into the back of the man's neck, exposed above his coat collar. But the man slipped aside like a snake, ducking, grabbing her father's hand—and Benedict got his own knife in the chest. The Benedict behind the desk ran out of time and vanished.

The woman threw something that flashed as it spun at Erik. He ducked, and it sunk into Alex. Nikki finally thawed in time to cry his name and grab him as he slumped to the floor. The woman pulled out a strange handgun and sprayed the air with it, eerily quiet. The blade stuck in the base of Alex's throat, blood welling where curly black hair was poking out of his t-shirt collar. He gurgled, looking at Nikki with blank eyes, and turned into an awkward, inert sack of meat.

Then Erik grabbed her around the waist and fugued out the window. It was a thirty-foot drop, so he'd had to fugue again before they hit the ground. She went rolling and sprawling across the west lawn. Sitting up, she saw him pull a baroque-looking dart out of his cheek and another out of his forearm.

發

"And then?"

"Then he went, 'Don't you ever do what you're told? Get out of here!' and passed out on me." Her mouth twisted. "So I did. Almost made it, but they caught up at the door and…" She gestured at her shoulder, the one he'd pulled the dart out of. "I remember seeing you, and that's about it until I woke up on your sofa and heard them come in."

"And all this happened where?"

"Santuario. And we'll be here all night if I have to explain where that is."

"…It's through the door in your dad's office," said Peter. She didn't deny it. "So are you going to call the police?" he added, feeling this was possibly a stupid question.

"No. I'd rather not get them killed. I—I've got to go back," and she looked up, through the front window in the direction of the Palazzo, invisible in the night and the mist.

"What happened to the psycho? Er—Erik, I mean, not Mr. X."

"Mr. X?"

"Well, that's what the guy called himself."

She snickered. Then laughed out loud. "Oh, Lord..." and it came on hard and fast. She dropped her face down onto her arm and pounded the table as it broke out of her.

Peter scooted his chair closer. "Okay. It's okay..."

"Mr. X... oh, Christ..."

"It's not that funny."

"I know it's not," she choked, but there was no stopping her. Peter patted her back until she got a grip. "All right. I'm okay. Thanks." She breathed slowly, stifling giggles or sobs, and blotted her wet face with a napkin. Peter held his coffee off the table in his free hand until she recovered. "I dragged Erik out of the line of fire and down into the cellar, but then I had to stash him behind a wine rack and run for it."

Wine rack made Peter think of wino for some reason, and that helped him make a connection. "Oh," he said. "My God. Those creeps X and Y—" He stopped as she broke down again. "Sorry."

She bit down on her knuckle. "What about them?"

"They saw us here. Or he did. He was the homeless guy on the sidewalk when we came in."

"Shit!" She got sober again, fast. "We need to go."

"Go where?"

"Excuse me?" Lindsey the barista was back, collecting the empty cup and plate. "Were you guys in here earlier?"

They both looked up sharply and Nikki said, "Why?"

"Well, because...hang on." She went behind the counter and came up with Peter's briefcase. "This yours?"

"Oh—yeah." Peter's alarm faded. "Forgot about that. Thanks," he said as she brought it over.

"*De nada*. You guys see the shooting?" she asked. "It was right after you left, that's how I remembered you."

"The shooting?" Peter echoed.

"You should've practically walked right into it." She waved in the direction of Market Street. "I didn't see anything, but there were cops all over the place."

"Um." Peter felt queasy. "I remember something like that, yeah."

Nikki was staring at Lindsey with an odd expression, which she then turned on Peter. "You remember?" she said. The phone rang behind the counter. "Come on, let's go!" she added as the barista went to answer it.

發

The night was chilly, the fog getting thicker. Moist air wafted into Peter's face and soothed his bruises. Light collected in coherent globes around each lamp. The traffic light changed to diffuse green. Nikki took his hand, tugging him across the street. Peter was pretty sure he didn't have a cracked rib. It still hurt to breathe deeply, so he was none too happy with her efforts to hurry him.

"Are we going through that door?" he asked.

"We? No. I've involved you too much already. Let me send you someplace safe."

"Send me? You mean like…*whoosh*? No thanks. Anyway, are you sure it's not safe for me here?"

They reached the other side, where a pair of barricades with yellow POLICE LINE DO NOT CROSS tape wrapped around them straddled a man-shaped tape outline and a large reddish-brown stain on the sidewalk. "Very sure," Nikki said, and gripped his hand tighter.

Peter's neck prickled as if a marching band accompanied by a motorcade was tromping over his grave blaring out "Oye Como Va." "Is something wrong?"

"We're in the wrong timeline. It happens sometimes when I'm panicking or in a hurry. I jump to the wrong place. You're not supposed to be here. I've got to get you home before I leave." She sighed. "Come on."

"Wait." He hurried after her. "What are you talking about? Wrong how?"

"I better check on my mom, too. If they know who she is, where she lives..." She shuddered.

"Wasn't she with your dad?"

"Oh, no," Nikki said. "That was Lady Varian. The new one. Mom divorced him when I was little. She lives here in San Francisco. Runs a clinic." She trotted up the steps and tried the front door. It didn't budge. Peter peered into the shadowy recesses of the lobby. Nobody around and the security office on the far side was dark. "Do you have a key?" Nikki asked.

"Back in my apartment."

She glanced up and down the street, said, "Brace yourself," took his hand, and pressed her nose to the glass.

"What are you doing?" Peter suddenly noticed two people in the lobby: a girl in a short black coat and a man in a suit, completely off-balance, and he didn't often see himself from behind, but—

In the same second, Nikki yanked him, or rather something yanked her and she didn't let go of him. He stretched, overstretched, then snapped. The glass between him and the interior of the building was no longer there. Instead of hitting it, he stumbled forward over the black-and-white mosaic floor inside, his bruised ribs singing in pain.

"Fugue," Nikki said, trying to steady him. "I'm not very good at it."

Peter looked back to see two figures standing outside, her pressed against the glass, himself looking puzzled...and they disappeared. "Could we not do that again?"

"No promises." She tested the security office door—it was locked—then headed for the elevator. "Do you like Hawaii?"

"Hawaii?" Not for the first time that evening, he felt his head spin, but he was grateful for the distraction from the impossible thing that had just happened. "Why?"

"Okay…New York? Miami? Puerto Rico? Any farther than that and you'll need a passport to get back."

"No, I don't want to go to Miami! Look, we need to talk about this…"

The elevator creaked, settled and opened its gilt cage doors. Nikki grabbed the rotating control and set them rattling upward into darkness. "Peter, I can't protect you. I should never have dragged you into this. Please don't make it harder."

Peter propped his battered self against the wall. He had first seen her here, the moment his day took a left turn into madness. "Maybe I could help protect you," he pointed out.

"Those two took out my father and both of my brothers! Dad's survived since the Renaissance—a couple times over. Erik fought in the Napoleonic Wars, both World Wars, and all over the Middle East. On both sides. For *fun*. I appreciate the thought, but what are you going to do, throw a briefcase at them?"

She stopped the elevator on the mezzanine and walked out. Flushing and pushing his glasses back up his nose, he went after her. "Let me at least see you get there okay—"

She stopped in front of the Human Resources office and tested the door handle. "Wait a second…"

"What for?"

She stared at the door as if she were trying to bore a hole through it. "Okay, go in."

Peter didn't move. "Am I going to end up in Uzbekistan?"

"No. Nothing is going to happen." He glowered; she gazed levelly back. "Nothing will happen," she repeated.

He opened the door. Nothing happened. He stepped into Human Resources.

"What was all that about then?"

"We should be back in the right timeline now," she said. "Does anything look different to you?"

Peter shrugged, looking all over the office and back out at the mezzanine. "No."

"Well, I'm going to check." She gave him an uneasy look. "Would you stay here a minute? I'll be right back."

"Check what?"

"If we're in the right place. Please. Trust me. Stay here?"

"Okay, but can I ask you something?"

"This is not the best time," she sighed. "Really, it's not."

"I know, but look, I've had the worst night imaginable…well. Okay, it wasn't as bad as yours. But I just had two maniacs kick the shit out of me and try to stick a rusty needle in my brain. Why did you come to me? If you didn't think that I could help?"

"I don't know. I was about to pass out, I had to go somewhere. You were the last person I saw outside Santuario. Your face just came to me. I'm sorry," she added. "It wasn't grade-A thinking."

"Well," said Peter, feeling a knot loosen in his stomach. "That's okay."

發

She had to be sure she'd gotten the poor guy back to the world that he hadn't been murdered in, but didn't want him to see that the difference between the one timeline and the other was the presence of that bloodstain and crime scene tape on the corner. He shouldn't have to find out he was supposed to be dead. She would hate having to tell him it was her stupid brother who'd killed him.

She hurried, but even from the inside, the front door could not be opened without a key. Outside, the fog had gone away on little cat feet; the street was almost clear. A street light here, the trolley track with swooping wire there, the shadow cast by the edge of the sidewalk slanting off that way, adobe wall across the street, part of the tall building that housed the coffeehouse, patterned like that, glass reflecting this way, a row of theater posters just there, a column that must be edited out, everything muted by darkness.... *There, now step outside*. Erik could fugue in a heartbeat, but it was harder for her to imagine a mere shift in perspective than an entire new scene.

The air was soft and humid. This timeline seemed three or four degrees warmer than the original. But she must be imagining it—one guy's death would hardly affect the weather. She hopped down the steps and saw there was no barricade on the corner. No tape outline. No blood. No crime scene. Finally did something right today.

發

Peter slumped into a chair. He had a few minutes to get a grip. At least he hadn't imagined anything—well, except.... He poked himself in the sternum. Tape outline on the sidewalk notwithstanding, he must have hallucinated being shot. But a pair of vicious thugs had beaten him up, and a girl he might be falling in love with (he was less sure about this now) had snatched him through a doorway into… into…. He wanted to end that sentence with "another dimension," "a land beyond imagination," or "a world he never made," whatever that meant. Saying that she had snatched him through a doorway into that place across the street from work where he sometimes had lunch just didn't have the same ring.

Anyway, to finish the list, the thugs had apparently murdered his boss. Peter noted that, while he had no idea why anyone would kill Mr. Benedict Varian, he somehow wasn't surprised.

He hefted his briefcase onto the nearest desk, his bruised core muscles complaining, and opened it. Mr. Sanders' report, densely printed gibberish, stared him in the face. He took it out and dumped it in the HR inbox. If Mr. Varian was an obituary, then he, Peter, was out of a job. Nobody else at the firm wanted a 25-year-old gamer pretending to be a stockbroker.

He took his smartphone and stowed it in his pocket, then left the briefcase, with its detritus of paperclips, broken pens, and gum wrappers, on the floor next to the wastebasket. Now he felt ready for…what?

Nikki didn't want to take him with her through the secret door to this mysterious place, this Santuario. But Nikki wasn't here.

So why not try again him—

發

He was in the outer room of Mr. Varian's suite. The door to the inner sanctum was locked and the Venetian blinds were down behind the glass partition. He looked at the glass, picked up the swivel chair from behind Elaine's desk, and swung it hard. It was like a dream, the way his impulses translated directly into action, with no time to think about whether this was a good idea.

There was a satisfying smash. He dropped the chair, grabbed the wastebasket, and bashed the remaining shards out of the frame. As the last crash died away, he heard somebody clear his throat. He pushed the blinds aside and stepped through the frame into the room.

Mr. Sanders sat behind the antique desk. He pressed his fingertips together and produced one of those smiles made by people who understand that smiling is expected of them. "Mr. Chang," he said.

Peter remembered that Mr. Sanders was actually a nice guy, very trustworthy. So he didn't bolt when the client approached, extending his hand and taking Peter's with a sidelong, snapping motion. And then it was all okay. He stopped wondering what Mr. Sanders was doing there. He was comfortable with slumping backwards and letting his client support him with one arm. It was okay when Mr. Sanders took a brass straw out of his breast pocket and stuck it straight up Peter's nose, even though it hurt and he could feel blood trickling down. Even when the client shoved harder and he felt and heard something crack inside his head.

Then Mr. Sanders put his lips on the other end of the straw. And Peter felt something other than blood being sucked out of him, and his thoughts began to disappear—

—self?

He was sitting in the Human Resources office with his teeth fastened in his coat sleeve, stifling a scream.

He unclenched his throbbing jaw, touched his nose, pushed his glasses into place. There was no pain there, only a vivid memory of pain. He staggered back toward the exit, trying to silence his breathing, which effort only made him sound like an asthmatic coffeemaker. He caught the door handle in the small of his back, grabbed and twisted it, and backed out onto the mezzanine—where he bumped into Nikki when the elevator dinged and she stepped out. He yelped, she jumped, they both spun around, then he tried to push her back into the cage.

"Peter—what the—?"

"Shh! For God's sake, don't go in there!"

"What? Why?" She let him hustle her into the elevator, but grabbed the lever and held it in place.

"Someone's in your dad's office. Down!" he urged.

"Who?" She shut the doors and the elevator creaked and descended.

Peter gulped air as though breathing had just become possible. "This client I met earlier today."

"...And that's a problem?"

"He drank my brain!"

The lift whined to a halt, the mezzanine floor level with their heads. "Say that again?"

"With a straw!"

She looked at him as though he were raising snakes in his hat. If he had not been so unnerved, he would have to admit she had a point. "He drank your brain with a straw?"

"You have to believe me!"

She let the elevator lurch and settle on the ground floor, biting her lip. "I believe you, but..." The gate-like doors rattled open. He scrambled out and urged her on with frantic gestures. "...but you seem awfully healthy...."

Peter tugged her out of the elevator. From the corner of his eye, he noticed two other people in the lobby, but thought nothing of it. "Well, obviously he didn't actually, but he will...er, would, but..." She came along with no resistance, but not much effort either, as if bewilderment had overcome volition. "Look, I did not imagine it," he said. "I couldn't have!"

"No kidding!" Mr. X said. "You should be in a coma."

Nikki gasped. Peter skidded to a halt, then put himself between her and them.

How could he not have noticed? They leaned on either side of the front door, Ms. Y holding the same weird-looking gun X had fired at him earlier.

X lurched forward. "Hello again. Here I am to add purpose to your meaningless little lives." The lobby acoustics did horrible things with his voice. "Oh, and here Ms. Y is to kill you."

"Run if you like," Y invited.

"Don't!" Peter said, trying to shield Nikki from both of them at once. "They want a clear shot."

"Who are you? How are you following me?" Nikki demanded.

"Wherever you go, we can follow, Daddy's girl," said X. "So come along quietly now…"

"…and we won't get hurt?" Peter asked.

"Oh, I wouldn't say that. That would be a fib, wouldn't it, Ms. Y?"

"It would."

"You bet—" X's face changed in mid-menace. Y's head snapped up. She sprang behind a marble support column, jerking X after her, just as a man in a long black coat leaned around the door to the security office and opened fire.

Nikki flung herself to the floor, dragging Peter down with her. The noise filled the space; Peter's ears rang. Chips of marble flew from the columns. He buried his face in the floor. When the shooting stopped, he dared to look up. Erik was using the security door as cover. He dropped a clip out of his pistol and slapped in another. "Nikki, over here! Move!"

Ms. Y snapped her arm around the column and fired back—not with the dart gun, Peter noticed, but a staple semi-automatic in basic black—three flat cracks. Nikki tugged him. She might have shouted; he couldn't hear her. Moving seemed a bad idea, but to oblige her, he wriggled forward on his elbows. Then, once more, he felt stretched and snapped, and had the sense of disorientation and altered perspective. He was all the way across the room, next to the security office. Nikki scooted inside as Erik leaned out and sprayed the room with high-velocity lead. Ms. Y's bullets punched into the door in return. Gibbering in shock, Peter crawled after Nikki. Inside, he fell over, curled into a ball, and stayed that way until the next pause in the battle.

"What are you doing here?" Nikki gasped.

"Looking for you, of course."

Peter smelled leather, cigarettes, and gunsmoke, a faint but irritating whiff of ammonia. His gaze started at the man's square-toed boots, then traveled up the long black coat to the gun, and the pale eyes that glanced down and dismissed his entire existence.

"How did you get here?" Nikki asked.

Ms. Y opened fire again. Bullets thudded into the outside wall. Papers hanging on a bulletin board overhead broke free and fell on Peter. Erik leaned out and blasted back. In the silence when the clips on both sides were dry, he said, "I woke up in the wine cellar, I went to the clinic to get detoxed, and then I came to see if you were here." He raised his gun as Ms. Y fired twice into the door, as if knocking on it.

"Let's talk!" Mr. X yelled.

Erik's mouth twisted. "Okay," he called. "Talk."

"All we want is your sister. We won't hurt her. Give her up and you can take off."

"Huh. Let's see, let me think," Erik responded. "Fuck you."

Ms. Y emptied another clip and lead mushroomed out the interior of the metal door.

Peter's back cramped up from the strain of cowering. He picked up the paper that had fallen on him. It was the security guards' duty roster. He wondered where R. Norris, midnight to 6 am shift, had gotten to. Then his brain kicked into gear. This was the security office. It contained a phone. He grabbed it, punched 911, and got a busy signal.

"You could keep them talking," Nikki was saying.

"I don't negotiate with ephemerals."

"But we might find out something about—"

"Cut it short." Erik braced himself against the wall. "I've got one more clip after this. There's a door back there you can use." He pointed down a narrow hallway running into darkness at the back of the room. "The juncture where I ran into you in Paris, okay? I'll be right there."

Peter punched 911 again and got a busy signal.

"Why should I trust you?"

"I just saved your life. Twice!"

"Oh, yeah. Thanks."

Peter tried one more time and then banged down the receiver in frustration.

"Don't overwhelm me with gratitude, just get going. And ditch the douchebag, will you?"

A fresh hail of bullets battered the door. Erik waved Nikki away. Peter picked up the phone again, then fumbled and dropped it as she pulled him down the dark hallway. It ended in an emergency exit rigged with a fire alarm. Nikki stared at it for a long moment, which changed into a longer moment. Peter shifted from one leg to the other. Behind them the firing stopped and then in the sudden, ringing silence came the sound of Erik changing clips.

"What's the matter?"

"Don't throw me off. I can hardly remember what the place looks like. It's been years…got it," she said. "Go through."

"After you."

"Open the door!"

"Go!" Erik roared from the other end, and a fresh exchange of gunfire began.

"Okay!" Nikki shouted. "Stay close if you want to come with me." She pushed the bar. The fire alarm went off, compounding the hellish racket. Humid air wafted into Peter's face and he boggled at daylight in a completely different city.

Her breath hit his ear. "Sorry, Peter. At least it's not Miami." She planted her shoulder in his back and shoved.

The world turned sideways. With a yelp, he tumbled through the doorway.

.

CHAPTER THREE

Peter landed in wet grass. Winded, he rolled over, hoping to see a doorway that he could scramble back through. He saw a canopy of gently swaying leaves. No door, no Nikki. There was a soothing, crashing sound, as of waves on a beach. A fragrant wind blew a few drops of warm rain into his face. It wasn't really daytime —the sky was full of soft twilight. The peace and quiet, after all the gunfire, made him feel dazed.

"Hey, you aren't supposed to climb the trees." Peter twisted and saw a lean guy in swim trunks, who said, "That tree is protected. You shouldn't climb."

"I wasn't climbing it." He scrambled to his feet.

"You dropped from the sky, huh?" The guy had a whistle around his neck. Peter inwardly quailed in the face of even such scant authority as this. "Maybe you'd like to carve your initials too?" He glowered and strolled off to watch the ocean, leaving Peter to gape at his surroundings.

He stood under a big banyan tree on the edge of a grassy park that fronted one end of a wide avenue. The avenue divided a long crescent beach from a line of hotels stretching at least a mile. He smelled salt air and flowers. Soft rain pattered on the sidewalk. He'd seen ads for the place. Only the ads were full of girls wearing dental floss, and drinks with pieces of fruit on sticks, and the sky was so blue it hurt.

She had sent him over two thousand miles away. Leaving her alone with her brother and two people who wanted to kill her. She was in danger and she had dumped him like…well, like a douchebag. Peter looked up at the sky and yelled.

The sky answered. The rain went from pattering to pounding, then the clouds opened up and dumped a bath over him. He scooted closer to the banyan tree. Its canopy cut the deluge down to windblown spray.

"No climbing!" the lifeguard barked.

"Okay!" Peter took his glasses off and pointlessly wiped them on his sopping shirttail. "It's not a compulsion or anything. Where can I get a cab?"

The lifeguard pointed to the nearest hotel, a gilt and white edifice with a K, a P, an L, and a lot of vowels in its name. "Concierge will call you one."

Peter plunged out, noticing as he left that the banyan did, in fact, have graffiti carved into its massive, dangling roots: "Hang Loose," "I.D. & N.V.," and so on. He ran, or rather sloshed, toward the hotel.

發

He couldn't dry out, even after the rain stopped bucketing down. The post-squall atmosphere was humid enough to swim in. He gave the cab driver nearly all the cash he had on him, then sat on a bench outside Honolulu International and dumped out his shoes.

A local behind a check-in counter told him there was a flight for San Francisco in two hours at an absurdly high last-minute rate. Peter handed over his debit card and accepted his boarding pass. He had a bruised face, no carry-on, and he squelched when he walked. The screeners took one look and yanked him out of line. After ascertaining that he had nothing metallic but his keys, nothing electronic but his phone, and no containers of liquid unless his clothes counted, they recommended he freshen up before getting on the plane.

"Sure," said Peter. "Do you have a towel or a clothes dryer I could use?"

He did the best he could in the men's room with paper towels, and reached his gate in time to shiver in the air conditioning until they announced his flight. The plane had rows of two seats on either side and five in the middle. His seat was in the very center on a crowded flight. At cruising altitude, he reclined the entire two inches and sank into misery. Notwithstanding chill and cramp, he was very tired. Somewhere over the dark Pacific, he drifted….

發

In his dream, he had plate mail armor and a mighty broadsword. These were standard elements of a dream he sometimes had after playing a massively multiplayer online RPG all weekend, but this did not feel like a game. A dark fortress reared up before him: two colossal towers, three great portals, and a façade of tall, arched windows. A single light shone in the highest window of the right-hand tower.

He advanced. Thorns like fishhooks caught in his armor. The place was surrounded by briars and brambles. He hacked with the broadsword and plunged forward, repeated the process innumerable times, and eventually broke through to the front courtyard.

The fortress looked like a very tall, gnarled old tree. Its flying buttresses were massive roots digging into the pavement. Branches twisted up the mullion between each set of doors and formed columns on either side. Their tops and the arches were leafy with carvings.

He pushed through the central portal and a huge inner door and found himself in a vast space crowded with people. It was a cathedral, and they packed the nave and the choir, filled the balconies and stood in the aisles, praying or chanting or singing. The sound filled the space, palpable as the light pouring in like honey through the high windows. The floor trembled, his back teeth vibrated. He felt that the sound was made by the light, or the light was made by the sound. The people didn't notice him, but they were praying for him, for the success of his quest.

He climbed the spiral stairs that ascended the tower with the lighted window. They were high and narrow and went a long way up. Water poured down the stairs in a rush and a roar, trying to sweep him away. Stones fell on him, fire tried to block his path. A middle-aged woman with a face as familiar as his own shook her head at him, disapproving. On one landing, he fought an angel dressed in black and couldn't lay a blade on him, though the angel also couldn't hurt him through his armor. On another landing, a slavering ghoul asked him a riddle, but gave away the answer. The air became thin and cold and the wind whistled in his ears.

When he reached the top, there was a door, gray as driftwood, with a silver latch shaped like an infinity sign. He went through. She was there in a cold garret room. In a black dress with a tight bodice and lace swirling around her ankles and way too much black eyeliner.

"Peter," she said. "You're too late." Then she turned and walked through the wall. Instantly, the tower shook and its walls began to crumble. He lunged after her and banged his head into the seatback in front of him as he woke up.

A few hours later he shuffled stiffly off the plane into the white spaceport atmosphere of San Francisco International. He made one stop in one of the molded-plastic restaurants, not to get the breakfast burrito and coffee his body craved, but to grab an abandoned newspaper, which told him that today was the Friday it was supposed to be. He escaped the airport into a cloudy late morning. He couldn't think of anyone he could call for a ride and plausibly explain how he just got back from Hawaii—except Jack, who didn't drive—so without enough cash left for a cab, he got on the BART.

Tall houses standing in rows looked solemn and unreal. Power lines swooped by and views of choppy gray water came and went until the train dove underground, and he saw his reflection in the glass. He looked rough, hollow-eyed, with a bruised chin and damp, slept-in clothes.

The dream had been so strange—a cathedral, and a girl who refused to be rescued, although that last part was at least consistent with what he knew of Nikki's character.

After thirteen miles, the subway pulled into Civic Center off Market Street. He thought about just going home. Calling in sick, or even quitting. He was fed up with being beaten, hunted, insulted, and ditched, and with Varian Financial and all things Varian. But he took the escalator to the street, ran northeast a few blocks, and reached the Palazzo Building breathing hard and nine hours too late.

A pair of cop cars had pulled up in the no parking zone out front. Inside, the foyer walls, columns, and security office door were riddled with holes and festooned with yellow tape. Official-looking people were doing forensic-looking things with tweezers and tape measures. He went up to a short, lab-coated woman who was extracting a bullet from the column X and Y had hidden behind.

"Was anyone hurt?"

"Who are you?"

"I work here," Peter said.

"Well, this is an ongoing investigation, which means no comment, move along, go back to your lives, citizens, unless you have a statement to give."

Peter didn't want to give a statement no one would believe. "Please. I have friends who might've been here. Was anyone hurt?"

"Peter!" Mr. Slinky called from inside the descending elevator cage. "Over here!" It dinged and its doors rattled open. Abe was there too. Giving up on the cop, Peter got in with them. "I want to speak with you in my office," the manager said. "I've been trying to reach you all morning. The calls went straight to voicemail."

"Is she all right?"

"Who?" the younger Mr. Slinky asked as the elder closed the doors and raised the cage off the floor. Peter had often thought it must be weird to work at the same place as your father, and vice versa.

"Nikki!" he exclaimed. "Nikkole Varian. Is she okay?"

"Miss Varian?" the manager said. "Why? Was she here when all this…" he waved at the bullet-ridden lobby beneath them, "this…"

"Cap-popping?" Abe suggested.

"…vandalism took place?"

"Vandalism?" Peter said.

"No bodies. No injured people," the manager said. "Nobody was here when the police arrived. Nobody saw a thing, not even the security guard."

"Asleep in the break room," Abe said in hell-to-pay tones.

"What about the boss?" said Peter. "Where's Mr. Varian today?"

"Hasn't come in," said Mr. Slinky.

"Take it easy," Abe said to Peter. "You're twitching like a bug on a griddle. Look like you had a bad night."

"Everything is under control," Mr. Slinky said, and Peter's jaw dropped. "We'll talk about it in my office."

The elevator opened on the third floor's hive of cubicles. Phones rang, scanners hummed, fingernails clacked, suits strode in every direction with tablets and frowns, and someone was reading off strings of numbers in a loud voice. Elaine, in a black and white dress with flapping sleeves, swooped down on the elevator. "Hey, look who finally decided to show up. Could really use that Andersen report about now. Where've you been?"

Peter stared. Jetlag sang in his head. "Oahu," he said, then grabbed the lever and shut the gate in her face. "Why are they acting like everything is normal?" he demanded as he sent the elevator downward again.

The manager raised an eyebrow. "Because everything *is* normal. There's been an incident downstairs, but that doesn't concern everyone. And I want to speak to you in my office."

Mr. Slinky's face no longer reminded Peter of a boulder. He looked more like a short, round pony with blinders on. "But the old man is dead, isn't he?"

The manager raised the other eyebrow. "Who told you that?"

"Nikki did. Who told you?"

Mr. Slinky had no eyebrows left to raise. His whole face widened and he exchanged a look with his father—who only smiled and shrugged. "We need to have this conversation in private."

"Later!" Peter opened the gate and plunged out.

The suite doors were open, so he strode right in. "Where do you think you're going?" Elaine demanded. She must have come down the stairs pretty fast in those heels. Noticing that the glass partition was unbroken, Peter went through the inner office door. "I'm calling security!" she shouted. He closed the door and flipped the deadbolt.

The office looked just as it had the last time he'd really seen it—before the vision, hallucination, whatever it was, of Mr. Sanders shoving a brass tube up his nose. The heavy, antique furniture looked blank, lifeless—as if no one owned it anymore. He found the right panel and pushed on it. Nothing happened.

He did all the pushing, pulling, shifting, turning, and tweaking he had done before, to get it out of the way and to see what he might have overlooked. Then he moved ledgers, opened cabinets, shifted knickknacks, twisted light bulbs, opened and closed windows, pushed on other panels. He tried knocking. The knocks rang flat, as though off a masonry surface underneath. Nothing continued to happen.

He went through the desk drawers, moving things inside, trying different combinations of buttons on the telephone, holding the receiver down. He examined the underside of the desk and the rest of the furniture. He climbed up on the desk and inspected the ceiling, shifting acoustic tiles and sneezing as dust fell on him.

He stood in front of the panel and said, "Open sesame!" He leaned his forehead against the panel, banged it, and swore.

Someone knocked on the office door.

Peter realized that no one had shouted at him or tried to break in for the last ten minutes. He twitched the blinds aside and saw the office manager, hands clasped behind his back as if he were prepared to wait for years. Elaine was nowhere in sight. Peter opened the door.

"I'm fired, aren't I?"

"In a manner of speaking," Mr. Slinky said. He came in and relocked the door behind him. "This will do for privacy. You better sit down." Peter sat with a thump. All his muscles sang with release of tension. Mr. Slinky took one of the smaller chairs on the client side of the desk.

"You're right," he said flatly. "Mr. Varian is dead. We were told early this morning."

"Who told you?"

"Mr. Dromio. His majordomo. Like a property manager," he added, for Peter's edification. He took a sheaf of papers out of his jacket. "Mr. Varian left behind instructions with regard to you in the event of his death. I will carry them out as best I can. Although the circumstances make it difficult."

The papers were folded together in thirds, tied with a black

ribbon, and sealed with wax. Mr. Slinky broke the seal, untied the
ribbon, and spread them out. Peter couldn't read them upside-down
because they were hand-scrawled in a script full of long, drawn-out fs
and other curly things. The paper was pinkish-brown and each sheet
had a different grain.

Mr. Slinky put on his reading glasses. "Skipping over the wherebys
and heretofores," he said, "Mr. Varian leaves you controlling interest
in the firm, and ownership of the Palazzo Building."

Peter listened to this calmly. He asked Mr. Slinky to repeat it.

He did.

"No," said Peter. "I still don't get it."

"The firm and the building are yours. Or will be. When this can be
probated. In about seven years." He turned the parchments around so
that Peter could read them. There was a paragraph naming Theodore
Slinky executor of the estate, Abraham Slinky as backup executor;
there were bequests describing corporate shares and real property
with his name mentioned, and there was a page where it was signed
"Benedetto Niccolò Variano," and witnessed by Alexander Varian
and Dromio Illegible Scribble.

Peter sagged back in the chair as the world came crashing around
his ears.

"Why?"

"The old man never explained his interest in you to me." Mr.
Slinky gathered the parchments and folded them together along the
same creases.

"Would you tell me if he had?"

"Mr. Varian was in the habit of not telling anyone anything,
not unless he had to, or he intended the world to know it. So, yes,
I would." He retied the packet so that the same parts of the ribbon
made up the knot. "And here is all that I do know. When you were a
baby, the old man paid for your initial medical care. You were sickly,

some problem with your lungs. He put you in a position to be adopted by Mr. and Mrs. Chang and made sure the process went smoothly. He took an interest in your education and saw that you received a few opportunities you might not otherwise have gotten. When you were old enough, he told me to hire you in your current job, and to keep an eye on your performance. Especially how well you did picking stocks."

"Patronage," Peter muttered in a daze.

"Yes, that."

"I get the whole company?"

"No. First it's necessary to prove that Mr. Varian is dead."

"That's a problem?"

"In order to get a timely death certificate, it's usually necessary to produce a corpse. Mr. Varian's killers apparently took his body."

"Why would they do that?"

"You knew he was dead before I told you, seems like you might answer that question." Peter shook his head wordlessly. "Was Miss Varian was here last night? Were you in the building at the time?"

"It was afterwards. It was a crazy guy dressed like a flasher, and a blonde paramilitary kind of woman, and Nikki's brother Erik trading shots with them." He described most of the events of the previous evening. "And then she sent me to Hawaii. I don't know what happened after that."

"Well," said Mr. Slinky, and Peter felt that he was picking his words with care, "she is not in there." He jerked his head in the direction of the panel. "Or so they tell me."

"What *is* in there?"

"Mr. Varian's estate."

"In another timeline?"

"More of a pocket dimension, I'm told."

"You've never seen it?"

"I've never been through that door."

Peter examined Mr. Slinky's placid face in disbelief. "Are you some kind of advanced organic robot?"

"No. Just a man from a family with a tradition of keeping another family's secrets."

"No interest at all?"

"Plenty, once. But I gave up trying to get in a while back. Seems ordinary to me now. All companies have closets full of skeletons and mysteries. This one is just deeper than some."

"Does anyone else know?"

"My father. Elaine. Everyone else…merely understands that you don't ask too many questions if you want to keep your job."

"And that's why you don't tell the police," Peter said, in a sudden, blinding grasp of the obvious. "Because he was killed in there. You can't show them a crime scene. What are you going to do?"

"When the time seems right, report him missing. They'll probably treat it as a kidnapping, what with the scene downstairs. If he doesn't… turn up…in seven years, I can have him declared legally dead. Then the will can be probated." He picked it up and tucked it back in his jacket. "In the meantime, I have proxy authorization to run the firm. You can stay on, learn the business."

"I want to talk to somebody in there," Peter said. "That guy you mentioned. Mr. Dromio."

"I'll let him know when I see him."

"I want to see him now." The thin, heady wine of exhaustion made him reckless. "I'm the last person who saw Nikki."

Mr. Slinky smiled for the first time. "I'm sorry. I don't have a pager number for anyone through there. Mr. Dromio will get in touch when it suits him."

"That's how it works? What if there's an emergency?"

"Mr. Varian didn't consider anything that could happen to this firm to be an emergency, Peter. I gather it's only a small part of his holdings, and not one that held his attention. He's had his fingers in a lot of pies. For most of my time here, he didn't come in to the office more than once a month. He didn't take an interest…until you were hired."

Peter turned his chair and stared at the panel.

"Trying to get a handle on the moment?" Mr. Slinky asked.

"Waiting for the graphical user interface to show up." He shook his head and got up. "I'm going home. Maybe everything will make sense after I have a hot shower and three or four beers, get a pizza delivered, play a little Warcraft, and sleep in."

"That reminds me," said the manager, taking a section of newspaper out of his jacket. "You might not want to go home right away. You might want to talk to a lawyer first."

發

Nikki slammed her studio door and leaned against it, ears ringing in the sudden quiet. She was back on the Île St.-Louis in La Belle Époque. A hundred and twenty years and more than six thousand miles lay between her and X and Y. She didn't know how they had reached Santuario, found her at Peter's, or known she'd gone to the Palazzo, but they could not reach her here. Could not. Not possible. No way.

Her shaking fingers found the bolt and shot it home.

She'd come here after sending Peter to safety, not the Vigoureux Fountain where Erik would be waiting, because she needed a breather. If you sup with the devil, use a long spoon. Let him wait.

No one kicked at the door or broke into the room. She heard the clip-clop and rumble-rumble of traffic and the underlying song of the Cité.

Afternoon sun poured in through the mansard roof window and her work-in-progress almost glowed. Notre Dame, stretched up into a surreal shape like a huge old forked tree with hanging roots and carved foliage. Like Yggdrasil, over a river green as absinthe. It wanted a few more layers, realization of detail. Her fingers itched to pick up a brush. She hadn't been ready to leave. If she had stayed, she could have gotten in a whole lifetime before seeing her father and Alex killed. All the smells welcomed her and made her feel safer: wine, oil paint, turpentine, canvas, garlic sausage, sex…. Edvard had obviously left right after she did. Perhaps just as well. She would've cried on his shoulder and prolonged the breaking-up process.

The smell of wine was rather strong, actually. She went around her easel, and there was the bottle of burgundy she'd bought for lunch, smashed on the table, dripping and pooling on the floor. Some of her canvases had gotten splashed. A chair lay on its side, and a couple of cigarettes had been stubbed out on a clean plate. *Men!*

It was a relief to be angry. A flush warmed her, her hands stopped shaking, her stomach settled down. She gathered up her work, every last door, archway, window, bridge, passageway, and labyrinth, wiped them with a towel, and restacked them. *Victorian men!*

She righted the furniture and put the food away, slamming the plates down too hard. Though she was furious, she felt clear and sharp, her mind racing.

…Victorian men who are upset…

She changed out of her jeans and Peter's t-shirt into a period-appropriate man's shirt, waistcoat, and trousers, put her hair up under a cap, and unbolted the door. The hall was empty, so she went for a bucket of water from the tiny communal bathroom. When she opened the door, a dozen brown roaches ran from the light. She filled the bucket at the sink, careful not to touch any surface, then stalked back to her room.

She loved this little garret under the mansard roof of a typical Haussmann building in the heart of Paris. Its privations meant nothing to her. She was proud of that. What had Edvard said? *You have some other life you intend to resume when I have ceased to amuse you.*

…Victorian men who have reason to be upset because their lovers have not been honest with them.

She did not want to be fair, dammit.

Putting the bucket on the floor, she took a fresh look at the mess. Tried to imagine Edvard the Monk, in his tight collar and knotted cravat, after she had walked out on him, smashing a bottle of wine and then deliberately not cleaning it up, even though it had spattered onto artwork. The picture wouldn't come.

She thought of him taking his hat and slinking away to his suite on the Rue Lafayette to scribble in his journal, something along the lines of *One day suddenly the scales fell from my eyes and I saw a Medusa's head and I saw life as a thing of terror.* That seemed far more likely.

She went to the closet where she kept the turpentine, rags and cleaning supplies. The handle was always stiff, but this time it stuck fast. She jerked harder, but it stayed stuck. She wrestled with it until it went beyond an annoyance into absurdity, a struggle that brought heat and pressure behind her eyes. The stuck handle was a stupid little thing, but she couldn't cry about the big things—her home, her father, Alex. They were too big; she would never stop. Blinking hard, she braced a foot against the wall and yanked with all her might.

She stumbled back as the door flew open.

Edvard fell backward out of the closet like a tower collapsing: horribly slow, supports buckling, beams flung outward, a deep rumble, an explosion of dust, the clatter of falling debris, the echo of her scream. His head smacked the floor. Too late, she unfroze and caught him by the shoulders.

Upside-down to her, his face gray, eyes wide open, as in *Self Portrait with Burning Cigarette*, the startled expression fixed in them until they rotted. Bruises livid in a line around his throat. Cold blood oozed from a wire buried and twisted up by his left ear.

She watched her hands crawl over him, like strange frantic animals attached to the ends of her arms. They verified what her eyes said: cold, still, no breath, no pulse.

Sometime later the room grew dark and chilly. Her face felt stiff. She staggered up, legs cramped and numb, and her joints popped with a sound like eggshell cracking. She turned up the gas. The light made everything ghastly: the garret narrow and cold, floor stained with dark fluid, gritty with broken glass, grimy beams not improved by cheap theater posters. On the easel, a dying tree above a toxic river. The rest of her canvases, each one a meticulously painted dead end. The dead man's face staring into the void through the window.

She ought to do something for him. Put him on the bed, untwist the wire, close his eyes, put the sheet over him. Alert the authorities. Raise the hue and cry. Little things, useless things, she should be able to do them.

Instead she put her coat on, pulled the unfinished painting off its frame, and rolled it up with the rest of her canvases. They made a heavy, awkward bundle. She didn't look at him again as she let herself out.

He had almost no family; so many of them had died young of brain fever or tuberculosis. He himself had died—would, in another timeline, die—an old man, after a long, respected career, during the Second World War. But not here. Not where she had intersected his life like a walking blight.

Strange how long it took her to move from the fact of his death to consideration of how and why it had happened. But not surprising, because she already knew. The answer was on the table, where two hand-rolled cigarettes had been stubbed out on a plate. She should've guessed after he shot Peter just for being around her.

The roll of canvas banged her knees as she descended the narrow spiral into the pit of the lower floors. Again she stopped outside the landlady's door. Madame would have to deal with what Nikki had no strength to face. And it would bring her trouble—with the police, with renting the room again. She slipped all the paper francs she had left under the landlady's door and went on. It wasn't enough; it would have to do.

Cold wind cut through her coat when she emerged from the hotel. The temperature had suddenly plummeted as it sometimes did in spring. Parisians shuffled along the street, collars up and heads down into the wind. Gripping the roll of canvas close, she headed south across the Pont de la Tournelle, along the street above the quay to the Pont de l'Archêveché, pausing to rest here and there when the bundle got too heavy.

Her arms ached by the time she reached the right place. In the middle of the bridge, in a pool of light from the streetlamp, against the stone rail. Where Edvard caught up with her. Where they talked for hours. Where they created another world. She pulled out the one unfinished painting, then hefted the bundle onto the rail and pushed it off. There was a splash and several canvases separated from the mass, turning face-up, flashing color and form. Then the dark current whisked it all into the blackness under the arch.

She straightened. Just then, the streetlight overhead flickered and died, leaving her with blue afterimages in her eyes. She walked across the bridge in the dark, hunched and shivering, with her last canvas rolled under her arm.

Erik was waiting for her on the other side, Notre-Dame's medieval bulk looming behind him. He was dressed in period for a change, in a gendarme's greatcoat and hobnail boots. As she approached, he took a last drag off a glowing cigarette, then flicked it into the river. She walked past him. He turned and fell in step. "You didn't make the rendezvous. I got worried."

She said nothing.

"I wanted to talk to you about these," he said, showing her a dart like the one Peter had pulled out of her. "I've seen them before." She said nothing whatever, walking west toward the front of the cathedral. "The Hunters use them. They've found a way into Santuario."

Again, she said nothing.

"Did you find the gift I probably shouldn't have left for you?" he asked. "Unusual weather you're having," he then said, after all these openings had hung in the air for a few moments. "Isn't it?" The wind was tearing the new blossoms off the chestnut trees. It was like being pelted with dry snow.

Nikki opened her mouth, just to see what would come out. "Parricide."

"What?"

"It was you." She stared straight ahead, her eyes cold and dry. "You murdered Dad and Alex."

"I only kill ephemerals."

"Those two were professional assassins. They were working for somebody else. Dad said as much."

"That's logical, as far as it goes, but these are Hunters' weapons." He gave her a dry look. "How do you connect me?"

"How'd they get into Santuario? Someone had to show them the way. It was your misbehavior that made Dad tell Dromio to reprogram the servas, so most of them were conveniently out of the way. Even if those are Hunters' darts, you could find some easily enough. And it's quite a coincidence that twice when they showed up, you were there to save me."

"You think that gun fight was faked?"

"Not necessarily. To you, they'd be disposable once they served their purpose." He didn't answer, so she went on. "I suppose you'd have come to Peter's place just in time, too, if they hadn't screwed that one up. You hired them to take Dad out, and terrorize me, and send me crawling to the only man who could protect me from the scary bad guys…didn't you?"

They were crossing the worn limestone parvis in front of Notre-Dame. A large number of bundled-up Parisians were going in through the great portals for evening Mass, seeking shelter or perhaps an explanation for the unseasonable cold.

"That," said Erik, "would have been brilliant of me. I wish I had thought of it. But the fact is I didn't."

Nikki turned and struck him. It was no limp-wrist slap; she cracked it loose-armed from the shoulder and his head twisted from the force. "You said you could follow me anywhere. Have you been helping them do it?"

A red mark bloomed across his cheekbone and the bridge of his nose. "Don't do that again!"

She saw him whole, as if at the wrong end of a telescope. "You know what? I won't." She walked on. "You can tell them it didn't work," she called back.

He came after, pushing through the other pedestrians, talking fast. "Nikki, it's bullshit. Nikki…where are you going?" He grabbed her arm. She glanced at him, then looked away, to the foot of Notre-Dame, by the portal of the Virgin. "You can't go back, it's not safe. I'm telling you—"

She fugued across the parvis, twenty yards, his grip wrenched from her arm, in full view of a dozen locals heading for the same portal. There were screams and yelps. A jostled citizen who had seen nothing turned and gave her a frigid stare. "Excuse me," she said, dodging around him.

Another scream told her that Erik had followed, appearing out of the night just as carelessly. "Nikki!" He pounded after her. "I did not murder our father, all right?" He reached for her, restrained himself for a moment, then grabbed her by the shoulder anyway. "Don't you realize, you're the only one for me? Do you really think I'd jeopardize us by killing him, on the off chance you wouldn't find out it was me?"

She could not find words to express the honest answer to that. She let it show in her face instead: a freezing—not contempt, she didn't have enough strength—but indifference. His hand fell and she went through the ancient portal.

發

Abe was waiting for Peter in the elevator again, with the firm expression of a man who has made up his mind about something. "It seems like you're in a spot of trouble," he said quietly.

Peter had a section of the *San Francisco Chronicle* folded under his arm and it tingled as if radioactive. "Guess so."

"I want you to have something," Abe said, and took a khaki pouch with a faded *U.S. Army* stencil on it from his trouser pocket. From this, he extracted a small, flat brown rectangle.

When he handed it over, Peter saw a traditional Chinese character engraved on it—it was a mahjong tile. "Uh…thanks. Why?"

Abe got the elevator moving downward in its usual atmosphere of rattles and creaks. "It's been in the family a while. An old Chinese lady gave it to my grandfather, actually, way back when he saved her life in the big one of 1906. He worked here too," he added, irrelevantly. "Anyway, it's good luck. I carried it through two tours of duty in Korea and never got hurt. I think you might need it now."

The character still had little flakes of green paint clinging inside its grooves. Peter thought it was qīng fā, the Green Dragon. The old ivory was so smooth it felt greasy, although the back was scratched up. "Oh, no, Abe, I can't take this, it's your good luck," he said, and handed it back.

Abe received it with a half-hopeful, half-sour expression. "You sure?" He opened the elevator door in the lobby. "Not even to save the world?"

Peter was nervously eyeing the officers and forensics people working in the lobby and didn't pay much attention to this question. "The world's going to have to save itself, I've got enough on my plate."

He tried not to hide inside his coat collar as he went through the lobby. But none of the cops glanced his way. He tottered across Market Street, hyper-vigilant for police cars, vaguely noticing more colorful vehicles whizzing by, the sun breaking through the clouds, pigeons pecking a muddy half-doughnut in the gutter, pedestrians pedding, junkies junking—in short, life going on. Even the police tape and barricades from last night had been removed from the sidewalk. He made it to the coffeehouse. The bell clattered, but no one looked around. Relief was followed by the fear that everyone was deliberately not looking at him. Three people at separate tables were reading the newspaper. But he couldn't back out without it looking weird.

In the lunchtime line, he tried making a call and a chilling voice said she was sorry but his cell phone account had been deactivated. Deactivated? He looked through the phone, finding no new emails, voice messages, updates, or texts, then shoved it back into his pocket. Hunger, he decided, was making him freak out more than necessary. By the time he reached the counter, the smell of coffee and pastries made him feel faint.

"The chili, a BLT on sourdough, the pasta salad, a brownie, and a mocha grande."

"Coming right up." It was the same barista—Lindsey —looking frazzled. She flew at the cash register, fingers jabbing keys, the energy of a frayed electrical wire.

"Double shift?" Peter asked.

She groaned. "All the shooting last night. That cow Missy refused to even come in today. I've got to find a better job." She thrust his debit card back and blinked at him. "Weren't you in yesterday? Did you leave this?" From behind the counter, she took his briefcase.

"Um, yeah—no. I mean, yeah, but didn't you already give me my briefcase last night?"

"Not that I remember. Do you leave it behind a lot? Or is this one not yours?"

"Well, let me take a look." He took the case aside to let her deal with the next customer and thumbed the combinations on both sides. There was the Sanders report he'd left in HR last night.

Underneath that was his smartphone. He picked it up. He removed the one in his coat pocket. Same model. Same case. Identical pattern of wear. He thumbed through the menu of each phone and found the same list of apps, contacts, text messages, downloaded music. But the phone from the briefcase had two new messages on it—both from Mr. Slinky—and did not have any pictures of Honolulu (which he'd taken in the cab on the way to the airport so that he wouldn't wonder later if he'd been dreaming). He returned the old phone to his pocket and used the new one to make the call again.

"Hi, Pete."

Enough tension to catapult a quarter-ton boulder through a castle wall went out of him. "Hey, Mom."

"How are you, sweetheart? Did you get my message last night?"

"Fine. Yeah. Things are a little weird at work today, that's all." She tried to invite him to dinner and he declined— "Just wanted to hear your voice."

"Well, get out of the basement once in a while, hon." Disappointed but quintessentially Mom. He mumbled through the goodbyes and punched off. Using a paperclip, he put a long scratch across the back of the functional phone.

The barista gave him his mocha. "So?"

"I don't know how I could have lost it twice in one night."

"Ha," she said. "I lost my car keys in the shower last week. Ask me how that's possible. That's heck of a bruise you've got there. Were you in a fight?"

"You don't remember that either?"

She shrugged. "Hey, it's been a long night."

At a corner table, Peter opened the *Chronicle* and reread the story about the two paramedics found dead in his apartment. Perusal at leisure revealed that the situation was less dire than he'd thought. He was not identified by name or description, and though his address was given, they'd left out the apartment number. He checked other news outlets online and was reassured. The police might be searching for him, but the public at large really wasn't looking at him funny.

The part of Peter that trusted cops and thought it good to do what other people said to do told him that he should go turn himself in before they came and kicked down whatever door he hid behind. He hadn't done anything wrong. He even had an airline ticket stub in his pocket and photos on his phone that proved he had been in Hawaii last night.

And what about my voice on the 911 tape? What about Jack and Elaine and all the other people who saw me in San Francisco that evening?

Well, the other part of him said, *perhaps the cops won't get around to asking them.*

Before he could kick himself for thinking something so stupid, the barista showed up and plonked his order down, her single tuft of blonde hair standing on end. "What shooting were you talking about?" Peter asked her. "The one outside, on the corner, where—somebody got killed?"

"Whaaat?" Her pierced eyebrows quizzed him. "No, nobody killed. It was a rampage in that fancy old building across the street.

Like somebody went postal, only it was after work, so nobody got hurt. Weird, huh? And pointless. Dude must have been crazy."

"Uh, yeah, God—all that marble defaced, when will the senseless violence end. So nobody's been shot around here recently? You don't remember telling me about a—a different shooting, do you?"

"Um. No? One's bad enough. Third shift in SOMA is for the birds."

"Yeah. Thanks." He stared after her, trying to make the gears in his mind mesh, then gave it up as a bad job and fell on the food. He shoveled chili, wolfed bread and bacon and pasta, gulped brownie and mocha. If he could have unhinged his jaw and engulfed it all at once, he would have. Proteins, carbs, sugar, and caffeine hit his bloodstream. He gave his brain another shove to see if it would go.

First problem. Cops wanted to talk to him about two dead people in his apartment. It was unlikely to be a short conversation, and might end with him staring at blank gray walls for a long time.

Second problem—not really a problem, but a puzzle. His remote, scary, pocket-dimension-dwelling boss whom he'd barely known had been controlling his life from behind the scenes. Had known him as a baby pre-adoption, even. How? Why?

Third problem. He had two smartphones, and the barista did not remember seeing him the second time last night, and someone had both been shot and not been shot on that corner outside, and what had Nikki said about the wrong timeline?

Final problem—an entire set of problems unto herself, including the previous three—Nikki. He watched the barista as she halved a bagel with one stroke of a bread knife, flung it into the toaster oven, scooped cream cheese onto a plate, snatched a bowl from the microwave, and splashed hot coffee into several cups. How simple today would be if he had fallen for *her* yesterday. He could be relaxing with a second cup of mocha, working up the courage to talk to her.

Ten minutes later, he marched back into work. Still not a single officer in the lobby looked at him twice, not even the one he'd been talking to. Peter was used to invisibility, but under the circumstances, it made him check to make sure he still cast a shadow.

It was still lunch hour and the third floor was quiet. He surveyed an acre of fabric boxes and found them squat and misplaced under the graceful vault of gray-white marble. Daylight came in by tall arched slits a long way from his workspace. He fired up his computer, mentally flipped off the firm's no-personal-internet-use policy, and let his fingers race over the keyboard, trying variations on Nikki's name on two different search engines. One hit in the Bay Area. A small credit card payment netted a short list of addresses and phone numbers.

He felt the prickle on the back of his neck familiar to cubicle workers everywhere. "Need another word with you," said Mr. Slinky. "What are you up to?"

"Since I can't reach Nikki's world, I'm looking for her in mine," said Peter.

"I see." Mr. Slinky lowered his voice. "What makes you think she'd be around?"

"She said she lives in San Francisco. And if they're really time travelers, then however long it might take from her point of view to come back, for us it would be now."

"If she came back."

Peter hunched his shoulders. "Yeah. If." He tried the most recent number on the list.

Brrrrrrrrt. Brrrrrrrrrt. Click. "Hi there, phone person, you've reached Nikki V.'s machine thingy. Talk into the box after it goes bing." *Bing.*

"Nikki? It's Peter. Pick up."

Boop. Click.

"Well?"

"Sounds like her." But she sounded more animated. And callow. It was a very Nineties sort of phone message.

The office manager coughed. "Isn't it possible that our time is the past for her? She could skip now and return to her own present."

"Don't think so. I have two identical phones, and the memory of an event that didn't happen—" Peter rotated his chair and stopped. A stranger attended the conversation. A bald guy in an old brown suit stood next to Mr. Slinky, like a praying mantis beside a teddy bear. "Um…"

"He's with me," Mr. Slinky said.

"Please, go on, Mr. Chang," the stranger prompted. Italian accent, more exaggerated than the boss's very slight one. "No one is listening. And I keep il Signore's confidences even now."

It was the guy he'd seen come out of Mr. Varian's office yesterday morning, looking like a spy or a butler. Peter plunged ahead. "I think she saved my life by pulling me into an alternate timeline. I think she makes new timelines when she goes into the past, at least if there'd be a paradox otherwise." He wished he had more than Physics for Liberal Arts Majors in his background; then he might at least sound authoritative. "If she returned to her present and it was our future, she'd go to the original timeline, not this one."

"Because?" the stranger prompted.

"Because in this timeline, the future will be different—it won't be the present she knows."

"Bravo." He clapped slowly, twice.

"This is Mr. Dromio, whom I mentioned earlier," Mr. Slinky explained. "He agreed to see you."

Mr. Dromio bowed. "The honor is mine. But I must correct my colleague. Lady Varian desires to meet you, and to learn what you know of the assassins and her unfortunate loss, and to discuss Miss Varian's whereabouts. I am come to conduct you into Santuario."

The manager looked startled. "You're taking him through?"

"Now, if you please."

發

Peter hovered while Mr. Dromio fiddled and pushed on the secret panel in a way that he was certain he had tried. It popped open. He stared down a narrow stone passage with a speck of daylight at the far end. It exhumed earthy scents and goosebumps formed on his arms.

"Be more on your guard here, eh?" Dromio said to Mr. Slinky. "We do not know how the assassins got in. If Signore Varian's children are targets, they may return."

A line deepened in the office manager's face. "You could have mentioned that sooner."

"I have been a trifle preoccupied," the majordomo said.

"If those killers are coming back, I'm sending everyone home."

"You will not stand watch to protect the family?"

"That was never in my job description," said Mr. Slinky. "I've got four security personnel. Except for the one who happens to be my father, none of them could find his ass with both hands."

Mr. Dromio turned away. "I see. Then do what you must." He motioned to Peter. "The lady is waiting."

"Okay." Peter turned sideways to fit through the opening—

發

A knifepoint hovered an inch away from his left eyeball. Dromio held the knife, his face all hard lines. Behind him, a woman in black stared with engulfing dark eyes. Peter couldn't move because a dozen or more hands were holding him in place, one even gripping his hair. "I can make you beg for death," the majordomo said.

發

Someone tapped his shoulder. Peter whipped around with a gasp. Mr. Slinky and Mr. Dromio stared at him, the former looking concerned and the latter suspicious. "Are you okay?" the manager inquired.

"What? Uh, yeah. Everything's fine." Except somebody was banging on kettledrums in his chest. But it was a hallucination. A flashback. Lucid something or other. Not real.

He squeezed past the panel. The tunnel was old, stones rough-hewn, mortar decayed, floor worn smooth. Cool in here like it really was underground. He looked back through the opening at the second-story office and felt a surge of—what had Nikki called it?—displacement shock.

Dromio slipped in, closed the panel behind him, and left them in the dark. He switched on a penlight, beckoned with it. "Were you afraid to enter here?"

Peter heard his own breathing and their steps, smelled dank earth and a mixture of sweat, wool, and machine oil from the majordomo. "A little," he admitted. Somebody was still beating kettledrums in his chest, but they slowed from prestissimo to allegro. "How does this work?" he asked. "Nikki said only family members could get in here. Are you—?"

"She exaggerates. This is a permanent doorway. Anyone with the right information could enter. But that information is difficult to come by." A few steps on, he added, "I wonder about you, Mr. Chang. Like that flunky back there with his four guards, you are a man of the twenty-first century. Loyalty to your *patrone* is not first on your list of virtues, is it?"

"Uh, no," said Peter. "Afraid not."

"Then why are you here? This is not in your job description."

"I'm trying to find Nikki, make sure she's okay. Anyway I'm curious. Who wouldn't be?"

They had nearly reached the other end and he could see a grassy slope through the doorway, with cracked marble blocks arranged like benches in four or five concentric semi-circles.

"You might pay dearly for your curiosity," Dromio said, and gestured Peter out first.

He stepped out into sunlight through a doorway set in a free-standing chunk of brick wall—where no tunnel could possibly exist— at the bottom of a half-ruined sunken amphitheater of white marble with grass and moss growing in the cracks.

Surrounded by girls.

Strange girls, with four arms apiece. "Um," said Peter. They had fixed, bright smiles, pink-painted cheeks, and empty glass eyes—they were dolls, a dozen of them, life-size. They wore tight bodices, puffy blouses, and ruffled skirts cut above the knee, like a calendar full of St. Pauli Girls. Only with four arms. Surrounding him.

A thud and a click made him look back. Dromio had closed the door behind them. "Er, what...?" said Peter.

"They are Mr. Varian's servas. Leave them to me." The majordomo stepped forward, exuding authority. "*Attenzione!*" Creaking slightly, the automatons swiveled toward him. Dromio pointed at Peter. "Seize him!"

As one, they trundled forward.

CHAPTER FOUR

*P*eter tried to bolt between the automatons. Multiple hands clamped onto him and jerked him to a stop. He struggled. They didn't budge. They looked awkward, like he could push them over and they'd be too heavy to get up again, but once they laid hold of him, it was like being chained between concrete walls. He saw a metal chassis under a dress, and sprocket gears exposed at the elbow and knee joints, just before they grabbed every part of him still free and within reach.

At the top of the amphitheater steps he saw a woman, very pregnant, her belly rounding out a full-length black dress with a train and a black veil over her hair. Her face was taut and cold with pronounced cheekbones, pale against all the black, her eyes huge and dark.

"What's going on?" Peter demanded from an awkward position.

Dromio brushed a speck of dust off his worn coat. "You are being detained."

"Why, for God's sake?"

"Search your conscience," said the lady. "Search particularly for the names of your co-conspirators and for the details of your plot against my husband."

"You let in the assassins who murdered il Signore and his son," Dromio said almost in the same breath. "You will tell me who they are and why you hired them before you die."

The sky whirled. "Excuse me, what?"

"Must I assist you with your memory? Because I can do that." He seized Peter's coat. "I have ways of making you talk." He produced a knife with a pronounced point and held it an inch under Peter's eye as Peter yelped and struggled. "I can make you beg for death. In fact," he added, "I have an entire phrasebook of clichéd threats at my disposal and I am not afraid to use it."

"Y–you're making a mistake. I'm not—I haven't—Christ!"

He heard a click, caught some movement out of the corner of his eye, and focused on it in preference to the sharp metal point in the extreme foreground. The door in the ruined wall creaked open again. Wrapped tight in her coat, looking windblown, pink, and miserable, Nikki came out of the tunnel and stared.

"What the hell are you doing?"

"Miss Varian!" Dromio lowered the blade. "You are safe!"

"I'm here, anyway. What are you doing with Peter Chang?"

The majordomo gestured with the knife—Peter squeaked as it missed him by an eyelash. "This is our traitor."

"He is not!" Nikki exclaimed. "Erik is!"

"That cannot be!" The woman, who Peter assumed was Lady Varian, came partway down the steps. "His own son?"

"Possible, my lady. You know they were estranged." Dromio frowned at Nikki. "You have proof of this?"

She shrugged. "Just motive and circumstance."

"Well, even so, it would not rule him out." He brandished the knife at Peter. "They could be in league."

"Uh, no."

"Not likely," said Nikki.

"Nonetheless," said Dromio, "I will find out to my own satisfaction."

"Forget it!" Nikki snapped. "Columbina, the rest of you, let him go!"

"Yes, Miss!" said all of the robot girls at once— chirpy and tinny like a bunch of wind-up birds. Every grip holding Peter off the ground let go. He landed on his back in the grass.

"Just a moment, Signorina," Dromio growled. "I am charged with your safety, among other things. I will not allow even you to interfere with this matter. Seize him!" he told the servas. They bent and grabbed Peter again, hauling him to his feet, his glasses hanging askew.

"I said, let him go!"

"And I said, seize him!"

Peter yelped as they all jumped for him, grabbing places already feeling bruised. "Could we make up our minds, please?"

Nikki gave Dromio a look in which rage faded into confusion. "They obey every member of the family and myself," he explained. "The only person with the authority to countermand any order given them was your father."

"Release him and don't restrict his freedom again," Nikki tried.

"Yes, Miss!"

Peter pushed his glasses back on and scooted over next to Nikki. "Can I mention how glad I am to see you right now?" Busy with a staring contest, she spared him a distracted scowl.

The lady came down the steps, managing her train with one hand. "Nicoletta, be reasonable...."

"Reasonable?" She turned as if to forestall an embrace. "I'm not the one with a knife here."

"We are trying to protect you and to avenge your father!"

"Not this way, you aren't!"

"You are making our defense difficult," Dromio said. "With contradictory orders, the servas may suffer a breakdown just when we really need them."

"Then stop giving them orders that contradict mine!"

"This is an unseemly argument," said Lady Varian. "With the dead not yet buried."

"Apologies, my lady." The majordomo put the dagger away. "We must settle it now. Another attack could come. The servas are our first line of defense. One person must be in command of them. We must have a master of Santuario."

"And just who would that be?" Nikki demanded.

發

Peter perched on the edge of a settee, in what he supposed was a drawing room paneled in antique walnut, set with tall, mullioned-glass windows and furnished with pieces of upholstered hardwood so baroque that he didn't even know the names of most of them. He hardly dared move for fear of knocking over some expensive unidentifiable thing. He sweated. Despite the late afternoon sun pouring in the windows, a fire blazed on the wide hearth.

He was following a debate between Nikki and Dromio as though his life depended on it, because it probably did. They'd already had an argument over whether he should be allowed to listen to this one, Nikki winning it by refusing to let Peter out of her sight.

Dromio paced in front of the fireplace and flourished pieces of parchment, arguing that Signore Varian's will provided that Santuario passed to his oldest surviving male offspring, and since it would take time to determine who that was and how to find him, Erik was probably most eligible to take over temporarily —

—and Nikki, standing in front of Peter, interrupted before he could expound upon this. Her father had expressed his intention to disinherit Erik for his behavior.

Dromio replied that while il Signore had expressed displeasure with his older son, he had not written him out—however, he added, to forestall Nikki's outrage, the old man had as good as done so by stripping Erik of the authority to command the servas and the other mechanisms on which Santuario's defenses depended.

Good, Nikki said, then—

—in which case, the majordomo interrupted, care of the estate devolved upon the next surviving male child with the gift of timewalking.

Nikki said that with Alex dead, there weren't any she knew of.

Dromio said there were several who had gone missing, including illegitimates, but he meant one currently present and born in wedlock, though posthumously. They looked at Lady Varian. She reclined on some sort of backless sofa with an ornate screen shielding her from the fire and watched the two of them lock horns, one hand resting on her belly.

Nikki said she would let anyone other than Erik take command of Santuario's defenses, but Dromio and Lady Varian were not heirs and (here she turned the air blue and the lady's cheeks scarlet) she would not permit them to kidnap, threaten, or stick a knife into the eyeball of a friend of hers.

Dromio said that Lady Varian stood in for the true devisee until he was identified and located, and that it was her duty and his own to protect Santuario and the Varian family as she thought best. Nikki said that if they were going to torture people, it wouldn't be in her name. Dromio invoked Interdimensional Security, the Real World, and What's Best For You, Young Lady. His pate developed a sheen that reflected the fire. Nikki looked ready to kick the furniture over.

Meanwhile, a serva trundled into the room. She—it?—shoved a mug of something hot into Peter's hand, then wrapped a theater curtain around his shoulders. On closer inspection, he saw it was a velvet cloak lined with cashmere. "Um, thank you, but I'm fine."

"Miss Varian gave orders to make you comfortable," she answered. "You've had a shock." And fussed around him, squeaking and rattling, adjusting the cloak and plumping the cushions.

"I'm getting used to them. I just want to listen to this—hey!" She picked his feet up and shoved an ottoman under them. Peter yelped as hot liquid sloshed over his fingers, and she caught the mug in her fourth hand and put it down. "Look, I'm comfortable, okay? Very comfortable!"

She stopped in the middle of mopping up his sleeve. "Very good, sir," and trundled out. Peter shrugged out of the cloak, sniffed the hot drink, which smelled of rum and spices and made him wonder if they thought he had been rescued from drowning in the Gulf of Alaska, and decided against it.

"…What on earth made you think Peter had anything to do with it anyway?"

Dromio had been pontificating at full steam, but now he paused. "Il Signore warned me that Mr. Chang might have the ability to reach Santuario."

"How?"

"I presume that he or one of the family told Mr. Chang how to do it. I can't imagine how else."

"I didn't. Why would he? When did he ever tell an outsider anything?"

"Further, Mr. Chang has been working at the San Francisco office for just a few months. All the other employees have been there five years or more. He stands to benefit by the death, for he is heir to the Palazzo Building and the firm. And he admitted he was in the building at the same time as the assassins."

"That's because I brought him there," Nikki said.

"You did?" Lady Varian put in.

"Yes. I was drugged during the attack. I took a walk while hazy and ended up at Peter's place. I took Peter to the Palazzo Building with me, then sent him away for his own protection."

"You revealed your father's secrets to this man?" said Dromio.

"Don't change the subject. You've got the wrong guy."

"I have heard enough," Lady Varian said. A wisp of cloud covered the sun, dimming and softening the light cutting through the windows. "We have made a mistake. Mr. Chang must be innocent of conspiracy."

Muscle worked in Dromio's jaw. "My lady, it would be wise to be certain."

"If my husband confided in Mr. Chang, then he must have trusted him. You cannot imagine il Signore putting trust in anyone he had not made sure of? Then let us be done with the matter." She strained to rise. Dromio and a serva assisted her. "Sir, my apologies." She held a languid hand out to Peter. "You were brought here on my orders and, it seems, over-hastily."

Peter got up belatedly. "Oh, it's—it's okay." Even if it wasn't, Lady Varian's manner slapped a restraining order on complaints. He shook her chilly fingers, then realized he was supposed to kiss her hand. But she had already pulled away.

"Okay, then," said Nikki, and all the fire went out of her. She turned toward the window.

"Nicoletta, " Lady Varian said. "I know this is unpleasant, but we ought to settle it. I want you to understand. I loved your father, but we must think of the future, of our safety."

Nikki ran one hand through her curls. "What do you want settled?"

"One of us must have the management of the estate and its defenses. For the child's sake, and my own, I want to protect Santuario. But I prefer to remain friendly with you. How does that sit with your disposition?"

"You seem up to the job," Nikki admitted. "I can't say for certain that I am."

"I appreciate the vote of confidence." Lady Varian hesitated. "You truly believe that Erik arranged the murder of his own father?"

"I think so, but…" Nikki sighed. "Yes, I believe he did."

The lady addressed Dromio. "The servas must be told to detain him should he arrive. How long will it take for you to make them to accept my commands over those of others?"

"It is a simple operation." The majordomo put on a business manner. "But I must do them one by one. I have spent much time preparing them for combat. I do not want to pull them all away at once and leave the portals unguarded."

"Then I pray you, sir, be about it."

"By your leave, my lady. Miss Varian." He bowed twice, ignored Peter, and withdrew.

Nikki turned to face her stepmother. "Did Dad say or do anything that seemed like…maybe he thought this was coming?"

Lady Varian cooled her cheeks with a fan. "Not that I perceived. Why?"

"I just wondered why he was so anxious to reconcile with me, you know, right around the same time."

"I assume," the lady said delicately, "that he wanted peace in the family coincident with the arrival of a new member."

"Maybe." Nikki sounded as if she doubted it. "Anyway, where is he? And—and Alex? I want to see them."

"Oh, my dear…" Lady Varian sank down upon the backless sofa. "Now I recall, you do not know. Your father's body was…stolen."

"Oh, yeah," Peter said. "Mr. Slinky said that X and Y took it with them."

"When you and your older brother disappeared, I ran for help. I met Dromio bringing the servas to our aid." The lady's voice turned bleak. "But when we returned to the study, the assassins were gone, and so was his body. Only Alessandro was left behind and so much blood…"

發

Peter went with Nikki to find her younger brother laid out in a room that had all the structural details of a chapel—nave, choir, columns, arches in white and rose marble—but nothing to indicate which, if any, religion might be observed in it. A serva keeping vigil gave a squeaky curtsey as they passed. "Are you comfortable, sir?" she asked Peter.

"Uh…yeah. Thank you."

A stone slab occupied the middle of the room. Peter gazed down at a guy whom he could have passed every day on Market Street without surprise. Alex Varian, even dead, looked like someone who worked for one of the Bay Area tech giants—young, nerd-pale, uncomfortable in a suit, a well-padded midsection, a dense black beard to provide definition to his chin. Someone who wargamed on weekends, communicated in grunts and jargon, could've sat comfortably in Jack's basement for days. He'd been cleaned up for display: no blood or visible wound.

Nikki cried quietly, without drama, for five minutes. She brushed straggling hair away from her brother's face, touched her lips to his forehead, and walked out. Hugging his jacket around himself, Peter followed.

"He was brilliant," she said. "And one of the good guys. He didn't deserve that."

They emerged from the chapel into its long shadow on the eastern crest of the steep hill that made up most of Santuario. Warmth lingered as the day grew old.

"Where is this again?" Peter, still trying to deal with displacement shock.

"It's an estate that Dad bought in Tuscany sometime in the 1600s after he made his first pile of money. He took the place with him into a timeline of its own and cut it off from the rest of the world, except for doorways to various times and places that he set up for supply lines and…other commercial ventures."

Peter's first impressions had been edited by terror. He'd seen the steep hill reinforced on the heights with stone walls, and a late-medieval fortified villa with one great square tower gripping the top, looking very much like a place you could go into and never come out of. Servas had conducted him through a courtyard, a warder's portal set in massive doors, a tiny foyer, and up a flight of stairs long, narrow, and steep enough to ensure the visitor was out of breath and defenseless when he reached the top. Then it flowered into a vast and graceful space—fluted columns branching into high arches, rows of tall and narrow windows set in the upper half of the outer wall, great chandeliers with hundreds of lit candles, ceiling frescos like a pagan Sistine. It made him feel like an ant in a gilded bathtub.

Now he looked down over wildly beautiful gardens, each planted with orchards or spilling greenery and flowers over its terrace like an overgrown pot. Most had a centerpiece of some kind: there were sundials, water clocks, armillary spheres, regular clocks, a huge geared mechanism of corroded copper. Statues and a few structures, too—bits of ancient Greece, Rome, the Middle East, and China transplanted. The terraces were all outlined or bordered by tall royal jasmine hedges. These were sparse and well-clipped near the top but grew thicker and wilder toward the bottom, forming a hedge maze on the valley floor, spanned by the massive and ancient-looking aqueduct.

Oddly, the steep round hill stood in the middle of a steep round valley, with identical terraced and hedged grounds all the way up its slopes, as if the hill had been turned inside out and stretched. "What happens if you climb out of the valley?"

"You come right back here." The view left Nikki unresponsive.

She stood and gazed impassively, like a statue to some virtue espoused by early Christian martyrs.

Peter touched her hand. "So what happened after you got rid of me?"

"I met Erik in Paris. Were you okay in Hawaii?"

"I was fine. Don't do that again."

"I couldn't take you with me. Couldn't leave you there."

"Thanks for not leaving me," Peter said, "but it seems a bit rude to send someone a couple thousand miles away to someplace he doesn't want to go."

Briefly, she came back to life and looked solemn. "Rude. Got it."

"So what happened in Paris?"

"Nothing much." She turned her head; the gleam went out. "I just realized that Erik could be behind it."

She descended the steps that cut through a terracotta wall shoring up the slope. He followed. "Mind if I walk with you?"

"No. You probably shouldn't wander around alone."

"Why, do you think that—that Dromio still wants to, er…"

"Cut your eyeballs out?"

"That, yes."

"Dromio is loyal to the family. Thing is, with Dad gone, I don't know what that means. It may be he doesn't either."

They wandered through a garden bright with anemones, marigolds, and yarrow. Nikki seemed to find it jarring. She strode restlessly from one end to the other. A pair of gray doves skittered away with alarmed peeps and hid under a hedge. She studied a headless marble nymph atop a splashing fountain. Then she squatted on her heels near the edge of the terrace, her back against an olive tree. Peter sat on a bench nearby and breathed in the sound and smell of water on stone and watched her profile.

"Why don't you, um, I don't know, go back in time and warn your father? Just keep all this from ever happening?"

"Well, for one, Santuario doesn't split and doesn't allow paradoxes. That's the way Dad wanted it. One stable singular place among all the shifting timelines. We can't walk backwards here."

"Then go back somewhere else."

"That would violate the taboo," Nikki said.

"What taboo?"

"It would split his timeline, create two of him." She seemed uncomfortable talking about it.

"He'd mind that?" said Peter. "He struck me as...such a survivor, you know, at any cost." Even without spending much time around him, the vitality and impact of the old man's presence had been obvious, enormous—he seemed to take up all the space and all the oxygen in any room he occupied.

She picked at the bark of the olive, pulling bits off. "He was that. But not at the cost of interference from the future. He didn't want another one of himself showing up, usurping his place, being with his wife, taking over Santuario. If you think about it, it's hard to cope with the idea of being duplicated. I would hate it. Even Erik wouldn't interfere with a family member's personal timeline...I think."

"Do you really think Erik hired those two?"

"I'm not sure any more. Why would he want them to take the body? Don't get me wrong, he's a complete bastard. The thing is, my theory of why he would want to kill Dad and Alex and send those two after me kind of...requires the universe to revolve around me." She flung a handful of bark over the edge. "And forgive me for sounding like this might not be totally obvious, but it doesn't."

Peter noticed for the first time that she was not really pretty...or rather, that her level of attractiveness varied a lot with lighting and mood. Right now, she looked blotchy: lips bitten, nose raw, freckles prominent.

"Mine could," he said. His ears grew warm and sound faded out so that he could barely hear the water splashing on the stone, or the doves calling to each other.

Nikki blinked at him as though he were just now coming into focus. "You'd be better off as far away from me as you could get."

"Maybe," he agreed. "But still."

"Erik murdered my last lover," she said evenly.

"I'm not afraid of him," Peter lied.

"Then you're an idiot!" She flung another piece of bark. "Anyway, you know, this is not the best time to talk about it." He nodded. Couldn't argue with that.

They sat awhile without speaking, Nikki hugging her knees and Peter finding the ground in front of him of intense interest. The precipitate declaration hung in the air and then seemed to fade away. The doves strolled and pecked about the lawn with sleepy twitters. Pale orange light on the valley's eastern wall began to fade and shadows softened and blurred into each other, like spreading pools of watery ink.

"Nikki?"

"Yeah, Peter?"

"You're crying."

"I know."

"What are you thinking?"

Her tears welled naturally like blood through a bandage, not even disturbing her expression. "He—my dad—called me home trying to make up." Her voice shook. "He wasn't perfect, God knows. I mean, look there." She pointed out a big, graceful bronze armillary sphere mounted on the back of a dragon in the garden below. "He stole that from a fifteenth-century observatory during the siege of Beijing in the Boxer Rebellion," she said. "Half the stuff here is loot and the rest was picked up for a song when the owners were desperate.... And I never forgave him for leaving us when I was little. Mom didn't want him back, I don't blame her, but he didn't even get in touch again until I was fifteen. But he was the only father I had, and I…I blew him off. I left again, first chance I got."

"Let me help."

"I want you to let me take you back out that door, and to go back home and forget that you ever met me."

"Sorry. Can't."

"Why's that?"

Peter's smile was wry. "The police want to talk to me. X and Y left two dead paramedics in my apartment."

"Oh." After a moment, she raised her head, blotted her face on her sleeve, and added, "Fuck."

發

Peter hoped to feel better after a good night's sleep. He'd been shown to a guest room with a big canopied bed and furniture probably priceless to an antique dealer. But the mattress was too soft, with so many pillows at the head it seemed he was expected to sleep folded at a sixty-degree angle. He also heard a continual *clack-clack-clack-clack-clack*, like someone pedaling a bike with cards stuck through the spokes somewhere below the floor.

Exhaustion overcame him anyway and he was halfway through his first R.E.M. cycle when a chilly hand shook him.

"Gah!"

A pink-cheeked face with fixed smile painted on white celluloid loomed over him in the light of one candle. "Is there anything I can do to make you more comfortable, sir?"

"Well, you could let me sleep!"

"Very good, sir." The serva curtsied, let the gauze curtain fall, then whirred and creaked her way out of the room.

Peter got out of bed, put his glasses on, and crept after her. His door opened onto the mezzanine that ran around the great central hall. He watched the serva trundle along the balcony and disappear around a corner. Her shadow lingered on the floor as she receded, for a moment joined by a second shadow not feminine enough to belong to a serva. Dromio was checking up, making sure he wasn't carrying out a plot to murder the family in their sleep.

Peter wedged a gilt chair under his doorknob and retreated back to bed, burrowed down into a sweat-dampened hollow he had made in the pillows, and sought oblivion. But the unfamiliar room weighed on him like a tomb. He twitched, tossed, dozed, and woke when the grandfather clock downstairs struck two. Dozed again, just below a troubled surface, a half-lucid sleep that stretched on and on. He thought the night must be nearly over, and then the clock struck three. He sat up and hunched around his knees.

He didn't know what he was doing here. Nikki did not like him in that way and probably never would. He knew that wasn't a fair observation—he'd known her two days, and she had just lost half her family and had killers looking for her; it was hardly time for starting a relationship. But just now, at this never-ending three o'clock in the morning, the rejection seemed worth a grown man's crying over. So he cried, muffling short sobs against his knees, until he felt drained. When he lay down again, sleep came on so fast he didn't even notice.

發

He advanced on the fortress, armor buckled, broadsword in hand. It looked more than ever like a great tree, ancient, gnarled, rooted through the center of the earth. But light still burned in the right-hand tower window. He went through the vestibule, where dead leaves crunched under his boots. It was very cold and he began to be afraid.

Inside, the cathedral was again crowded with people. The deep humming of voices that prayed, chanted, and sang in different languages and multiple octaves faded away as he came in. Every man, woman, and child in the place turned to stare at him.

Thousands of faces, disappointed, despairing, reproachful. His parents, his co-workers, even Jack was there.

"She ran away," Peter said. Then embarrassment consumed him. Offering excuses to these people: stupid, stupid, stupid.

Someone tapped him on the shoulder. A small, middle-aged woman with a disapproving expression showed him an ivory tile with a green Chinese character on it. He couldn't read it; its meaning kept changing every time he tried. She pointed in the direction of the apse. There was a cross up there, smaller than a pin at this distance. Even so, he could see that the figure hanging from it was not an icon. It was bleeding, dripping from the toes into a crack that ran the length of the cavern. The crack was deep and full of writhing blackness that hurt his eyes to see.

"You should hurry," the woman said.

He ran for the stairs. The crack ran through the base of the tower, splitting the inner core. Beetles bled out of the wall and bounced down the steps. He climbed past them, jumped a gap in the steps and a deep fissure through the floor of a landing, full of the same insects. He pushed his way to the top again.

The angel in black was there, sword in hand. But instead of trying to stop Peter, he was trying to batter down the final door.

"Let me help!" Peter said.

"Away with you, traitor!" said the angel, drawing back for another try. As he rushed the door, Peter flung himself shoulder to shoulder with him. They slammed into the wood with a crash of armor. It burst inward. The angel fell down on the threshold. Peter tripped over him and skidded on his plate mail into the room.

Nikki looked down at him. Too theatric to be real: black lace dress piled up on the floor, face white as a mask, dark-ringed eyes. Without a word, she turned and walked out through the wall.

It cracked. Black beetles spilled out of it. The tower shook. The room broke open and began sliding sideways and down. He scrambled to his feet just as the floor gave way and tumbled down in a rain of stone and bugs and bits of mortar, and he woke up gasping.

CHAPTER FIVE

*P*eter looked rough the next morning. Nikki had slept a deep murky swamp of a sleep in her old room—which looked just as her nineteen-year-old self had left it, vintage posters and early paintings still on the walls—and did not feel she had quite emerged from it yet, but he seemed positively groggy. She wanted to tell a serva to get him some clothes because he seemed to be starting his third day in the same shirt, but there were no servas to be found.

Also there was nothing on the sideboard in the breakfast room except coffee and bread rolls.

"*Scusi*, Signorina," Dromio said. "The servas have been reprogrammed for defense, so the house is a little short on comfort."

"Well, thank God for that," Peter muttered, helping himself.

"Are you enjoying your stay?" Dromio asked.

"It's a beautiful place."

"We so rarely have guests."

"Have you tried not assaulting them?"

"We try to make them comfortable."

"Was there something else?" Nikki asked.

"Your pardon, Signorina," said Dromio. "In fact, there is. In all the excitement yesterday, I neglected to give you a message from your father."

Nikki put her coffee down so nothing would happen to it. "What message?"

"Visit the first Unseen Room."

"Excuse me?"

"That is the message. 'Visit the first Unseen Room,'" he said, gaunt as a bird of ill omen in his rusty old suit. "It's the one in the sub-basement."

"What's that supposed to mean? We don't go in there!"

Dromio adjusted his lapels. "Il Signore told me years ago that in the event of his death, I was to instruct each of his surviving children to go into that room in turn."

"And... what is an Unseen Room?" Peter put in.

"It's a room we never look inside," Nikki said, clutching the arms of her chair. "Dad built one on every floor in case somebody needed an emergency exit. I used one to get to your place the other night. Once we see what's really in the room, it's harder to use it to timewalk anymore. Its potential is diminished. Understand?"

"Um..."

"Good." She frowned at Dromio. "Did he say why?" The majordomo smiled and she answered herself. "Of course he didn't." She drank the coffee, wolfed down the rest of the roll. "Good a time as any, I guess. Want to come, Peter?"

"Signorina, your father intended for you to visit that room alone."

"Did he say that?"

"No," the majordomo admitted. "But I doubt it occurred to him you would have a guest present."

"Well, I don't see how it matters."

They were halfway out of the breakfast room when the majordomo raised his voice. "Be careful down there, Signorina. The place is a bit of a junk room. You know how it is in a great house. Whatever is not wanted, but cannot be discarded ends up in those rooms. After all, the family never goes in them. It may be a little disturbing."

With that cheery expression ringing in her ears, Nikki led the way down the grand marble staircase, to the terrazzo floor of the great hall. There wasn't a serva to be seen, even though keeping the mosaics, the chandeliers, and the column tops dust-free was a full-time job in itself.

"Do you trust him?" Peter asked. "He could've shown Mr. X and Ms. Y how to get in here. He backed your stepmother for the run of this place instead of you. They both survived. And he gives off those…" he waved his hands, "scheming grand vizier vibes."

"Those come with the job." She took him along a back hall that served as a neutral zone between upstairs and downstairs. "If he were a traitor, we'd already be dead."

"But you're scared," he observed.

Peter seemed to care—unlike Dromio, who was duty-bound, or Lady Varian, who thought her a threat—but he saw through her when she would rather be opaque. "I just can't figure what this is about," Nikki said. Her father must have left a legacy or a message in the Unseen Room because his children would never look there. So it was something he didn't want them to find until after he died, and she dreaded any secret he had kept that long.

They went down a stair of gleaming hardwood and through the laden shelves of the pantry. The air smelled like she could eat a slice of it, cold with pepperoni. Then through the buttery and wine cellar, where it became chilly and fragrant with grapes aging in oaken casks.

…Her father among the vines, big callused hands gripping the grafting knife and the billhook. Sunlight hot where she rested her head on his chest, bringing out the sweetness in the scent of earth and wool….

She lit a lantern and they went down another stair of worn, scuffed hardwood. A hum, punctuated by the odd *clack*, permeated the gloom, as did a reek of cleaning solvents and linseed oil. Peter made a startled sound—they were in the engine room's antechamber, which held card files and workbenches, and on the other side of a glass wall were the engines. Floor to ceiling, row upon row and rack upon rack of mills, gears, rotating drums, flywheels, and pulley belts, all slowly spinning and clacking and humming. Cams and shafts connected the upper half of a serva mounted over an old-school printing press, slumping like puppet with one dainty hand resting in the job case in a compartment of lead Ts. Nikki gave Peter the minute he seemed to want to gape over the thing.

"Why this, though?" he asked after goggling. "Why these gigantic mechanical processors instead of a lightweight collection of integrated circuits?"

"Dad was comfortable with this." She watched the gears spin and the barrels clack. "He was a Renaissance man... I mean, that's when he grew up. These engines made sense to him. He didn't want any technology he couldn't understand, or repair. Alex goes—used to go—on and on about recursive algorithms and Turing degrees, but to Dad, this was never more than a mechanized filing system. It didn't need to be portable."

The chemical fug made her eyes sting. She led him out through an airtight door and they went down stairs of splintered plywood. The air changed again, becoming musty, oily, damp, and warm. There was a muffled noise of pumps: the hydraulic power of the aqueduct, running the engines from underneath. Serva tracks led through the dirt, down narrow hallways of cracked cement and naked pipes and shadows fleeing the light.

"What disturbing things," said Peter, "was Dromio talking about?"

"Probably just stuff that got moved down here over the years. Like Dad kept a gallery of portraits. All of his wives through the years, up on the wall in chronological order. They were his own work. My mom was in there, Alex's mother, Erik's, some I never met, probably girlfriends too. Eleonora had them all taken down; I noticed this morning. I expect they ended up in one of the Unseen Rooms."

"Didn't that upset you?"

"Almost as much as those portraits being there all together in the first place." Her shoulders twitched. "My mother was the first late-twentieth-century woman he ever married, but I bet she wasn't the first to object to them."

They went down a final stair cut into the bedrock, so old the steps were worn down in the middle. At the bottom was a heavy black oak door. She got a dry sensation in her throat and found she couldn't swallow. Careful not to think about the Piazza San Marco or anyplace else she'd rather be, she lifted the latch and the door opened with a patient creak.

A small, subterranean room, unevenly dug; a couple of timbers, dark with age, shoring it up. Walls plastered and whitewashed and clean. Despite Dromio's junk room comment, there was nothing in it—except a coffin on a stone table. Her first thought was that Alex had been moved in here, but the coffin was too small.

She pushed inside, raising the lantern, and stared at the plain white pine box. The weighted door shut behind Peter as he followed. She moved around to the other side, tugged the latch up, and lifted the lid.

Yellowed bones with scraps of long dark hair clinging to the skull, some ancient cobwebby fabric, originally white. Probably a woman. Not too horrible, the smell of decay was faint. There didn't seem to be anything else in the coffin, though she didn't want to go questing through the moldering dust and decayed satin under the skeleton to be sure.

"Why would he want me to see this?"

The door creaked, the lantern flame dipped, all the shadows jumped. "Nikki," Peter said in a remote sort of voice.

The room wobbled, and the coffin lid slipped from her fingers and fell closed. Not Peter, but an apparition stood in the doorway. Gray-bearded, with the powerful build and robust features that only artists under patronage give to old men. His cloak, a warm soft black from Rembrandt's palette, let his face dominate the room. He carried a bouquet of white roses in one hand. At Peter's voice, he turned.

"What in God's name are you doing here, Chang?"

"I. Uh. Er…" Peter stammered.

"Do not answer!" The apparition advanced, spearing a forefinger at him. "Tell me nothing, nothing at all. Don't say a single comprehensible word!"

"Um?"

"That's acceptable." The apparition turned toward her, his voice and gestures softening. "You also, Nicoletta. Tell me nothing. If I forget myself and ask a question, do not answer."

He came forward, hands extended. She flinched back and he let them drop. But his warm breath washed over her face. Okay. A ghost would not smell like puttanesca. "Dad?"

"Yes, *figlia mia.*"

"Never mind Peter. What are you doing here? Don't you know you're supposed to be—"

"Dead? I am aware." He was trying to gentle her with a low voice and soothing gestures, but dammit, she wasn't a horse. "Do not tell me how it happened. I must not learn anything of the future, especially the time, place, or manner of my death. I must not avoid it."

The room spun. "You… haven't avoided it?"

"I haven't yet reached it," he said.

"Then you didn't… you're not…" Her own voice seemed disconnected from her. "You came here from…?"

He cupped the side of her face with warm, roughened fingers. "From just after the time you left home on your nineteenth birthday."

At which time she'd called him an autocratic pig and swore that wild horses wouldn't drag her back to Santuario, but guilt could wait. "How could you reach your future, Dad?" She gripped the hand on her cheek, held it tight and got it wet. "You always said it was impossible!"

"No, I always said that timewalking is a matter of visualization. To reach the future, you need only know what it will look like. The servas have preserved this room exactly as it was on that day. All I had to do was imagine you in here, and if you followed instructions, that would only occur upon my death."

"But then you couldn't use it as an Unseen Room again."

"We have seven. I could spare one to come see you." He pressed her hand. "So tell me nothing or I'll end up with paradox and duplication when I return."

"...You won't be staying, then."

"No. The longer I stay, the greater the danger."

He gave her a little time to recover, but insisted that Peter wait outside. "I did not risk visiting the future just to discuss intimate family affairs with an outsider present."

"If it's such a risk, why did you come at all?"

"To make peace with you. To explain why I have been so, well, 'overprotective' is the kind word. And to deliver these." He opened the coffin, and scattered the white roses among the bones.

"Who was she? Why's she down here?"

"She was your sister Gabriela."

Another sibling she'd never heard of.

He took her hands. "Her mother was a Florentine lady of good family from the mid-seventeenth century. You know my weakness. I need a woman around. Often, my feeling runs no deeper than that." She drew a sharp breath; he inclined his head as if to acknowledge she had cause for resentment. "Not so with my Bianca. We found great joy in each other—for a time. Then, as women do, she became disenchanted when she accepted the truth: that she would grow old at a mortal's usual pace, and I would not."

"That's not all there is to it, Dad."

"No," he admitted, and she wished she hadn't said that. "But even granting my character flaws, marriage is difficult between our kind and ephemerals. We become wary of investing our hearts, as you may have discovered. I held aloof, knowing that in a few decades, she would be gone. Our daughter resented me much as you have. Like you, she was restless, discontented. When her mother died, she too ran away. In her case, I pursued. A father's duty in those days, and the Hunters were more numerous."

He let her go and began to pace the small room. The lantern on the floor flared in the wind of his cloak every time he turned, making monstrous shadows on the walls. "I knew she had gone back to the juncture that her mother came from. But I did not find her in her grandfather's house or the local nunnery or anywhere she could take legitimate sanctuary. I was reduced to making inquiries in the street, directed to a disreputable house in a sordid corner of the city." He stopped in the darkest part of the room with his back to her. "I found her dead."

"Dead how?"

"With the metal straw driven up into her brain."

"The Hunters?"

He nodded, then turned back into the light. "I lay in wait for her seducer and killed him before he knew I was there. He had the look— short, with Nilotic features but pale skin.

"She had not intentionally strayed from virtue." *Unlike you*, he didn't say. "They control their prey, I've told you, by the scents they exude. If I had given him time to react, he might have paralyzed me or terrified me. That is why we have automatons to defend Santuario. That is why I tried to keep you here, even though they have not been seen in decades. Although I did not restrict you as much as I did her because it was partly me, my severity, that drove her—"

He stopped speaking.

"Why do they hate us?" she asked.

He seemed glad to change the subject. "Several reasons. They drink a person's memories along with the fluid, and no doubt they want the secret of timewalking, although I don't believe they can gain the ability that way. A Seer once told me they could not, at any rate. Further, we know what they are and it is a secret they would not have commonly known. And finally…well, they are simply parasites, monsters, with a nature to work evil, even on the other bloodlines. Especially the Telepaths."

This last came out unusually vehement, even for him on this subject, and for a moment his strong-boned face in the amber lantern light seemed fanatical.

"I wish you had told me more of this before," she said.

"Well, now I know that in my future I must not tell you *too* much," he said dryly, for of course he would not want to break the taboo by creating a second, better-informed version of her. "But as for the past, at first you were too young, then you were gone. For all I knew, this was my only chance to tell you everything."

She looked down. "I'm sorry, Dad. I wanted you to love me."

"I know. I did." He clasped her. "I do."

"You loved somebody." She smelled earth and sugar-cured tobacco and closed her eyes. "Not sure it was me."

"I had my expectations," he admitted. "But it was you nonetheless. With your barbed tongue, provocative dress, and black eyelids, it was you." He released her. "I should not stay much longer. Is there anything you want to ask me?"

"Yeah, about a million things, but—"

"But even the questions will violate the taboo, eh?" She nodded. "I can imagine," he said. "You do not seem significantly older, and I am unlikely to die a peaceful death. Well. Besides the one regarding the Hunters, I can give you two warnings. I won't ask how Peter Chang came to Santuario, nor how much you know of him already. Do not trust him excessively."

"Peter?" She was incredulous. "Why?"

"He is the son of a Seer." As she boggled, he added, "I have seen no power in him, but it may come. And the Seers are manipulative; they can be very dangerous."

"How'd he come to work for you then?"

"It was a debt I owed his mother. And I had hoped he might be useful."

"Who was she? What debt?"

"She was a fortune teller in Old San Francisco, around the turn of the century." Benedict seemed impatient with these irrelevant questions. "I had stayed too long in one place. Hunters tracked me down, laid an ambush. She warned me. Her price was that I save her son."

"From what?

"From the Great Quake." He made an irritated gesture. "He had some lung disease as well. Consumption, they called it then, I don't remember what it turned out to actually be. It couldn't be cured in those days."

"So he's from the past. Over a hundred years. And he doesn't know."

"You'd be wise not to tell him, to have nothing more to do with him."

"...I have to say that sounds ludicrous."

"Well, I did not come to argue," he said dryly. "I am dead now. You must find your own way. I suppose there is not a hope of seeing you married before I die? Don't answer that."

"Why didn't you tell him, though? How useful could he be if he didn't know?"

"If he ever showed a sign that he'd inherited the gift, I would have told him," Benedict said. "But otherwise, what would be the point? I'd have had to reveal my own nature, without having any reason to trust or burden him with it. Use your wits, girl." He embraced her again, which took the sting off, then said, "One last warning."

She hung on to the cuff of his doublet, reluctant to let go. "What's that?"

He gently disengaged and collected his cloak around himself as if gathering in all the darkness in the room. "Beware the unraveling," he said.

發

After the first shock, Peter thought that his boss must have survived and escaped from the assassins, but apparently this was a younger version who knew nothing about any of it.

He didn't mind being expelled from the room, although Benedict's order to leave was peremptory and rude. It was Nikki's last chance to talk to her father. But as he sat on the cold subterranean steps with only his smartphone for light, it began to get tedious. He played a game, changed the wallpaper, fiddled with his keys, rubbed the worn-smooth stone of the step that his rear was going numb from sitting on, checked his watch...

...Wondered what would happen if he went back in.

He didn't mean to disturb them, but suppose he just—

發

He grasped the iron latch. It was dreamlike, without volition— to think of doing something was to do it. He eased the door softly inward.

"—are manipulative, they can be very dangerous."

"How'd he come to work for you, then?"

The door creaked and alerted them. He saw the family resemblance in their change of expression, though hers paused at chagrined as his passed on to affronted. "I said stay out, Chang. This is a private matter!"

But there was another scene, a simultaneous, fainter overlay of the first. There was a second Benedict Varian. Where the first merely glowered and spoke coldly, the second turned purple, advanced and— to Nikki's evident astonishment—screamed at him. "Liar! Spy! Get out of my house! Stay away from my daughter!" A great, clenched fist flew at him, blotting out the light—

發

The door creaked, the lantern shone in his eyes; he gasped. Nikki came out alone.

"Peter? You okay?" Behind her, the cellar was empty except for the coffin.

"Yeah—uh, yeah, I'm fine." He blinked. "He's gone?"

"Well, yeah, he had to leave. He's dead." But she was smiling. It lit the stairwell by ten candelas, raised the temperature five degrees, and hit him like a pound of sand tied in a sock.

"Damn," he said nonetheless.

"You wanted to talk to him?" She slipped by and looked back, losing some of the smile, seeming to remember that he had interests and feelings too. "What, about patronage?"

"It goes way back," he said, climbing the worn bedrock steps after her. "Apparently he even arranged my adoption."

He half-expected her to say *I didn't know you were adopted*, which was the most common reaction, but instead she said, "You know anything about your birth parents?"

"Not a thing. No records."

"I'm sorry. I didn't think to ask him to talk to you."

"That's okay. You had a lot to think about."

The slog back up through the basement levels—plumbing, engines, pantries, and wine cellars—to the main floor reminded Peter of the dream he'd had for the second time last night. The unending stairs, the struggle to reach the top of the cathedral or whatever it was, just in time for the princess to walk out and for the whole place to collapse. But Nikki remained elated—a purposeful stride, a firm set to her mouth, a brave little scrunchie imposing order on her hair. She didn't look like she might jump out of a tower any time soon.

"Hate to admit it, but Erik may have been right," she said. "It's time to consult the Book of Days."

"Which is?"

"An index to our database of timelines."

From the main hall, they went up two more flights of graceful old marble stairs, worn down in the middle. Then Nikki used a complex key she'd snagged from the buttery in an ornate lock on a set of doors on the third-floor mezzanine. They opened onto a long, high-vaulted study with tall, narrow windows overlooking the terraced gardens on the west side. Such a high proportion of ethereal blue sky was visible through them that the room seemed to float. The walls were floor-to-ceiling bookshelves: history, geography, art, economics, and physical sciences, mostly. A slate floor, very clean even though this, Peter realized, must be Benedict's study, the scene of his murder. A massive desk gleamed dark with the warmth of heartwood in its depths, a brass-and-leather-bound book the size of a small coffee table chained to it. Beside that was a large windup box: a glass-walled cube full of gleaming brass barrels and gears in a rosewood frame and gilt fittings, bolted down, a hand crank sticking out one side.

Nikki perched behind the desk in an ebony chair that made her look about twelve. She unlocked the book with a key from a desk drawer and started turning over the pages. Peter observed upsidedown that each page was divided into several entry spaces and moved around the desk for a better view. Each space had a mounted photograph, a few handwritten notes, and a card in a slipcover. The photographs were of monuments—the Great Wall, the Coliseum, the Parthenon, Michelangelo's *David*, the Eiffel Tower, the Golden Gate Bridge, etc.—and natural landmarks, and buildings, some famous, some he didn't recognize. Old inventions, too—chain pump, printing press, Jacquard loom, a mechanical serva-like doll, a duplicate of the windup box—and a few important-looking, long-dead men. Most of the last were not photos, but small portraits in a very realistic style.

"Coordinates," Nikki explained, "for junctures we haven't seen or can't remember." She flipped to the back. The last quarter of the pages were blank except for a handwritten index at the end. She consulted an entry and flipped forward again.

On the page where she stopped, a two-and-a-quarter-inch square hand-tinted photo caught Peter's eye. "That's the Palazzo!" It had clearly been taken with a simple meniscus lens on antiquated rollfilm, probably with the first type of Kodak Brownie. The three-story edifice looked much taller among the buildings that had surrounded it back then. He twisted to read the caption. The sharp slanted handwriting was as familiar as the signature on his paycheck, but he could only decipher *15 Ottobre 1892 – 17 Aprile 1906.* "What's it say?"

"This was one of Dad's ventures," Nikki said disparagingly. "A big land grab and stock buyout during the Panic of 1893. Then he sold off everything except the Palazzo right before the big earthquake in 1906. But more to the point, this is the most recent juncture where he ran into the Hunters. And before you ask—"

"What are the Hun—?"

"—the Hunters are another family. A gifted bloodline like us, only they aren't Timewalkers, they're immortals."

"...Immortals," said Peter. "Okay. Why do we care?"

"There was a feud between them and us. They hunted Dad for centuries in different timelines. They haven't been heard from in a long time," she tapped the caption, "but Dad was convinced they're still around. And...those darts X and Y used? Erik told me the Hunters use them. I wasn't interested in his opinion at the time, but..."

"But it's worth checking out," Peter agreed.

"Dad would've described an encounter with them. I hope." She slipped the card accompanying the entry out of its cover. It was stiff and translucent with an intricate fretwork of holes. She fed it into a slot in the wind-up box and turned the crank.

There was a *rattle-rattle-bing*, then a faint *clack-clack-clack-clack* started up from somewhere below. Somewhere being the engine room in the basement, Peter realized. "How long will this take?"

"It has to print out, and then a serva brings it up."

"Okay. So tell me about these Hunters."

She drummed her fingers on the desk. "Remember telling me that somebody tried to drink your brain? Did that really happen?"

"Uh... It can't have? Because I'd be dead."

"But that's what they do. Dad said they're like vampires, consuming brain matter and fluid to live forever. That's nonsense, right? It'd be like eating nothing but pork, it doesn't even have antioxidants. But it would explain why they took his body. You see why I'm asking. Did one attack you or not?"

Peter rubbed the bridge of his nose. No pain. He had bruises where X and Y had hit and kicked him, but where Mr. Sanders had shoved a brass tube into his skull, there was no trace. "No...it seemed real, but it didn't happen."

"Pretty weird thing to imagine."

"Strange coincidence, yeah," he agreed. "Like when your brother shot me."

"Okay, but…" She looked up sharply. "Oh, right. I forgot—you said you remembered that."

"You remember it too?" Peter fumbled through his pockets and showed her his pair of identical smartphones. "He did shoot me, didn't he?"

She stared, fidgeted, sighed. "…You must have picked one of those up when we ended up in the wrong timeline. Yes, he did. You died. You shouldn't remember that. It didn't happen to *you*." She looked uneasy. "Tell me about this guy who didn't drink your brain."

"Mr. Sanders? A new client. When I first met him, he…I can't actually remember my first meeting with him. I think he made me forget whatever it was we talked about."

"They do that," she said. "Pheromone control."

"What, they exude Rohypnol or something?"

"Or stuff to make you like them, or fear them, whatever."

"Ah." Peter shuddered, thought for a bit, then said, "Remember what X said when we got down to the lobby and they were there waiting for us?"

"'We're here to kill you'?" She gulped. "I've got a visual memory, I don't recall exact words very well."

"He was surprised to see me. He said I should be in a coma." Peter rubbed his nose again and pushed up his glasses. "I think…I know this is crazy, but I think Mr. Sanders really was in your dad's office waiting for you, and would have attacked me if I'd gone in."

"…And X knew it! This Sanders, is that his real name?"

Peter shrugged. "It's the name a lot of real assets are in."

"He must have given you a business address, phone number, email, and all that."

"Well…yeah." She looked up at his tone. "It's just that…he drinks brains," he reminded her.

The ethereal light in the room went gray as a cloud crossed the sun. Her face lost warmth and detail. "Yeah. They're monsters, Pete. But I'm not running away. Not this time."

"No... but..."

"You don't have to come with me."

Peter raised his eyebrows. She seemed to realize what a stupid thing that was to say. "I just meant that maybe this is one of those 'dust off and nuke 'em from orbit' situations," he said.

"I don't need nukes. I only need coordinates."

"And then what? Are you going to kill him?"

"I'm going to make sure they never hurt my family again."

There was a rap on the open door and Dromio cleared his throat and came in, looking gaunt but flushed, with a stack of paper. "As I mentioned earlier, Miss Varian, the house is short on servas at the moment, so I took the liberty of bringing this up."

"Thank you." Nikki put both hands on the desk as if planting a flag on it. "Right here please."

He placed the stack, ink looking still damp on the pages, where she indicated. If he had a comment on her occupation of her father's study, he kept it to himself, but his attitude certainly did not convey approval. "Also, luncheon is served on the north veranda. Her Ladyship requests your company for a council of war. Mr. Chang is welcome too."

Peter's stomach rumbled. Nikki hesitated, but agreed. "Okay, this can wait a bit."

She left the data behind, but Peter saw her unstick the hand-tinted photo of the Palazzo Building in its glory days from the Book of Days and put it in her coat pocket.

發

Lady Eleonora Varian, draped in black silk, stood at the edge of the veranda amid the budding greenery of spring. The sun had returned, the breeze was soft, warm, smelling of moist earth and early flowers. She gazed out over the valley where the riot of gardens was spanned, on this side, by the great aqueduct. Mist drifted off the high waterway, descended and wound through the supporting arches. She turned, showing her strong, lovely profile against a pale blue dome of sky—Nikki wanted to paint the scene, call it *The Dowager's Reverie*, and set fire to it.

"Well-met, Nicoletta, Mr. Chang. Signore Dromio. Please join me."

Apparently the prohibition her father usually observed against masters and servants eating together had been suspended for the duration of the emergency: the table was set for four. Nikki salivated to see a tureen leaking exquisite wisps of steam, panbread, olive oil, a salad of field greens, a blue-veined cheese, and Muscadine grapes.

Dromio pulled out Lady Varian's chair and she took it with due gravity. Nikki grabbed her own while he was occupied. Circumvented, the majordomo uncorked a chilled Arnais and filled the glasses. Peter lowered himself onto his seat as though there might be a landmine strapped under it. She caught his queasy look. "I assume you aren't going to poison Peter while he's our guest?"

"Nicoletta!"

"Certainly not. I do not believe Mr. Chang is a threat to Santuario at the moment."

"Or any other moment!"

"Enough!" Lady Varian's cheekbones flamed. "We have settled the question of Mr. Chang. We are here to discuss our position and our options."

"*Mi dispiace.*" Dromio bowed. "We do not know how the assassins gained entrance, so we must assume they could do it again. Five servas now guard each doorway. They have orders to capture anyone belonging to the family and to kill all others who attempt entrance. As for options—well, we do not yet know what we face."

Lady Varian rested both hands on the table. "I have been wondering if we should bring the rest of the family here, even the illegitimates and the giftless. For their protection, and our own."

Dromio lifted the lid from the steaming tureen. "A worthy idea, my lady. And yet..." he bent to serve her cioppino. "They will be difficult to find. Some may feel bound by filial duty, but many are estranged, and others may have become so in their years away. How can we be certain none of them is the traitor who let the assassins in?"

Lady Varian wrapped her fingers around the bowl as if chilled. Her expression became abstracted and bleak, and Nikki felt slightly ashamed of herself.

"I don't think there is a traitor," she said. "If it was the Hunters who sent X and Y, they could have gotten the secret by questioning one of us under the influence of...whatever they use for that. Or slurped it out of somebody's brain."

Lady Varian was jolted out of her distraction. "What in God's name do you mean?"

"They suck out information along with the goo." She twiddled her fingers in the direction of her skull. "Cioppino over here, please."

Dromio slipped a dipperful of crab, shrimp, fish, and fresh tomatoes in wine sauce into her bowl. "Did you enjoy the visit, Signorina? Or should I say, the visitation?"

Nikki put her spoon down. "You knew I'd see him?"

"I did." Well, of course, Nikki realized. Servas maintained the Unseen Room and Dromio programmed the servas. "But I was forbidden to tell you."

"See? Him?" Lady Varian rolled a grape between her fingers.

"Il Signore, my lady," Dromio explained. "Before his death, he arranged to visit each of his children posthumously."

She absorbed this slowly and frowned. "Only his children?"

Peter coughed and spewed bread crumbs. Dromio patted him on the back and said, "He had...messages for them which he did not entrust even to me."

She put the grape back on her plate, where the rest of her food remained untouched. "And what of his unborn child?"

"There were no instructions as to him. Probably, il Signore had not gotten around to making arrangements."

"An unfortunate oversight, then? Perhaps it would not be importunate to inquire what was said, Nicoletta?"

"There were no dramatic-pause messages," Nikki said dryly. "It was just saying goodbye. And he warned me about the Hunters again. Reminded me that they slurp brains."

Lady Varian folded her arms around her belly and bent forward in her seat. Dromio served Nikki a wedge of panbread. "Perhaps you questioned il Signore about the enemies we face—what did he say?"

"I couldn't ask him directly. It would have caused a paradox and another personal timeline. But yeah, something he said—" In spite of her father's warning against him, a protective impulse made her leave Peter out of her revelations. "The guy who hired X and Y is probably a Hunter named Sanders."

"I know that name!" Dromio paced. He had not yet sat down, nor put any food on his own plate. He rounded on Peter. "A new client of the firm, is he not?"

"Huh?" Peter looked up from his plate, jumping as if guilty by association. "Yeah, he is."

Nikki was thankful he didn't mention having met the man— Dromio's paranoia would've known no bounds. As it was, he said, "Then perhaps you betrayed us unintentionally. And you remain the only employee who knew how to get in."

"I don't know how to get in!" Peter said.

Dromio tightened his lips. "No matter," he said. "I will investigate. Strike at the root of the problem. I will pay a visit to San Francisco this afternoon, and this enemy will trouble the family's peace no more."

Lady Varian's eyes were huge and dark in her pale face. "Just like that? All alone?"

"I will not wait for another attack, my lady." The majordomo made the stiletto up his sleeve appear in his hand.

"I'll go with you," Nikki said, after weighing Dromio's undeniable competence against her recurring impulse to smack him.

"But it would be catastrophic to lose you, signore." Lady Varian gripped the arms of her chair. "With my husband gone, the estate will fall to pieces if the worst should happen."

"No, lady. Not for many years. There are stores enough to feed three people for decades, and the servas can repair each other. This is the duty left to me by il Signore. And I will take the necessary precautions. The brainsucker will not see me coming, I assure you."

"Not with my help, they won't," Nikki agreed. "And vengeance is *my* job, by the way."

"Nicoletta, don't be absurd."

"Your father would never permit it." Dromio said.

"My father is gone!" She smacked the table, making Peter jump. "So I'm not asking him. Or you."

"Hm!" The majordomo turned to Lady Varian. "I need only your leave to go, my lady."

"You have it. Godspeed."

"Thank you." He turned back at Nikki. "My apologies, Signorina, but you stay here. And Mr. Chang as well, since he knows too much to be allowed to expose himself to the Hunters again."

"I don't take orders from you," Nikki said with a cold feeling down her spine. "So what are you talking about?"

"What did you do?" asked Peter.

"Something I advised il Signore to do years ago, when his daughters' inclination to stray manifested." Dromio stood, all poise, clearly prepared for this confrontation. "He declined on the grounds that he could snatch you from death if necessary. Since I lack that power, I will protect you as he would wish, but by my own means. You will find, Signorina, that you cannot leave Santuario. I have stationed servas at every exit and they are programmed to prevent you."

In the moment of shock that followed, Peter recovered first. "But...she can override them." He indicated Lady Varian.

"No."

"What?" the lady gasped.

"I beg your pardon, my lady." Dromio inclined his head. "My loyalty is to the family. I never had to question what that meant so long as il Signore lived, and I don't wish to begin now. I carry out my duty as nearly as possible in accordance with what he would want. I reprogrammed the servas, in the event of conflict, to follow my orders, not yours." He raised his hand as if to forestall reproach. "You need not fear. You will be quite comfortable."

"Comfortable!" the lady exclaimed.

"They will serve you in all things, except where il Signore would wish otherwise."

Nikki's hackles rose. "As interpreted by you."

"Of course." Dromio turned the calm eyes of a fanatic on her. "Should I trust your interpretation? Or his?" He nodded at Peter. "It will all be for the best. But if you do not agree, you can reproach me when I return." He made the knife disappear, bowed, and walked off the veranda into the gardens.

Once Peter stopped worrying about arsenic in his Arnais,

the meeting had been one of his increasingly rare opportunities to process the weird shit that had befallen him and improve his odds of overcoming post-traumatic stress disorder. Plus, it was catered. So he'd mostly paid attention to the interplay of cioppino, focaccia, and gorgonzola dolce on his palate, not the Varian family drama. He'd seen his dead boss come back to life, learned of an ancient race of brain-sucking vampires, confirmed that Nikki's brother had murdered him in another timeline, and figured out the identity of her enemy, all within a couple of hours. Enough. He tuned out.

Until Nikki banged the table and Dromio explained that he had subverted all the servas and that they were trapped in Santuario. Trapped together, Peter noted, sneaking a gander at the breasts, lips, freckles, and curls sitting opposite. In a luxury villa with great food, wine, and scenery, and Mr. Creepy Schemer wouldn't be around because he was going to go deal with the sinister Mr. Sanders and the homicidal Mr. X and Ms. Y.

"There must be a downside to this," he said.

"Yeah," Nikki snapped. "Like, 'suppose he never comes back?'" She leaped to her feet and sprinted after the majordomo.

"That's a point," Peter admitted.

He was talking to himself. Lady Varian stared after Nikki and Dromio with horrified shock. "I trusted him." Spots of red burned in her cheeks. "I trusted him!"

Peter rose. "Uh, I'd better—she might—excuse me." He went down into the nearest garden and followed angry voices around a line of cedars, past a great bronze astronomical sextant, and through a gap in the jasmine hedge. On the other side was a drop-off where a terracotta wall reinforced the terrace. Nikki was blocking Dromio's way down some steps cut through the wall, spitting-mad. "I'll reproach you right now, you—"

"Machiavelli?" Peter suggested.

"—jerk! You know my father wouldn't want this!"

Dromio's pate glistened like it was the previous argument all over again. "Since it's the only way I can protect you in his absence, he would."

"He'd want us to have a way out!"

"Not if he knew you intended to confront the Hunters, Signorina."

She pressed the attack from the moral high ground. "No matter how overprotective Dad was, he'd never have locked us up!"

"Indeed?" The majordomo gave ground, Peter thought, in preparation for a classic pincer movement. "Are you certain?"

"I'm certain you're betraying him!"

"What I do, I do for your own good, and the good of the family!"

"Who are you to judge?"

He turned white, then red. "Who am I? I helped build this place! I served your father all my life! I know what the Hunters are capable of." He seized her by the upper arms and shook her. "There is no one else!"

"Hey!" Peter grabbed the man's shoulder, but a sharp elbow got him hard in the solar plexus. A whoof of air went out of him and he sat down in the gravel as purple spots bloomed in his vision. "Leave him alone!" came Nikki's voice. There were scuffling noises, a smack, then an instant's silence.

"I forget myself," the majordomo said. Peter's vision cleared to reveal Nikki with her hand on her reddened cheek, looking shocked, and Dromio flushed and frowning. "I do not lay hands on you. Pardon me." He bowed, then went around her and down the steps.

"Oh, no, you don't!" She whirled and ran after him.

"Uh, Nikki..." Peter wheezed.

She disappeared. Peter sat up and peered down. She had gotten below Dromio, again blocking his way. "You're a traitor!"

"You are a wayward child." He pushed past her.

Peter used the wall to help himself stand. "Could we possibly talk about this like reasonable people?"

Nikki got in Dromio's way again. "Judas!"

He pushed past her again. "*Sciocca bambina!*"

"Quisling!"

"*Monella!*"

"Backstabber!"

They stood nose to nose on the terrace below, among beds of peonies and bittersweet. Dromio's retort came so low Peter barely heard it: "You don't believe il Signore would have approved what I am doing, eh?" He sidled around her and she turned inside his orbit. "Did he tell you what happened to your sister Gabriela?"

Peter hurried down as she replied sarcastically, "What happened to my sister Gabriela?"

"She was a wild one. Just like you." He paused to button up his suit coat and adjust his cufflinks, but the ritual did not seem to calm him. "She ran off. Il Signore tracked her down to some Florentine brothel, killed the monster who seduced her, brought her back, and locked her away until she died."

"She was already dead," Nikki corrected him.

"Is that what he told you?" The majordomo shook his head. "No. The Hunters did not kill her. Il Signore kept her in a room that was windowless and kept dark, so that she could not see to fugue her way out. She lived another five months."

"You don't know what you're talking about!"

"I brought her food so that she could not suborn the servas. You can still see the room, it's second to the right of the tower." Dromio waved upward. Peter saw again the way the great villa gripped the top of the hill in broad stone claws and cast a black shadow over the gardens. He saw projecting battlements and pinched windows—and one had indeed been bricked up.

"He didn't care that much about anybody's stupid chastity!" Nikki was saying.

"Not since then. She hanged herself. After that, he abdicated the responsibility. You, he let run wild. But to protect your life...he would do what was necessary." The majordomo's mouth twisted. "I will not suffer anyone to call me traitor. I was il Signore's man then, and I am now." He bowed to Nikki without apparent irony. "And, once again, goodbye."

She stayed frozen until he disappeared over the edge of the next terrace, then made a thick sound, half-growl and half-sob, and went down the steps. Peter caught up, took her hand, and gently tugged her to a stop. "I don't think we can talk him out of this."

"He's gone nuts. He can't handle it himself. We have to do something."

"Well, you could bean him with a rock from here...."

"And if it killed him, where would we be?"

"Ah. Right." He let her hurry him down the next set of steps, through a hedge and a flowering peach orchard, and along a path that followed the base of a terracotta wall.

They saw Dromio reach the sunken amphitheater where the door he'd brought Peter through hung in a piece of jagged brick wall, surrounded by five or six tiers of white marble blocks half-smothered in grass. Five servas stood in a semi-circle, three facing the door and two the other way, all cradling old-fashioned carbines in their upper arms. Dromio had reached them, his bald head bobbing, a visible target. Nikki stopped on the brink and picked up a small chunk of broken marble. Her hand trembled, but she dropped the rock and fugued instead—just as Dromio went past the servas and through the door.

The servas closed ranks as the door shut behind him. "Good afternoon, Miss," they piped in unison.

"Move aside, please."

"Sorry, Miss," they piped. One added, "Master Dromio's orders for your protection, Miss."

"I am the last scion of the bloodline left in Santuario. No one's orders can supersede mine. Stand aside!"

"Sorry, Miss."

She fugued past them to the door. There was a collective gasp and a flurry of mechanical arms. Eight brass-and-celluloid hands clamped on and hoisted her off the ground before she could even touch the latch. Twelve more tried to catch her various limbs as she struggled.

"Oh! Don't hurt yourself, Miss!" They rolled forward, holding her aloft, then lowered her onto one of the marble block seats. Four trundled back while the last one dusted her off and smoothed her disarrayed curls.

"Oh, leave off!" she snapped, and it rotated and scooted after the others. "Well, that was undignified," she admitted as Peter came down.

"There's got to be a way to disable them," he said. "Sand in the gears? Sniper from the battlements? Pipe bomb? It's not like they're alive," he added at the look she gave him.

"I don't know what classes you may have taken at Berkeley, but I can't make a pipe bomb. Anyway, we shouldn't leave this door unguarded. X and Y got in this way. We'll have to try a different door." But then she slumped, head in hands, all fire gone.

Peter sat by her, took off his glasses and rubbed them with his shirttail until they were theoretically clean. When he hooked them back over his ears, the horizon line, where a bell jar of perfect blue met the inside-out wall around the valley, came into focus.

"It can't be true, what he said about your dad, Nikki."

"It can't be."

Actually, Peter had no idea whether Mr. Varian would put his own daughter in solitary confinement or not. He could list quite a few accurate descriptors about his boss—brusque, authoritarian, secretive, generous, resourceful, innovative—but he really didn't know the man. Still, it was easy to guess that Dromio had lied just to mess with her— and it had definitely messed with her. Her face was dark and clenched, her chin trembling.

"It can't be," she said again.

"We should get going," he prompted. "We don't know when... oh, hey." He finally processed what she had said earlier. "...You're right! X and Y had to come in this way, didn't they?"

"Well, yeah, this is the only door to that timeline."

"Maybe we shouldn't hang ar—"

There was an enormous noise and something hot struck him an enormous blow.

He was lying on his back and he could not see or hear anything. It seemed to be raining, but there was no sound. Then there was gray light and...not rain but dirt, pieces of wood, bits of metal falling on him. His glasses were filthy and smoke obscured the sky. Scraps of burning cloth or paper drifted down. He felt sandpapered. His feet were sticking up over the marble bench he'd been knocked off of. Something had exploded....

Turning his head was slow like underwater. She lay a foot or two away. She seemed about to speak.

He tried to touch her and discovered the rags that his arm had become.

發

"We need to go now," he said, getting up.

"Why?"

"They're coming!"

"Really."

"Come on!" He tugged her arm. She had said "Why?" with an apprehension that matched his alarm, but "Really," with flat suspicion. She seemed about to ask how he knew; instead she grabbed his hand and turned her back to the door. There was a jerk as she lunged, and he saw her vanish a split-second before her grip stretched him out and snapped him forward.

His eardrums protested a sudden change in air pressure and then he stumbled and barked his shin on a low wall that hadn't been there a second ago. He gaped up at the great villa which was suddenly towering right over them as if it had grown a giant stone hand and snatched them back to its hard bosom. They were back on the north veranda. "Shit!" He sat down abruptly, strings cut. Then he lost interest in his usual role of sitting around with his mouth hanging open until somebody explained what was going on. "You said you weren't any good at fugue!"

"I'm getting better," she said.

She was staring back down at the amphitheater which, from here, looked like a target—rings of white marble and green grass with the door in the wall at the center, in a semicircle of servas. Peter joined her and they were both watching when the door was blasted apart. From a safe distance, he boggled as great jagged splinters of wood were driven into the earth and black smoke billowed and broken bricks rained down on marble.

"That might've killed us!" Nikki said.

The shattered doorway loomed through a veil of smoke, which thinned and drifted away as Ms. Y came through, surveying the carnage over the sights of her semiautomatic. Only one serva was upright—it lurched drunkenly in a circle around a pitted metal stick that had been its leg, wearing a corona of burning celluloid—and she promptly shot it. The rest were smoldering shapes strewn on blackened earth. Mr. X skulked in behind her in a hunch of shoulders.

"Come on, away from here!" Peter urged. X and Y were too far away for any accuracy, he hoped, with a handgun, but their position were still too exposed. They retreated, Nikki lingering and looking back, past the table where white bowls of red cioppino were attracting flies, into the cool and shadowy house.

Two sets of footsteps, one heavy and one squeaky, approached along the flagstones of the hall. They both jumped, but it was Lady Varian, gripping a brass telescope in one hand and clutching a serva's upper arm with the other. Her face was drawn tight around eyes that engulfed them in bitter comprehension. "So the enemy is within our gates," she said. "What of the traitor, is he dead?"

"Dromio?" Nikki's voice shook. "Oh, God, he must be, he would've run right into them."

"Unless he was in their camp all along," Lady Varian said. "That, too, would explain how they got in."

"Now what?" asked Peter.

"We must barricade ourselves in the tower." The lady was pallid, breathing fast. "The servas will not obey me, except for this one. Can you handle any sort of weapon?"

"Me?"

"You are the last man here."

She clearly would have preferred almost anyone else. Peter tried to rise to the occasion without mentioning first-person shooter games. "Um, well—"

Nikki turned pink under the freckles. "We're not sacrificing him just because he's got a Y chromosome!"

"Nicoletta, I really do not have time to reason with you—"

"We can't fight them!"

"Then what are we going to do?" Peter demanded.

She squeezed her eyes shut. "…I don't know yet. Barricading the tower might buy us some time. Or —" They sprang open. "We can keep on fuguing!"

"But we're like, in a fishbowl here!"

"Right, but we can go from the bottom to the top of the hill in five seconds flat." Her eyes blazed with feverish hope. "They have to walk. We'll wear them down."

"How many times can you do that? With three of us?"

"I'm game to find out!"

"No." There was such authority in Lady Varian's voice that Peter started and Nikki actually shut up for a moment. "You may do as you think best. But I will not be jolted around from place to place in an undignified effort to outrun our enemies. I will retire to the tower with Clarabella."

It was Nikki's turn to be nonplussed. "This is no time to—to go down with the ship, or whatever you're thinking of—"

Peter bit his lip. "Nikki?"

"X and Y will kill you—"

"Um, Nikki…"

"—they aren't the kind of people who accept honorable surrender, or…or spare the women and children—"

"I am a Sforza!" Lady Varian snapped.

"What has that got to do with anything?"

"Nikki!"

"What?"

"We'd better go with the tower plan."

"Why?"

"Well, look at her." Lady Varian's face had flushed and beads of sweat stood out on her brow. Her belly seemed, in the last hour, to have visibly swollen under the black silk. Even as they stared, she shuddered all over and her knuckles went white on Clarabella's arm. "Speaking as a layman," Peter said, "I think she's going to have a baby."

"What, now?"

"My apologies." Gallows humor tugged the corner of the dowager's mouth. "You see, my dear, not being able to avoid my traditional role in life, I must ask the young man to embrace his."

發

The majordomo could hardly have made the situation worse if he really had sold them out, Peter thought. Lady Varian reported that one or two of the servas from each quintet stationed at the other doorways had left their posts to converge on the explosion site, but Peter privately doubted a dozen automatons could catch X and Y. The rest were still guarding places where attack wasn't coming. "Barricading the tower" turned out to mean dropping a bar into a slot behind a door. It was a solid oak slab bound and studded with iron, but that only made it a barrier to anything short of explosive force. Finally, Clarabella turned out to be the only serva that Dromio had not reprogrammed to follow only his orders—because her job was taking care of Lady Varian when she went into labor.

"Well, someone has to," Nikki said wryly.

They got her up the stairs into bed in her own room, all dark wood and red draperies, with her mechanical midwife to attend her. Then Nikki dragged Peter out onto the battlements at the top.

The wind was stronger up here, blowing in from the northwest, and shadows were crossing the hill as the sun slipped in and out of clouds in advance of darker ones on the horizon. Peter scanned the grounds futilely. A quarter-mile of terraces, walls, hedges, and orchards lay between the villa and the last place he'd seen X and Y. The servas, diligently searching outward from the blackened, smoking patch of turf, were having no luck. The assassins could be anywhere.

"Are there any weapons?" he asked.

"There's an armory. If you know how to load and fire a black powder musket."

"Why so primitive?" He was beginning to find it less charming.

"We've got to get out of here," Nikki said.

"Not without—"

"No! God, no. I'm going to have a baby sister or brother. I mean, we've all got to get out of here."

"How?"

She came close and pointed down the hill, directing his gaze at the exploded doorway. "No servas guarding it now," she pointed out.

Peter blinked. "Oh! Yeah…but…X and Y could be expecting us to try that. Maybe they're just waiting for us to show ourselves there."

Nikki turned away, fidgeted, seemed to debate with herself. From the room below came a muffled cry. She turned back, looked him in the eye. "Are they?"

"What?"

"Are they waiting? If we try for that doorway, what will happen? Can you see?"

Peter felt like he had run smack into something he had been groping for in the dark.

"It came true—" he said, with a wave at the explosion site below.

"You saved our lives," she agreed.

"—and you weren't surprised. What are you not telling me, Nikki?"

"There are other talented bloodlines," she said, very fast. "There's Timewalkers and Hunters and Telepaths and there are also Seers. You're one of the Seer family, apparently. That's probably how you knew Erik shot you even though it wasn't you. You had the vision, precognition or whatever, before I split the timeline."

Peter searched himself for a reaction, but the revelation just got in line behind all the rest of the weird shit that he had yet to fully process.

"How long have you known that?"

She avoided his eyes. "Just since this morning."

"What else did your dad tell you?"

"Not much. He said he owed your mother a debt for warning him about a Hunter ambush."

"...He knew who she was then, obviously!" There. Outrage was a reaction.

She hunched a little, defensively. "He didn't tell me her name. She's long dead, though, that much was clear. I'm sorry I didn't ask more. I've had a few things on my mind."

"Is that why you didn't tell me sooner?"

"No," she said miserably. Her freckles were prominent. "Dad didn't want me to trust you—he said you were dangerous. I didn't really believe him, but it was weird to think of you...changing."

"Changing?"

"My perception of you, changing. Seers are scary—I mean, I've never met one before, but a Timewalker of all people can appreciate how much power they have, knowing what will happen instead of just, you know, having a pretty good idea what's supposed to happen but might not. Look, this is no time to argue, is it?"

"...No," Peter admitted. "How does this work?"

"I'm not a Seer. I have no idea."

"...Right. Okay," he said, hoping to calm her down. "Let me just...give this a try." He hadn't actually tried before. Even the vision outside the Unseen Room had just sort of sprung on him when he was merely thinking about going in. He took the deep breath that all uncertain endeavors seemed to require and stared down at the shattered doorway in the amphitheater a quarter-mile off. With its door missing, it framed the darkness of the tunnel in broad daylight. The tunnel, leading back to what he still thought of as the real world.

He tried asking the question out loud: "What will happen if we—"

發

It was like two thousand people shouting in his ears. Angry, frightened voices multiplied beyond his comprehension, blended into white noise, shattering his comprehension. His vision blurred into staccato flashes of events too fast to register. Everything he perceived was swept away in a flood of confused sensation, as if the world was made again over and over, different each time. There was a face, a stern, middle-aged woman's face, all tightened and pursed up with disapproval.

And everything went white.

CHAPTER SIX

*P*eter clapped hands over his ears, staggered, made a convulsive movement, and went down like he'd been hit with a rock.

Nikki caught him, but couldn't keep him standing. He was limp as a wet towel. She got him down to the stones of the parapet and rolled him over. He lolled, eyes unseeing behind smudged glasses before they closed.

In a flash of eidetic memory she saw Alex with blood gushing from his neck, Edvard, bug-eyed from the buried wire—"Peter? Peter!"

She found a pulse in his throat and sagged in relief. She dragged him back from the edge, casting a fearful glance down the hill, so full of trees and hedges and shadows, and tried to rouse him with shaking and slaps. He was out cold. She waited, with his head in her lap, but minutes went by, and Lady Varian cried out again from below, and more minutes went by, and he didn't stir.

He was not going to wake up in time for his vision, if he was having one, to be any use. She would have to do something to save them herself.

Jump down to the door, she thought, *to spring the ambush*; and if it turned out there wasn't one, she could come back for Peter and her stepmother. That was a plan. Not a good one, but better than nothing. She stood at the wall of the parapet getting ready to fugue and searched the gardens below for any trace of X and Y—a glint of metal in the foliage, a hint of movement other than the servas or the wind stirring the branches—but there was no sign.

It was then she really looked at the hedges, tracing the maze-like paths between them near the valley floor where they crowded closer and thicker and more overgrown, unexplored and unseen...

Then she went down to Lady Varian's room. "There's something else to try."

Her voice resonated in the bedchamber—one of the largest in the villa, decorated to her stepmother's taste in dark mahogany and crimson damask with lots of embroidery—and got attention. "I do not understand," said Lady Varian. She lay, between contractions, with her eyes closed, breathing like a steam engine, gripping Clarabella's hands.

"The hedge maze. I never explored the whole thing. There are plenty of corners I haven't looked around." How had she never thought of it before? "Dad knew what he was doing even then. All I need is one place I haven't seen. Can you walk?"

"If I must. Are you certain this is for the best?"

"Better than getting trapped here. Clarabella, help her up to the top. I need you to carry Peter."

The deep shadows were inundated with the scent of jasmine. The hedges were—though not uniformly—eight feet tall and three feet thick, unkempt, overgrown almost into archways on top, and full of long thorns, dark leaves, and white buds. They were not spaced evenly, so the passages and spaces between them did not all look alike. Nikki could just glimpse the top of the tower through a gap. This was as far into the maze as she had been able to see.

"We are still here, Nicoletta."

"Not for long."

"We are farther from safety. I fail to see any improvement in the situation." Lady Varian bent over and shuddered. *"Dio mio!"*

With Clarabella's help, she had put her gown back on, but her hair was loose and she was flushed red and shaking, holding Nikki's hand in a painful grip. Nikki led the way, taking rights and lefts at random. Her stepmother walked as though carrying a heavy basket of laundry through the ninth circle of Hell. The serva followed with a creaky, squeaky gait and Peter hanging down her back.

"What, pray tell, are we doing?"

"Getting lost."

"That should not take so long." Nikki didn't answer; the dowager didn't push. "Where will we go?" she asked.

"Dad's present timeline in San Francisco."

"I am not familiar with it."

"It should be safe." X and Y had come from her alternate timeline; their counterparts in his had never found her as far as she knew. "He's got a deal with a private hospital. They won't ask for identification or insurance or anything. It'll be strange but you'll be taken care of while I…while I figure this out."

Lady Varian compressed her lips in response like Queen Victoria— *We are not confused.*

The hedges grew shaggier and more overgrown and tunnel-like. Foliage closed out the sky. A few more twists and turns, and she no longer had any idea where they were or which way they were facing. "I think I'll try here, it ought to be far enough. And you can't come, Clarabella, so give him here—Shit!"

Ms. Y appeared, sudden as a tiger out of the underbrush, at the other end of the passage. She was alone, breathing as if she had run all the way. She had lost the brown leather jacket and her exposed skin glowed with perspiration. The object in her hand was not the black semiautomatic handgun, but the baroque dartgun, steadily aimed. Nikki didn't see a movement, didn't hear a sound, but felt a tiny blow and jolt of pain.

"Ow!"

"What did you do to my partner?" Ms. Y demanded, advancing.

The shot hurt like a cigarette burn and she could feel it spreading. But she had hold of Lady Varian's hand, and she seized Peter's as the serva released him to slump toward the ground. "I don't know what you're talking about," she said, and yanked them both around the corner with the strength of desperation.

Stretch. Snap. Gone.

發

Peter woke up...on a gurney in an institutional-green hallway, with bright light, bustle, and the smell of sterility and cleaning products piercing his aching mind. A young woman in scrubs, with the sort of healthy glow so many medical professionals had, especially in advertisements, was bending over him. The first thing she did, after asking if he knew his own name, was to demand ID and proof of insurance. Benedict Varian's no-questions-asked arrangement with this clinic was so effective, as he learned later, that nobody blinked when Nikki stumbled in dragging an unconscious man and a woman in labor, but it didn't extend to non-family members.

Since he felt okay other than the headache and a lingering fuzziness, he declined to be admitted. Waking up in a hospital gave him an initial sense of sanctuary, of the crisis being over except for picking up the pieces. He wanted to believe it but did not dare. He asked after Nikki and was directed to a window, redirected to the front desk, told to wait, told to come up, sent to another window, made to produce his driver's license, told to wait, and then finally called and sent back to a small room.

Nikki was there with Lady Varian, who was propped up in a hospital bed, fully dressed and clutching a sheet in both hands. Lady Varian's face was flushed and damp and rigid-looking, as if she were clenching her jaw in an attempt to smile through agitation. A middle-aged woman, with the authority provided by professionally short graying hair and a stethoscope draped around her neck, was talking to her. Nikki glanced at Peter, then did a strange double-take, as if she hadn't recognized him at first, and threw her arms around him.

"Are you okay?" he asked, hugging back with surprise.

"I'm tired," she said. "And frightened. And tired of being frightened. And—well, anyway. You?"

"Uh, much the same." He wanted to ask after Lady Varian, but not right in front of her, even though they were speaking in low voices. "Where are we? How did we get here?"

"San Francisco. I found another way out after you keeled over. Details later," she added.

"Yes, it's a higher risk after age 35," the doctor (Peter assumed because of the stethoscope) was saying, "but you're progressing well and you're in good hands here. So let's not go borrowing trouble. Now, you need to let the attendant prep you, okay?"

At this point, Lady Varian noticed that Peter was in the room and drew the sheet up even more. "Am I permitted no modesty here?" she demanded.

"Apologies." The doctor drew the privacy curtain around the bed, then moved Peter and Nikki out into the hallway by the sheer force of her glowering.

"I could just kick that man," she said when they were out of the room. "Why didn't he bring her in sooner? It's not as if he never heard of prenatal care!"

Evidently, this was the continuation of an earlier discussion. "Uh, Mom," Nikki said, startling Peter—the woman's nametag said Dr. Veronica Murray—"this is Peter. Peter, this…is my mother."

"Uh, hello…"

"Pleasure," Dr. Murray said crisply. She gave him an odd look, as if he had his fly undone or something stuck to his face, and shook his hand in a distracted way. "Now she's got to learn to cope with modern obstetrics on the fly!" she went on.

Given time, Peter might have guessed they were related. Dr. Murray had Nikki's coloring, though one shade paler; Nikki's facial structure, one step less robust; and Nikki's build, but a little shorter and finer boned, and of course with the difference age made. But it was strange to recognize another, apparently ordinary, person who knew who and what Nikki was, and who had known Benedict and had been to Santuario.

"Is she going to be all right?" Nikki was asking.

"You know I'm not the OB-GYN here. But she seems fine. Past her prime, certainly, but so far it all looks textbook. No thanks to your father!"

"Speaking of whom," Nikki said, "I really need to talk to you, Mom." With a direct look at Peter.

"Oh, right. Sorry."

"Well, I can spare a few minutes," Dr. Murray said. "This way to my office."

"I'll meet you out front," Nikki told him.

Peter wandered back to the waiting room. Then, feeling disoriented, he stepped outside to get his bearings. The clinic occupied a glass and steel edifice with a sharply overhung corner entrance and broad steps down to the street. The street plunged westward toward the skyline with the TransAmerican Pyramid in the middle distance and the far end of the bridge on the horizon. A cable car rattled by, all brass, polished wood, and bright red paint, in case he hadn't gotten the point: he was on Powell Street just below the crest of Nob Hill. Afternoon light suffused thin, zigzag-pattern clouds, but it was cold; the wind rattled the leaves on the spindly urban trees.

He took out his pair of identical smartphones. The time and date caught his eye and he was nonplussed to realize he had been away just half an hour. He put away the phone that didn't have a scratch on the back and started to check his email—

"Young man," someone said in a cracked voice.

Peter looked around and flinched back from a Buchenwald skeleton in a floral dress—actually an old woman, skin almost blue and an oxygen tank slung under her walker—who had just emerged from the clinic. "Uh, yes, ma'am?"

She patted his hand, apparently with some dry twigs wrapped in parchment. "There you are, dear."

Peter unfolded the dollar bill she had tucked into his palm. "Um—"

"We can all do with a little help." The starvation victim or terminal cancer patient or whatever she was gave him a ghastly smile and marched away. That is, she shuffled away, but with determination. Reaching the bottom of the ADA-mandated ramp, she half-fell into a waiting cab.

"—thank you?"

Hm.

He put the phone away, went back inside, and visited the men's room. A human wreck greeted him from the mirror—rumpled, bruised, hollow-eyed. He brushed the dust off his suit, cleaned his glasses, washed his hands and face, and slicked down his hair. Then he slunk into the waiting room, where he was relieved to find that nobody else seemed inclined to help out the less fortunate.

It was an ordinary waiting room. Chairs, magazines, potted plants, Muzak, receptionists, and sick people. But it needed upgrading: the upholstery had tears, the plants were wilting, the magazines yellowing though only a month or two old by the dates. He used the dollar in the coffee vending machine, gulped a third of it (too nasty to drink at any temperature less than scalding), sat down, and tried to think.

One question demanded his attention: How did X and Y keep finding them? When Nikki had shown up in his apartment out of the blue, they had arrived in less than an hour. They had followed her to the Palazzo Building, out of all the places she could have gone. They had come into Santuario itself as if knowing she was there— admittedly late, but time ran differently there.

Was there any reason to think they couldn't track her here to this very clinic in the next, say, twenty minutes? Should he try to find out? The thought made him shudder. What had happened had felt like sensory overload, what he imagined an epileptic seizure would feel like. His immediate takeaway was—*don't try that again!* Let the visions, if that was what they were, come in their own time. They seemed to show up before things got dangerous anyway.

He stood up with the intention of going back to find Nikki again. But just then, she came into the waiting room. He breathed with relief and greeted her as she nearly walked past him.

"Oh! There you are," she said.

"Here I am," he agreed. "How'd your mom take the news?"

"She was upset, of course. And I didn't know how much to tell her. I didn't want to worry her, but she needed to know some things."

"Lady Varian's still okay?"

"Yeah. They said it'll be another hour or three...."

"We may be dead by then."

"Right." She buttoned up her coat. Her disheveled clothes still looked good on her, though she was pale and strained. "Let's scarper."

"Do what?"

"Come on."

Peter gulped another third of the harsh coffee and tossed the cup on the way out. "Where are we going?"

"My place. It's only a few blocks from here." She hurried through the foyer and down the steps to the sidewalk, but there she hesitated. "Uh...it's downhill. This way." City noise welcomed them back, traffic did its crisscrossing thing, dust, dead leaves, and scraps of newspaper danced in the gutter. It was really cold for September; the wind cut to the bone.

"From the Italian *scappare*, to escape, to run away," she explained.

"You're thinking what I'm thinking," he surmised.

"I expect so."

"But—" He looked back. The hospital occupied an ordinary building, big plate glass windows and doors, open to the public. Not even a security desk. "What about your mom and Lady Varian and the, uh, the incoming? They could be taken hostage, or killed, or..."

"I know. But we can't protect them by hanging around."

"Well, but—" Slightly aghast, he said, "Are you just hoping that X and Y will come after us and leave them alone?"

"No. I'm planning to be back before X and Y show up." She pushed back hair that the wind tumbled into her face. "We can't protect them now. But it's never too late to come back. This is the right juncture to turn things around on them when we're better prepared."

"What's so special about it?"

"We're at the event horizon."

Peter waited for an explanation, but she seemed preoccupied, uncertain, almost startled, it seemed, by everything she saw. Her head swiveled across the skyline, taking in trees, buildings, trolley cars as if she were confused by them. They walked past a travel boutique, a coffeehouse, a real estate agency, and a leather shop before he gave up. "The what?"

"What we call it when we can't walk any farther into the future because of never having been there before to know what it looks like," she said finally. "The point in any given timeline at which we can only travel forward, you know, minute by minute like everybody else."

"Okay..."

"Nothing to do with black holes. I guess when Dad first heard the term, he thought that's what it should mean."

"Sure, why not? Why shouldn't he redefine astrophysics terms to suit himself?"

Nikki shook herself and gave him more attention. "Anyway, this is my timeline...the one I made for, well, for you to be alive in. I've never been any farther than this in it. This is the event horizon, the ultimate now. And when we're ready to take X and Y down—"

"What?"

"—we can come back to this exact moment and do it without causing a split. We don't want two timelines—you know, one in which we don't come back and protect my mother and stepmother and… the incoming. You see," she gave him an earnest look as if to impart a revelation, "you really can't fix anything by returning to the past. You can only escape. Okay...I think this is it."

She led him to the front security door of a three-story faux-Victorian house subdivided into rental units, in need of more pale blue and white paint and maybe replacement windows. The balconies showed signs of occupancy—a rusting barbecue, a half-dead potted orange tree, a little brown dog pushing its nose through the slats—but the place was quiet.

"You *think* this is it?" Peter repeated. These houses were all architecturally similar, but they had a lot of variation in color and placement and the little gingerbread-house decoration around the windows and roofs; they weren't that easy to mix up.

"Let me make sure." She pressed four intercom buttons in sequence. The security gate buzzed and they got out of the wind, entering a hallway with worn-down black and white tile, six mailboxes, and minimal lighting.

Peter felt he was missing something. "Nikki, are you okay?"

She handed him a dart. "Not really—" and headed up a set of worn wooden spiral stairs.

The dart was the same as the one he'd found in her shoulder three days ago, brass and glass shaped like a stinging insect. Its ampoule was empty but for a trace of green liquid. Green, not clear. "Shit!" he said, and scrambled after her. "You didn't pass out?"

"No, that's not what it does. It's interfering with me. I tried to pop over here half an hour ago while you were sleeping," she said. "You know, grab a cup of tea, be back before anybody missed me, but I—I couldn't remember what the place looked like."

"You mean you can't...?"

"We were lucky the stuff didn't take effect immediately. I can't pull up images that should be in my memory, not clearly enough to timewalk anyway."

"Then we're stuck here?" He offered the dart back, but she wasn't paying attention, so he kept it. "Look, maybe it's time we call the police."

"No. Memory isn't the only way. Alex wasn't much of a Timewalker, but he could do it with a photograph. There's no reason I can't."

"Then where are we going?"

She showed him the hand-tinted photo of the Palazzo Building taken with an antique Kodak, which he had last seen pasted in the Book of Days.

"...I'm not going to get a hot shower, a clean shirt, or recognizable coffee any time soon, am I?"

"I'd suggest you don't come, but...if I fail and don't come back, you'd be in more danger here."

They arrived at a door painted deep enamel blue with a brass number 9—actually a 6 hanging upside-down, as Peter saw by the 6-shaped patch of cleaner paint above it. "Fail at what exactly?"

"We're going to find my dad." For the second time she looked like her father's daughter and he felt chilled. "Taboo be damned," she said, "there's a baby on the way. These monsters have to be stopped." She unlocked the door with a key on a drain-plug chain around her neck and locked it again when they were inside.

"Then what are we doing here?"

"I have an Unseen Room of my own."

It was a two-bedroom-one-bath, the rooms tiny even by Bay Area rental standards, but careful organization, large windows, and northwestern exposure made it seem spacious. Peter noticed because of the contrast with his own apartment, which was twice the size but cramped. The place smelled like oil paint, solvents, and varnish and sun-warmed sheets washed with bleach and fabric softener, something he hadn't smelled since leaving his parents' house.

One of the bedroom doors, painted enamel green, was padlocked, presumably so Nikki wouldn't accidentally discover what the room behind it looked like, and he pondered how odd it must be to live in a place you hadn't seen all of. Just now, however, she was looking around the place, checking out the tiny kitchen and bathroom, as if she had never seen any of it. She touched a landline phone, a 90s-vintage white plastic answering machine with an unblinking light, then picked up a coffee table art book with *The Scream* on its cover. She frowned and put it back with a decisive thump. "We're gonna need clothes."

"Nikki, where—what's this?"

A painting had caught Peter's attention. She used the main room as a studio and the works covering its walls appeared to be hers. They were of buildings in various and often mixed architectural styles, with walls, doors, archways, windows, and connecting bridges arranged in ways that did not always make sense. It was impossible in several of them to tell whether the view was interior or exterior. Although they all contained numerous exits, they conveyed a sense of confinement, of obstacles where there shouldn't be any.

The one that had drawn his eye was no different in that regard, but it stood on the easel, still damp, blurry in the details compared to the finished ones, and it was of something familiar.

Nikki regarded it as she had everything else in the last twenty minutes—mildly amnesiac. "...It was going to be Notre-Dame," she said, "but then I had other ideas...I can't remember now what they were."

The structure in the painting looked impossibly tall, and more like an ancient tree with two forks and exposed roots made of yellow-gray limestone than a gothic cathedral. Peter felt as though the room they were standing in, particularly the floor, had no solidity and might fall apart any minute. The sun went behind a cloud billowing up from the northwest and all the warmth went out of the air.

Nikki betrayed a similar unease although for a different reason. "This had better wear off soon." She strode into the bedroom, changing the subject. "I'm not sure I have anything that'll fit you...."

Peter was about to follow when he heard the roar of a powerful engine coming from the street below and a shriek of brakes. He peered out the window, trying to show himself as little as possible, just in time to see a sleek black Jaguar sling itself into a no-parking zone directly below the window.

"Nikki, they're here!"

She came back as Mr. X and Ms. Y sprang out of the car—Y from the driver's side.

"They're beginning to remind me of zombies. Or killer robots," Peter said, although their body language—Mr. X's particularly— showed agitation and rage. There was no attempt at stealth. Ms. Y slapped something against the security gate. He couldn't identify it, but as they took cover behind a mailbox, he guessed. Subtlety had left the building. A second later, sound impacted his ears, the windows rattled, and a dog started barking, high-pitched and excited, echoed by several more along the street. The air outside was full of gray smoke and fluttering flakes of scorched paint.

"Do you have a camera? Take a picture in here!" said Nikki.

"We have to go!"

"We need a photo of this place because if this drug doesn't wear off and we don't find my father, we won't be able to get back!"

He fumbled with one of his smartphones and snapped a photo while she shoved a key into the padlock on the green door. The phone's battery read 13%. He turned it off.

There was a thudding sound, as of someone taking the spiral stairs three or four at a time and colliding with the walls along the way. Nikki threw the padlock aside and stared at her old photograph as she twisted the doorknob. "Hang onto me!"

A gunshot disabled the bolt on the blue door just as they tumbled through the green one.

發

Cobbled pavement materialized underfoot. A brisk ocean wind rearranged the twilight sky and blew some of the fog out of Nikki's head. "Okay," she said, breathing easier. "Seriously. They can't reach us here."

"Are you sure?"

"Well, there are Hunters around here somewhere, but we're a hundred years away from X and Y."

Peter opened his eyes and his jaw hit the paving.

The arc-lamp streetlights were just coming on, and great Victorian block and brick buildings loomed over them. Naked power lines and telegraph wires netted the intersection, humming and sparking. COCA WINE for FATIGUE of BODY and MIND blared in letters painted ten feet high on the side of a building, reminding all time-travelers to be careful what they drank. Homburg hats, muttonchops, and sack coats paraded by. Shirtwaists and button-boots glided along the sidewalk, a swish of poplin fringe against kid leather. Traffic didn't cruise—it rattled, jingled, and clip-clopped on the cobbles, squeaked, clanged, and grated along the rails. The air stank—sewage, manure, coal, and tobacco smoke.

"It's in color!" he said, and she was grateful for the giggle that pushed itself out of her chest.

She held up the photograph of the Palazzo Building until she found the matching original: three stories of granite arches and windows in the Italian Renaissance style, all new from foundation to rooftop, suffused in cold amber as the lowering sun broke through seething cloud cover.

"Your dad's here?"

"Should be. He built the place. Let's go see."

The locals were staring at them, curious, befuddled, cold, and in a couple of cases, outraged stares. She sighed for the contemporary clothes they'd had no time to change into. Their clothing didn't exactly look out of place in this juncture, but it did look inappropriate on them. Blue jeans, worn exclusively by working men, neither concealed her gender nor sanctioned it. And though Peter would just look foreign if he were by himself in his oddly cut suit, together they were a mixed-race couple. His presence made her a whore; her presence made him a fiend.

She dealt with the hostility in the usual way: by moving too fast to register it. They crossed the street, dodging a Model A and a cab drawn by a bay Standardbred. Peter tugged against her grip—"Hey! Did you see that woman?"

She steered him around a steaming puddle. "What woman?"

"She was right there!" He pointed at a blank arch in the Palazzo wall. "A lady in a *tangzhuang*, and—"

"A what?"

"—and she was just gone!"

"I didn't see anything."

"Maybe I'm having visions again...."

A doorman blocked their way into the building, subtle as a billboard in royal blue with gold trim. A black guy, stress lines sunk deep in a still-young face probably just from being born here in the Progressive Era. His voice was deep and unexpectedly steady. "Can I help you, miss?"

She tightened her grip on Peter, who was wobbling a bit and inclined to stray. "Is my fath—is Mr. Varian in?"

"Do he know you?" the doorman asked.

"He will. I'm his daughter."

The doorman rubbed his jaw. "First a fortune teller, now a white gal in men's clothes hangin' off a Johnny Chinese say she's Mr. Benedict Varian's daughter. If that don't beat all."

"I am though. Could you please let him know?"

Peter was searching the man's face. "Abe?" he blurted.

"Who?" said the doorman.

Nikki couldn't see any resemblance, but then she wouldn't be able to, would she? It was so disorienting—"He's not Abe."

"Sorry," said Peter. "You remind me of someone."

"You don't remind me of nobody," the doorman retorted. "My name is Tom. Tom Slinky."

"Oh." Peter laughed. "Oh, my God."

Nikki twitched—they were drawing attention. "Are you going to let us in?"

He shifted a bulge from one of his cheeks to the other. "Well, miss, when I took this job, Mr. Varian, he told me some outlandish relatives might drop in now and again." He reached back and pulled out a flexible speaking tube mounted on the inside wall. "So I will ask him, anyway." He pressed his lips to the mouthpiece and blew a whistle mounted inside it on a piece of cork, which he then removed. "Mr. Varian, sir?" he said into the mouthpiece. "Sorry to disturb you, but they's a gal out here says she's your daughter?"

She'd hoped to surprise him, having an idea he might make tracks if warned. But he'd know the taboo was already broken, right? He'd storm and bluster and pontificate, but he wouldn't—would he?—try to avoid her....

"Sir?" Tom repeated into the tube. Silence, except for the whistle of an amplified draft. "Sir?" He replaced the tube on the wall. "I guess he ain't in just now, miss, or he ain't answerin'. It's after hours and, frankly, it ain't a good time when we're closing down. Why don't you come back in the mornin'?"

"I'm sorry. I'd better see for myself." She took Peter's hand. "Brace yourself."

"What f—oh."

"Hey!" the doorman yelled, and there was a momentary spike in ambient street noise as passers-by tried to decide if they had really seen two people vanish from the street.

Peter was coping with fugue now. "It looks exactly the same," he observed of the lobby, with its marble pillars, black-and-white floor, and vaulted ceiling.

"Does it?" She was trying to ignore the problem with her memory, it felt too much like amputation. "Probably is." Although there was a fug of cigar and cigarette smoke that wouldn't be there in Peter's time.

The gilt cage elevator, all shiny and almost new, rattled its gates open. "Hey!" The doorman spun around and ran in. "How did you—hey, you!"

There was no operator, so Peter grabbed the lever. "I'm sorry," Nikki called as the cage rose. "It's an emergency. Listen," she said to Peter, "I should mention Dad won't be pleased to see us."

"Because of the taboo?"

"Yeah. I'm splitting his timeline by coming here. Not just this one, his personal timeline."

"But you have no problem doing that to us ephemerals."

Heat came into her face. "Well, yeah. You—they—usually never even know that it happened." There had been a perceptible edge in Peter's voice. He didn't push it, probably remembering that he was still alive because she had split his timeline, but she felt a pang. He probably regretted the near-declaration he'd made to her yesterday. She'd always thought that a great trauma would numb a person to lesser wounds, but it turned out they hurt more, as minor irritants sting a raw abrasion.

Bing. Mezzanine level. She stepped out and changed the subject. "Awfully quiet up here." Tom Slinky was thudding up the stairs, but silence reigned otherwise—no footsteps, no chatter, no typewriter click or stock-ticker clack.

"I guess no one's working late."

She couldn't remember where her father's office was supposed to be, but Peter did. The outer doors were locked. She squinted through the crack between them, fugued through, then opened them for Peter. Tom had reached the mezzanine, so she shot the bolt behind them. Stark electric light revealed an outer office. Peter looked bemused at it—the quaint furniture, the green-shaded lamps, the speaking tube, the pigeonholes, the blotting paper. "Wow."

"Hey!" came Tom's voice. He banged on the door. "You're trespassing! Open up!"

"We won't hurt anything," she called, then tried the inner office door. It opened. But the room beyond was dark, and smelled of carpet and furniture moved but not cleaned under. Switching on the light showed dusty rectangles on the floor, clean squares on the walls. The bookcases were all empty and stacks of books were all around, some in wooden crates.

"You goin' to get me fired, I'll call the po-lice!"

Peter closed the inner door, muffling Tom's shouts and thuds. "He's closing down and moving out."

"Sure looks like it." Her eye fell on a stack of documents left on the desk. She switched on the desk lamp and leafed through them. "Notice of pending corporate dissolution. Bank drafts to creditors. Paychecks...all stamped 'in lieu of notice.' A letter closing accounts already sent," she brandished a carbon, "to Pacific Gas and Electric. I'd say he's already cleared out." She dropped the stack back down on the desk.

"Well, we know where he went, right?" Peter went behind the desk and prodded the panel. Sunk in thought, she didn't answer. "Shouldn't we check?" he prompted.

"I've told you. You can't reach the past in Santuario."

"Um...we're in the past."

"If we go through that door, we'll arrive later than last time we were there. Dad won't be there."

"Okay. Can we reach a different one of his timelines?"

"I don't have coordinates." Nikki kicked herself for not grabbing more pictures out of the Book of Days when she had the chance. "We'll have to backtrack along this line. I just need something to give us a fix. A picture in a magazine or something."

She sat down at the desk. The big chair still held an impression—hell, it was still warm—and smelled of Cavendish pipe tobacco. He couldn't have been gone long. Blinking, she went through the documents again.

"Maybe he hasn't left quite yet," Peter offered. "He could still be in the building."

At the bottom of the pile was a folded copy of the *San Francisco Examiner*. "No, he's definitely bailed." She passed it to him. "Check the date."

"April 17, 1906?"

"Uh-huh, so tomorrow is...?" A San Franciscan, he must know that date as well as he knew September 11, 2001, or December 7, 1941.

"Shit!" he said succinctly.

"Yeah, that." She looked toward the window and the seething

sky. "Nine or ten hours to go. I can't imagine Dad cutting things any closer." She sagged on her elbows.

"Maybe there's a picture in here you can use?" Peter riffled the *Examiner*.

"Doubt it," she said absently. She was thinking. Back in the clinic, before her mother showed up, Lady Varian...Eleonora...had thoroughly unnerved her by begging her to stay. That icy dignity had finally cracked. She pleaded with Nikki not to abandon her among strangers in her travail. In that moment, Nikki had hated her father. Death was no excuse, the taboo was meaningless, he had no right to run out on them. She had done it herself, but she never claimed to be the all-powerful, all-knowing *pater familias*. Rage rose hard enough to choke her...

...but it was really a frozen lump of tears. She had been prepared to be furious with him. But oh, how she had counted on him being there to be furious with.

As a child—three? four?—she'd had this dream: She was in her mother's house in San Francisco, where she'd lived for half of her childhood before the divorce and almost all of it afterwards, down in the basement. It was an evil-smelling place, so dark it made no difference whether her eyes were open or shut. Nonetheless, she could see beetles—big, black beetles that lived in cracks in the walls, chewing up the mortar and shifting the cinder blocks. They were swarming out to get her. That they would get her, no matter how she ran, screamed, or stamped on them, was so inevitable that every second she found herself not yet gotten was a surprise.

Eventually in the dream, she found the stairs going up and began to climb. But the steps were too big for her. She had to use her hands to scramble up each one. After a long time and enormous effort, she got near the top. There were only three more steps to go. But she had run out of strength. Couldn't climb any further. Just could not get up the last three steps. The basement door was open. She could see Mommy and Daddy in the kitchen. They were arguing, sharp and hurtful. She called to them. They did not respond. She kept calling—*Help! Come get me!* They were wrapped up in their own concerns and did not hear her.

"Are you all right?" Peter broke her reverie with that odd expression he got sometimes.

"Sure." Still warm, still breathing, what did he expect her to say?

"These aren't good enough, are they?" The pictures in the newspaper, he meant, blurry and grayscale, detail lost in the printing, and she shook her head. "What do we do?"

"I don't know," she said.

"Hm." Peter sighed. Then he took his glasses off and sat down on an office chair, laying the *Examiner* aside. "All right. Hang on a minute."

"What are you doing?"

"We need more information." His face relaxed and went blank.

"Uh, Peter? No. No, don't do that!" But his eyes were already unfocused. Whatever he was looking at wasn't in the room, at least not yet. She leaned over him. "Peter?"

He flinched. For a second, he seemed to see her. "They're coming!" he said. Then he jerked upright as if shocked. "Recursive…" he said, twitched again, and collapsed off the chair onto the floor.

"Oh, shit!" She took his head in her hands. He lolled. "Well, that was helpful." More sarcasm than she'd use if he could hear her, and she regretted it—he'd only done this because she was near the end of her rope. *They're coming.* "Who is coming?" He lay there and twitched at her. The only sound was traffic from the street and the wind blowing through bare wires. "We're over a hundred years in the past, you know. They can't. Get. Here." Well, unless, of course, Erik really was behind it all, she realized, turning absolutely cold. "Oh, shit, oh shit, oh, shit…"

She elevated his feet on a roll of carpet in case of shock, switched off the light, locked him in the office and crept out to the mezzanine to reconnoiter. If it was Erik coming—and it could be, he could've found the engine records she'd left on Dad's desk and figured out where she'd gone—she wasn't in any physical danger. But Peter was.

Doorman Tom had given up thumping and gone away, probably to find help. Perhaps Peter just saw local police coming, nothing to worry about. The lobby was empty, all stark shadows under crude electric light, and the sky outside was darkening. She summoned the elevator and hopped aboard. It creaked and rattled and echoed in the empty space. A clock tower, City Hall perhaps, began to sound the hour: *bong...bong...bong...* On the fourth stroke of seven, all the lights went out.

She stumbled into a corner as the cage screeched to a stop. Stuck halfway between floors. She blinked, afterimages leaping on her eyeballs. *Somebody cut the power!*

Well, yes. She found her wits. Dad had closed the PG&E account. He wouldn't leave the gas and electricity on during the Big One; that would be wasteful and irresponsible. She tried to pry the cage doors apart, until she remembered that a Timewalker couldn't be confined in anything she could see out of and fugued down to the floor. Misjudged the distance a bit in the dim light and landed on her ass. Grumbling, she waited until her eyes adjusted, then headed for the front door.

And stopped short as it opened, and a distorted shadow fell through with a crack of streetlight. Her heart lurched in one direction and her brain in another, as if they could not agree which way she ought to run. The shadow half-stalked, half-staggered inside and turned into a golden-brown woman in a flak jacket carrying a gray man in a flasher coat limp over her shoulder like a sack of grain. Nikki didn't exactly recognize them, but they couldn't be anyone else. She put her fists on her hips. This couldn't be happening; she refused to believe it. "What," she demanded, "are you doing here?"

Ms. Y gave her an odd look, first annoyed surprise, then grudging satisfaction. "Didn't I tell you?" Mr. X said, muffled behind her back. "Put me down. I can walk now." He staggered and half-fell against the wall when she let him drop. "Fucking precog," he said hoarsely.

"You mean—" she cut herself off before saying Peter's name. How did he know? Nothing about any of this made any sense. But the mezzanine was in her line of sight, an easy hop and a dash to safety—

"Hold it," said X. In the half-light, he looked like a corpse propped against the windowsill. "Don't fucking run away again, little girl, or Ms. Y will go upstairs, break down a couple of doors, and step on your boyfriend's neck until it breaks."

"Go ahead," Ms. Y invited.

"And then we'll head back to the twenty-first century and pay a visit to the expectant mama," X added. Nikki froze in place. "That's better," he said. "Now we talk." Ms. Y gave him a scornful look.

Nikki's chest felt tight and her fingertips were cold. "Are you working for my brother?"

"We don't discuss that," Y said, while in the same breath, X said, "Shit, no." To his partner, he added, "Don't interrupt. I know what I'm doing." She gave a shrug and faded back into the shadows until all Nikki could see were her eyes when they caught the light in gold.

"If he didn't send you, how did you get here?"

He pushed away from the wall and leaned instead on the podium just inside the front door, where Tom had his speaking tubes clipped in a row. "I borrowed the image from your mind and walked through the portal you left open." He grinned. "Told you we could follow you anywhere."

Cold struck down Nikki's spine. Answers were falling into place—like the huge stone blocks of a trap set in a pharaoh's tomb. "You—you're one of the Fourth Family." That was how they'd followed her. That was how he knew—well, everything. His grin got impossibly wider, shark-like, and she added, "I didn't know a Telepath could follow a Timewalker."

"Neither did I, until I tried it. But the clan sits on its collective ass droning *om mani padme hum* to keep from going batshit. No wonder no one ever found out before." Leaning heavily against the podium, he fished under it and brought out a kerosene lantern.

Nikki licked her lips, edging back unconsciously. "What have you done to me?"

"Clipped your wings, sweetheart." He struck a match and lit the lamp, releasing the smell of kerosene. "The drug is a visual memory inhibitor. Which means I don't have to put up with all the crap in your head anymore." The lamp threw a circle of jaundiced light up on his face. "And," he added, "you can't leave."

She glanced up and fugued to the dark mezzanine in the blink of an eye. "Yes, I can," she called.

Ms. Y emerged from the shadows, semiautomatic tracking. "Kneecap," she suggested.

"We're still talking." X turned up the lantern flame so that the flickering light almost reached Nikki. "Don't go back to your precog. We're not having you grab him, pop out the window, and get lost in the Tenderloin. I've had it with chasing you, bitch. Make me do it again, we'll butcher Chang, your mama, your stepmama, and your new baby sibling, and break both of your legs."

Ms. Y growled. The wind whistled outside. She tried one more time. Home—the most basic, most familiar image—wouldn't come. Her father's face. Edvard's. Peter's. All blank. "Get down here, little Miss Varian," X said.

"You're bluffing about Mom, Eleonora, and the baby," Nikki said, not moving. "If you have to follow me, you can't get back without me."

"True," he conceded. "But your boyfriend is available. Here and now, baby girl, you have to deal with us. Come on down."

This is responsibility, Nikki noticed in surreal moment of calm. And it was simple, it was rational. A moral imperative, the incontrovertible conviction of a dream. Almost nothing to do with X and Y. *You must do it, it is to be done.*

"Why?" she said to Mr. X when she stood down in the lobby again, looking only at him, though golden eyes and the muzzle of the gun stared into her back, and Y smelled rank, like a big predatory cat. She'd never been this close to them before.

X knew what she was asking, of course, because he didn't respond with threats. He must be the most understanding kidnapper and murderer that ever lived. "The Hunters need you," he said.

"Then you're working for Sanders," she said. They did not deny it, nor look surprised, nor let their faces give away anything but lack of denial. The black-and-white tile floor crawled in the flickering light and shadow like something alive. She seemed to see everything like a four-year-old would—as if for the first time and through a lens of fear. X was a haggard psychotic ghoul, Y an oversexualized killing machine, neither of them human. Maybe it was the drug, maybe the effect of stress you couldn't escape, or maybe they really looked like that. "What do they need me for?"

"To save their race," X said.

"What?" Oddly, as she later realized, it did not occur to her that he could easily be lying. "Then why kill my father? That's not conducive to getting my help!"

"Big Daddy Timewalker wouldn't have let you. He was in favor of genocide. I sympathized," the Telepath said, his eyes sunk in hollow sockets behind prominent cheekbones, "but he had to go."

"And Alex?"

"Collateral damage."

"...You cold sonova—"

"That's enough," Y said.

"It is," X agreed. "You're coming with us."

"Oh, yeah? How? If I can't access my own memory—" Of course there was the photo on Peter's cell phone, and it was too late to suppress that thought.

"We prepared for that, too," X said, and held up a digital camera. The screen displayed the interior of an apartment that Nikki found attractive until she realized it must be hers and that she was unable to recognize it.

"I can timewalk with a photo," she admitted, "but I don't remember the place." Her nerves were provoking too much honesty, not that it mattered. "I can't be sure we'll end up in the right juncture."

"Why not?" demanded Ms. Y.

X explained for her. "Corresponding points in different timelines can have similar coordinates. Or a place can look the same for a long time. We could end up in a different timeline, or in the right place but a couple of years off." He snorted. "Give it your best shot. I took that picture literally seconds after you left, it should work fine. Anyway, we're not staying here for the big one."

"But I can't just leave—"

"Yes, you can."

"They'll eat him alive here!"

"Or Ms. Y can put her boot heel through his spinal column. Your choice." The Telepath chuckled without any humor. "You people always have the choice."

CHAPTER SEVEN

He stood on a bridge above the bay with the city at his back. It was in the right place to be the Oakland Bay Bridge, but it was a wooden footbridge, extraordinarily long. Two figures walked toward him out of a blood-red eastern sky. He heard or felt a scream of existential horror from all of nature—as if the vision was expressing the utter futility of his life. Then he recognized the figures and realized it was, in fact, pointing out the brevity of his life.

They looked as they always did—the gray man like hammered shit, the golden woman like a really cool way to die. But X was wearing mirrored sunglasses, the sky, sea, city, and bridge reflected in them, and as he approached, Peter was reflected too. And Peter, as he saw in his reflection, was also wearing mirror shades clipped onto his usual glasses, and X was reflected in them in his reflection. And Peter was reflected in that reflection, and X in the next, and so on and—

Vertigo hit him. Forward became down. He toppled with a cry. X flew toward him, falling in the opposite direction. They passed through each other. Peter plummeted down a well of mirrors, faster and faster, until all the images and sounds blurred into static and white noise, and then went black.

發

He woke up in the dark on a hard surface. Not a hospital gurney this time.

There was enough light to make out the looming corner of a desk. He was...on the floor of Mr. Varian's office, head throbbing, eyes gritty, a taste in his mouth like salt and ashes. He remembered the bridge, the red sky, dark figures, mirrored glasses, falling. What the hell?

Well, whatever the hell, assuming these visions were accurate at all, X and Y seemed to be coming their way. Even the past wasn't safe from them. "Nikki?" No answer. He sat up. "Nikki!"

A streetlight cut through the blinds. Harsh and bright, not a subdued modern light, and it made his headache worse. He was more than a century away from home and hadn't brought any aspirin. He scrambled up, found himself stiff and chilled—*how long have I been lying here?*—and lurched to the door. It wouldn't open. Hunting for the light switch, he instead found a pair of pushbuttons set in a metal plate. Pressing one down popped the other one up, but neither turned the light on. He resorted to one of his phones in its capacity as a flashlight. It showed him the bolt securing the door—on this side and he hadn't locked it.

His glasses were on the floor where he was just about to step on them. He put them on and went out, deactivating the phone again to conserve power. The outer office was also dark, but dim light flickered under the outer double doors. These doors were bolted from inside too. This puzzled him until he recalled Nikki had fugued through to open them in the first place. She must have gone out the same way. He shot the bolt back and shoved the doors open.

Tom the doorman was waiting for him outside, holding a kerosene lantern. He looked stressed, which increased his apparent age and family resemblance to Abe Slinky. "You finally comin' out of there?"

"Um—yeah," said Peter. The mezzanine was dark, the whole

building was dark except for Tom's lantern. "Sorry about that. We didn't damage anything. Have you seen my friend?"

"You mean that gal that calls herself Miss Varian? She gone."

"Excuse me?"

"She gone."

"How gone? Where?"

The lines in Tom's face deepened into chasms, although it could have been an effect of the light. "Devils took her."

Peter squeezed his eyes shut, rubbed them, opened them. The doorman was still there with the same expression. "Devils?"

"The devil in the long gray coat and the she-devil with the roscoe."

"...Oh, those devils," Peter said, his pulse starting to sound in his ears. "How? When? How'd they get here? Where'd they take her?"

"I went out looking for the po-lice, lucky for you I didn't find none. So I was coming back in the front door. I see them two with your gal. She wasn't happy, but she wasn't fighting, neither. They all marched into the back and opened the door to the broom closet. Where, I don't mind telling you, there ain't enough room to swing a newborn kitten. They all go inside and they don't come out again. When I open it, they ain't there. That's all I know."

"That's impossible...." Peter stared at him, then ran to the mezzanine rail. "Nikki!" he yelled into the dark pit of the building. "Nikki!" *Eee!* said the vaulted ceiling. Shadows of leaves shifted on the lobby floor. The building breathed cold, musty drafts.

"She gone," Tom repeated.

Peter gripped the rail. "You're sure? Have you heard any other noise in the building? Could she have come back out some other door?" The doorman looked at him as if a pink petunia was growing out of his forehead. "Sorry I'm blathering, but have you checked everywhere?"

"There's nobody here but you and me."

Peter waited to feel something other than shock. It was like getting tapped with a sap; you wouldn't even know how hard until you woke up three weeks later in the coma ward. After a few seconds, he laughed. "One of my predictions came true." Now he knew why the others—or some of the others—hadn't come true: because he'd acted on them in time. "What a useless talent!"

"Now come on." Tom shifted. "Ain't no time for hysterics."

"They kidnapped her. Forced her to timewalk out! She's going to get her brain sucked out! I don't have any way to reach her. Or get home. This is April 17, 1906! It's the perfect time for hysterics!"

"Well, you can't have 'em here," said the doorman. "I got to lock up. I don't ask who you are. I don't want to know."

Protest seemed futile. Peter followed Tom down the back stairs to the lobby. In the light from the street, he saw the elevator cage eerily suspended halfway between ground floor and mezzanine. "Power's out?"

"Turned off. I was s'posed to be home an hour since."

A minute later, Peter found himself out on the sidewalk. Traffic had died down, leaving only a few stragglers in homburg hats. Victorian buildings, over-bright arc lamps, quaintly worded billboards, a curlicue brass hitching post planted in the cobbles where he remembered a steel bike rack set in concrete. It looked unreal. Fog was creeping in, blurring the edges of things like a hand erasing chalk lines.

Tom locked the front door of the Palazzo with two turns of a large key and came down the steps. He had replaced his splendid blue and gilt coat with a tweed jacket and a workman's cap. He glanced at Peter, shifting his jaw for a couple of seconds, and apparently compassion got the better of his determination. "You got someplace to go?"

"I...guess I'll just hang out here. For when she comes back."

The doorman eyed him with sour pity. "It seem to me, when a gal disappear off the face of the earth like that, she ain't coming back."

"But if she does, this is the only place she'll know to find me."

"You'll get yourself rousted."

"I'll what?"

"The po-lice? Don't want no Chinamen hanging round the Palazzo."

"Yeah...okay. I'll be careful. Um. Thank you for everything...."
He squinted at the man. Perhaps it was the light, or the change of
clothes, but Tom looked even more like a younger Abe. His skin had
grayed enough to show the darker flecks of freckles. "Do you live
around here?"

"Folsom Street."

"You, um, might want to come in to work early tomorrow." In
his time, the old Palazzo looked much the same as now. Company
literature said it had escaped the Great Earthquake almost unscathed.
It must be reasonably safe. "Really early. Like, before five a.m.?" A
deeper crease appeared between Tom's brows. "Seriously," Peter
urged. "You should come in before dawn. Bring your folks. Your
friends. Everybody you care about. Just camp out in the lobby." He'd
seen the photographs of the city in the aftermath—it looked like an
atomic bomb had hit it.

Tom shook his head. "What is it everybody around here knows
except me? You're the third person today to tell me that. Come to
work at four in the morning, stay inside."

"You wouldn't believe me," Peter admitted. "Just do it, please?"

"Well, you're the first to say please, I'll give you that." Tom put his
cap straight. "Good night to you."

He walked off, leaving Peter to feel that he was watching the last
boat sail away from a desert island. A bell, a rattle, and a clip-clop
sounded, and a horse-drawn tram came along, jolting and rattling
over the cobbles. Tom hurried after it. He had nearly reached it when
the other shoe fell on Peter's head and made him chase after. "Hey!"

Tom glanced back with evaporating patience. "What?"

"Third time? Who else told you?"

"You go bother somebody else, John Chinaman!" Tom shook off his grip and jumped onto the rear step of the tram. "Hook it!"

"Mr. Varian could've told you." Peter jogged alongside. "Who else?"

"It was Madame When, the fortune teller. She told me."

"Madame When? Who's she? Where can I find her?"

Tom's face traveled into hitherto unexplored realms of puzzlement and annoyance. "You don't know her? You ain't fresh off the boat. Everybody know her. In Chinatown!" he yelled as the tram clattered away.

Peter ran out of breath, stopped to catch it. He staggered back to the Palazzo and sat down on the steps. Dark except for the streetlights, quiet except for horse trams and a few people strolling the sidewalks; mist muffled the city noise. He fingered his smartphones, longing to check one of them for texts, email, the internet, the time, any kind of connection, but it would just run itself down searching for a signal.

X and Y had Nikki. However they'd gotten here, that was the salient point. They must've taken her back to the juncture where they all, himself and Sanders included, came from. Peter shuddered, then tried to calm down. Nothing was happening to her now, it was in the distant future. Plenty of time to save her if he looked at it like that, the problem was living so long. Why had she gone so tamely? Even drugged, that didn't sound like the girl he knew. But Tom could not have been lying, he didn't know enough, couldn't guess what lie to tell.

And why couldn't he have fallen for the barista? What was her name again? He wouldn't be here, stranded in a strange city. Cut off so completely he might as well be dead.

He pressed fists against his eyes. His head throbbed, his chest felt tight. As far as everybody he knew was concerned, he was dead.

Well, what are you going to do? Sit and wait for them to be right? Because if Nikki could come back, she'd already be here.

Peter rubbed his face on his sleeve. *Thank you, voice of harsh reality.
Don't mention it. Well?*

He stared at the skyline, which unnerved him by being so alien
and so familiar at the same time. Somewhere out there, somebody
named Madame When knew there was going to be an earthquake
early tomorrow morning. Unless she was a fraud who happened to
be spot-on one time, like a broken clock, she must know Benedict. Or
she might be a Seer. He hadn't accepted that there were such things as
Seers. But what else was there to try?

Light, clipping hooves sounded in the mist. A hansom cab
appeared, like something out of Sherlock Holmes. He made up his
mind and hailed it. "Hey! Hello! Right here!" The driver, looking dour
under a pulled-down cap, whipped up the horse to accelerate past him.
"Hey!" snapped Peter, seeing no other possible fare. The driver made
a universally understood gesture and drove on his way.

…Right. He was a member of the Yellow Peril. A Celestial. A
Chink. He should probably skip cabs and streetcars if he didn't want
to get roughed up, verbally abused, arrested, or shunned. He'd have to
hoof it a mile or two and just avoid people as much as possible.

That horrible cup of coffee-machine coffee seemed even longer
ago than it really was. He could hardly believe that he had thrown
half of it away.

About five years later, according to his feet and stomach, he
reached the place where Chinatown was supposed to be.

It was, in fact, Chinatown, just not one he'd ever seen before. He
stood shivering in the mist at the intersection where the Dragon Gate
should have been, looking up a steep, narrow street between rows
of falling-down-drunk Victorian houses. They slumped and piled

on each other for support, rickety wooden balconies and jury-rigged staircases built out over the street. A veneer of China had been tacked on with the paper lanterns and dragon flags. Incense, lacquer, and fried noodles overlaid the miasma of horse manure and waterfront. But it was basically a western slum. All along the way, he'd been ambushed by bits and pieces of the San Francisco he knew—surviving buildings, the shape of the hills, the names and layout of the streets. But this...he had never lived in Chinatown, but his paternal grandparents did; he had visited often, watched the parades and eaten the moon cakes. He didn't recognize anything.

Easy to see why. A stiff breeze would knock this place down, let alone...he tried not to finish the thought. Chinatown, poor and flimsy and horribly overcrowded, had been completely destroyed.

Would be. In a few hours.

He squared his shoulders and trudged up the hill. The streets by night were busier here. Men coming home from work, men going out to work, men hanging around teashops and food stalls...they were all men, wearing long tunics and queues under work hats, except a few in dirty western clothes, or shorn like prison inmates, and of course, the white tourists—sailors and addicts and generally sleazy individuals. Peter became conscious of his haircut and two-piece suit. Though the suit wasn't terribly clean and must seem a bit odd, he looked like a rich man—like a foreigner. All the way here, he'd been invisible; now he was the most conspicuous person on the street.

He walked faster, tried to look as though he knew where he was going, and shortly got into a fish market. Now men were hawking and haggling and calling their wares, tubs of dead fish, live crayfish, and ghastly squid lined a confusion of walkways, paving stones glittered with scales and brine under the harsh lights. Cantonese rang in his ears. The rhythm was familiar, but many of the words were strange, or strangely pronounced.

"Excuse me," he said to an elderly fishmonger, fumbling for half-learned and half-forgotten phrases. "I need...Madame When?" The name must be Wen, but he didn't know which inflection to use, so he just pronounced the English word and hoped for the best. "Do you know her?" The old man looked at him askance. "Do you speak English? Know someone who does?" He flushed hot asking this. The fishmonger flicked a fan at him—*shoo, fly*—and went on extolling the virtues of his octopuses.

A bell tolled once for the half-hour. *Old Saint Mary's!* he realized. Something else had survived—would survive. His pleasure at the familiar sound was short-lived. Time was running out. He pulled a coin out of his pocket and showed it to the old man. It had the wrong date, but who would squint at a quarter in the dark? "Please. Madame Wen?" He tried a reasonably common pitch variant that meant *glorious jade*.

The fishmonger's lips thinned, but he plucked the coin from his hand with rough fingers and pointed across the market. Peter followed the direction indicated, getting jostled all the way, and found himself at the hole-in-the-wall doorway of a tea shop. Fragrant air drifted out, calming and lifting his spirits a fraction. Hoping it was the right place, he ducked through a curtain into a dim, warm room, perfumed by tea, just big enough for a few low tables.

There wasn't anyone serving, but there were five customers. Four sat together at a single table—two older men arguing in a rapid Taishan dialect that Peter had no hope of following, one thin clerk clicking a wooden abacus, and one just sitting there, a stolid, heavy-set young man. Peter's bully detector, honed through years of public school, sounded off.

The fifth man sat by himself, engrossed in some kind of game with white tiles or counters. Where the others were straight-backed and formally attired, he slouched in a shabby robe, a baby-faced, middle-aged man, fat in the midsection and scrawny everywhere else. Peter took about a nanosecond deciding to approach him first.

"Excuse me...." Peter saw the man was playing with mahjong pieces, but he wasn't playing mahjong. He had set five or six suited tiles up on end, and he used the Red Dragon piece to knock each one down, doing kung fu sound effects like a little kid playing with action figures. Peter smiled. "Excuse me," he repeated. "I need Madame Wen?" It occurred to him that this might not be not her real name, but he soldiered on. "Do you know where—"

The big young guy from the other table leaned over and smacked the man on the back of his head. "Hey, Lucky Wen! This banana wants your wife!"

Two of the others chuckled, but the oldest man stopped arguing to say, "Be silent, nephew! You are rude to interrupt."

"Who, me?" The nephew put on an innocent expression. "I didn't come barging in here."

Peter recovered. "Your wife?" he said. "Um...sorry, I, I just—" But Lucky Wen looked up and Peter stammered to a halt as he met the man's astonishingly warm and sympathetic eyes. The smack had almost put his nose in his tea, but he looked at Peter as if nothing and no one else existed.

"*Lei ho*, Jun-fan," he said.

Nonplussed, Peter said, "Uh...hello who?"

The oldest man at the other table coughed. "Do you know this intrusive person, Mr. Wen?"

"Oh, yes!" The man called Wen stood up and put his hands on Peter's shoulders. "This is my number-one son!"

Peter opened his mouth but nothing came out. Jaws dropped at the other table. "Your son?" said the man who had been arguing with the oldest one. "You have a banana son?"

"I—I think you may—" Peter began.

The guy with the abacus spat on the floor. "A lot of nerve to come in here!"

"Oh, no, no," said Wen. "He has just done well for himself. That is not a bad thing."

Peter bit off the end of his sentence. Perhaps it was just the dialectal difference, but the word "banana" sounded more pejorative than he was used to, and it was clearly safer to be somebody's son. "Uh...thank you...Baba," he managed.

"Well, that's Lucky Wen all over," the second arguer complained. "He has his wife, he always wins at fan-tan, and now he's got a rich son!"

The big nephew snickered. "Yeah, but he's a loser. Totally hen-pecked."

The older man cleared his throat again. "Tell me, what is your number-one son doing here? Just come back to visit his father, after all these years of you not mentioning him?"

Wen drew himself up and linked his arm through Peter's. "He has come back," he said proudly, "to save me from the Great Earth Dragon!"

"The Great Earth Dragon?" echoed the second arguer. He and the nephew and the abacus wielder looked at each other, then looked away, grinning. "Did your wife tell you about the Dragon?" said the nephew, and snorted. The other two doubled over and pounded the floor, turning red, faces pressed into their sleeves.

"Please." Wen smiled. "I don't mind if you laugh."

"I mind." The older man, who still hadn't unbent, scowled at the other three.

They got control of themselves under his eye, straightening up. The nephew wound down last. "Lucky Wen takes all the fun out of it anyway," he grumbled.

"The Dragon is no joking matter!" The older man turned back

to Wen. "Chastise your wife!" he ordered. "And explain," he added, "why your son speaks Guangdong dialect."

"Oh! Well, he is really my paper son," said Wen, smiling broadly.

"Ah." The older man was satisfied, and being satisfied, dismissed Peter's existence from his mind. "Back to business, gentlemen. Mr. Cheong, our interest rate applies to gross profits..."

The others picked up the thread, the abacus clicked, and the discussion became rapid and, to Peter, unintelligible. With a flush he realized that they had been speaking slowly, using simple words, to talk to Lucky Wen.

"Come, Jun-fan," Wen said. He swept his mahjong tiles into a cloth bag and threw it over his shoulder. "Your mother is waiting."

Peter trailed him outside. The fish market was closing down, stalls being packed into astonishingly small packages, men streaming away, cats coming out of hiding. The mist had drifted away and vernal stars shone small and cold. Old St. Mary's was bonging out the hour. He counted the strokes while Wen led him out of the square onto California Street—and there was the cathedral. A streetlight shone full on the clock face, which agreed it was ten o'clock. Words were printed in gold underneath: Son, Observe The Time And Fly From Evil. Ecc.IV.23.

"What the hell is going on?" he said in English.

Wen's expression did not change. "Your mother is the one who understands foreign-devil talk."

Peter switched back. "Who are you?"

"I'm your father," Wen said with surprise, all innocence.

"You've mistaken me for somebody else," Peter told him. "Or this is a—" he could not find a word for "scam" in his vocabulary. "A lie," he finished.

"Actually, this is a plan to find you before you get into trouble. Something you seem very ready to do. They thought you were a police informer."

"How'd you know I'd be there?"

"Your mother told me," as though that should be obvious.

"Madame When?" Peter asked dryly.

"Well, that is what foreign devils call her. Her name is Wen Sze Chu-kheng."

"How did she know?"

"She foresaw, of course. She told me this afternoon, when you were a little baby boy. You don't remember me," Wen said sadly. "But you've grown up so tall and healthy!" He clapped Peter on the shoulder.

Fifteen minutes, Peter estimated. Fifteen more minutes he could stay on his feet. Ten, if he had to comprehend any more weird shit. Then he would just keel over on the pavement, wherever he happened to be. "What," he asked distantly, "is a paper son?"

"Oh, that's a person whom you say is your son on the papers the foreign devils make you write when you come to Gold Mountain, so that they will let him in. I had to say something to explain why you don't speak Taishan dialect." Wen smiled and rubbed his belly. "It is not as easy as you might expect, to make people believe you are simple. It helps if you really are a bit simple."

"What's the real reason I don't speak your dialect?"

"I don't know. She didn't mention it. But I suppose that the Timewalkers," Wen said the word in English, slowly as if uncertain of the pronunciation, "did not teach it to you?"

Peter closed his mouth so fast, he bit his tongue. "Okay," he said, in a smaller voice. "What is this all about?"

Wen gave him a sidelong glance, all compassion. "Your mother is much better at explaining things. And you've come a long way. We don't have much time, but you're tired and probably hungry. Come home with me and we'll sort it all out."

Peter had been waiting for somebody to say that.

發

There was another steep, narrow street with old Victorian houses built on split levels and leaning at precarious angles. A figure stood, arms folded, under the only streetlight on the block. Following Wen, Peter approached, feeling hazy and detached with fatigue, and the figure resolved into a small, shabby middle-aged woman with gray-threaded hair wound into a tight bun. His first impression was of a stone mask of a face, with eyes that weighed him up much faster than he did her. His second was that he had seen her before.

"Well," she said, "you finally got here. Come inside, Jun-fan."

Although he hadn't minded when Wen called him that, to her he said, "My name is Peter Chang."

She sniffed. "I know what I called you. You only just found out." She spoke quickly like the men in the teashop, but this time Peter could follow it. "How could you know which is your real name? Come." Without giving him time to think of an answer, she went around one of the decrepit houses. Wen gave an encouraging nod, so Peter tried to smooth down the hackles she had raised. He followed Wen and the strange woman—Madame Wen, or Chu-kheng—down an alley, through a door set below the main level of the house, and down a half-flight of stairs into a room dimly lit by a single gas jet.

It was a small cellar with a brick floor. It smelled of coal, gas, and damp, but mostly it smelled like steamed buns. There was a rough wooden table and a pair of old chairs with split-cane seats. A black iron kettle set on a coal-burning stove was just starting to sing. The stove and a low-burning kerosene lantern provided all the light. Chu-kheng swung the kettle over to the table where tea things were set out ready. Peter swallowed. His throat was so dry it felt like gulping a fishhook.

There was a ceramic oven, and cast-iron pots and pans, two-pronged forks, ladles, tongs, and things hung from hooks along one wall—a lot of cookware, considering the poverty of the rest of the room. A folding screen sectioned off one corner, a wooden chest rested on rough-sawn baulks of timber. A doorway showed a smaller, darker room and the edge of a bed made up on the floor. That was it. Except: on top of the chest was a basket half-full of white cloth.

Lucky Wen hung his bag on a hook, turned up the gaslight, and plumped down in one of the chairs. Seeing Peter ill at ease, he beckoned. "Come. Please. Come sit."

Peter's feet hurt, but elders were entitled to precedence. "There are only two chairs," he pointed out.

"You are the guest," Chu-kheng snapped, busy with tea preparation. "Sit down."

So he did. Every muscle quivered like a snapped guitar string.

Chu-kheng made tea with brusque, efficient motions—she warmed the teapot and cups, offered the leaves for her husband and Peter to examine, rinsed them, scooped off the debris, discarded the first brew, then finally allowed the leaves to steep. Her face looked as if all soft earth and detritus had been washed away years ago, leaving dry stone courses behind, and the prominence of a pink, peeling nose. He saw nothing of himself in it. Nonetheless, he'd had time to piece some facts together and reach an inevitable conclusion.

"Why'd you give me to Benedict Varian?"

She held up one finger and sniffed the steam from the teapot. Peter twitched. This hardly seemed the time for the full gongfu ceremony. But with a slight nod, she poured out the tea—first Wen's, then Peter's, then her own. Wen tapped the table for thanks, lifted his cup with an appreciative murmur, and looked expectantly at him. Even without picking his up, Peter could detect an aroma that made his head spin and his parched tissues scream. He raised the cup, inhaled the steam, and sipped. An exquisite liquid heat with subtle hints of peach and orchid rolled down his throat. He shuddered all over—not the least because caffeine was about to enter his bloodstream—and drank deep. Wen and Chu-kheng drank their tea in the proper three tastes—one to sample, the main drink, and an aftertaste. Wen smacked his lips.

Chu-kheng put her cup down. "So. You figured that much out."

"I'm not an idiot."

She stared for a moment. "No," she agreed at length. "You are not that."

"Tell me why."

"Very well." She leaned against both hands on the table. "You were born in this house in the Year of the Wood Snake. Our first son. Our only child." Her face didn't change, but Wen lit up the room and thoroughly discomposed Peter with a smile of pure happiness. "That same night," she went on, "I dreamed that the Great Earth Dragon awoke. I saw the city fall and burn. I saw this ceiling collapse and kill everyone under it."

"I see." What he saw was her standing next to her husband under great smoke-blackened timbers supporting a ground-level floor of unfinished planks, looking even heavier in the shadows than it probably was. Whatever she'd seen, it hadn't driven them away. "Then you know the big one is coming in six or seven hours, right? So that didn't work out very well, did it?"

"You've come back," she agreed. "But you are a man now. You had your safe, comfortable childhood. What drives you now is none of my doing."

"...Yeah. Okay." Heat prickled Peter's face. He covered it by finishing the dregs of his tea. "You know what drives me?"

"Of course." Chu-kheng put the kettle on the stove to begin a second brewing. "Ask what you came here to ask."

"How can I rescue Nikki?"

"I don't know." The kettle, its water still hot, whistled almost at once. She brought it back and warmed the pot and cups again. "I know who she is only because I foresaw this conversation. If I ask, you will tell me—she is a Timewalker, Father Varian's daughter, with whom you are infatuated obviously, though you won't say so. And that she has been taken by Hunters back to the time you came from. I don't know how you can find her or save her. It's too far away. It isn't in my future."

"I didn't realize that was a limitation."

"You don't yet understand what madness you would suffer if it weren't."

He could imagine, now that she mentioned it. "Can you tell me how to find Mr. Varian?"

"He's gone." She poured the first brew. "He got what he wanted here, some of the riches that support his hidden kingdom, and he moved on, taking you—the baby you—with him. It was our bargain. He will not be back, not in my lifetime anyway."

Peter wiped chilled sweat from his brow with the back of his hand and stared at the table. A crack in the wood harbored ancient caked-in flour, though the surface was scrubbed raw. It began to blur. He felt like an overstretched and frayed piece of bungee cord. "Is there anything you can tell me that would help?"

"Yes." She strained floating leaves out of the tea. "I can tell you how to escape this time and place and go back to your home."

"If you want to," Wen said wistfully.

Peter definitely wanted to, if that were the only thing going. "How?"

"Through the secret door in Father Varian's office."

"Um..." He didn't ask how she knew about it. "I've never been able to open it. Anyway, that'll only take me to Santuario, not..." Then he remembered what Nikki had said. *Time passes differently in Santuario. If we go through that door, it'll be later than when we left.* And if it's later there.... "But if I go back out the same door," he finished the thought out loud, "it'll be..." he could not remember *twenty-first century* in Cantonese, "...my time?"

"Exactly."

"That'd be good," Peter admitted. Nikki had to be there somewhere. He'd be able to look for Mr. Sanders, search the city, call the police.

Chu-kheng checked the tea and lifted the pot. He reached for it in the same instant. "Let me do that." He poured for them both, as a young person was supposed to do for his elders. "What?" he said, flushing as Wen beamed at him and even Chu-kheng's face softened half a point on the Rockwell scale. "You say you're my birth parents? Okay. It's weird, but it fits the facts I have."

"Welcome home, son." Wen turned away and snuffled.

"Oh, Chri—oh, don't do that, Baba." Peter squirmed. He longed for the way his dad, Corey Chang, occasionally popped into his life, said, "How's it hanging?" and disappeared before Peter finished saying, "Fine." He couldn't possibly live up to what this man thought of him.

"All right." Wen mopped his eyes on his sleeve and turned back around with an effort at composure. "All right. I suppose you have to go back?"

"She's in trouble."

"You're better off without her," Chu-kheng said. "That whole family is trouble."

"Um...that didn't stop you from giving me to them."

"It was the best of a bad set of choices."

"So is this. And, no offense, but I just met you. I have a life back there. Parents and...well, parents."

"Of course." She turned back to the stove to start another brew. "Well then, you must. And you can. I have seen."

"You said you couldn't see that far?"

"True. But I have glimpsed a potential future in which we meet again." She pinched his ear. "That isn't likely to happen if you don't save this Timewalker girl."

"Um—okay, I guess not." He fidgeted with his cup. "She must be in my timeline because the kidnappers live there. But it's a big city. It's a big planet."

Wen patted his shoulder. "You worry too much about the future."

"He is a Seer," Chu-kheng said.

"I'm really not."

"Well, you will be. Drink your tea."

Peter drank his tea. It seemed to rinse him out. He felt light-headed, but sharper, with some of the accumulated poisons of stress and fatigue washed away. "They've drugged her with something that keeps her from timewalking," he said. He felt in his coat pocket and took out the brass dart Nikki had handed him. "It might wear off, but…"

She paused while bringing back the kettle and picked up the dart, avoiding the point of the needle carefully. "A Hunter made this." She began the sentence as if asking a question, but turned it into a statement before finishing.

"Is there an antidote?" He didn't know how she would know if there was, but he was ready to grasp at straws.

She was silent for a moment. "I don't know," she said at last, "but perhaps we will be able to find out. Now," she said, cutting off his next question, "you take a bath. And eat. There isn't much time."

Peter shut his mouth. She had him at "bath." And he reminded himself again that whatever was happening to Nikki wasn't happening now.

發

The light of a winter sunset suffused a set of small rooms. White plaster walls were covered floor to ceiling in oil paintings, mostly of confusing architecture. She knew she'd painted them. Hardwood floors, careful arrangements of eclectic furniture and bookcases to make the most of the space. As unfamiliar as if she'd never seen any of it in her life.

Through picture windows, an unknown city, faux-Victorian mixed with postmodern architecture, spread down the steep hill to the bay, under a herringbone pattern of high, thin clouds. A soaring red bridge on the horizon crossed to a distant arm of land, half-concealed in lower, darker clouds pierced by the lowering sun. The bridge must be The Bridge, and that tapering skyscraper shaped like a pyramid must be The Pyramid, so this had to be San Francisco post-1975, but other than that they could be in any juncture.

If it wasn't her timeline, at the right time, Eleonora and the not-yet-born baby weren't here (although her mother might well be). X and Y couldn't hurt them.

"It is," said X, "they are, and we can."

"You're sure?" asked Y.

"Of course I'm sure! Same time, same place, same assholes!"

"Then call in."

"You do it," he said, rubbing his head. "I've got enough to deal with."

The city through the window looked, not just strange, but surreal. All the buildings listed to one side as if sinking into the pavement. The slope looked steep enough to tumble everything into the bay. All of the surfaces—walls, roofs, pavement—looked brittle, like marzipan in the cold orange light. All the cracks and shadows seemed deeper and blacker than they should be, and the bridge like it ought to collapse under its own weight.

Had it all been so fragile before? She couldn't remember ever thinking so. Maybe X was lying. Maybe it wasn't her timeline.

"I'm not," he warned, "and it is."

"I'm gonna check," she said and fugued.

Gunshot. Breaking glass. But she was on the street corner outside. The wind was surprisingly cold. A dog started barking, a spatter of glass fragments hit the pavement, somebody shouted. She fugued to the opposite far corner of the block, well out of Ms. Y's line of fire. There was more shouting, but farther away. A little old man begging with a cardboard sign saw her show up. How ephemeral he looked, face so thin, veins so blue, Band-Aids over his cheekbones, unraveling fingerless gloves, his face coming undone with surprise.

She read the street signs on the corner because she didn't recognize anything. It was uphill. On Powell Street. Three blocks. She could remember that because it was abstract information, not the concrete visual memories she had always relied on. Three blocks uphill and against the wind as fast as she could, and she knew her mother's workplace by the clinic name on the side of the building in brushed steel letters. It had a glass corner front with a steep overhang, like an iceberg about to break loose. She climbed the outside steps to the front door.

If Lady Varian wasn't here, she could grab her mother and keep on running, fugue horizon to horizon until she was out of X's range. They could go halfway around the world like that. She could find safety, find Peter, find another way to vengeance.... She cut through the sick and anxious people in the waiting room to the front desk. The receptionist there was tiny, had ears sticking out thin as bone china teacups, an incongruous person to hold the hammer over her head. Nikki remembered a name, but could not recognize her.

"I need to see Eleonora Varian?"

The receptionist looked confused—because she didn't know the name?—then brought the hammer down. "Sure, go right back, they haven't moved her." Because she'd seen Nikki twenty minutes earlier and wondered why she was asking permission. "Are you okay, hon?" she added, perhaps noticing Nikki's fingers trembling, or seeing in her face that she was trapped in her own body and it seemed to be trying to suffocate her. "Do you want me to call your mother?"

"No! I mean…I'll just go on back, I'll probably run into her…." No, she wouldn't, or at least she didn't intend to. Her mother was made of thin blue steel; Nikki could tell her *I am surrendering to the people who killed Dad and Alex* without fear it would break her, or that she would reproach Nikki, disown her, call it a Timewalker thing, or in any way shirk the emotional burden. But for exactly that reason, Nikki couldn't tell her, for there was nothing that ephemeral Dr. Veronica Murray could do to protect herself or Eleonora from a Telepath and whatever Ms. Y was. And Mom was, well, something Nikki always counted on but seldom appreciated because she was always there, like oxygen, and it was impossible, unthinkable not to protect her; it would be like choosing not to breathe. She followed the sound of a woman breathing hard and crying in pain, relieved not to meet anyone on the way.

On first meeting Eleonora, she'd thought her beautiful. Rossetti's work had come to mind, and a painting of the Empress card from a Tarot deck she'd seen once in a Haight Street gallery. The woman whose belly anchored her to the bed seemed nothing like that now, although she couldn't picture either work to compare her with. They had finally put her in a hospital gown, which she must find appalling, and one nurse was readying instruments while another gripped her hands and chanted instructions.

They all seemed preoccupied. Nikki slipped in silently, using the privacy curtain to reach the small bureau unseen. She eased the drawer open and found the few items Eleonora must have been carrying: her reticule, her rosary. She put her wallet and the keys to her apartment in with them and left before the contraction ended. She went back through the waiting room, outside and down the steps.

The sidewalk under her shoes felt cold and fragile, like a crust of snow over deep powder. The freezing wind was pushing her back down the hill; she let it have its way. Dead leaves lost their grip on their twigs and sailed off into the void. The gray man and the golden woman climbed toward her, clouds blood-red and swirling on the horizon behind them.

"How can I be sure you'll leave them alone?" she said when they met.

"You can't." X came up close on one side. "But we probably will."

"We have more urgent things to do," said Y, crowding her on the other side.

"You should've kept running. Should've said, 'Fuck that bitch. Fuck that dweeb.' Cut your losses." X grabbed the edge of her coat, pulled it taut, slipped two fingers into one of her pockets, as familiar as if it was his own coat, and came out with the old Kodak photo of the Palazzo, which he stuck in his own breast pocket. "Family responsibility? Way overrated."

They walked back down three blocks and put her in a sleek black car parked in front of the apartment building. X got in back with her while Y pulled away from the curb like a shot out of a cannon.

"Of course, if you had, I'd have shot you when next we caught up." X massaged his temples with his free hand. The skin over his forehead and cheekbones looked slack, rubbery and bruised; his eyes lay in deep black holes.

"You can't hit the broad side of a barn," Y said.

"*She'd* have shot you," he amended. "You try hitting a target when you're looking at it from three different angles and forget which one is yours," he told his partner. "Family!" he said to Nikki. He seemed in a garrulous mood, like he was running a fever. "They go on and on about responsibility to your gift. Some gift! Hearing everybody's thoughts, do you know what that's like? It's a sour, greasy purple hangover with broken glass in your eyeballs. It's a thousand separate staticky broadcasts of random noise and imagery blasting you day after day and you can't shut down the receiver. It's swimming in everybody's shit, it's a shitstorm, a typhoon in a sewer driving through this city so fast—Slow down!" he barked as Y launched the Jag off the crest of a hill, landed, and shot down the slope in a squeal of tires, leaving a significant percentage of rubber behind. They were driving toward the tall buildings and the water.

X clung to a panic handle, his face as gray and insubstantial as dishwater. "You know what it's like when I kill somebody? It all just... stops. Everything, all the broadcasts shut down. I don't know why, it's like the moment of death overwhelms everything else. Just for that one moment, it's peaceful. It makes me weep—God, will you please slow down?" as Y blew a red light, dodged an oncoming cable car, and kissed a delivery van, underlining its logo with sparks and black paint. "Shit!" He folded over his lap, arms wrapped around his head.

"I'm crazy about her, though," he told Nikki after he'd recovered a little. "I couldn't live without her. She's...her brain is quiet. Like a still pool. Some kind of Zen thing, she does meditation and shit. Never worked for me, it's the power of positive thinking versus fucking Godzilla. But her, she stalks through the whole world like it's a jungle, she's absolutely quiet. Her mind has nothing in it but death. The first thing she notices about a person is the fastest way to kill him. I love the way she looks too," he added. "Half the people we meet imagine her with no clothes on, it's fantastic...."

"You talk too much," Y said.

"Well, she thinks too much. I'm just trying to calm her down. I can't deal with how fucking freaked out she is!"

Ms. Y stopped at the next red light, twisted in her seat, and aimed an odd-looking gun. Nikki only had time to gasp and shrink.

She took the dart out of her arm with numb fingers. The ampoule had a trace of clear amber liquid in it. It fell slowly out of her hand, bounced off the back seat, and rolled under the front.

"Problem solved," said Y in a slowed-down distorted way, and everything quietly went away.

CHAPTER EIGHT

The bath was a tin washtub just big enough to sit in, filled at a communal pump and heated with water from the kettle. Drying off with a blanket, Peter found a paper package on the bed, along with his suit, which had been thoroughly brushed. He opened it and found a clean dress shirt with lightly starched collar and cuffs.

Five hours to go, and they had taken the trouble to get him a new shirt.

Peter had a quarter-century of luxury and entitlement behind him, so he managed not to cry. He did up the buttons, put on the suit, left off the tie, rubbed his glasses with a clean part of his old shirt, and went back into the other room. Chu-kheng was stirring a pot on the stove. His stomach growled. She glanced up and back down. He sat at the table. "Thanks," he said conscientiously, inadequately.

She made a grimace that seemed to be the closest she could get to a smile.

"Where's Lucky Wen?"

"Gone to see someone who can make your antidote."

"There's someone around who can do that?" He perched on the edge of the chair, unable to quite relax. "That seems really unlikely. Who?"

"A Hunter."

Peter started. "You know one? Are you sure it's safe for him to go?"

"Nothing is safe. But it's survivable. He will return."

He supposed that she would know. He wondered how she had found a Hunter and known him for what he was. It must have happened much the same way it did to Peter—she happened to meet one and had a vision that warned her away.

Speaking of warning visions.... "How are you going to escape the earthquake? Are you leaving town or what?"

"Your father and I will stay in Father Varian's former place of business for a few days. It's already deserted. No one will disturb us there. It will be safe."

"Tom Slinky is going to let you in?" he guessed.

"That was the price of my advice to him."

"Even though Mr. Varian gave him the same advice. And so did I."

"He is fortunate in his acquaintances." She ladled up a bowl of soup and gave it to him with a plate of steamed buns. As she leaned close, he caught a whiff that made him wonder if the food was okay—a yeasty, almost-spoiled scent. But he was so hungry it stabbed him from the pit of his stomach. He shoveled a chopstick-load of hot noodles into his mouth, added a bite of bun with sweet bean-paste filling, and was reassured. Chu-kheng sat opposite and he noticed the front of her tangzhuang was stained or damp, as if she had spilled some soup. Her eyes flickered over him like checkout-scanner lasers.

"What?" he said with his mouth full.

"You're quite tall. They cared for you, fed you well in that future time. Father Varian kept his word."

He chewed and swallowed. "You didn't have to send me away, did you?"

"I never have to do anything," Chu-kheng observed.

"But it wasn't because of the earthquake. You could've just left the city. What was the real reason? Don't worry," he added, though she looked as though this was the last thing she might worry about. "I can handle it."

"We wanted you to have a better life. I saw the opportunity."

He understood. He approved. He was glad he'd grown up with unlimited hot water, automated laundry, abundant food, a large well-lit home, affectionate parents, a tolerant pluralistic society, and a million ways to entertain himself with an electronic box. He was ecstatic. At gunpoint, he wouldn't trade places with his infant self.

"Also, you were very ill," she said. "A weakness of the lungs. We did not have the medicine to cure you."

"Oh. Okay." His mother Destiny had constantly embarrassed him with stories of the month he'd spent in a hospital oxygen tent; it was what she had in place of difficult birth stories.

"So what's wrong?" Chu-kheng asked.

"Well...you...you aren't what I imagined," Peter said. "You know. As a kid." He had pictured a soft, shy, pretty birth mom. As he got older, he added uneducated, addicted, abused, poverty-stricken, or simply too young. Someone who had loved him, but had no chance and no choice. Not this tough old woman. All his life, he had been grieving a person who'd never existed.

"Well," said Chu-kheng, "if it's any consolation, you aren't what I lost."

Peter remembered the tea-shop bully calling him banana and bristled. "What, not Chinese?"

"Not a child."

"Fair enough," he said after a pause.

She rose and retreated to the cookstove. Peter heard footsteps and dust fell from cracks in the ceiling. Lucky Wen came in, breathless, damp, and vibrant. "Whew!" he exclaimed, and dropped into the chair that Chu-kheng had vacated, making it creak. "Hello again, son. What a friendly and agreeable person that honorable doctor is." He scratched the back of his neck under the queue.

"Well done, husband," said Chu-kheng, clinking dishes together.

"Did you get the antidote?" Peter asked.

"What? Oh, no." Wen took the last steamed bun from his plate. "I just gave the dart to the honorable doctor. He said he'd have to examine the substance first."

"We'll visit him on our way," Chu-kheng said. She opened the wooden chest and took out an armful of clothing. "Come, husband. It's time to get ready to leave."

發

"Question," Peter said half an hour later when they emerged from the cellar into the alley. The dark houses on either side were pitched on a slant, already sagging as if they knew they would soon fall and burn. "Why'd you wash the dishes and sweep the floor before we left?"

"Ah, mysteries," said Wen.

"The way that can be explained is not the eternal Way." Chu-kheng hoisted a rucksack full of food and water bottles onto her shoulders and grunted under the weight.

"Let me carry that," Peter offered. Wen also had his bag, but Peter had seen him pack only money, papers, quilts, and mahjong tiles.

"You had better keep your hands free and your wits about you."

Besides their bags, both of them appeared to be wearing all of the clothes they owned, which in Wen's case was enough to make him waddle. He went first. At a poke from Chu-kheng, Peter hurried after him, and she followed several paces behind them. Wen strolled down the alley like a particularly complacent lord of creation, but as soon as they reached the street, he glanced back. She gave a tiny nod and he strolled on.

The fog was creeping back, the stars swirling in and out of obscurity. Old Saint Mary's sounded a quarter after one. Everyone still on the street looked a bit more wasted, a little more desperate, a trifle more likely to fall down in a puddle and spend the night there. A white man stumbled up the stairs from a basement to the street and tottered away, reeking of sickly-sweet fumes. Someone tugged on Peter's coat with a whiny mumble—a dark shape squatting against the wall, right under the overhang. This was so familiar and yet so far from home. He put a quarter in the outstretched palm. At the next intersection, he questioned Chu-kheng out of the corner of his mouth. "Did you warn anybody else?"

Between arc light and black shadow, her face looked more than ever like a stone mask. "I told everyone who would listen to an old Chinese woman."

"...Shit." He had an impulse to go back and drag the beggar away from the wall, but his intention would probably be misconstrued.

Within another block, they left Chinatown behind and walked among newer houses and storefronts. Peter had been disoriented, but now he recognized the street's downward slope, the harbor lights and the smell of the waterfront. This wasn't "on the way" to the Palazzo Building. "Four hours to go," he said. "What if this guy doesn't have the antidote ready?"

"He will." She had caught up with them. They walked closer together in the places where they were not welcome.

"All will be well," said Wen. "Trust in heaven. Anyway, here it is." He pointed out a house standing in no-man's-land, not part of their rickety slum, but not one of the grand mansions of old Nob Hill either. A tall, narrow façade, like the older apartment buildings Peter was familiar with, though evidently a single residence, it gathered the street around itself for camouflage. Light gleamed yellow between the drapes of the tall, narrow windows on the ground floor.

"They expect us to use the back entrance," said Wen.

"Not this time," Chu-kheng said. "Listen to me, Jun-fan. Don't show surprise or fear when you meet this man. Hunters are good at reading people, but you needn't make it easy. When he asks you questions, answer truthfully. But don't offer information."

"I hope you know what you're doing."

"There's nothing to fear," said Wen. "He is a friendly and agreeable gentleman."

"Really?"

"You will see," said Chu-kheng.

Unsettled, Peter followed them through a gate in the iron railing surrounding the house, and up the steps from the sidewalk to the front door. Wen reached for the gleaming brass knocker.

A white girl in a black dress with an apron opened the door. She was gorgeous in a stock California way, with hair like corn silk, but her expression was cold and vacant. "Yes?"

"Um—hello—"

"We have returned to see the honorable doctor?" said Wen, apparently under the impression that anyone could understand Cantonese if he spoke it slowly and loudly enough.

"You were told to show us in," said Chu-kheng in English.

"Come in," said the girl. Peter had been told to fill out forms at the DMV with more warmth and personal interest. She led them into an entrance hall. It glowed in the lamplight with varnished wood and polished brass. On either side were rooms probably referred to as the parlor and the drawing room. The furniture looked even more antique than, to Peter, it really was, and static. Frozen in amber. Almost a glaze in the air.

"A guy lives here?" he asked. It was the kind of place where you wouldn't dare use the good towels.

The girl gave him an empty smile. In his own time, he might have mistaken her for a strippergram in that tight, frilly housemaid's dress, even though it covered her from throat to ankles. "This way."

She proceeded down the hall. Lucky Wen trailed after her, rubbernecking shamelessly. Chu-kheng followed, stiff under her load, and Peter brought up the rear. They passed several doors and climbed a half-flight of stairs. At the back of the house, the girl tapped on a final door. Peter was trying to identify the predominant smell in the house—furniture polish? formaldehyde?—when someone said, "Come in." His blood turned to ice.

Chu-kheng gripped his arm. "Remember." She went in after Wen and the girl.

And there, like an incongruous figure in a bad dream, was his mystery client, Mr. Sanders, leaning against a table.

"Lei ho!" Wen exclaimed. "Wonderful to see you again, Doctor. May I?"

"Baba!" Peter lunged into the room—too late. Wen snagged Mr. Sanders' hand and pumped it with both of his.

"Good of you to see me again at this hour. This," and Wen gestured extravagantly, "is my number-one son! You already know my wife, of course. Please excuse me. My wife will have to talk for me. I don't know your foreign tongue, and you don't understand a word I'm saying, do you? Too bad. But no matter, I trust my wife. She'll tell me all about it afterwards. Please, go ahead, don't mind me."

Mr. Sanders managed to get his hand back by the end of this speech. He pushed the corners of his mouth upward with as much effort as if he were bending a crowbar. "Ah. Yes. Good morning, my dear..." he patted Wen's shoulder "...fellow." He turned to Chu-kheng, eyes flickering over Peter without a sign of recognition along the way.

The same cold dead eyes, bloodless skin, shell-like face. He didn't even look any younger. He wore a satin dressing gown over a formal shirt, old-fashioned tie, and well-creased trousers. Against the wall behind him, framing his head and shoulders, was a cabinet full of...of brains, and other organs, and whole fetal specimens in jars. The room kept up the preserved-in-amber motif of the rest of the house, but scratches in the lacquer and smudges on the glass suggested actual use.

A cabinet of bottles and vials stood in a corner, anatomical charts hung on the walls, and a brass caduceus and ornamental mortar and pestle rested on the desk. The air was close and smelled of formaldehyde.

It was like finding Darth Vader at dinner. Without having a blaster pistol handy. Peter switched his stare to Chu-kheng, a marked contrast in her shabby layers, and suffered a moment of paranoia.

"Madame When," Sanders said.

"Doctor Sutorius," Chu-kheng responded. She gave Peter—on the verge of bolting—a glare that nailed his feet to the floor.

"I received your message. Inconvenient hour to choose."

"It could not be any sooner or any later than this," she answered.

"I'll take your word for that. It is the least of the surprises you have sprung on me tonight." Sanders spoke urbanely, with more... Peter had to pick a nearly obsolete word out of his vocabulary...class than he remembered. But he looked agitated—leaner, hungrier, more stressed. "You're dressed for traveling," he observed. "Leaving the city, are you? Or the entire juncture?"

"Neither." She was as unaffected as a little gray rock. "Nothing that you fear is true."

He licked his bloodless lips. "I've met your messenger of course..." indicating Wen, who strolled around the room, examining jars and humming to himself.

"My husband."

"Ah. Apologies." Sanders gave Wen another painful bend of his mouth and Wen returned a smile. "I've met your husband. But who is this impulsive and well-dressed young man?"

"My son. Jun-fan—Doctor Sutorius."

"Er." Appalled to hear the word doctor, Peter managed, "Hello."

"He is afraid of me," Sanders—or Sutorius—observed, after a pause during which Peter failed to shake his proffered hand.

"He's confused."

"He's terrified."

"He'll get over it," Chu-kheng said, lancing Peter with another glare. "You know why we have come."

"And you know what I am going to say."

"Of course. But say it to my son."

Sanders-Sutorius eyed Peter as if he would like nothing better than to feed bits of him to a starving vulture. Then he rose from the desk and paced. Peter took the opportunity to swallow his heart back down into his chest and resume breathing the stale air. Sutorius came to one end of a track worn in his carpet, turned, and showed them the ampoule that Nikki had given Peter and Peter had given Chu-kheng. He shook it so that a few green drops ran down inside the glass. "I made this. I know my own work, even if I never saw it before."

Peter opened his mouth. He closed his mouth.

"And I've definitely never seen it before," Sutorius continued. "That being the case, there must be another...me. And that means there is at least one Timewalker involved." He dropped the ampoule on the desk and his voice dropped into a cold register that distracted Wen from a bottled fetal kitten. "What are you plotting, Madame When? And with whom?"

"Calmly," Chu-kheng advised.

"Calmly?" Sutorius cried. Peter jumped and Lucky Wen banged into a low-hanging Tiffany lamp and set it swinging. The doctor smacked his fist on the desk, seriously agitated. "I just lost three of my men! Calmly?"

"There is no plot," Chu-kheng said, as Wen grabbed the lampshade to stop it. "You are in no danger from Timewalkers now. Benedict Varian is no longer in the city. He left early this evening and will not return in my lifetime at least."

"He eluded our ambush," the doctor said. "Was that your doing?"

"Yes. I warned him."

"Then I see no reason I should trust you, Madame."

"You will, though. Benedict Varian's survival was necessary. I work entirely for my own and my family's interest, but on this occasion, that interest coincides with yours, just as on that occasion it coincided with his. There is a Timewalker in the case. But not one you've met. She isn't born yet."

"That means nothing!" All the refinement slipped from Sutorius' voice; it was raw terror and fury. "Before I make any bargains with you, you will tell me. What is the bitch's name?"

"Mom," Peter said.

She waved him off. "You don't need the name," she told Sutorius. "You don't know her. She doesn't know you. We keep it that way while we do this business."

Sutorius came face to face with her. They glared at each other like a pair of idols, one tall, lean, and brittle-looking, the other squat, blunt, and stolid. "I could force you to tell me," he said.

"No, you couldn't," replied Chu-kheng.

He apparently noticed for the first time that his housemaid was still in the room. "Ilse! That will be all. Go back to bed. Forget what you've heard here." The girl, unmoving until now, turned without a word. She still wore the same smile—Peter saw well-developed muscle in her face and complete vacancy in her eyes. She went out and closed the door behind her.

"That was careless," Chu-kheng observed.

"No matter," Sutorius said. He stalked Peter, who froze in place. "Your son is not a Seer?"

"Not quite."

"Interesting." Dr. Sutorius' pupils and irises were nearly indistinguishable from each other. Though he stared, Peter got the impression he wasn't really looking, not with his eyes anyway. He inhaled. "You are still afraid of me."

"...Well, yes," Peter admitted. He could feel sweat beading on his forehead.

"Your suit has been dipped in chlorinated solvent," the doctor observed. "And you've eaten a lot more corn and beef than rice and fish in your lifetime. Let me see those." He indicated Peter's glasses.

He didn't feel any emotion that seemed too extreme for the situation. If San—if Sutorius was influencing him with pheromones, it wasn't obvious. But then, it probably wouldn't be. He slipped his glasses off and handed them over.

Dr. Sutorius tapped the polyurethane lenses and examined the plastic-coated earpieces. "Very interesting." He gave them back. "You're not from here-and-now. You came with the mysterious Miss Varian." There seemed little point in denying it. "You could tell me her name," Sutorius added.

"If you try to force it from him, we won't be making a deal," Chukheng said.

"You certainly are confident that you have something I want." Sutorius turned back to Peter. "What's your involvement? Why do you want the counteragent to this substance?"

"She's been drugged and kidnapped and I want to help her," Peter said.

"By whom? By me?"

"Um..."

Sutorius laughed and shook his head. "So you come to me for help? Like little lambs to the slaughter?" He went back to leaning on his desk, leaving Peter to breathe relief. "We have reached arrangements of mutual benefit in the past, Madame, but you wouldn't count on me to help one of that breed against myself. Even a different self from another timeline. You couldn't—well, if you were anyone else, you couldn't—even be sure I'd let you leave here alive, especially after that confession. What's up your sleeve?"

"A fair trade," she said.

"That being?"

"I know how and when you are going to die."

Peter stared. Wen, examining another brain in a jar, said, "Ha!" in delighted tones and went on humming.

"When?" said Sutorius.

"What time is it?" Chu-kheng responded.

"Today?"

"Before dawn."

"How?"

"That, I tell you for the antidote. And you let us leave with no trouble." Chu-kheng said. "And stop bamboozling my husband," she added with exasperation.

"It's instinctive," said Dr. Sutorius. "I have to make an effort not to do it."

"Then make one. Do we have a bargain?"

"Yes, of course. But why don't you tell me first? As a gesture of good faith."

Everything was going to be all right, Peter realized. Dr. Sutorius' proposal was quite reasonable—he was a decent and friendly guy—and Peter felt sure that Chu-kheng would agree. But she flared her nostrils in a deep, defiant whiff and said, "You can't stop testing my patience, can you?"

His voice fell flat. "I can try other methods—"

"They won't work." Her face was at its stoniest. "This is the offer. You trade a drug which may...or may not...save a Timewalker's life for information that will certainly save yours. Or you say no. That's all." He bared his teeth and she added, "You know I have never deceived you."

He closed his eyes for a few seconds, then went behind his desk and sat down in the chair, pressed his fingertips together, and produced another bend in his expression. "Very well." He opened a desk drawer and took out a tiny vial of dark amber liquid. "Here it is."

"You made it already?" said Peter.

"I needed it myself." He indicated the glass ampoule on the desk. "That was a disturbing experience, thank you very much. The effect would be worse for a Timewalker."

"How does it work?"

"It produces selective amnesia. You can remember events, smells and sounds, spoken words, and so on. But you can't remember what anything looks like beyond generalities. Classes of objects are not a problem. That chair is a chair. Specific objects—that chair is one of a set my grandmother had in the dining room—no."

That accorded with what Nikki had said. Peter's heart thudded. "She needs to remember in order to timewalk."

"Hence a useful substance for anyone trying to hold one captive without keeping him unconscious," said the doctor.

"Give it to him," said Chu-kheng. "Time is short."

"Inject or ingest," Dr. Sutorius advised. He tossed the vial underhand and Peter caught it.

Lucky Wen rubbed his hands and bustled forward. "I'm so glad we could do business, Doctor..."

Sutorius ignored him. "Now tell me."

"How do we know this is what he says?" Peter asked. The vial was smaller than a free cologne sample. Obviously he wouldn't get a second chance with it.

Chu-kheng looked blank and distracted for a moment, then said, "It is." She patted Wen's forearm. "A moment more, husband."

"She knows," said Sutorius. "Tell me."

She did. Graphically. He listened with growing agitation, consulted a gold watch from his dressing gown pocket. "That doesn't leave me much time." He looked around the dispensary at all of his cabinets and specimens. "You could have told me before."

"You had nothing I wanted until now."

"I could have sold my property. Transferred my interests. Built up a practice in Oakland." He began pulling papers out of drawers and piling them on top. "I'm going to be ruined!"

"You'll survive to make another fortune," Chu-kheng said. "That concludes our business. Kindly recall the other part of our bargain."

"I have more important matters to concern me, thank you." Sutorius hefted bundles of stock certificates and banknotes out of a floor safe. "Show yourselves out."

"Um." Peter hesitated. He leaned forward over the desk. His coatsleeve brushed over the ampoule that had contained the visual amnesia drug. "Can I ask you something?" The doctor glared, which he took as permission. "You, uh, Hunters—" he'd almost said brainsuckers—"you seem to mostly get along okay with Seers...."

"Enlightened self-interest. You Seers are difficult to control—" with a pointed look at Chu-kheng, "and harder to kill. You tend to see it coming. Forbearance and trade are our best options." He shoved papers and loose twenty-dollar gold coins into a valise.

"Why do you hate Timewalkers so much? Is there an actual reason or is it just one of those feuds that's gone on so long that nobody remembers why?"

Sutorius looked at him as if wondering whether anybody could really be that ignorant. "I remember why." Flat expression, flat voice. "We asked a simple favor. It would have cost them nothing. We would have gone our own way and never troubled them again."

"What did you ask? What happened?"

"Ask Benedict Varian, if you are ever his son-in-law. But don't assume his moral superiority." He spat. "Have you spoken to any Telepaths?"

"Telepaths?"

"They prefer our company to that of the Timewalkers," the doctor said. "What does that tell you?"

"…That I still have no idea what's going on," said Peter, although he vaguely remembered Nikki mentioning… "What telepaths?"

But the doctor refused to say more and Chu-kheng said, "Come, Jun-fan."

發

She walked in darkness. A warm numbness wrapped her, or if not warm, at least an absence of chill.

She was not cold, frightened, grieving, hungry, thirsty, tired, or anything in particular. Scary, painful things were far away and unimportant like everything else.

The ground was pale and gritty. There was dark scrub-brush, barely distinguishable by the light of remote stars. A highway—or something like a highway—was streaming headlights somewhere to her left, a few hundred yards or several miles away. She didn't look directly at it—the lights were too harsh—but kept it in her peripheral vision as she walked. It was a direction, something to follow so that she didn't have to think about which way to go. There might be a destination, but it was far away, so far that she didn't have to think about that either.

She walked. For a long time, or for no time at all. The number and intensity of the lights and the pattern of brush to bare ground were the only things that changed, and those not very much.

There was nothing to remember or worry over or be afraid of or feel bad about. Nothing to feel or to think or care about. Everything was okay because there wasn't anything. She was apart, unseen, off to the side. Walking in the dark without effort, purpose, or care….

An eye-watering stench roused her. She opened her eyes. A man with a cold, smooth face, harsh light above making a black corona of his hair, leaned over her. "Peter Chang," the man said. She wanted to slip back into the darkness because the smell was irritating and the light was too bright. "Is there any way he could reach this juncture from where you left him?"

Pain grew in her chest because she was too close to sleep to release whatever swelled it in words or tears. *No, Peter's lost.*

Had she said that out loud?

"And your brother. Erik," he said. She must have. "Would he break the taboo on duplicating another Timewalker's personal timeline to rescue you?"

Not sure she understood the question, but—*bet he would, the bastard.*

"Thank you," he said. "That's all I needed to know." The smell and the light went away. She fell back into darkness and went on with the endless, pointless, comforting journey.

Sometime or no time later, the smell came back. It pierced her, dragged her up from the darkness like a hooked fish. She identified it—ammonia salts. The same man stood over her, radiating the stench. "Get up," he said.

She sat up, put her bare feet on the cold floor, and stood.

"Wake her all the way," said a creaky voice. She kept her eyes down on the white tile and didn't see who spoke.

"Why get attached?" said the man.

"I want to know what she is, not what you make of her." The voice was creaky, like dried-out leather. Accented with guttural French, or some patois.

"Very well."

Nothing seemed to change. But she felt…confused. She squinted directly at the man despite the harsh light. Hard mouth, cold eyes, an expression blending irony and sadism—he was not a highway. He was a prison wall. A set of bars. A truncheon, a thumbscrew, a spray can of sodium pentothal.

"Well, now you know," he said.

"Come out of that corner, girl!" said the other speaker, and Nikki realized she was cowering flat against the wall. "Come sit down."

The other speaker was a crone, a witchy old hag dressed—Nikki blinked—dressed like the Goth ideal of a wicked fairy in textured layers of bombazine and black leather corsets. She sat at a small table with an empty chair opposite. Nikki didn't move. The man, looking so much like her father's description of a Hunter that she must be projecting, came toward her. Looking at him, she knew her body as meat and bone, something easily cut, stabbed, shot, beaten, broken, or raped. The room was small, laboratory-white, lit by a globe in a wire cage, containing only the table, the two chairs, a hospital trolley bed, a toilet, no windows, one door—

She crossed to it in a blink, tried the handle. Locked. No light showed through the cracks, they must know that trick. She tried anyway and was slammed back into the room and bounced off the far wall.

The man put her in the chair while she was dazed. The old woman sat opposite with a gently ironic expression on her face. All in black against the cold white background. "Come on. Wake up."

The man had gone. Breathing harsh, painful dry throat, occipital bone throbbing, Nikki stared. "You...who're you?"

"I'm chairman of the board of directors," the crone said. "In charge, to the extent anyone is around here." She was very old, her skin worn so thin it seemed translucent where it wasn't spotted brown, and veins knotted around the knuckles of her hands like gnarled tree roots. She was well made up, however, and projected a certain chic. "One of your monsters," she added.

"A Hunter?"

"Not so frightening you can't even stay in the same room, I hope."

"I would rather not negotiate in a cell, thank you." Her voice numb and frigid.

"This isn't a negotiation, *chère*," said the crone. "Are you thirsty?"

…Parched. Bathed in sweat like she'd broken a fever. There was a bottled water on the table she'd been staring at, but now she shrank away. "No."

"You should be. We sped up the diaphoresis of narcotic from your system. Don't be stubborn, girl, you're already breathing whatever we want you to breathe. Drink."

They'd even left the plastic seal in place, but—"No. Thank you."

"Drink."

She watched her hands reach for the bottle, peel off the plastic, unscrew the top, and she drank until it was gone.

"What'd you do to me?"

"I disengaged your impulse control with a combination of neurotransmitters. Helped that you wanted to drink it, of course. We have more powerful agents. You've experienced Mr. Sanders' favorite dissociative. That one overcomes almost any resistance—except to what a person really, at her very core, doesn't want to do."

Nikki shuddered. She tried to reach for the shield of anger but couldn't find it. "Don't go all deer in the headlights," the chairman added, "but you need to know. This is not a negotiation."

"Then why are we talking? What is it you want?" Her memory filled in some gaps. "The Telepath said you were in danger and needed my help."

"We are. Grave danger. You're going to help us escape."

"From what?"

Eyebrows plucked into perfect arches rose. "From your family."

"…You from us?"

"You're the youngest, I believe," the crone observed, "and your father was not a forthcoming sort. You might be unaware of the Florentine Massacre of 1896?"

"I never heard of it."

"Hm!" Prejudice confirmed. "Well. Your family and mine have feuded in a disjointed, opportunistic way for centuries. But we grew tired of a war that, since it was with Timewalkers, could never really be won. We sued for peace. Since neither side would share the world with the other, we proposed that your father should give us one of our own by sending our entire race back to a time before the Timewalkers came into existence." A strain entered the creaky voice. "It seemed a perfect solution...."

"I doubt he saw it that way."

"He pretended he did. To him, it was a perfect opportunity."

"For what?"

"To have all the Hunters of this timeline gathered together in one place and one time."

"...Oh."

"About a third of us survived," the chairman added.

Nikki's head felt stuffed with cotton. The white room swam. "This happened in Florence? Was it the time one of you killed my sister Gabriela?"

"Mm...not that I'm aware," the crone answered. "That doesn't mean it didn't happen. We've seduced or killed several of your family members, or people close to them. And in other timelines too, no doubt, though I won't be held responsible for that. We aren't claiming the moral high ground here."

"Well, thank God for that."

"Indeed. Well. We've lived scattered and in hiding for the last hundred-odd years. Until our Mr. Sanders became very clever and developed the visual memory inhibitor to prevent you from timewalking except as we permit."

"...With pictures."

"Yes...well, not literally in this case. There's no photograph of where we're going, there couldn't be. But we save our memories as well as you do, and for much longer. And we've discovered a way to isolate and transfer them." She made a gesture as if injecting herself through the temple and Nikki felt her innards curl up. "We'll give you visual coordinates when the time comes."

She forced herself to stay in the chair, but she was flat against the back of it. "And—and if I refuse?"

"We'll persuade you."

"Why tell me? If this isn't a negotiation, if you can turn me into a good little automaton, why even discuss it?"

"Because I can doesn't mean I must." She sighed again. "*Chère m'mselle*, I don't want to frighten you. I know of no harm you personally ever did to us, though others will insist on phantom atrocities in timelines we know nothing of...."

"Well, I really, at my core, don't want to help you. I want you all to die horribly."

"Yes, I see that. It's an unpleasant way to live. Better if you accept some responsibility for your father's crimes and help us put an end to our feud."

"Like you've accepted responsibility for Alex? Or Peter?" Because if she couldn't reach him, he was dead by now.

"Ah. Yes. Your brother." The crone flattened her mouth in a simultaneous smile and frown. It might be intended to convey sympathy, but in Nikki's eyes it did a poor job. "Well then, it will take some time to persuade you. But there's no great hurry."

Nikki wondered how much the old woman knew. She had to assume X and Y had told her everything. If her mother, Lady Varian, and the baby were threatened, her defiance must collapse. "So what happens to me and what's left of my family after you force me to open your door back to the good old days?"

"We'll leave your relatives in this timeline alone," Madame Chairman said, crushing Nikki's rather feeble hope of ignorance.

"They're harmless. But you'll have to come with us."

"…What?" She shoved back from the table with a screech of chair legs on tile. "Why?"

"Because our only other alternative is killing you. You can still timewalk with images supplied from outside. And the rest of your family can, of course. Even the ones we've previously killed could show up to butcher us in our moment of weakness, all gathered together as we will be."

"That would violate the taboo on duplicating personal timelines…."

"Would that really stop you, your father, or your older brother, under the circumstances?"

"…No…but Peter…what if I did agree to help you?" Hypothetically. "Would you let me go?"

"You could make that promise and I'd know whether you were sincere." Gently ironic tone again. "But you live as long as we do. And you are a Timewalker. If—no, *when* you change your mind, we'll face the slaughter today. Right now. My people can't trust yours to keep promises. I can't ask it of them knowing they'll be killed if I'm wrong. You'll open the door for us. And then you must come with us, or die. It needn't be unbearable—you can live with the same privileges we enjoy—but you can never timewalk again."

Frozen half out of her seat, she stared at the crone gazing mildly and implacably back. "Stay with Hunters for the rest of my life in some juncture before the Renaissance?"

"Oh—before the Bronze Age," the crone said. "I can't tell you exactly when and where. Another of your family might trace you and learn it. But we would like to enjoy our safety for as long as possible."

"What would stop you from drinking my brain, or turning me into a puppet or a pet?"

"There are those among us who mean you harm," the chairman

acknowledged. "Perhaps not as many as you think. We don't consume human brain matter for food, you know, only for information or for raw material. We're omnivores, in fact, though your father believed—or it suited him to believe—otherwise. And you'll have my protection, though it will depend on my continuing to maintain power and position."

"Then your protection won't be free, will it? You say I won't be allowed to timewalk, but don't you mean except for your purposes?"

"I won't require you to use your power for my benefit, but you might feel constrained to by circumstances, unless you found another protector." She made such a deep grimace that a crack appeared in her makeup. "Such is life among us, my girl. We're players in a game of love and power and dominance. When we're together, we mingle— literally. Each one's essence influences the others. That's why I look this way. I've aged myself beyond the influence of our more common pheromones. But even I'm not free."

"Sucks to be you?"

Her pouched eyes swallowed the sarcasm whole. "You're a prisoner of people you've been taught to fear, who are responsible for your father's murder and your brother's death—of course you can't trust me. You can't even trust your feelings since I could be influencing them."

"Are you?"

"Yes. I'm encouraging you to tell me the truth, and I'm countering your excess adrenaline. Panic won't help. Listen, *chère*. You'll have to trust someone or go mad, I've seen it happen. So far as I can, I'll preserve you as you are, free will and all. But that's all I can promise. Think about your options in an abstract way. Don't believe what I tell you, just consider what you'd prefer if it were true." She left a moment's blank silence, then, "Will you help us?"

"No."

She sighed, not surprised but not happy. "Very well." She rose, slow, creaky, and absurdly fragile, and turned toward the door.

Nikki tensed. The cell went black. She sprang forward physically as she heard the door open—but collided with someone who shoved her back hard. The door snapped and locked shut. The light came on and Sanders was back in the room, regarding her with cold dead eyes.

發

The city, the night, the street like open arms—Peter plunged into them, gulping moist air. Down toward the waterfront, mist blurred the too-bright lights and the skyline. Old Nob Hill was quiet as only three in the morning could be, just the background grating of iron wheels, but his pulse banged in his ears. He rounded on Chu-kheng as she and Wen descended from the house. "You could've told me it'd be Sanders!"

"Who?" said Wen.

Chu-kheng spread her hands, raised her shoulders, and turned down the corners of her mouth. "You did better this way."

"Did we just hand him the drug he used—is going to use—on her?"

"No." She swept past, herding her husband. "It's in your coat pocket." Peter started—he'd been sure nobody saw him palm the ampoule. "Hurry, we must board the streetcar before he sees it gone. Anyway, he told you himself he is not the same man."

"The same as who?" said Wen.

"Okay, branching timelines, but—" Peter scrambled after her. "He's the same person and he had it for hours, he's got the idea. He could use it on her someday!"

"Who could?"

"Dr. Sutorius!"

"But for you that has already happened," Chu-kheng said. "And if you try to save her without the antidote, you will die, or at least I will not see you again, which is significant. Dr. Sutorius was the only person who could provide it."

"The doctor...is your enemy?"

"Uh, no, Baba. It's more like he could become my enemy."

"As things stand, you have a chance, you have a remedy for the girl, and you have a way to return to her." She walked on stiff-legged, without a backward glance.

Peter checked the tiny vial, glinting in the streetlight. He stepped his nervous system down from Defcon Two to its normal state of jangle. "Okay." He followed, turning south at the cross-street, stretching his stride across pavement cracked and gleaming black with puddles. "But I can't believe you know that guy." They were walking at her pace—a forced march—and she looked worn down, pink showing through thin skin. "Let me take that," Peter said, reaching for the rucksack. She gave it up this time without a word.

Wen waddled along in mild bewilderment and kept looking back. Once the cold lights of Dr. Sutorius' house disappeared, he cleared his throat. "The honorable doctor is not really a very good man?"

"No," said Peter. "Not really."

"That is open to debate," said Chu-kheng. "By his lights, he only does what he must to protect his own. But he should know better than to threaten me."

"Whatever he did, it worked on me," Peter said. "Why couldn't he make you answer?"

"I chose not to."

"But—"

"Ahead of time. I saw the ways the meeting could go, and committed to the path that would get what you needed."

"He couldn't make you change your mind?"

She stopped and poked him in the chest, hitting one of his bruises. "Heed this, Jun-fan. If you foresee the paths, if you know the likely outcomes beforehand, not even the Hunters can seduce or frighten you into changing the choices you have already made."

"Good to know."

"Indeed."

"The thing is, I suck at foreseeing the paths."

Wen patted his arm. "Nothing to be ashamed of."

"I'm not ashamed," said Peter. "I didn't ask for this. I didn't enjoy the experience of having my brain sucked out of my head in full sensory detail—" Wen audibly choked. "—but if foreknowledge can give me an edge, I'd better use it."

"You aren't as bad as you believe," Chu-kheng said.

"When I try for a vision, I get white noise. Then I pass out."

"That won't happen next time."

Peter started to say "How do you know?" but stopped himself in time.

A clop and a clang startled him as an early-morning streetcar rattled up, passed by with a bit of damp paper flapping in its wake, and stopped at the corner. "Come!" commanded Chu-kheng, and scurried after it. He ran with the rucksack bouncing painfully on his shoulder, scrambled on, and pulled her aboard, and Wen skipped onto the back step as it pulled away. It was a lucky chance; Peter saw a burly figure pacing the end of the street, swinging a truncheon on its loop. A place for getting rousted, as Tom would say—great granite and marble banks and fortresses of law loomed on both sides of the street, dark and silent.

"Fifteen centee, Johnny," said the rear driver—there was one in front with the horses, and this guy in back with the steering wheel. Wen clanked a few coins into the box. The other passengers were dark, hunched shapes on wooden benches. They took the last one with Peter squeezed against the window. He was grateful not to be trying to negotiate these streets on his own. Although he did see something familiar—they were passing the funny old Montgomery

Block building, sitting on the future site of the Transamerica Pyramid. He'd seen it on postcards and the historical landmark sign in the Pyramid's lobby.

"You know," Wen remarked, "your mother's gift is good fortune to me. It helps me win at fan-tan so I can send money home without working myself to death. That's why they call me Lucky Wen." He winked. "But it makes her unhappy to see the evil that lies in the future. She can't live in the moment like me. I would hate for that to happen to you. Maybe you shouldn't try."

Peter's glasses fogged up. "Uh—thanks for the thought. But it's too late. I get visions without trying. I'd rather get some kind of handle on it." He rubbed his lenses on his new shirt tail. "What am I doing wrong?" he asked Chu-kheng.

"Probably, you're looking too far ahead," she said. "More paths branch off with every choice you make. You can't look down all the roads at once."

"The farther you look, the more interference you get?"

"The farther *you* look, yes."

"Hm," Peter said doubtfully. It hadn't seemed that far to him and he didn't remember making any choices.

She thawed to the subject. "Only two kinds of visions come easy to a beginner. Sudden dangers and inevitable events."

"What are inevitable events?" He'd had the sudden danger one several times now.

"Sudden danger visions are as if you see a snake in your path," she explained anyway. "It's obvious because it's close and shocking, and because you have only two choices—encounter it or avoid it. An inevitable event is like a mountain in the distance. Fixed, immovable, unchanging. You can see it from far away, and though your road forks a thousand times, all ways lead to it." Her voice sank low, as if she'd lost it in some memory.

"What kind of events?"

"Such as the awakening of the Great Earth Dragon less than two hours from now," she said. "Nothing can alter that. No action of ours can preclude it."

"I haven't had that vision," said Peter, discounting his dreams. "I hope that means I won't be here."

The clock at City Hall was striking four when the streetcar stopped on Market Street near Seventh Avenue and they disembarked and approached the Palazzo. Peter looked around for cops but luck— or Madame Wen's vision—was with them again and the street was deserted once the car rolled on.

Without surprise, he saw Tom waiting for them in the shadow of the front door. Wen greeted him with outstretched hand and smiles to make up for the lack of common language, but the doorman hurried them inside, locked the door with a clank, and pushed up the cap that concealed his eyes.

"You'd be gonna losing me my job, but I 'spect it was lost already," he said to Chu-kheng. "Mr. Varian cleared out today just like you said, and sent everyone away." To Peter he said, "So, you found Madame When. And she took a shine to you."

Two bewildered women and two excited boys came into view. "My family," Tom said. One woman was young and sweet-faced, the other gray-haired and aggrieved-looking, and the boys were in the seven-to-ten range. Peter couldn't guess which one might be Abe's father. They seemed to be having the time of their lives setting up camp behind the stairs at the back of the lobby with a picnic basket, blankets, and a storm lantern.

"When the clock strikes five, you put that lantern out," Chu-kheng said. "No fires!"

"Yes, ma'am," said Tom. "Where will you folks stay?"

"In Father Varian's office," she answered.

His eyes widened and he shifted uneasily. "I'll get trouble for that."

"No one will come until the day after the fires die down," she said. "No one will ever know."

"Why you want to stay there?" he asked.

"I need to use the secret door," Peter said. A light rose in Tom's eyes. "You know it's there," Peter noted.

He nodded slowly. "Plenty times someone come out of there that hadn't gone in, or went in and didn't come out. I thought that was what you and your gal was up to, before. I don't speak of it. I don't want trouble."

"You will get none from this," Chu-kheng said.

He worked his jaw back and forth for a minute. "Well, I hear you usually get your way, Madame When." He fished his keys out and led the way up the stairs.

His boys ran ahead, all whoops and giggles. "I'd like to run that!" The younger one pointed at the gilt cage elevator suspended below the mezzanine.

"I hope you have better things to do with your life," Tom told him.

They all trooped along the balcony to the office suite door, Wen slinking on exaggerated tiptoe, one finger on his lips and his eyes rolling, to make the boys laugh. The inner office was just as Peter had left it: dusty, dark, empty except for the books on the floor and the documents on the desk. "Don't touch nothin'." Tom raised the wick in his lantern and the wall panels glowed in response. "The old man's really gone, ain't he? Where'm I gonna get another job without a reference?"

"He made arrangements for you to stay on," said Chu-kheng, "and look after the building while it's being leased."

"Is that so?" Tom's brow furrowed up in a reaction too complicated for Peter to describe, although he totally understood it. Patronage.

"I'd better get going," Peter said.

"Yes, you should," Chu-kheng said, and Lucky Wen lost his clowning manner and looked stricken.

"Um, but how—" Peter turned toward the wall where the panel should be.

"You already know how."

And he did.

He hugged her and Lucky Wen. She was stiff. He was attacked by sniffles. "Thank you for everything. I promise I'll come back if I can. Please don't, Baba...." He shook Tom's hand and waved to the boys, who were busy crawling through the empty bookshelves, then went behind the desk. In this juncture, the panels were too new for him to distinguish the right one immediately, but he took his best guess based on his memory of its position and felt pretty confident of the result.

Now he just had to do what Timewalkers did. Of course his memory wasn't as good; he couldn't visualize something he'd seen once or twice like Nikki could. But he didn't need to remember what Santuario looked like in the past because he could see it in the opposite direction. All he had to do while he pressed on the door was wonder what would happen if it opened....

He started, scared of another attack of white noise, but it was impos—

發

Pushing the door open, he went down the dark cool stone tunnel toward gray light. He came out through a shattered doorway at the bottom of the amphitheater halfway up the hill of Santuario. Heaps of twisted metal smoldered, smoke and ash stung his eyes, blackened grass crunched underfoot. The burning serva had fallen over and died. Wind was whipping up the ashes, shaking the trees, bringing storm clouds—a hard rain, as the song had it, was going to fall. The beautiful terraced gardens lay under shadow. The fortress gripped the summit like a vulture whose wings obscured the sky.

發

—sible to stop. The panel swung open when he pulled back.

"Ooooh," Wen and the boys behind him said in unison.

"There, you see," said Chu-kheng.

She and Wen stood there, looking small and quaint somehow with their layers of shabby old clothes, under the bags they hadn't put down yet. "Come with me," Peter proposed suddenly.

Clearly, this idea hadn't struck Lucky Wen before. His eyes lit up. "Oh! Yes, why not?"

"Not this time," Chu-kheng said.

"But why not?" Wen repeated.

"It will end badly if we do. If Jun-fan goes alone, we may see him again, although it is not certain."

"Is there something I need to know?" Peter asked while Wen subsided into disappointment.

"I have seen nothing that I need to tell you," she answered, with a certain smugness. "If that changes, perhaps I can get a message through. Go on now."

Peter turned and plunged through the opening. Before he could look back, the panel closed behind him as if weighted, leaving him in the dark except for the irregular gray blob of light at the far end. He walked toward it and it slowly grew into the jagged shape of the doorway X and Y had blown to hell.

As Nikki had said, he was arriving later than when he'd left. A cold draft brought the smell of burnt things, but also a scent of approaching rain. He neared the threshold and saw through the doorway all the burned broken servas lying in charred grass, the marble benches above the crater, the lush gardens rising up toward the dark fortress. Just as he had seen it in the vision. He emerged—

And ducked as Erik's fist whistled over his head.

CHAPTER NINE

*P*eter didn't see—or didn't *see*—that it was Erik. He saw a fist coming at him and his nose meeting the back of his skull if he didn't duck. He dove to the ground, rolled through ashes and pieces of wood and bits of sharp, cooling metal and scrambled to his feet. Then Nikki's brother stepped out from behind the broken wall.

I have seen nothing that I need to tell you. Thanks, Mom. Meanwhile another vision fell on him—

發

Erik coiled up and spun around, unleashing a kick that dislocated his jaw before he could blink.

發

He twisted and scrambled back. A boot tore the air in front of his face. Miraculously untouched, he backed away. The Timewalker advanced. His mirrored shades flashed, his long black coat flared in the wind, stormclouds gathered around his head, the earth turned black in the prints of his motorcycle boots—in short, he looked pissed.

"You!" he observed.

"Me," Peter agreed, edging back around a burnt chassis and a heap of broken bricks.

"Nikki's little ephemeral. Ching, wasn't it?"

"Chang."

"The Hunters sent you?"

"Um...nobody sent me." He backed into a marble block and hopped behind it. The guy was crazy. Not sociopathic, but truly batshit.

"Tell me where to find the man who murdered my sister," Erik said.

Peter blinked. "Nikki's alive."

The Timewalker's face tightened as if Peter had said something that hurt him. "Really. Then where is she?"

"That's complicated." Peter raised his hands in a pacifying gesture. "We can talk about it, if we can just calm down a little first. I think you're projecting some hostility that isn't—hey!" He dove forward over the marble bench. Erik fugued behind him, then aborted the attack that might have paralyzed Peter if he hadn't seen it coming. Heat rushed through Peter. He jumped up and charged the bastard, who blocked his punch without effort. "You want a piece of me?" Peter snarled unoriginally. The ghost pain didn't cripple, it goaded him. He threw a clumsy left hook and a wild right. Erik vanished. Peter stumbled.

The Timewalker stood a few yards away up the steps— "I want to know how you betrayed her!"—and vanished again.

Peter ran from a frontal assault that would have left him with broken ribs. The prescience was working automatically now, like an electric pulse stimulating muscles he hadn't known he had. "I didn't!" he yelled. "I'm trying to find her!" He struck back, missed by a yard. Erik fugued so fast he blurred, kicking up plumes of ash. Peter punched air and turned in circles like a confused basset hound.

"You're going to tell me," the Timewalker said from behind his right shoulder, and unleashed another barrage that had Peter jerking around like a puppet on strings to avoid it.

"I might if you weren't such an asshole!" He tried to see where and when to throw a punch that would nail the guy but there were too many variables. He could do effective defense, but not offense, not at the same time anyway.

He'd been in one fight before, at age thirteen, pushed to the wall by a hulking juvenile delinquent. Suddenly he was that boy again—no coordination, no technique, just a raging need to pound someone's face in. But Erik's face was never where it was supposed to be, any more than Peter's face was present when Erik tried to hit it. He went flailing after the Timewalker in a red haze. It was like trying to fight somebody in a dream—safe, but so frustrating he would wake up grinding his teeth.

Then he became aware of another factor: endurance. If he ducked those fists eleven times, he'd be too tired to duck the twelfth. The nerve strike would get through on the tenth try. The sixth footsweep would take him down. Fear began to take the place of rage. He'd have to fight his way back to the broken arch, make a break for it—

At that instant, fuguing from point A to point B, Erik lost his footing on a flywheel poking out of the serva wreckage. He lurched, caught himself, and almost got to safety, but Peter's fist flew out at just the right second and connected hard below his left eye. The Timewalker staggered. Then, as Peter came at him again, he sprang back and pulled a pistol out of his coat. "Dodge this, twinkletoes!"

It was the same gun, close enough now that Peter could read "Glock 42 Austria .380 Auto" engraved on it. He froze in mid-lunge. Avoiding bullets was not in his new skill set; when an object traveled hundreds of meters per second, it didn't help to see it coming. Still, a heady wine surged in his veins. He wouldn't have expected to last five seconds against Nikki's brother—and Erik had called it quits, not him. "Chickenshit!" he gasped, and doubled over to catch his breath.

Stupid thing to say to a man who had shot him once already, but Erik didn't take the bait. "If the brainsuckers did send you to kill me," he said, "their standards have declined appallingly."

"You tried—" *huff* "—to kill me!" *gasp*. Peter straightened up and shook out his aching hand. Erik hadn't broken a sweat, but at least there was a reddening mark on his cheekbone.

"If they didn't send you—" Peter took a large step to his left. "—then how is it," the Timewalker said, six feet closer with arm cocked to pistol-whip him across the face, only of course Peter wasn't there. He pointed the little black hole of death at him again. "How is it you see me coming? Just like the first assassin knew exactly where my father would end up when he fugued, and got him with his own knife. You're a backup agent. You got into my naïve little sister's confidence and sold her out."

Something glimmered at the back of Peter's mind about X and Y knowing where certain people would be at certain times, but the main effect of these remarks was to sober him completely. "I'm not working for the Hunters. Thing is, I'm a Seer. I *do* see you coming."

"You're one of the Third Family? Then I ought to kill you on principle. I fucking hate Seers," said Erik. "Anyway, that doesn't stop you from belonging to the brainsuckers. They'd love to recruit one of you fortune tellers. And if you're not with them, how did you get in?"

"In here? It's pretty obvious you just picture where you're going."

"You'd have to know what it looks like first."

"Nikki showed me." He hoped that stung.

Mirrored shades glinted over the gun sight. "So you *have* seen her lately."

Peter wiped the sweat from his face and pushed his glasses back up his nose. He dusted the ash and soot off his coat and trousers—just cleaned, dammit—for good measure. "Look, I've got someplace else to be just now. I've got to go rescue Nikki, actually, so are you going to kill me or not?"

Erik snorted. "You tell me."

"...You're not."

"Not yet." The Timewalker grabbed him by the lapels. Since it was the alternative to being shot, Peter didn't try to dodge. Erik hauled him around to face Santuario's central hill. The sky was gray and gloomy behind the old fortress-villa on top and the wind battered against its walls. Everything blinked. There was no stretch-snap, like when Nikki dragged him somewhere. Erik fugued smooth as a shot across an air-hockey table. They were standing under the fortress wall on the south veranda, where lunch was still congealing on the table. The serva Clarabella was slumped in a heap by the low outer wall, all six limbs askew. One glassy clockwork eye was still. The other had a bullet hole punched through it.

"She didn't seem pleased to see me," Erik explained.

"Go figure," Peter said through the roaring in his ears.

The Timewalker shoved him toward the table. Sheltered from the wind, black flies buzzed over cold cioppino in bone-white bowls. "Four places set. Last I knew there were only two people left. Nikki was here?"

"Yeah, we had lunch with Lady Varian and—and Mr. Almost-As-Paranoid-As-Present-Company Dromio." Peter smoothed out his shirtfront.

"The assassins crashed the party? And only you escaped to tell me about it?" Erik scratched his chin stubble with the front sight of the gun. "So tell me about it."

"Nikki got me out."

"And what happened to her?"

"They grabbed her," Peter said reluctantly. "Not here. After we escaped. They caught up again."

"Tell me how they managed to catch a forewarned Timewalker," Erik said, shades glinting cold.

"They shot her with this." Peter shook the ampoule from his sleeve into his palm and showed it to him.

"That's just ketamine or something. I took two hits and still managed to fugue. She'd have had time to escape before going under."

"You might notice, genius, this isn't the same stuff." He held it up to the light. "Whatever they used the first time was clear yellow and this is green. She said she couldn't remember what anyplace looked like. So she couldn't, y'know, blink out anymore, and they grabbed her. That's all I can tell you."

"But they left you alone?"

"I wasn't with her at that exact moment," Peter admitted.

"Tea leaves tell you to stay away?"

"I...I did see it actually," he said. "But the vision came too late. They were gone by the time I came out of it." At Erik's scowl, he added, "Look, I just found out I can do this. I'm not Nostradamus!"

"How did they find her?"

"That, I don't know. It's freaky how they keep showing up. It's like they just know where she is." Again he had a glimmer of an idea. If he could just get a few minutes of peace and quiet to sort it out....

"You're the common denominator. You've been with her every time they caught up."

"How could I have told them where she was?" Peter protested. "Do cell phones work across timelines? Is there an interdimensional paging system?"

"You're a Seer? You'd have known ahead of time where she was going, you could have left them a message."

"I could have hit her over the head with a wine bottle, too. She trusted me," Peter said. "I was trying to protect her."

"Then what are you doing here?"

"I was—" Peter started to answer, then felt his kneecap shatter. In an instant of more agony than he thought any human being could endure, he learned how to shut down a prescient vision while in the middle of it. The question was a trap. A truthful answer would make Erik more suspicious, not less.

"Quicker than that. You should have gotten your story straight ahead of time."

The entire trip into 1906 had to be left out, Peter realized. Erik would never believe X and Y had reached Nikki in the past and he couldn't explain it himself. "I was looking for help," he lied with unfeigned reluctance. If there was anyone whose help he didn't want, it was Erik's. "I can find out where they took her. But I can't storm the castle by myself."

The Timewalker pulled up a chair and sat down. "Suppose I swallowed this whole cock-and-bull. How can you find them?"

"The assassins—they call themselves X and Y, by the way. The Hunter they work for is named Sanders. He infiltrated your dad's firm as a client. I worked there. I have access to the client files." He mentally bashed his head against the wall to subdue his own objections and said, "We could track him down."

"How do you know they work for him?"

"He was in the Palazzo the night they killed your dad. Sitting right in his office during that shootout you had."

"How do you know this Sanders is a brainsucker?"

"I foresaw him sucking out my brain."

"You what?"

"I...had a vision of going into Mr. Varian's office and finding Sanders there. He put me under and stuck a straw up my—well, you know how it goes."

The Timewalker stared hard at him for a moment, then got up and started pacing again. Peter didn't relax. He had to be thinking up more holes to poke in the story. But a moment later, he turned back with, "Okay. I'm in. But do you know what I'll do to you when I find out you're lying?"

"Uh...don't you mean 'if'?"

"Do you know?"

"Obviously," said Peter, not bothering to check.

"Good." Erik took off the shades. The time since Peter had last seen him without them had not been kind: his eyes were red and raw and his face looked like wax mixed with stubble and scraped too thin over the bones. "You *are* lying—or you've been brainwashed—and your story is a setup. The brainsuckers imagine I'll be easier to take down on their turf. I don't give a fuck. Nikki is dead, and all that's left is revenge. Shut up," he added as Peter opened his mouth to protest. "I was on my way to search the timeline the assassins came from when you stumbled in. I had no idea where to start looking." He slid the shades back on. "You can lead me into their trap. And we'll see who it closes on."

Peter stared. "You are mindblowingly paranoid!"

發

Erik disappeared, needing more ammo, he said. Peter took a second to see what would happen if he tried to escape the Timewalker's company at this point. It was scary, painful, and unavoidable given that he had only the one doorway out of Santuario. So he went inside, descended to the kitchens, and washed the soot out of his throat with some cold black coffee he found in a saucepan. He had reached the point where caffeine was essential but no longer helped.

The kitchens were quiet, with low lighting and pleasant warmth. He took a few minutes to think about X and Y and Nikki and made a connection that should have been obvious before, although he was too tired to trust his brain processes and did not accept it as conclusive. As for Nikki's brother, there was something wrong with him—well, more wrong than usual—and he should probably find out what, if he could work that into his schedule. But Chu-kheng had foreseen him coping with the guy, apparently, so he would carry on.

He went back up and met the Timewalker—looking bulky under his buttoned-up London Fog—on the veranda. A patter of drops was just beginning and the wind smelled sharp and heady. They fugued back down to the amphitheater floor. Ashes swirled and were laid to rest under a sprinkling, then a pounding, then a deluge of wind-driven rain. Peter jumped into the tunnel and escaped with his clothes slightly damp. Erik stayed outside a moment, staring back up the hill. He came in with water streaming off his hair and coat. "Move it."

Peter moved it. No gun was visible, but the back of his neck prickled as if one was. The smell of scorched earth gave way to underground scent and the tunnel roof pressed down heavy and black. He trailed one hand on the wall. "Why are you so sure Nikki's dead? Because X and Y went to a lot of trouble to catch her if they were just going to kill her."

"The brainsuckers like it fresh," Erik said.

"In my...in my dreams, she's still alive," Peter said.

"Your dreams."

"You've got no hope at all? Even if she is dead, couldn't you visit the past and find her again?" He doubted the taboo meant anything to him.

"If I choose."

"Well, do you?"

"Want to take care of this first."

Peter stopped before banging his nose into the secret panel. "We're here."

"When were you last in this timeline?"

"Friday afternoon. The day after your shootout."

"That's later than my event horizon," said the unseen Timewalker. "So?"

"So, you open it. No point in splitting the timeline and creating another Nikki to be avenged."

"Rescued," Peter said.

"Say that again," Erik said. "Say it one more time."

"I don't get how you—"

"I'll tell you once." An icy voice, but the ice was cracking. "This is my doing. I could have protected her, but I let her go. Right into the hands of the Hunters. So it's too late for anything but revenge. You lead me to it, fine, I won't kill you, but shut up about her being alive. I know she isn't."

"But how do you know?"

"Open the goddamn door!"

"Okay," Peter said, almost sorry for him: he was, like all bullies, so limited—a Timewalker able to go anywhere, do anything, yet unable to escape the hell he carried around with him. "Hang on...."

He opened the door and his eyes adjusted to the dirty-dishwater light seeping in through the Venetian blinds and he saw—

"Christ!" He tried not to gag.

"Problem?"

"Nothing that'll bother you." Peter pushed the panel open.

It was like opening a fridge full of spoiled meat, in that the office smelled terrible and was as cold as if the air conditioner had been left on full blast for days. It was also noisy because a major traffic jam seemed to be happening just outside the building. Peter's eyes adjusted to the light and focused on the dead man lying just behind the desk, half-buried in a cascade of paper.

He heard a *foop!* noise from behind him, as of displaced air. Erik, shades propped on top of his head, appeared on the far side of the desk, crouched, and turned, checking every corner over the sights of his .380.

"It's safe." Peter edged out to avoid stepping on the corpse.

The Timewalker used the muzzle to crack the blinds on the glass partition and checked the outer office. "Who asked you?"

Peter ignored this, his gut lurching. Dromio hadn't gotten far. He lay prone, but with his neck twisted far enough to expose the face, lips and gums pulled back from the teeth, cheeks sunken and livid. The dusty black suit seemed to be covering something more caved-in than it used to be. "Jeez!" He tugged his shirt collar over his mouth and nose. "How long has he been dead?"

Erik checked out the windows, put the gun away, came over and dripped rainwater from his coat onto Dromio's face. "They killed him?"

Peter had no doubt he had been killed; nobody's head could rotate that much. "He left right before they came in; he must've run into them. But he looks like he's been here for days!"

Erik swiped up some dust from the desk with his forefinger. "Did the place look like this when you left?"

"More or less. Although…" Peter became aware that the papers, both on the desk and spilled over the corpse to the floor, were yellow and curling up at the corners. Dust was thick on the shelves, books, lamps, windowsills. The antique furniture looked…more antique, as if someone had gone over it with a sandblaster and crackle glaze finish for that cool distressed look. "…No," he said finally. The room's chill dug in under his skin. "Are we in the wrong time?"

"No."

"Why not?"

"You couldn't reach the wrong time."

Peter turned one of his smartphones on. It searched briefly for a signal, then settled in to work. "7:43 p.m.," he observed, "and it's the same evening." Only an hour after he and Nikki had left the clinic on Powell Street. "I saw Dromio alive in this room eight hours ago. What's going on?"

Erik kicked some of the paper off of the corpse, substantially adding to the dust in the air, and exposed an object that had been concealed in the drift—an antique desk lamp. He picked it up. Peter saw a small impact crater in its base, like a pock in a windshield. Erik set it back down on the desk. As it touched the surface with a tap, the spiderweb cracks spread. The lamp fell clattering into a dozen shards of Bakelite and the light bulb shattered.

It was as if the thing had been dipped in liquid nitrogen—Peter didn't want to touch it, in case it burned his fingers. "Uh—was that supposed to prove something?"

"Yeah." The Timewalker produced a caustic twist to his mouth. "This is Nikki's timeline. I remember. She split the original line to save you—"

"When you shot me?"

"—when I shot you. That's funny."

"Why?"

"Because you're going to die."

"…You mean in an obvious, eventual sort of way?"

"No, I mean soon."

"What does this being Nikki's timeline have to do with it?"

"Can't you see it coming?" He turned curious eyes on Peter.

"Just tell me."

Erik got a sort of muscular twitch to one side of his mouth that in anyone else might have passed for a grimace of pain. "This is how I know she's dead."

Out of the corner of his eye, Peter saw Fate creeping up behind him with a tire iron. "Explain."

Erik crouched and patted down Dromio's corpse. "Anyway, what was he doing here?"

"Nikki told him about Sanders." Peter leaned back as dust sprang up from the dead man's coat. "Explain."

"Oh, I see. Like you told me."

"Yeah," said Peter. "And just to be sure you wouldn't suspect a thing, I left him right where you'd trip over him."

"I never said you were a competent tool." Finding nothing, he rose and shouldered Peter out of his way, reaching for something behind him.

"You know, 'excuse me' works pretty well," Peter snapped as the Timewalker bent and grabbed something from under the desk. "Explain!"

The something was a small handgun of the sort carried by agents who don't want to ruin the line of a tailored jacket. Notwithstanding the late Mr. Dromio's sartorial handicap, Peter supposed it belonged to him; X and Y wouldn't have left one of their own behind. Erik eyed Peter sidelong over it. "The timeline unravels when the Timewalker dies," he said.

"Explain that."

"It splinters. Disintegrates. Falls apart. Ceases to be. How many synonyms do you want?"

"...What happens to the people living in it?"

Erik shrugged. He blew a layer of dust off the little gun, imitating a low whistle of wind.

"Wait. What—the whole? —what? You mean the whole world just..." He stammered, then managed to say, "Why would it?"

"Why not? All that you call home is just a tiny fragment of probability to us. Wouldn't exist if she hadn't interfered. Why should it survive without her?"

"I hardly know where to begin answering that," Peter said. "I mean—I think the burden of proof is on your side. Just because this timeline needed her interference to get started doesn't mean it would just...stop if she died! That has to...I don't know, violate some law about predictable rates of entropy or something."

"I wouldn't know. We didn't have entropy when I was a kid, just a lot of stuff breaking down."

"Nikki never said it could happen."

"She didn't know. Our father never told us. I found out the interesting way. When my sister Gabriela died." His expression went, for Erik, rather thoughtful, and when he spoke again, his hostility was not directed at Peter. "He was keeping her locked up in the dark. She slipped me a note, smuggled it out with her breakfast tray when Dromio one time was too busy to collect it and sent a serva instead. Asked me to take a message to some ephemeral friends in her nineteenth-century Florence. I was just a kid then. Fourteen. I went and the palazzos were all coming apart in the wind. You could watch it happening, the buildings eroding into blowing sand like..." He waved his hands as similes failed him. "I've seen some crazy shit, but the ground was disintegrating while I was standing on it. I got back, she was dead, and all of her timelines had gone the same way."

"Back up." Peter was starting to shiver. "You're reading way too much into this. You can't extrapolate Armageddon from a—a rapidly decomposing corpse and a fragile old lamp. Those aren't inexplicable events."

"Look out the window," Erik said. He slipped the tiny gun into his pocket, probably to keep it out of trouble rather than with any intention of ever using it.

The racket of engines idling and horns engaged registered on Peter. He went to the northwest-facing window and raised the blinds. The sky was spectacular—dark clouds shot through with purple and dull red from a sun dropping below the horizon like a brick—but not that unusual. The street was a parking lot in both directions, four lanes solid, but that was hardly a sign of the apocalypse. The stoplight was out of order. So were three cars within his line of sight: tire ruptured, hood raised, smoke drifting. He wasn't high enough to see beyond Market Street, but he could hear horns, voices, sirens…the city buzzed like an angry hive. Not your average Friday evening commute, maybe, but not a universal catastrophe….

But if it wasn't his imagination, if he wasn't remembering wrongly, there were patterns of decay everywhere he looked. More cracks in the sidewalk, more potholes in the asphalt, more erosion in the brickwork, more rust in the chain-link. The sumacs, which he was almost sure had been in late summer green that morning, were the crimson of burst capillaries. Across the street, a girl whose breath was fogging stood on a chair outside Cosmos Coffeehouse. He knew the barista, Lindsey, by her two-tone hair and café logo t-shirt. She was fixing a crack in the front window with duct tape, stopping occasionally to shiver and rub her bare arms and look around in doubt and confusion. The QUESTION EVERYTHING graffiti was nearly worn off the purple wall nearby, along with a lot of the paint.

"…Is there anything you can do?"

"Not even if I gave a rat's ass." Erik picked up another item from the floor—the stiletto Dromio had threatened Peter with. He gave it a cursory glance and dropped it on the desk, then picked up a piece of flannel with ties sewn to it like a surgical mask. Then noticed Peter staring at him. "What? One timeline? Out of hundreds that I know of—you think I can spare any tears?"

Peter skipped epithets and went for the jugular. "Your new sibling is here, by the way. Lady Varian is giving birth in a hospital on Powell Street right now."

"Boy or girl?" Erik asked. Peter shrugged, his throat feeling like it had closed up. "Well, I'll pick them up when I blow this shithole." He stuffed the flannel mask inside his bulging coat. His eyes caught a crimson gleam from the dying light. "So. Where can I find Sanders?"

"Uh—the world's about to end? How does getting revenge work with that?"

"Very quickly."

"You have a sense of humor like a two-by-four."

"I'm not joking. I've got to kill him before he stops existing."

"That's as pointless a —" As a video game. "If it's really true," Peter started over, scraping together a few of his battered wits, "if Nikki's dead and the universe is collapsing and you can't or won't do anything about it, why should I help you?"

Erik apparently gave the question serious consideration, because he didn't answer it with his .380. "Do you think it's really true?"

Peter remembered what Chu-kheng had said about vision and inevitable events. "Nikki isn't dead," he repeated.

"Well, there you go." Spoken with an undertone of *you poor delusional sap.* "If she's still alive, the brainsuckers have her, and you'll be a little spot of grease on the wall if you try anything without me. So. Where?"

"…I need my computer." Peter headed for the door. He'd have taken his chances on the grease spot, but Nikki's life was at stake and anyway he couldn't stop the guy from coming.

The planters in Elaine's office each contained something dead—leafless stems, frost-burned petals, desiccated corms—and her furniture was raising a second generation of dust bunnies. The thought of Elaine reminded him of their late boss, which suggested another objection to Erik's theory. "If the timeline disintegrates when the Timewalker dies, why is Santuario still around?"

"Santuario isn't just another ephemeral timeline. It's outside time, self-sustaining and permanent. It doesn't need its creator."

"Oh...how special." Peter rubbed his head. The claim didn't gel with what Nikki had said about the place being a piece of Renaissance Tuscany. But Erik had a biased view of Santuario and everything else associated with his family. "Upstairs."

Great swathes of plaster were eaten out along the baseboards on the mezzanine where the sun hit on these late summer evenings. But the light now was gray, the air more like January than September. Unmoved by these portents, Erik jabbed the button to summon the elevator. In the same instant, Peter flinched. "Bad idea!"

"Is this a Seer thing?"

"Well, that, and a common sense thing." After a longer-than-usual pause, the lift was lurching and rattling its way up from the floor below. "That elevator was a hundred and ten years old this morning. If you're right...how old is it now?" It reached the mezzanine without a ping, hesitated, and opened. Peter backed away. Wild horses, assuming some happened to drop by and were so inclined, couldn't have dragged him into that rickety gilt cage. "Let's take the stairs."

"If you want to live a little longer..."

They got four steps before the cable let go—or more likely, the cage suffered terminal metal fatigue around the bolts. Screeches and clangs rang out as it careened off the walls, striking sparks all the way down. The final crash sent a tongue of fire licking up through the floor. Erik clamped Peter around the neck and fugued to the far side of the mezzanine, away from the oily black smoke billowing out of the shaft.

"You really saw that coming," he observed as the echoes died away.

"You're welcome!" Peter was still shaking.

"I'd have survived."

"No, you wouldn't have." The smoke was spreading through the lobby and mezzanine with unnatural speed. "Let's go, before the automatic sprinklers come on," Peter said. "Assuming they still work."

They did. The fire alarms went off and a burst of cold water hit him just before he ducked into the stairwell. Cursing, he climbed after Erik. The steps had their original treads and were worn down in the middle. The walls made clanking noises, as if the pipes supplying the sprinklers were freezing and might break any minute. But the third floor, when they emerged onto it, was dry, quiet, smoke-free, and well-lit. Someone had forgotten to turn the lights off, or was working late—and just as Peter made this observation, another premonition slammed into him.

"If you shoot him, I won't help you!"

The office door nearest the stairwell opened just as he started to speak. Abe Slinky, looking like a wise old cadaver in a decent suit, leaned out. "Peter!" he exclaimed—and had to cross his eyes to focus on the business end of a .380 semiautomatic. "Uh…"

Then Erik's comprehension caught up with his reflexes. "What did you say?" Peter repeated it. "You're bluffing," said the Timewalker, "but never mind. Are you sure he's not gonna tip off the brainsuckers?"

Peter wasn't bluffing; he'd had a vision in unnerving clarity of Abe shot and himself tackling Erik, followed by a loud noise and everything going black. His legs trembled with adrenaline. "He's just the security guard!" he said.

The Timewalker uncocked and put the gun away. "What the hell, you're the Seer."

Despite knowing in advance how it would end, Peter sagged with relief. "Are you okay?" he asked Abe. "I thought Mr. Slinky, I mean your son, sent everybody home."

"Mm-hm, I'm fine, thank you." The lines in Abe's face seemed to be in a state of continuing expansion, as if somebody had thrown a stone into a pool, but he was recovering. "I came back. Thought someone ought to keep an eye on the place. Was that the elevator crashing just now?"

"Yeah—you should get out of here, it's not safe."

Abe adjusted his headset and frowned. "Why is the place falling apart?"

"Yours not to reason why," Erik snarked.

The old man blinked at him. "You're Mr. Varian's oldest boy. The one he was so disappointed in."

"Yeah, lucky for him he had more. Are we done here?"

"What's going on, Pete?" The old man waved around the third floor: dead plants, discolored cubicle walls, PCs, copiers, and scanners fuzzy with dust, black smoke seeping in from the elevator shaft, OSHA posters yellow and curled. "Why is everything breaking down?"

"The—the timeline is…unraveling, apparently."

"Unraveling?"

"Apparently."

"Oh." His rheumy eyes flickered and went still. "Oh, my goodness," he added.

Peter felt he hadn't gotten the point across. "He says it means the world's falling apart and we're all going to die."

"I know what it means," Abe said sharply.

"You know?" Erik scoffed. "My father told you?"

"Don't be a fool, boy." The old man stood upon his dignity. "*My* father told me."

"That a timeline will be destroyed if the Timewalker who started it dies?"

Abe stared back. "How's that now? No, nothing like that. He told me that the old Chinese fortune teller—the one I already mentioned to you?—she foretold to my grandfather that the world would end in my lifetime, unless I gave you a message from her." He tapped Peter on the chest. "Close your mouth, son, you're catching flies."

"Mah—" said Peter, and swallowed. Memory was making him flush. "Madame When was the fortune teller? That tile was a message for me?"

Enough smoke reached the floor at this point that the sprinklers came on. Almost immediately came a noise like a pipe bursting somewhere in the wall. "What an all-fired mess," Abe observed, raising his voice above the racket. "You'd better come with me, Pete. I'll see if I can't find it for you again."

發

He led them first to the basement, where water seeped down the walls and the wreck of the cage smoldered and sparked. Moving too slowly for Peter's comfort, he hosed it down with retardant foam, then shut the water main and the fire alarms off. Then they repaired to the security office on the first floor. Erik skulked after. He had argued against being sidetracked, but Peter was firm. "It's a message from the most powerful Seer in my family! We can't afford to miss it!" He finished the argument by walking off, leaving the Timewalker to put up or shut up.

The security office walls were cracking. Fallen plaster lay around the edges. Erik slouched against the bullet-ridden door as if yearning for Ms. Y to come back and play Killzone with him. Abe's chair creaked when he lowered his lightweight body into it. Peter hovered, dripping and shivering, while the old man sorted through a desk drawer with arthritic fingers.

"This is Madame When we're talking about?"

"Your great-great-grandma or something?"

"Something." *Why didn't she just tell me whatever it is?* he wondered. *Or warn me about the world ending—if it is. She must not have seen it yet, then.*

"I thought you were adopted," Abe said. He took a brass key out and inserted it into the lock of a second drawer. "Anyhow, the story goes that my Grandpa Tom saved the old lady's life in the big one of Aught-Six. Old Tom was the doorman here and he risked his job by letting her stay inside. You probably heard this place was one of the surviving buildings...."

"I know that part of the story," Peter said. "I never heard about any message, though."

"Well, in her gratitude," Abe jiggled the key in the lock, then took it out, "she foretold to Grandpa Tom that he and his descendants would prosper so long as they continued to work here at the Palazzo." He tried the key again. It didn't budge. "She also said the world would end in a century unless her message got through to you—which it won't if I can't get this damn thing open." He dug a can of Three-in-One oil out of the first drawer. "My father Walt was there with Grandpa when she made the prophecy. He was only seven years old and the whole city was falling down and burning up around him, so it made a real impression. And Grandpa Tom did do well working here, considering the times." He shook up the can and sprayed the key. "So did Daddy when he took over. Always good business, good neighborhood, good tips. While his older brother, my Uncle Daniel, had run off and got himself killed in the Great War. That settled it for him—damn." He rattled the key in the lock. "Rusted solid."

"Want me to shoot it?" Erik offered.

"What do they say about a man who has nothing but a hammer?"

"Don't keep him waiting?"

The old man removed the key again and sprayed inside the lock. On the fourth try, it unlocked with an audible pop. The drawer was empty. He tugged on its back wall. It didn't budge. He worked it back and forth. "Wood's swollen up." With a few maneuvers he removed the entire drawer from desk. Peter had a vision—not a Seer's premonition, just an insight—of hundreds of old men with toolbelts and assorted screws puttering around, putting one little thing or another to rights while the rest of the city fell to pieces around them.

In a space behind the false wall was the khaki pouch with a faded "U.S." stamp. The musty smell of canvas emerged when Abe picked it up. "Yeah, my father gave me this and told me the story when I was, oh, nineteen?" he said. "I didn't believe the end-of-the-world part. But like I told you—two tours of duty in Korea. Never a scratch. So I hung onto it. Didn't think I'd ever meet the Peter Chang I was supposed to give it to. Even after you came to work here." He fingered the canvas for a few seconds. "But once things started looking unsettled around here, I thought it best to just give it to you." He extracted the mahjong piece and handed it over.

The Green Dragon lay in Peter's palm, silky-smooth and the color of teak. The Timewalker leaned over to see and said, "So what?"

"Turn it over," said Abe.

Two columns of characters had been cut into the back, crudely, nothing like the graceful calligraphy used for the Dragon. Chu-kheng had scratched them into the surface with a penknife, maybe, from Mr. Varian's desk.

Curiosity dragged Erik a step closer. "What's it say?"

"I don't know."

"You don't?"

"Wish I had a dime for every time I've had to say this—not every person of Chinese descent can read Chinese."

"You're screwed then. Can we go now?"

"It's all right. I had it translated." Abe drew a much-folded piece of almost transparent yellow paper out of the pouch and unfolded it. "The first line is a quote from *The Art of War*, chapter 11, verse 26. It says 'Prohibit the taking of omens.'"

"That's...a weird thing for her to say," Peter said.

"I looked up the commentary on the text." Abe referred to the paper. "Sun Tzu told his generals never to use magic spells to predict the outcome of a battle because the men would spook if things looked bad."

"Oh. Okay…" Peter could hardly be more spooked than he was already, and the message was contrary to Chu-kheng's previous advice. "And the rest?"

"The second line says, 'until you behold the enemy.'"

"That's it?" said Erik.

"Don't make any predictions until you see the enemy?"

"That's what it says," said Abe.

"Why?"

"Now how would I know?" The old man folded the paper and put it back. "Always took it to mean don't fret over what you can't fix. But that seems a bit weak for a message that's supposed to stop the world ending."

"Does that wrap it up or do you want to stop off for tea and fortune cookies next?" Erik said.

This was probably a slur on Seers rather than on Peter's Chinese ancestry, but it brought heat to his face. "Why don't you go blow yourself up if you're so bored?"

"What a good idea. Coming?"

Peter had to admit he was stymied. There was nothing more to gain here. "Thanks, Abe." He reluctantly laid the tile on the desk.

"I hope the old lady knew what she was about—hey, don't you want it?"

"It's still your good luck," Peter said.

Abe's gaze flicked at Erik. "I expect you're going to need it more." He slid the piece across the desk toward Peter, who caught it as it fell over the slippery wet edge. "Keep it." He began to fit the drawer back into the desk with single-minded care.

Peter glided his thumb around the ivory surface of the tile as he climbed the stairs. It was worn smooth enough to feel greasy. Chukheng had told him to foresee the paths before confronting one of the Hunters. Why would she tell him differently now? He was in the worst possible shape for riddles.

Meanwhile, Erik stuck close and eyed him through—what was the term? —cold slits. Like he had to squint because his retinas had iced up. "Not planning to shoot me after we find Sanders' address, are you?" Peter asked.

"Wouldn't you know if I were?"

Which was a point. Peter couldn't think of a comeback. They reached the third floor and found the cubicle plantation completely dark. Hundreds of itty-bitty lights and LEDs that should be twinkling weren't. He found a light switch and flipped it. "I have a bad feeling..."

"...the fuses have blown," Erik finished. "Any ideas?" The soaked carpet squelched beneath his prowling boots.

"Yeah." Peter headed into Mr. Slinky's office and located a Rolodex next to the landline, right where he expected a fifty-something-year-old man would keep one. The cards were saturated and some of them stuck together, but he managed to separate the S section without obliterating the address they wanted. "600 Montgomery Street, Suite 3900."

"The Pyramid!" Erik exclaimed. Peter had a sense of impending déjà vu—the strange feeling that soon he would be somewhere that would give him the feeling he'd been there before. The Timewalker plucked the card from the roll. "How do you know this is legit?"

"The firm sends documents by courier all the time. Nobody ever came back and said, 'there's no such business.'"

"Could've been brainwashed."

"Yeah...but Sanders would have to be there to do it, right?" He stuck cold hands into damp pockets. "There's no point to cloak and dagger stuff. We just have to go and see."

"You don't. You can see from here."

"Yeah…" Peter said uncertainly.

"So why don't you?"

"You want me to foresee…?"

"What's there? Who's there? Are they expecting us?"

"You want the fortune cookies now? I thought you were in a hurry."

"I've never been inside that building, as it happens," the Timewalker said. "Closest I can get in one jump is the street entrance. Gives them a good chance to spot us coming. Do you care?"

"A bit," Peter admitted. "They must have security cameras or…" and he remembered his guess about Mr. X "…something." His thumb circled the ultra-smooth surface of the Green Dragon. "But no. I'm going to hold off until we're closer."

"You bought it, didn't you?"

"What?"

"Your message." Erik barked laughter. "Your miraculous hundred-year-old message engraved in ivory and handed down father to son, surviving Heartbreak Ridge and God knows what, just to tell you—" poking Peter's chest "—don't use the one advantage you have."

"…You think it's fake?"

"I'm certain it's fake."

"And Abe Slinky?"

"Yeah, the harmless old fart. Brainwashed. He doesn't know he's an agent. The story's more convincing if he believes it."

"You think Sanders planted it?"

"Perfect way to defuse you." He leaned back and folded his arms. "Even stops you from checking to see it's been planted."

Peter gritted his teeth. "Okay, two problems with that theory. One, Sanders doesn't know I'm a Seer—"

"If he ever touched you, he knows."

"The only time he met me, I didn't even know. And two—" feeling far more certain about this, "—only Madame When would use a mahjong tile."

"To tell you not to try to predict the outcome until after you tackle a brainsucker? They'll finish you off like a milkshake."

Peter hated him for being the voice of his fears, not to mention planting a few new ones. He squeezed the tile in his fist. "You don't know what you're talking about." And Chu-kheng's voice came to his relief. *The future branches with every choice you make. You don't yet have the capacity to see all possible roads at once.* "She's reminding me to be careful about the timing. The future is like—like fractal broccoli—"

"You're telling me what—"

"If I try to predict the outcome too soon, the information overload will put me in a coma. That's all she's saying."

It shut him up for half a second. "In that case," Erik said then, "she went a lot of trouble to tell you something you already knew."

"Not half as much as it would've cost Sanders to fake it!"

"Touché," Erik said grudgingly. Silhouetted against the doorway, distant streetlight giving him a cold orange halo, he ruffled up his coat and resettled it on his shoulders. "Okay. Fine. Ready?"

CHAPTER TEN

They jumped from the dark, quiet office to the corner of a five-way intersection and were assaulted by headlights, blaring horns, helicopter backwash, and bitter cold wind. Peter blinked away the sensation that ice was forming on his eyelashes and saw traffic at a standstill, the streets locked up in every direction. Traffic lights were out for blocks. Commuters were climbing out of their vehicles, abandoning them in the middle of the intersection. A buzzing helicopter passed and repassed overhead, its loudspeaker barking out instructions nobody could understand. Sirens and gunshots and a howling dog sounded in the distance whenever there was a gap in the local cacophony.

If anyone saw them arrive, nobody cared. Erik laughed and spread his arms— "Welcome to Armageddon!"—and looked so much like a heavy metal poseur that Peter turned away before he could make the devil horns gesture.

The decay here struck him almost speechless. He could no longer hope that he had been imagining things—cracking pavement, potholes, windblown garbage, and creeping rust were not the status quo in this neighborhood. Under the ghastly light of flickering streetlamps, every surface looked like it had a skin disease.

"Is this going on all over the world?"

"No, it starts out local, then spreads. At least it did last time I saw it happen."

"Local to what?"

"The Timewalker's death," Erik said. "Sure this is the right place?"

They had arrived right across Montgomery Street—so much for Erik's concern about being spotted—from the Pyramid. Banded and spired in light, it rose in vertigo-inducing heights from the plaza where the old Monkey Block had stood a few hours ago in 1906. Peter looked up—and up and up—and though the Pyramid looked nothing like a cathedral or a giant tree, his impending déjà vu came home with a vengeance. "Yeah, I'm sure."

"Even though you aren't doing the Seer thing?"

"I think I saw this before. I just didn't put it together until now."

"Okay. Coming?" Rhetorical question—he was already stalking off. But Peter couldn't move. This was the place of his dreams. The fortress where his beloved lay in vile durance. The place where everyone was disappointed in him, where he couldn't do anything right, where the world was falling apart and he couldn't stop it. Where Nikki, if he found her, would walk out and leave him to fall and to die.

He could do it in the dream; he could not force himself in reality. He was not a knight in shining armor. He was a twenty-five-year-old computer gamer with no friends except other gamers and the ground was disintegrating under his feet and he couldn't even look at the future. Erik was walking away; in a minute he would turn around and see him paralyzed and probably shoot him.

His hands were stuffed in his pockets because of the cold. He found the Green Dragon in one and circled the ivory with his thumb. Why had she told him not to look? Was it a reminder or was she trying to spare his feelings, keep him from seeing the quest was hopeless, though that didn't seem like her at all....

Another thought occurred then: How did she know to tell him not to look? She'd said she couldn't see this far....

How can I save Nikki?

I don't know.

You don't?

I know who she is only because I foresaw this conversation.... I don't know how you can save her. It's too far away. It isn't in my future.... But I have glimpsed a potential future in which we meet again. That isn't likely to happen if you don't save this Timewalker girl.

He drew a breath so cold it seemed to cut his lungs. She could only know by foreseeing a conversation in which he told her. He could only do that if he and Nikki survived. It must be possible or she couldn't have seen it. He gripped the tile. It must be possible or this couldn't have reached him.

He moved. Put one foot in front of the other. Picked his way through the trash and jagged rips in the sidewalk. Caught up with the Timewalker. He didn't want to storm the castle in company with this man, but even Erik was better than no one.

"Look there," said the subject of this thought. Some way off, among the rest of the chaos, a dozen street-corner prophets with cardboard signs were proclaiming the end of the world, and blaming it on gays, terrorists, and God's wrath. A larger group, whose signs condemned corporate greed, environmental poisoning, and neglect of infrastructure, were shouting them down. Erik laughed. "Ephemerals!" he said.

"By the way," Peter said, to puncture his balloon, "there's going to be an earthquake."

"When?"

"I don't know. Soon."

"That should distract the brainsuckers," the Timewalker observed.

"Yeah. It'll distract a lot of people."

Erik pulled something out of his pocket and unfolded it with a snap—a compact set of binoculars, high-tech enough to give an orgasm to any paramilitary fetishist. He began to survey the Pyramid from the top down, counting floors. While he was occupied, Peter reactivated the phone with the scratch and tried calling his parents, and then Jack, to find out if they were okay, but he wasn't surprised when the calls wouldn't go through. He hugged himself and shivered. His jacket, wet from the Palazzo's fire sprinklers, had frozen stiff as cardboard.

Surprising so many people were milling around out here rather than huddling indoors. A pretty black woman with severely pulled-back hair and a tailored pencil skirt went by, her face drawn with cold or fear or both. She seemed familiar, like he'd seen her in a dream—and he probably had seen everyone here. His eye, following her, was drawn to the building right behind them edging the sidewalk. A postmodern skyscraper built sometime in the 1980s, it looked as weathered as if it had stood there a hundred and fifty years.

He stepped closer and scratched its concrete façade with his house key. The surface flaked and disintegrated like shale. "This is going to be bad," he said.

"The assault?"

"The earthquake! Can we hurry it up here?"

"Working on it." The Timewalker set his enhanced gaze on something very high. "There's the thirty-ninth floor. The highest one still lit. But the angle's too steep to fugue in. Maybe from the top of another building...."

"They've probably noticed us by now," Peter said. Especially if Mr. X—he cut off that line of thought. "Why not use the front door?" The Pyramid didn't have a front door—it had an open ground floor with massive supports holding up the building and a glass lobby with elevators in the center. But he wasn't wearing armor or carrying a broadsword, either, so why quibble over details?

"Sure." Erik swept the binoculars downward. "You want to take the stairs or the elevator up?"

He was being sarcastic, but before Peter could ask why, the sidewalk began jittering under his feet. A deep subsonic rumble vibrated his back teeth. "Out of time! Come on!"

"Stay put," said the Timewalker. "I'll get us in."

A few dozen people were in Peter's immediate field of vision—protestors, commuters, the black woman who'd paused at the bus stop. He took a couple steps forward and yelled, "Get off the street! Take cover! Run! Run!"

The rumble came back like the approach of a fully loaded freight train. The earth shook. Someone screamed. A slab of sidewalk cracked with a noise like enormous popcorn.

Erik grabbed him under the arms. Peter collided with something hard and lumpy under his coat, which he forgot about because just then everything including the ground under him disappeared. Light burst in his eyes. They were in a room—a conference room—in mid-air. He fell, his feet connected with the edge of a table, he windmilled his arms and toppled forward between two executive chairs to the floor, which was carpeted in pewter-gray and shaking like a wet dog. He clung to it and squeezed his eyes shut.

After a sickening moment, the rumbling tapered off, then subsided, and everything was quiet except the blood pounding in his ears and one inevitable car alarm going off. A pause—then another, stronger shudder. Peter hugged the floor. The lights swung back and forth, then there was a burst of sparks and they all went out.

His eyes adjusted—there was still light seeping in from outside. White dust fogged the air. Quite of bit of ceiling had fallen in heaps all over the room.

Erik laughed. He had landed on his feet on the table. "That wasn't so bad."

Peter coughed until his throat felt a little less like the Mohave. Interesting he hadn't had a sudden-danger vision that time; his decision to not look must have extended even to his reflexes. "I don't think that was it," he said. "That was just a foreshock."

"Makes sense." The Timewalker jumped down. "This timeline's in for the grand slam of natural disasters."

Peter stopped himself from hyperventilating by changing the subject. "We—we're in the Pyramid?"

"Fifth floor. Couldn't see enough to put us on the floor. The angle was too steep. Wish we could've gotten higher. But at least the security cameras should be out of action." He prodded Peter with his boot. "Hurt?"

"Uh..." He climbed to his feet, assessing himself on the way up: battered and coated in disintegrated wallboard like a piece of Shake'n'Bake, but intact. "...no, I'm fine." He blew dust off his glasses and put them back on. "But Christ," he added, and stumbled, because the floor had an unexpected slant, to the window.

The blackout extended several blocks, but a multitude of car headlights revealed the scene below. The skyscrapers were stripped of their façades as if they had sloughed a layer of skin and the steel bones were showing through. The air swirled with dust; the street was full of rubble and shocked faces—people staring upward after taking shelter in doorways, in cars, even under cardboard signs. Peter oscillated between horror and relief. "Don't see anybody dead," he reported.

Something went *teep*—a phone or a copier, a sound too innocuous to notice, and Erik chuckled. "Just wait a few minutes."

Peter's glare was wasted on him—he stood with his back to the window doing something indiscernible in the dark. "This is a big thrill ride to you, isn't it?"

"No, I take my revenge very seriously. It's not my fault *Götterdämmerung* is playing in the background."

He was buttoning up his coat, which—though it wasn't the reason Peter wanted to break his jaw—was a little weird. "What are you doing?"

"Inventory." He turned, fastening the top button. "Everything's here. Coming?"

Peter let it pass because he was overworked on the coping front. He scraped his eyelids on his chalky frozen coat sleeve. "The elevators will be out."

"I wouldn't trust them anyway."

The door wouldn't budge until they forced it out of its warped frame. It opened on a dark, dust-choked hallway in which somebody coughed and groaned and called hoarsely, "Is someone there?" Whoever it was sounded shaken but probably not injured and Peter wanted to keep him that way. He rounded on Erik. "If you shoot anyone except the bad guys—" he began.

"You'll what?"

"I'll think of something," Peter said between his teeth.

"I'm not wasting ammo on ephemerals."

"Promise?"

"Hope to die."

The hallway went quiet except for a distant scrabble of movement. One direction seemed good as the other, so without consultation they turned right. Peter moved with one hand on the wall, stumbling over chunks of debris and coughing frequently. The dust, mixed with God knew what carcinogens, took a lot of the fun out of breathing. Something around the next corner creaked rhythmically and diffused light shifted back and forth through the coherent air. It turned out to be an exit sign swinging on loose wires. Under it, a functional door opened onto a concrete pit of a stairwell. It closed behind them with a final, echoing slam. Emergency lighting revealed just enough to be scary—a landing silted up with rubble, walls cracked, steps crumbling. The vast space above them seemed to breathe cold, faintly whistling air.

Erik pitched his voice low for an unearthly timbre. "After you. If it turns out you set me up…"

"You seriously still think I did?" Peter swallowed bile he had no time for and addressed practicalities. "So if we happen to run into a bunch of brainsuckers on the stairs, you'll think I tipped them off?"

"Are we going to?"

"I don't know. You should probably assume the worst." *Especially if Mr. X is here.* But Peter didn't need a sudden-danger vision to tell him Erik wouldn't accept an "oops" and an apology for not mentioning earlier that Mr. Sanders had a Telepath working for him. "Trust me, I'll do a faceplant right here if I try this soon."

He began to climb. The rusting iron treads were solid, despite the stress-fractured concrete they were bolted into, and he could go quietly as long as he didn't dislodge any rubble. The ascent gave him a few minutes to think for the first time since—well, since meeting Erik, for like most bullies, he was really good at keeping Peter off-balance. Unfortunately what he thought about was Erik. The presence of a man with a gun concentrates the mind wonderfully, but what the mind tends to concentrate on is the presence of the man with the gun.

A door banged open a few floors above and somebody wondered aloud if the stairs were safe, while somebody else said there was no other way down and no one coming to help them in all this mess. There were echoing footsteps, then two women and a man appeared—worn-down middle-aged people smelling of cleaning products—like an oasis of the ordinary. They burst into questions, but Erik brushed them off—"Emergency! Shift your asses, this building's coming down!" He looked and sounded enough like Hollywood's idea of a plainclothes cop that they vanished down the stairwell like rabbits.

"Even the brainsuckers could just be evacuating," Peter observed.

"If we're going to meet them, tell me."

His voice was muffled. Peter saw a thick piece of flannel tied over his mouth and nose like a surgical mask. "What's that?"

"Filter mask packed with glycerin, lime, and activated charcoal."

"Where'd you get it?" The air was thick enough with dust that he would've liked one.

"Piece of Dromio's kit."

"Oh, yeah." In other words, he'd stolen it from the corpse. Peter stopped envying him.

There was this about climbing hundreds of steps in a dream: you don't get tired. After a dozen flights or so, it got harder to drag oxygen out of the air; the stuff seemed to be getting thin, though at least he was warm, even sweating in the damp wool suit. Every so often one of the treads gave way and he had to grab the rail. Every so often, the rail came loose from the wall and he had to trust the stairs. Just before the thirtieth floor, both happened at the same time. He toppled with a suppressed yelp. Erik stopped him and shoved him onto the landing. "Catch your breath."

"Thanks."

"Don't mention it." The Timewalker tugged the mask down and lit a cigarette with a flare from a death's-head Zippo. "Are we close enough yet?"

"No," Peter said, bent over, between coughs.

"What was that you said before?" he asked in a lungful of smoke. "About having seen this before?"

"Uh—I've had dreams about this, yeah." This wasn't exactly the medieval spiral stairwell from those dreams—but those were probably allegorical, he thought—his prescience trying to prepare him back when it could discern only an indefinite outline of events.

"What'd you see in these dreams?"

"Nikki. Here. Alive."

Erik shifted the coffin nail from one corner of his mouth to the other. "Bullshit."

"Funny…"

"What is?"

"You are," said Peter. "You want me to look, you've accepted everything else I predicted. But not this."

"Yeah." He flicked the cigarette lighter and held it high so that the shadows fled like roaches into the cracks. The walls were eaten away, iron rebar showing underneath, gravel bleeding out of the holes. "Go figure."

"You're assuming her death is the only possible cause for this effect."

"You're seeing her alive because you want it to be true."

Peter drew his brows together. There was something going on here that he just wasn't getting. "What do you want to be true?"

Teep.

Much louder in the stairwell than it had been in the conference room. It came from Erik. From the bulge under his coat, to be exact. The hard, lumpy bulge under his coat that Peter had collided with earlier. And if the sound came from a phone, he wasn't bothering to check it. He made no move at all. He looked as if he had just made a joke and was waiting to see if Peter got it. Peter's throat went even dryer and the air swam. The penny dropped as if from the top of the Empire State Building.

"Took you long enough." Erik flicked away his cigarette and stepped on it. "I guess you really weren't looking ahead."

"Wha—why?" Peter managed.

"Do you think the brainsuckers will let me keep my free will long enough to shoot them all? Even this won't protect me for long enough." He pulled up the filter mask, then reached inside his coat. "I need something to finish the job."

Peter had time to say only one more thing. *Bomb!* was his first thought and *Gun!* was the second, but what came out of his mouth was, "Goddammit, she's still alive!"

"You said." The pistol came up and there was nothing to do and nowhere to go, and Peter didn't even grasp why the Timewalker was going to kill him, it really didn't seem necessary—

There was a loud creak and a golden-blonde woman in a brown flak jacket leaned around the door on the landing above, head and arm together, and started shooting.

Erik was spun around by the first bullet. Dust and chips burst out of the rotten wall. Peter's ears imploded—it was thunderclaps in an echo chamber. He clapped his ears and dropped into a fetal curl. It was worse than useless because she had a clear line of fire and now he couldn't move. Still on his feet, the Timewalker fired back, a deeper boom. Peter reached up, grabbed the handle of the door on their landing. Locked. Ms. Y punched rat-holes in the wall around him. Erik fired again, then took a dive downstairs, disappearing instantly into the darkness. Peter was still hanging onto the door handle, and it suddenly turned under his weight. The door opened as if by someone on the other side. Peter half-fell, half-rolled through.

The door closing was nearly inaudible. He lay on lumps of wallboard and heaps of plaster in the dark. Someone grabbed him under the arms and dragged him away from the door over crumbling heaps and slanting floor. Then came a muffled explosion. Light outlined the door. Fire licked around its edges and he felt the heat as its paint blistered. Then both died down, and the darkness was complete again. Whoever was dragging him stopped, propped him up against a wall.

"Hello?" said Peter.

If there was any reply, he didn't hear it. He swallowed and winced as his ears popped. Gritting his teeth, he pinched his nose shut and blew. It was painful, but his ears cleared most of the way. He could hear wind whistling around the Pyramid and himself breathing in deep gulps. There was light seeping in from a band of windows all around a big open floor, whatever floor this was. Dark shapes of wrecked office furniture and larger piles of debris loomed around him, everything broken and ripped apart and unrecognizable.

Someone was crouching in front of him. Peter braced his heels and pushed up the wall into a standing position. The other person stood up at the same time as if mimicking him. Peter wasn't sure how that helped him make the connection, but he knew who the man was before he spoke.

"Don't look at the future," he rasped.

Whatever Peter might have expected him to say, that wasn't it. "What?"

"If you look now, we're all going to die. That shouldn't bother me, but it does." His voice had gone beyond hoarse. It rose from the burnt-dead embers of Hell. "I'm not the enemy. If you don't believe me—and I see you don't—remember we just saved your life."

He clicked on a flashlight, aiming the circle of light at the ceiling between them. If he'd looked haggard and ill before, he now looked like the guy from *The Scream*, wrapped up in a shapeless gray coat. Peter could hardly believe he was capable of standing. X grimaced and clicked the light off again. "We'll do better without it. Just don't look."

Something like a brain was still wedged in Peter's skull. Mr. X didn't have a weapon out, and he looked as if a slight push would knock him down, but he was Mr. X. Of course he knew about the Green Dragon, he knew everything Peter did.

"Actually," X said, swaying a little, "my name is Ladislaw. X is a stupid joke. Trying to impress my partner when I first met her, being all mysterious—'You don't need to know my name, call me Mr. X,' right? And she didn't miss a beat, she said, 'Then I'm Ms. Y.'"

"What do you mean, we're going to die?"

"If you use precognition within range of a Telepath, it sets up a recursive loop that results in total meltdown for both of us."

That sounded familiar. "How—how does that work, exactly?"

"You see the future and decide what you're gonna do, right? But I see what you see, I know what you decide to do. I change my plans. But you see what happens when I change my plans. You choose to do something else. But I see you choose something else, I change my plans to counter it, and so on, but it happens so fast we don't realize. When you look, you get everything at once, the whole spectrum of options expanded by my awareness, and I pick it up from you and in about two seconds, we blow our minds with data overload."

By the sinking of his stomach, Peter was sure he was speaking the truth. "Well, that explains…"

"…your dream about the bridge, and what happened in Santuario," X finished for him. "Yeah, I was there, I got the smackdown too. We're like two guys pointing tasers at each other. You know what happens when you're hit with a taser? Your muscles spasm and you fire back."

"That's not right," Peter said. "Maybe I can't look without frying us, but you're still reading my mind. You're doing it now!"

"I can't help that. I can't fucking turn it off," the ghoul said between his teeth. "Quit that! I can't stand when people feel sorry for me!"

Peter wondered how often it came up. He braced against the wall, then stopped as it began to give way. He stood still for a moment, just trying to catch up. "Okay. What am I doing here? Why did you save my life?"

"We need you to save the world, obviously."

"Obviously?"

"You hadn't noticed we live here too," X said sourly. "Nobody wanted you before everything started breaking down, but now? Hell, yes. She's on the forty-eighth floor. My employers moved her to the top level to get farther away from your friend the suicide bomber."

"You want me to find her?"

"She's not dead, so that can't be why the shit's hitting the fan." He shrugged. "Maybe it's her state of mind. Which is bleak. Lots of angst and despair. Fun for me, I can tell you, on top of all the fucking panic downstairs. Maybe the timeline is unraveling backward from her suicide in the future. I don't know. I'm taking wild guesses because that's all we have."

"What do you expect me to do?"

"Go cheer her up! She thinks you're dead. Give her a reason to live. Make her want this timeline to survive!"

"Why doesn't Sanders cheer her up?" He bridled, remembering Ilse's vacant smile. "Isn't that what brainsuckers do?"

"They tried!" X snapped. "They turned her into a manic smiling Stepford bitch. It didn't help. Speaking from personal experience," he added, "they can elevate anybody's mood, but if it doesn't get rid of the underlying problem, you might as well cure severe depression with rock cocaine."

"Why did they kidnap her? Why are they doing this to her in the first place?"

"God! Ask them! Get going!"

"It's not going to work. She's going to walk out on me. She doesn't—I can't—"

"She does. You can. You pathetic piece of crap!" X said. "Think I'm in any shape to give a fucking pep talk? Anyway, what else are you going to do? You've already decided, so quit stalling."

That was true.

"Take a different stairwell," the Telepath advised, handing him the flashlight. "Your buddy's coming back as soon as he gets the bullet extracted and the timer reset, and he could show up anywhere he's already been."

"Uh—didn't he already—?" Peter looked back toward the scorched door.

"That was a grenade. Something to clear the stairs. What he's got is enough to blow the top off the Pyramid."

"Why, for God's sake?"

"Because if he dies avenging her, she was wrong to reject him. Even a Seer should see that. Go! And don't look!" he stressed. "I need to be functional to deal with the guy when he comes back. If you knock us out, it's an even bet which way we'll go!"

Peter met Ms. Y on the stairwell, coming down. It was like meeting a leopard. Golden eyes, a haze of burnt explosives and musk. But she let him by without a threatening move; she even looked faintly amused. "I'm Allison," she said.

These stairs were just as dilapidated, so he went carefully. There was no one now to catch him if they collapsed. Soon he was breathing hard and sweating again. Nine flights to go. One foot on a step and then the other, another step and another. *And just keep going.*

Why?

He remembered the terminally sick lady who'd given him a dollar outside the Powell Street clinic.

Because you aren't dead yet and this is what live people do.

Four flights. Three. Two.

One.

Another door. Ordinary. Not locked. He doubled over for a few seconds to catch his breath and keep from vomiting, and then he eased it open.

"Come in, Mr. Chang," said Mr. Sanders.

CHAPTER ELEVEN

A dozen people sat and stood around a conference table in the highest, smallest room of the Pyramid, facing the doorway where Peter stood panting from the climb. Sanders was the only person he recognized. Nikki was not there. The room was dimly lit and half-destroyed.

"Is this him?" somebody croaked. A crone—literally the oldest person he recalled ever having seen—sat at the head of the table.

Mr. Sanders looked sleeker than he had as Sutorius, but just as angry, all rubbed the wrong way. "Yeah. This is the brave knight come to save the damsel in distress."

Peter bristled. Why not? The trap was sprung; if they wanted him dead, he was as good as dead. "Where is she?" he demanded.

"She's here," said the crone. She sounded vaguely French or maybe Creole—Peter didn't know enough to say. "Come in, Mr. Chang. We won't eat you."

"Or mess with your mind," Sanders added.

"Directly," said the old woman.

"Or you'd be a zombie now," Sanders said. All of them looked at Peter with burning eyes, twelve cats to one mouse.

"We will make a bargain with you," the crone said. "So take Ladislaw's advice and leave the fortune-telling alone. You will need to be conscious."

He had to assume they knew everything about him that X knew, which was…everything. "Who are you?"

"You may call me Carabosse." She said it like a joke, splitting her well-made-up wreck of a face in a grin. Peter didn't get it.

"This is the chairman of the board," Sanders said. "You call her Madame Chairman."

He shrugged. "I'll call her the Queen of England if you want. You guys are all Hunters?" They weren't what he expected because some were Asian, some black, some white, one Hispanic, and Madame Chairman could've been almost anything, but she didn't look like Sanders. On the other hand, they had great clothes—Madame armored in custom black Gucci that gave her almost a young woman's shape—like they were as rich and powerful as Peter would've guessed. "What do you want? What bargain?"

"Can you guess?" Madame asked.

"…Yeah." Cracked walls, broken chandeliers, table covered with plaster and gravel, debris and bits of God knows what all over the place—the elite conference room occupying the Pyramid's top floor looked like a bomb shelter. Blinds shrouded the whole panorama of windows like a blackout was in effect and everything was lit—or not—by a single battery-powered emergency lantern. Sanders wore Armani and antique gold, but he was standing in broken glass. "You need me to stop the unraveling too," Peter surmised.

"Well," said Madame, "we are prepared to let you try."

"And what do I get out of it?"

"That is what you get." Sanders snorted. "The opportunity."

"Wake her up," said Madame, "and make her deal with her monsters."

"Her monsters being…?"

"Us." She showed teeth. "Among other things."

"And if you can't," said a flushed adolescent boy leaning on the back of her chair, "we can suck your brain out in front of her."

"Yes, thank you for that, Mercure," the crone said sharply as everyone other than herself and Sanders seemed to lean forward. "I'm sure he had forgotten."

"What is it you want from her?" Peter asked.

"He doesn't need to know that!" Sanders crushed glass into smaller fragments under his Louis Vuittons.

"Oh, yes, he does," Madame said. "This is the time of revelation. Cards on the table. We need to leave this juncture," she told Peter. "We took the *chère m'mselle* to open a door for us to escape her family by. Now, of course, the matter is much more urgent."

"...Escape to where?"

The thousand lines of her face drew down. "To a time before there were Timewalkers."

"Before we had to live in hiding," Sanders said.

"Before there were so many of you mortals," Madame said, "so dangerous and so clever. When we were gods to you."

Hair prickled on the back of Peter's neck. "When you were the top predators, you mean."

"We're omnivores, but—as you say. If we're not welcome here and now," a little blood rose to her withered cheeks, "we wish to go home."

Peter imagined Nikki's reaction to this demand to turn the Hunters loose on primitive humanity. "So what's the problem? You killed her father, so she refuses to do it?"

"Oh, we can make her," the crone said. "Although it may take more time than we have—she's very stubborn. But the real problem is that not all of us are here yet."

"He really didn't need to know that!" Sanders snapped.

"When you deal with Seers, speak the truth!" Madame retorted. "We have family in the air who cannot land, on the road who cannot get through, in the city who cannot reach us. This world is falling into ruins. It must hold together long enough for us to gather."

"So you need me to do it," Peter said. "So again: what do I get out of it?"

"You won't do it without a concession?" Sanders scoffed. "You reek of noble intentions!"

Peter felt heat come to his face. "Why should I? You traumatized her, you're holding her prisoner. Even if I can help her, it'll just happen all over again!"

"We did nothing," the hag said.

His jaw dropped. "Kidnapping, chasing her through timelines, murdering her father and her brother—you call that nothing?"

"Bah!" She smacked the table and dust flew. "Poof! That is nothing. Trauma, we can fix. Grief, we can heal. It is only speeding up the natural process. What she has, we cannot cure speedily."

"What does she have?"

"What all her kind have," Madame said. "You lack words for it. And we do not use language to communicate such things. *Anomie*, perhaps?"

"*Weltschmerz*," someone else suggested.

"Immaturity," Sanders said.

"She does not connect. Does not commit. Does not take responsibility. Does not finish what she started." Madame cackled. "Too easy to move on, leave it behind, try something else. They never learn, those Timewalkers."

"Why would that cause this timeline to unravel?"

"Perhaps she has created too many?" A shrug. "I do not know all the Timewalkers' secrets. But yes," she added, "we need you. Bring her out of the darkness, stabilize the timeline while we gather. Once we are gone, we do not need her anymore." Sanders' eyebrows both shot up, but she overruled him with a glare. "You may both go free."

He didn't believe that, but he saw no other way to find Nikki. "Okay. Where is she?"

"First the bargain," said Sanders.

"What bargain?"

"You hand over the antidote I made for you."

Peter blinked. "Wait. What?" It had slipped his mind while he struggled to cope with Erik's threats, Dromio's murder, the world falling apart, the message from Chu-kheng, the earthquake, Y shooting at him, X rescuing him, the Hunters demanding that he help them. "That you made?" he stalled. "That was you?"

"Our Telepath friend saw in Benedict Varian's mind that you were the Seer's child," Sanders said. "I confirmed it when we met. I remembered you well after a hundred years, though you have a sort of generic corn-fed American flavor."

If he meant that to sting, it was lost on Peter. "But this is a different timeline! How can you be the same guy?"

"How could I not be? Your mother was no altruist, she didn't give warnings for nothing. I wouldn't have survived 1906 in any timeline you didn't visit. I paid my debt, though—X and Y had strict orders not to kill you. I knew you had not met me yet."

"He's not very bright, is he?" said the boy Mercure. "For a precog. Did you know I was going to say that?" he asked Peter.

"Miss Varian split this timeline off the original at some point after we met," Sanders said. "So yes, it's a different one, but no, I am not an alternate version of myself with no memory of you, if that's what you expected."

"Don't feel bad," Madame counseled. "Even the wisest Seer couldn't keep up with a Timewalker's machinations, let alone…well."

"I don't feel bad about that," Peter said. "I feel stupid for having forgotten you drugged her. That's what's messing her up!"

"The inhibitor isn't causing this," Sanders said.

"You screwed with her brain chemistry and the unraveling started! Do I have to draw a diagram?"

"If that were the problem, we'd have fixed it with one dose of oxytocin," Madame said.

"You told me that memory drug was a horrible experience!" Peter reminded Sanders. "You said it would be even worse for a Timewalker!"

"That must be why you stole it." The Hunter glowered. "Did you know how long it took to reverse-engineer that compound?"

"Did you ever try just asking her for help?" Peter demanded.

Except for Madame, who avoided his eyes, all of the Hunters laughed. "That didn't work out well the first time," Sanders said.

"What was the final body count, does anyone remember?" asked Mercure.

"That was Benedict!" Peter, putting together what Sutorius had told him. *We asked a favor. It would have cost them nothing. We would have gone our own way and never troubled them again.* "That was Erik and the rest! Not her!"

"And we should risk another massacre because one Timewalker might be different from the rest of her family?"

"If escape means that much to you, yeah!"

"We don't have time for this," Sanders told Madame—and then he turned so fast Peter barely registered it, and exhaled sharply in his face a familiar musky scent—

"Gently now," Madame said.

"I *am* being gentle," Sanders growled.

—familiar because he'd experienced it once, in a precognitive flash: slack muscles, paralysis, weird sense of peace. Somebody shoved a chair behind him. Sanders pushed him with one finger and he toppled into it. His arms and legs were like dead things, his tongue was a piece of rubber. "Monoamine blocker," Sanders explained. "Prevents the motor neurons from being stimulated and induces REM-state atonia. You'll be fine."

Mercure snickered. "The Telepath was right. Not much of a precog. Unless this is all part of his plaaaan." He made air quotes. Everybody laughed again, but this time the way people do when tension breaks rather than when something is funny and Peter realized, with astonishment, that they had been afraid of him.

Two of them riffled his pockets and put everything on the conference table: wallet, smartphones, mahjong tile, brass dart, and the tiny vial. Sanders took the last two items, unscrewed the lid of the vial and sniffed it, then put the cap back on and tucked both of them into his own breast pocket. He took the two phones, dropped them on the floor, and stamped them with the heel of one expensive shoe until they shattered. "I told you infatuation is only chemical. I should suck it out of you right now."

He breathed in Peter's face again. The musky scent evaporated. Peter got up and snatched the Green Dragon back, grabbing his wallet as an afterthought. Then he stared at his broken phones. "What was that about?"

"We only took her ability to visualize," said Sanders.

"So?"

"She can still timewalk with an image to focus on—we need her to open that door, remember? And you're not pulling a fast one."

Right, he'd had digital photos on those phones—Waikiki, Santuario, even Chinatown—and maybe five percent of a charge left on each. He extended his hand. "Give it back! Just give me the antidote back. She needs it. I can't help her!"

"Yes, you can," Madame said.

"But she can't do anything without…"

He fumbled for the word—it was *agency*—but it eluded him. Madame seemed to understand. "She won't use it. As she is now, she'll just run away and the timeline will shred itself."

"You have to give her a choice!"

"That kind always has a choice," Sanders growled. "That's the problem!"

"We don't *have* to do anything. We're her monsters," said Madame.

"Then I refuse!" Peter said.

A tinny rendition of "Ode to Joy" played, thin and startling in the dim-lit, rubble-strewn room. Sanders turned away, activating his phone. Mercure bared his teeth, as did several other people. Emotionally they were like a flock of birds, all changing direction at the same time. "Plan B," the boy proposed. "We try a taste of his spinal fluid. The bitch will rally to save him." And they all leaned forward with eager, wet eyes and mouths....

There was a distant rumble and the floor began to shake, then to shake hard. The Hunters gripped their chairs. Peter grabbed the edge of the table. A chunk of ceiling fell and struck Sanders, making him drop the phone. Another chandelier crashed. Everyone jumped or scrambled under the table and some tried to shield Madame with their bodies.

Most of the window blinds fell clattering to the floor. Apocalyptic darkness shone through the naked windows—the city in blackout. Then the windows shattered, bursting outward with a roar. Shrieks and car alarms became audible. Sirens howled, a freezing wind cut through the room, a blizzard of plaster danced across the table. A few seconds later came a prolonged crash like sudden heavy rain as tons of glass hit the pavement forty-eight floors below.

The shaking died away. Fragments of glass still clung to the frames by shreds of polyvinyl laminate, rattling in the wind. The Hunters began to pick themselves up, coughing on dust. Peter hacked stuff out of his lungs, his eyes burning and watering. If not for the broken windows, it would be unbreathable in here. Sanders shook out his battered hand, brushed off plaster, and cursed the loss of his phone. "That was Ladislaw," he said shakily, and began digging in the debris. "I think it was important —"

Madame, who hadn't budged, held up her withered hand to silence him. "You won't do it?" she said to Peter. "Suit yourself."

God knew how many people had been killed. Peter broke like a twig. "Okay! Okay. Where is she?"

She raised the lantern, dispelling the shadows that hid a second door, barely visible through the dust. "Up there."

"Up there?" He looked at the floor and steel underpinnings of the Pyramid's spire, exposed in the darkness above when the ceiling fell.

Before he could move, however, footsteps rang outside, then Ms. Y—Allison rather—burst into the room, semiautomatic in her hand, pointed upwards. "Kill the light! Close those blinds!" When nobody moved—and they couldn't close the blinds anyway, the damned things were on the floor—she lunged for the lantern in Madame's hand.

Then Erik appeared. Out of thin air. Peter knew instantly it was him, though he couldn't see his face in the dim light, by the way he was crouching on the table, looking like The Shadow in that long black coat and flannel mask, field glasses in one hand and pistol in the other.

"Tag!" he barked. "You're it!"

Peter heard only one shot, but saw muzzle-flash from both guns. Allison changed trajectory and dove under the table. Both had missed. The Timewalker fugued to the other side of the room, pivoted, and fired from the hip—not at her, but at the Hunters who were all frozen in place just like Peter. Three of them fell before he thawed.

He dropped under the table with Allison. She rolled to one side and fired over the top. The Hunters dropped, or ran, or died. Hands over his ears, Peter heard screams, thuds, shots from so many different angles Erik must be bouncing all over the place, and Allison rolled by whenever she had to fire in a different direction.

The Timewalker must have been on the roof of another skyscraper, he realized, to be able to see and fugue into the room when the window blinds fell. X had sensed his presence, had been calling to warn Mr. Sanders, but the earthquake interrupted—

—Somebody crashed into the wall in his field of vision, dropping a cell phone as he hit. Speak of the devil! Mr. Sanders slid down and fell over sideways, exposing a livid hole in his forehead, a bloody ragged exit wound on top of his skull, the shell of his face shattered forever.

Oh, God. Peter gulped. The guy had lived so long, worked so hard, gotten so close, and a single bullet was enough to destroy all that and he didn't care that the man was his enemy, that was not right, and it was not right that the world could be destroyed just as easily and he had to do something about it. He hyperventilated, enough dust in his lungs now to make him feel like someone was stabbing him through them.

He rolled out of cover, over the plaster and rubble and broken glass. He fetched up against the dead Hunter and ripped his coat open. A darker shadow, out of all the shadows in the room fell over him. Erik, of course. Not even looking at him, focused on Allison, but he took the time to take aim at Peter, who had half a breath left, and the short half at that.

He pulled the trigger, but the gun only clicked. Allison vaulted the table with a flying kick. Erik disappeared. She whirled and caught him upside the head like she knew where'd he'd show up—then the two of them were all over each other like a pair of rabid weasels, dust flying, every attempted blow a lethal one. Their empty guns lay in the debris.

Peter fumbled in Sanders' inside breast pocket, hands shaking. The smell of the dead man's relaxing bowels reached him despite the wind howling through the windows. He found the dart, which he tossed, an old-fashioned metal syringe, which he ignored, then the tiny vial, and then he staggered up and ran for the door, past Madame, still hunched in her chair, her expression virtually unchanged. He tore it open. Narrow, steep metal stairs, almost a ladder, went up into a blue-lit darkness.

He clambered up, cold rungs biting into his hands, into a high gulf of enclosed space—the interior of the Pyramid's two-hundred-foot aluminum spire—with an Escher-like support cage of girders and metal spiral stairs, all rusted and twisted from the unraveling.

It was quieter here, echoing with his steps and the fight below. The air was clear and cold. It smelled of machine grease, dust, and fried electrical wiring. The chill bit through his damp clothes and his breath swirled frost.

Nikki lay on the dirty floor a few yards from the top of the stairs like she hadn't moved since they dumped her there. He had expected decorous posture like a maiden sacrifice—it would've been more consistent with his dreams, anyway. No fancy black lace dress; she had the same coat, white blouse, and jeans. No goth eyeliner either, but her face looked like paper in the blue light.

He crawled to her, terrified the floor would give way. "Nikki." He smoothed the curls from her face. "I'm here." In the face of all evidence he added, "It's going to be okay."

Her eyes opened like holes in the ozone.

"What are you doing here?"

"Looking for you, of course!" He held out the capped vial with a trembling hand. "Drink this!"

"You were dead," she said.

"I'm fine! Not hurt a bit." He propped her up in his lap, offering the vial. She wasn't taking it. "Come on, this is the antidote."

"Is this real? Or are they making me think it's happening?"

"They can do that?" Peter blinked. No time for questions. "I'm real. Of course I—I'd say that even if I weren't. But—um—you made this timeline to save my life, remember? When your brother shot me outside the Palazzo, when we met. Does Madame know that?"

"Maybe I told them and they made me forget."

She was like somebody on the other side of a cold, dirty pane of glass, not Nikki at all. "Listen—you know the timeline is falling apart? Everything's disintegrating around us?"

She frowned and squinted. "She told me that. Is it true? Why would it be true?"

"If you drink this, you can stop it!"

"If I were doing it, they could make me stop."

"Will you forget about them?" Peter begged. "Please drink it. I need you to!"

She took the vial with ice-cold fingers. It slipped and fell and Peter nearly barfed up his own heart, but he caught it. He popped the lid off with his thumb, poured the few drops into his own mouth, then kissed her, quick and clumsy.

Her lips parted, and she swallowed, then pulled back and hugged him, burying her face in his shoulder. "You wouldn't believe what they told me." She shook with sobs.

He held her. "Don't give up. Remember when you told off Dromio?" he asked. "Remember when you said we'd turn it around on them?"

"I do now," she said, and quieted.

"Nikki, the timeline is unraveling," he said into her hair.

She sat up and her eyes focused. She looked at the trash and decay around them, the rust eating away the girders and spiral stairs. "Is it? It is. It really is." She sounded more like herself. "Dad told me. It's all going to fall apart," she said wonderingly, "with—with them in it!"

She pushed out of his arms and got up. Face pale, dirty, tear-streaked, but not broken, not hopeless; she looked alive with rage. "Then all I have to do is nothing!"

Peter scrambled up as his chest lurched painfully. "Nikki?"

She hesitated one second, then grated on her heel and walked away. He sprang after her, but she reached a door. A maintenance hatch or something that should've been locked, seeing as it went outside, forty-nine floors up. Perhaps it was, but when she touched it, the mechanism fell apart in a clatter and clank of plates, bolts, screws, and rust.

"Nikki, don't!"

"Wait," she said over her shoulder, stepped through, and was gone. The door stood open to an apocalyptic sky. Peter was—

He was outside—"No, not now!"—outside looking up at the Pyramid. At the same time and in the same place, he saw the cathedral—the façade, the towers, the flying buttresses. Then it was a huge ash tree with exposed roots. As in a dream, it changed every time he looked, but it was still the same, all its aspects were still there. The villa in Santuario, a globe supported on the shoulders of a slumping giant, a flat disc on the back of a giant turtle, a massive egg cracked down the middle, the gaping mouth of a vast cavern, and many other things.

Someone was speaking. A woman with a flat, business-like voice. "We're sorry, your account has been deactivated. We're sorry…" He looked down and saw his smartphone in his hand. There was a long scratch across the back.

He ran inside. The floor was shaking. The cathedral, with walls of natural stone and great ash roots for support columns, was disintegrating. Rocks crashed from the high ceiling, statues broke and slid apart, chandeliers rained burning candles on the multitude. A fissure ran down the central aisle from his feet all the way to the cross at the far end, and there were things writhing within it. He saw the door to the stairs, but turned his back on it. He ran up the aisle, alongside the fissure, toward the crucified figure. He jumped the cracks, dodged the falling stones, pushed past the terrified, rioting people.

The ceiling got higher, the walls farther away, the pews disappeared. It grew darker and quieter and the air got thin. Ice crystals formed on his eyelashes. The sword froze to his gauntlet like an icicle to a mitten. The aisle was gone. He ran through the fissure where millions of beetles swarmed, crunching under his mailed feet.

When he reached the nave, the cross was no longer there. Instead there was a throne cut out of massive dark rock. It was occupied by a god, powerful, ancient, grizzled, muscle-bound, with brooding features, a patriarch. The god's eyes were open and fixed above the knife that was buried in his chest.

God the father, not god the daughter.

Peter opened his eyes.

The floor collapsed under him.

CHAPTER TWELVE

The city's trees were in full summer green, shimmering and stirred by the breeze. The sky was lightly fleeced with wandering clouds, their shadows gliding over one street and leaving the next in sunlight. A working day but soft as a dream, traffic moderate, pigeons cooing and preening on a bus stop bench, a plastic bag drifting in the draft from the BART station entrance. There was a cute piece of graffiti written on the purple wall outside the coffeehouse: QUESTION EVERYTHING, with *Why?* in a different hand underneath.

Nikki crossed Market Street with the light and went through the glass doors into the Palazzo lobby. Abe Slinky was there to take her up the elevator that his grandfather had known.

"How are you this fine morning, Miss Varian?"

"Fine, thanks." His eyes were warm and kind. For the first time in her life, she thought to ask: "Have you always worked here?"

"Most of my life," he answered. "My father before that and his daddy before that, and my son the office manager now." He sounded, not exactly proud, not exactly angry, but it was all mixed in there.

"Is my father worth all that loyalty?"

He frowned, disappointed, but forgiving her at the same time. Which he must have been doing for the entire time he'd known her.

"It ain't about him. It never was." He stopped the elevator and opened the door for her, and Elaine shooed her through the outer office with a bright smile.

The inner office, with its stuffy, delicate old furniture, was full of sunlight. Her father bent over his desk—the same one he'd abandoned a hundred years ago—writing in formal slanting longhand on unlined parchment. The stuff that had no place here, but he'd always had his eccentricities and was rich and powerful enough to make everyone put up with them. He wore a charcoal suit that let the bones of his face and the jutting gray beard dominate everything else.

He was startled when she walked in. "I didn't expect you so soon." He looked robust when he ought to have been faded as old newspaper, like his future timelines, or translucent around the edges as this one seemed to be. He started to rise, to extend his arms. "It's so good to see you."

"What really happened to my sister Gabriela?" she asked.

He stopped. Gaped. She gave him a little time to comprehend. "You've come from the future."

"Yes, you spoke to me in the Unseen Room. Did you lie to me?"

"You're breaking the taboo."

"Please don't change the subject. Did she kill herself after you kept her in solitary confinement for five months?"

"You've been talking to Erik. Or perhaps to Chang."

"I will if you don't tell me the truth," and then he was silent and she said, "I see."

"You have to understand," he said. "She had been with Hunters."

"She was contaminated, was she?"

"They poisoned her against me," he explained. "It was as if they had killed her."

"Five months," she mused. "Was she pregnant?"

"What could I have done? Welcomed one of them into Santuario with open arms?"

Dust curled through shafts of sunlight under the force of his explosion. Everything in the room decayed a few seconds' worth.

"It's okay, Dad."

He gaped again. "What?"

"It's okay." Startling him further, she took his hand. It was large, warm, callused. He smelled of good cigars and, a little bit, of rich dark earth, and those things, although good in themselves, would be forever tainted for her. "I forgive you. That was a long time ago."

"Then why the devil are you crying?" he asked.

Peter fell into the conference room in a shower of debris, hit the edge of the table, and toppled into a heap that included a corpse, a chair, splintered support beams, marble chunks, and broken glass.

With a groan, he raised his head. The lantern, half-buried in garbage, filled the dim room with violent shadows—Erik and Allison still trading blows on top of the table like a pair of vicious dancers, barely slowed by fatigue and injury. Madame Chairman still occupied her chair as if presiding over their grudge match, a spatter of blood across her makeup. Dead people littered the floor. A few surviving Hunters cowered in dark corners. All the windows were broken out, the room was a skeletal enclosure high above the city, scoured by a wind that cut to the bone.

And here was Ladislaw, out of breath and coughing from a long climb through all the dust, doubled over in the doorway. "Y!" he yelled hoarsely, barely audible over the din. "Y! Holdout gun!"

The combatants were in a clinch, bleeding from nose, mouth and ears, Allison from some slash or bullet crease across the thigh, and Erik listing to protect the side he'd been shot in earlier. At Ladislaw's shout, she stopped trying to break his neck and stabbed her fingers into his injured shoulder instead. He yelped, vanished, reappeared slammed up against a spur of wall, out of the distance she could cover at a bound. He turned around with a small pistol—Dromio's little Walther PPK—leaping into his hand.

"Erik!" Nikki yelled.

She stood in the other doorway, the one to the spire, hair and coat streaming in the wind. She must have bathed and changed clothes— her blouse was green—and her face had lost the dirt and some of the strain and fatigue.

Erik was probably half-blind with blood and trauma, but he saw her. His coat hung open—Allison must have torn it—and little red digital numbers flashed from the device strapped to his chest that had made him bulge underneath it all this time: 06, 05, 04...

"No!" Peter wasn't sure who screamed that; it might have been him, but he thought it was Ladislaw.

Allison sprinted across the table, flew over the space, and kicked the little gun out of Erik's grip. She followed up with a brutal blow to the throat. As he went down, he scissor-kicked her legs out from under her. He rose to meet the elbow coming down hard into his gut and grabbed her in a bear-hug. He looked out the nearest window and then they were both gone.

The explosion lit up the dark clouds in red and silver, rocked the Pyramid, took out the tiny bit of glass left in its windows, and billowed out a mass of heat that felt almost pleasant by the time it reached Peter.

It took a minute or two for his hearing to come back. Then he realized the room was actually quiet. The wind had dropped off a bit. Ladislaw had fallen to his knees in the doorway. Everyone else stood, sat, or lay as if paralyzed. The floor was thick with dead people, bits of carpet showing under debris soaked with blood. A woman lay spilled out of a fallen chair near him, a third of her face missing. The boy Mercure was sobbing under the table.

Nikki made a sound like a child waking from a nightmare. She came further into the skeletal room, looking around until her eyes fixed upon Madame, who sat rigid.

"Congratulations, *chère*."

"I didn't—didn't do this," Nikki said. "This isn't my timeline. It belonged to my father. You started the unraveling by killing him." To Peter she added, "There's police tape on the sidewalk outside the Palazzo. I must have brought us here to the original one accidentally, when Y drugged me with the memory inhibitor."

"I didn't check which phone worked," Peter said. "And your message light wasn't blinking."

Nobody asked him what he was talking about. "Well." Madame said to Nikki, and gestured around the room. "You have what you wanted."

"No." Nikki slowly shook her head. "I broke the taboo. I made another timeline where—where my father didn't return to Santuario until after you killed him. He's alive. Another one of him, anyway. The unraveling should stop now. I hope it didn't get much past the city…."

She went to a window. Peter staggered over to join her. The street below, lit only by vehicle headlights, was so buried in broken glass it could be a scene from a Christmas card. But lights still blazed across the bay.

"My parents…" Peter said in shock. "Jack…"

"My mother," Nikki said softly, then added, "Don't call them. You're dead in this timeline."

"Is your father seeking vengeance?" Madame inquired.

Nikki turned back toward her. "I didn't tell him. I did what you wanted in that timeline. Sent you all back to ancient Sumeria or whatever. I'll do the same here for what's left of you. But I'm not going. You'll have to trust me not to change my mind."

Madame opened her mouth to speak—but a shriek cut her off. Peter, stunned and numb though he was, nearly jumped out of his skin before he spun around. Still on his knees, Ladislaw was screaming like an animal in unendurable pain. He struck his head against the doorjamb so hard Peter thought it would kill him. "Stop it! Get off! It's all meat! It's all shit! Get off me!"

"Jesus H!" somebody swore in a hysterical voice. Mercure.

"Are you doing that to him?" Nikki cried. Ladislaw thrashed as if drowning and tried to brush invisible things off him, then smacked his head again.

"You're doing it," Madame Chairman said. She got up and hobbled over and through the rubble to the nearest prone body. "Mercure, help me check everyone. See who can be saved. Mercure!" She slapped the boy across the cheek. Her hand, like a bundle of twigs, probably hurt; he stopped crying and moved.

"How can I be doing it?" Nikki demanded, raising her hands as if to clap then over her ears. Ladislaw's voice, wrecked by dust, wasn't that loud, but his agony was enough to shred anyone's nerves; Peter would give anything to make it stop.

"Your visualizations, unaffected by our inhibitors, are stronger and clearer than anybody else's at the moment, *chère*. You're throwing salt on his wounds." Some grudging honesty drove Madame to add, as she laid her hand on Sanders' forehead and closed his vacant eyes, "And he was habituated to Allison's pheromones. She was one of us. She was keeping him stable."

Peter's eyes strayed, in horror, to the window Erik and Allison had vanished through. There wouldn't be anything left but red mist, shattered bones, burnt pulp. Ladislaw screamed and keened and Peter tried to stop thinking.

Three more Hunters dragged themselves out of the rubble and dark corners of the room, battered and filthy but more or less unhurt. "Get everyone still alive together," the crone ordered. "And find the syringe with the coordinate pictures! We're getting out of here." But Ladislaw crawled, staggering on his knees, hands clenched over his ears, still screaming. "And somebody put him out. I can't hear myself think!"

"Can't," one of the other Hunters said dully while he and the others obeyed the first command. "The wind's too strong."

Peter wasn't sure what that had to do with it until he remembered they did everything with pheromones. He tried to make himself move, to help someone, to tend an injured person, but his impetus was gone. Every bit of energy and willpower built up over his lifetime seemed to have gone into kissing Nikki. She seemed equally at a loss.

He saw that Ladislaw had found Erik's discarded Walther—at least his hand had fallen on it. He picked it up, turned it this way and that, seemed not to know what it was. But then he lifted it toward Nikki. Then he lowered it again, turned it around, tucked it into his own mouth—

—prohibit the taking of omens until you behold the enemy—

"No!" said Peter, more authority than had ever emerged from his mouth before. A kaleidoscope of futures, multiplied by Ladislaw's eight simultaneous points of view, divided in half as Nikki fugued across the room out of the line of fire, then expanded exponentially by his own act of observation flowered in his mind.

And all went black.

CHAPTER THIRTEEN

The streets of the Île St.-Louis were noisy and cheerful in early May—pigeons flocking, urchins running through them, lovers walking on the quay, easels set up along the river, cyclists and cab-drivers swearing at each other, all the cafés open. Plenty of people around to notice a woman in jeans and an unfashionably cut coat with unfashionably short hair hanging loose. So Nikki stayed hidden in the doorway of her hotel, hoping no one would come in, until Notre Dame rang the half-hour.

Then she went up the curling spiral stairs to the attic floor. She rattled the knob going into the garret and Edvard flashed a look at her, in the act of stubbing his cigarette on a saucer. He was difficult to see clearly—the whole room, bathed in light from the mansard window, seemed to float.

A moment passed as, shocked and confused, he absorbed her strange face and stranger clothes. He was exactly the same but looked five years younger, standing by her surreal painting of the cathedral by a toxic absinthe river that she hadn't taken back yet, nor ever would in this new timeline. The remains of their cold collation was on the table—he had put the sausage back—and the bottle of wine as yet unsmashed. He'd seen her only ten minutes ago, but she was wholly changed.

"You have returned?" he asked.

"This is my studio," she said.

"I see."

Clearly, he did not. "You were right," she said. "I loved you because I knew it wouldn't last. That there wasn't any danger in it. I'm sorry."

He went rigid. "You became entangled with me with the intention of leaving me?"

"No. I was selfish and careless, but I had no intentions one way or the other."

"I am sorry," he said stiffly, "for what I said, for what I implied about your character and your work."

Her eyes were on the bulge in his waistcoat where he kept his pocket watch. It would be so tactless to ask him what time it was. "It was close enough to the truth," she admitted.

"Will you forgive me?"

"Yes, of course. But no more than that. You have to leave, *M'sieur*."

This formality obviously hurt. "You cannot mean—I cannot leave now—"

"Yes, you can. Go home, go back to Norway, don't think about me anymore."

"That is impossible!"

"I'm sorry, Edvard. It's over."

He began to pace, hands tucked and folded behind his frock coat. "Then you never loved me?"

"I can't say that."

Hectic red rose to his cheeks. She cherished how alive he was, for the half-second before he spoke. "But you must say that! You must say, 'I never wanted him. I merely used him! For my own excitement, gratification, ambition!' If you want me to go, you must!"

Oh, such drama. There was a rip in her heart, but she had to be quick and kind as a scalpel. "I never loved you, I never wanted you, I merely used you. Please go."

"You are a hateful creature, *M'mselle* Varian."

"You speak from hurt pride."

"I speak from a broken heart."

But he picked up his hat, took his coat and stick, moved to the door. She allowed herself to breathe. When he was in the doorway, every movement reluctant, she realized there was something else to say. "Edvard—"

"What?"

"I'm sorry. I had no right to read your journal. Or rather," she added, "I had no right to come here and get involved with you after reading it...to interfere with your life the way I did." To treat him, in fact, as though he were a tourist attraction—Edvard Munch, the Expressionist, Inc.—but she couldn't figure out how to explain that sin or apologize for it. She visited the past the way rich, idle useless people toured other countries, feeding on the cream of the experience and throwing the rest away. The grimy details never bothered her because she could always leave.

He wasn't looking at her, he spoke over his shoulder. "Do you not feel any responsibility for what we had?"

"Well, yes," she said. "But do you think we could rebuild on a foundation of your love and my guilt?" She had a sharper blade to cut him free. "Anyway, you chose me for the same reason. Because there was no danger I'd trap you in anything permanent."

There were many cruel words he could've said in return. She would've deserved them. She had slept, eaten, showered, waited, figured out what to say before coming here, where his emotions were still raw and angry. Timewalker privilege.

But he was a Victorian gentleman and let a freezing, disdainful look convey those words to her imagination. He walked out theatrically like an innocent man on his way to his execution. The studio door banged behind him. She stood at the mansard window and watched him come out at the bottom, hail a cab, and clatter away over the Parisian cobbles to go live his life.

Erik,

went the letter she wrote in charcoal on a blank piece of canvas,

I broke the taboo. There're two of you now. The one reading this is the alternate I created. By murdering my lover, the original you started a series of events that will culminate in his death. If you leave Munch alone, you'll be the only Erik in existence again shortly. If you come after me, you'll run up against yourself. Not a pretty picture, I'm sure one of you will kill the other, then be killed himself by the forces already set in motion.

I'm aware you can do the same to me. That's okay. I don't have to be unique. I'll just keep telling you—

go away,

Nikki.

發

The painful kaleidoscope vision of all the places Peter could be waking up in resolved themselves into: his bedroom.

It had its usual lived-in smell and was green with the underwater sort of light he got in the morning when the sun tried to make it in through the clematis, the curtain, and the unwashed towels and clothes accumulated wherever feasible, including the ceiling fan. But it looked solid and showed no more decay than the usual overpriced subdivided walkup rented by a guy of twenty-five. He was lying on top of his rumpled covers and the blanket over him was the same one he'd covered Nikki with that night.

"Nikki?"

Groggily, he pushed off the blanket, found himself still in his clothes. They were crumpled and white with plaster. His throat still felt raw from breathing the stuff. His head throbbed.

He rolled stiffly out of bed and moved to the window, blinking against the daylight. The yard looked as it usually did. Vines half-dead, grass the landlord needed to either water or get rid of, two jacaranda trees with clamshell seedpods dangling open, neighbor's potted marijuana leafy and flourishing, fence with no more than the usual peeling paint. A changeable mostly-sunny sky. Birds and shit.

He stumbled achingly out of the bedroom and through the living room. It had been ransacked, torn apart, and carelessly put back together, and dusty with what he suspected was fingerprint powder. His china penguin lamp was still gone. His landline telephone cord had been cut. His smartphone, he remembered, had been destroyed—twice.

So he fired up his laptop and sent an email to his parents—*I'm okay. Are you okay?*—before noticing that his mom had sent one inviting him to dinner just half an hour previously, and wondering what was wrong with his phone. He added another quick note—*please disregard that last.* He'd tell her he'd dreamed there was earthquake or something when he had his head back together. There was also an email from Jack telling him to pick up the new version of *Ultimate Fantasy* before he came over next time.

In the kitchen, standing up, he drank a full cold bottle of beer just to wash out the dust and put some carbs back in his body. The bathroom had yellow police tape on the door, more powder on the smooth surfaces, and dirty boot prints in the tub, but the absence of dead paramedics made it usable. While showering, he found minor cuts and fresh bruises as well as old yellowing ones.

His brain felt swollen and he shrank from looking, from experiencing more than one future at a time; he didn't know if he'd ever be able to stand doing it again. He washed off thoroughly and stood in the spray (shower therapy, his dad called it) until the hot water ran out. He toweled off, brushed his teeth, scraped a razor over his face, looked at his own harrowed expression, wondered if that was him.

He was somnolent and numb. Stunned. Something was on hold inside him. She must be okay or how had he gotten here, but there were no other answers and he could not go on with, well, anything, until he had some.

He picked up his clothes to toss onto the floor of his bedroom until he decided whether to dry clean or burn them. There was something hard in the pocket of his shed trousers. He pulled out the Green Dragon tile and held it on his palm for a moment.

He put on a bathrobe and went back into the living room. She was sound asleep on the couch under her coat.

發

They went for a walk in Yerba Buena after a late breakfast of cold pizza. It was nearly noon. They found a patch of grass free of couples getting snuggly under some camellia trees blooming with white and yellow tea flowers. Blackbirds twittered and the sun shone bright on the gardens, murmuring fountains and the nearby SFMOMA cylinder.

"Then it's all okay?" he asked.

"No, it's not okay. People died. That San Francisco is rubble and decayed infrastructure. Everything suddenly, senselessly fell apart and nobody understands why. There's a lot of fear and there will be more death, though they're blaming the earthquake to stop the panic. And it may have happened in all of my father's timelines."

"But it's not spreading anymore?" She nodded. "Why did it happen?" he asked. "I mean, just because he died…? Doesn't seem a good reason."

She wrapped her arms around her knees. "I went around some UC campuses and asked the physicists a theoretical question…."

"You've been busy."

"Yes, well, this is time travel. Some of them hectored me with 'the impossibility of the many worlds interpretation of quantum mechanics owing to its violation of the rule of conservation of energy.'" She recited this from a piece of notebook paper pulled from her coat pocket. "But some told me the rule wasn't violated because energy would be apportioned to each new universe according to its probability."

"Okay…"

"And one guy agreed with me that possibly some event could cause a universe's probability, thus its energy, to decrease." She put the paper away and started pulling up stems of grass.

"Like the death of the person who got it started?"

"I mentioned that but neither of us could imagine how it would work, what mechanism, so I'm kind of stuck on that point."

Peter changed the subject. "What happened with the Hunters?"

She rubbed her temple under her hair. "I sent them where they wanted to go. I don't know where it was, this Neolithic city like ancient Uruk maybe. They took X, I mean Ladislaw, with them. With their help and with fewer people around, he might get better."

Peter wasn't sure how he felt about that yet. "Was it a good idea to give brainsuckers their own timeline? I mean…they do suck brains."

She peeled a blade of grass into two pieces and sighed. "Have you ever supported a campaign to save Bengal tigers or timber wolves or something?"

"No, I've never really gotten into all that."

"But if you were concerned about biodiversity, or just thought that tigers were cool, you wouldn't be terribly bothered about all the gazelles they eat."

"I'm not related to gazelles," he pointed out.

"You are from one of the Four Families. For all we know, you could be just as closely related to the Hunters as you are to people who lived five thousand years ago."

"But basically you're okay with it?" he asked. "You're not just rationalizing a decision they made for you?"

"Up until I talked to Dad, I wanted them all dead." She discarded a handful of grass and stretched out. He did the same. They lay side by side staring up through the camellia branches, and the sky gave the impression that gravity might stop working any second and let them go sailing off into the void.

"Is he angry that you broke the taboo?" Peter said after a bit.

"Eleonora told him how with him gone, she had to flee Santuario and give birth to Julietta among impertinent strangers in the middle of an unraveling timeline. He'll forgive me. Or she won't forgive him."

Peter turned his head to look at her and she did the same at him. A camellia shed a few yellow petals that drifted down onto her hair and cheek. She lay very close. Beyond her, on the sidewalk, a worn-faced busker with a slouch hat had arrived and was opening the case that contained his saxophone.

"Well then. I've only got one more question."

She said, "I'm not a reward, Peter."

"…I know that."

"Don't be hurt. I mean this isn't a prize. It's not happily ever after." Her eyes searched his. "I have to make my father understand. If timelines unravel, we shouldn't make them, at least not for fun or for profit. If a feud threatens our existence, we should resolve it some way other than genocide. If he won't listen, I'm going to help the Hunters in his other timelines behind his back. And I have to break the taboo again for Alex.

"And I don't quite know how I feel about you," she added before he could speak. "How easy would it be to live with a guy who can see the future? But that's the position all my boyfriends have been in, so maybe it would be fair. You'd still be better off far away from me—"

"I'd know if that were true."

"—but if you wanted to, well." She swallowed and her fingers interlaced with his. "To be there. I'd be grateful for the company."

"That wasn't actually my question."

"...Oh."

"Yes, I would like to help," he added, "at least I think so—you haven't given me much time to consider, but I can't imagine going back to my job all day and gaming every night."

She turned pink. "I keep forgetting I've had recovery time that you haven't. Didn't mean to rush you, I just..." Her look was naked; she was holding back tears. "What was your question?"

"Would you like to meet my family?" he asked. The busker raised the sax to his lips and began to play the opening to "Stolen Moments."

THE END

ACKNOWLEDGMENTS

Thanks and much love to Calvin Johnson, Zak Jarvis, Sharon Mock, Robert Pritchard, Shweta Narayan and Allison Lonsdale, the best writers' group in San Diego. Thanks also to Carlos de los Rios and San Diego Writers Ink.

Special thanks and appreciation to my editors, Athena Andreadis and Kate Sullivan, and to a book cover artist who can read minds and express the madness found therein—Eleni Tsami.

And of course, to my dear family, Bruce, Autumn, Mom and Paula.

ABOUT THE AUTHOR

Lise pronounces her name "Lisa" but will answer to anything other than "lice." She started out writing fantasy role-playing game articles and books but has also written science fiction intermittently over the last 25 years. In her day job, she is an attorney, handling indigent criminal appeals and writs in the California Courts of Appeal. She also invented the traffic sign which reads "Resume Being Unprepared To Stop." She lives with her husband Bruce, daughter Autumn and two shaggy dogs in La Mesa, California. Her best writing occurs in various coffeehouses in La Mesa Village.

The ADVENTURE
CONTINUES ONLINE!

Visit the Candlemark & Gleam website to

Find out about new releases

Read free sample chapters

Catch up on the latest news
and author events

Buy books! All purchases on the
Candlemark & Gleam site are DRM-free
and paperbacks come with a free digital version!

Meet flying monkey-creatures
from beyond the stars!*

www.candlemarkandgleam.com

CPSIA information can be obtained
at www.ICGtesting.com
Printed in the USA
LVOW03s1445161017
552626LV00002B/532/P